the MOMENT

ISBN: 979-8-9888601-2-9

Cover design: Lori Jackson Designs LLC

Cover photo: Ren Saliba

Editing: Brooklyn Kerr

Grymm Publications LLC

For the overthinkers in us all.

May you find a way to …

EMBRACE THE
Moment

Playlist

Character List

Not all of these characters will make an appearance in this book, but will be around.

As Above band members

Rex Thompson— vocals, guitar, songwriting
Finland Montgomery— guitar, backup vocals, songwriting
Tobias "Toby" Jeffers— bass, rhythm guitar
Mac Thompson— drums, nickname designator

Sentry Security

Ian— Head of Security, Rex's detail
Lugh— Second in command, Toby's detail
Peach— Fin's detail
Jordan Kauffman— Mac's detail
Jonathon— The floater

and more …

A Note from the Author

Welcome to the chaos.

Population: *As Above*

First and foremost, I would like to thank you for taking a chance on this book when there are literal millions of others out there. In my opinion, not nearly enough rock stars, but hey, someone's gotta write them, right?

If you have been with me for awhile, you know that this story was previously published in February of 2023. In March of 2024, it was removed from Kindle and Amazon.

Since then, it has been reedited, reproofed, recovered, and reformatted. The story as a whole, though, has remain *unchanged.*

But if you think you've read this before, I promise you … *no you haven't.*

While this work is wholly fictitious, there are some traumatic elements that I have done my best to portray based on the direction of my characters. No two experiences are the same. No two traumas dealt with in the same manner. Events encompassed in this book are strictly the way that my characters have chosen to deal with their *things,* and is, in no way, any kind of *diagnostic* or *self-help* book.

Having said that, there is a list of content warnings that can be found at the back of the book, just after the acknowledgements.

I want you to enjoy this story. So, please, heed any warnings and reach out with any questions.

Your mental health matters to me.

Keep in mind, this book is a spicy romance.
There are lots of *fucks*. Tons of *dick*.
And should only be read if you are 18 years, or older!

Enjoy.

Blurb

He has had his name chanted by the thousands but all it takes is her to bring him to his knees.

Powerhouse vocalist, Rex Thompson, never knew what his life was missing.

Until she shows up, all sexy curves wrapped in black silk, and rocks the foundation of everything he's ever known.

And she doesn't even know his name.

Aria Scarlett has been content with taking the backseat as those around her reach for their dreams.

But then that comfort zone shatters when a tatted stranger crooks a finger in her direction, and alters the very fabric of what she thought she knew.

Once the blindfolds are off and the illusions wash away, Rex and Aria are an instant spark of connection with only one thing in their way.

Will Rex's fame be too much?

The Moment is an instaburn rockstar romance, the first installment of the As Above series, and can be read as a standalone.

"I write what I feel, I say what I mean, you can't buy
sincerity." —A Day to Remember

Contents

Chapter One

Aria

"How would I even start such a thing?"

I'm exasperated, pushing hangers to the side of the rack like they're the last thing I need.

Cuz they are.

"I don't *know*," my sister shout-giggles over the rack to me as she pushes the same clothes to the side, discarding the piles that normally bring us treasures.

I shake my head and spin to the final rack behind me. We've been through the entire store, aside from this one lone display that isn't really a display of anything, and I've still come up empty-handed.

"Maybe post some pieces online for sale? Start small?" Aurora joins me in my quest of the last section to sift and starts separating the articles of clothing for me.

She holds pieces out for my judgment, only to receive a scrunched nose or a shake of the head in return.

I'm on the hunt, mentally preparing to make the perfect pair of jeans to go with the upcycled outfit, but I'm missing a vital piece.

Except I don't know what that piece is.

And I don't know what the rest of the outfit is. Or what kind of style it falls under.

It's just there, sitting in the back of my mind, waiting for the perfect moment to pop up.

"Right … like I need more time on socials, computers, and shit." Blowing a tuft of hair that's fallen from my short pony out of my rolling eyes, I flick more items to the side.

See, I'm a social media manager for a local tech company that gets all of its traction online. I enjoy it, I guess, but it's nothing like altering a dress to fit my frame or adding the right sized pockets to… well … everything.

Why can't girls have pockets, too?

The final set of hangers remains. I can see each item and know it's not the thing I'm in search of, but I still touch each article in hopes that the feel will encourage and inspire. None of them match the vision in my head, but maybe if I touch them, they'll turn out to be the one? I'm grasping now, considering this search has been going on for days, but a girl can dream, right?

"I'm just saying, Ari. You need more."

A heavy sigh escapes me as I turn to give my sister my full attention. My junior by only two years, this woman in front of me had the guts to pursue her passion from the moment she got her hands on it. A full-time photographer since straight out of high school, my baby sister has accomplished the one thing I wished I could one day do.

Follow her dreams.

I could've, but I didn't. I made other choices that led me here, constantly pushing my passion to the side for more money, better hours, easier life.

It hides in the darkness of my sensible apartment where I keep it to myself. Designing and altering clothes for myself to wear that actually fit right, feel comfortable, have functional components, and look fantastic.

Maybe a thing or two for others as gifts I've yet to see them wear. I'm good at it for myself, but not as much for others yet.

Which is precisely why it's been filling up my closet and not walking down any runways.

Taking in the sight of my sister, I pull her against my chest for a quick squeeze. I'm not sure that her words require a response, so I leave it alone.

For once, when I pull back to look at her pretty face, I don't see the same disappointment there. Instead, I see something else making her gaze twinkle with a newfound mischief.

Something that leaves me feeling uneasy.

She snickers when my face drops, which earns her a shoulder punch and gains me a look of hurt flashing across her high cheekbones and long lashes.

"We have a surprise." *We* … I roll my eyes knowing that she means Cedar, our best friend, is engaged in this shenanigan. Which only serves to twist my gut up with dread. "It's something different, and I can't wait to tell you about it."

"Oh, no." I already regret the decisions they've made without me as my sister clasps my hand and leads me out of the underwhelming thrift store.

"You need out of your head. That's all I'm saying."

Much to my dismay, we make it back to my apartment in record time, thanks to my sister's reckless driving. My palms are already sweating when I find my best friend perched on my couch with snacks at her side and a movie on the TV.

"Ari." She hops up with arms wide, crumbs falling all over the floor in her wake, as she tosses herself in my arms like I didn't just see her this morning.

These girls practically live here, too, despite having their own places to crash. And I honestly love it almost as much as I love giving them a hard time about it.

It's nice to have them around for moments like these. Someone to come home to since Chip passed.

Tonight was supposed to be a girls' night in, but now I'm in hell, wondering what they've done, and I don't think I'm coming out anytime soon.

"Ari, listen." Clearly, I'm more in my head than in the room, so Cedar begins to twist our embrace to gain my attention.

Aurora was right.

Shaking my head, I bore into one set of green eyes that match mine to some ocean blues, and I can already feel the determination in them both. The admiration.

The stupid love.

They want better for me, and I like that. Even if they go about it all fuckered up.

Which I never agreed to be okay with.

"We booked you a surprise trip," Aurora says, her hands locked together at her chest, almost in a sort of plea for me not to freak the hell out. "It'll be so much fun for you."

Too late.

"It's out of your comfort zone," Cedar warns, but her face suggests that there's nothing to worry about.

I pull in a slow, deep breath as the emotions in me build. Some weird combo of exasperation and excitement. Panic and curiosity.

Cedar loosens her arms around me to give me the room to breathe but not enough room to run.

It does nothing to ease the churning of my stomach.

"But you're totally going to love it," Aurora finishes.

"I know you two have pulled off some shit if this is how you're acting." I'm terrified of what they've actually done. I can't lie about that. But I'm also curious as hell.

It has to be a vacation of some kind. It can't be that bad, right?

Shit, am I really okay with this?

They share a knowing look, then swing their gazes back to me.

"You're going to a *blind shoot*." Aurora hops, squeals, claps, and all that weird happy dance jazz she's prone to do when it comes to any kind of photography shit. I must wear a confused look on my face.

I am.

She lands back on two flat feet, her dark blonde hair settling around her shoulders like a cape, and grins at me.

My sister spins on her heels, light as a feather, and floats over to the couch, only to flop into the cushion like an anvil from the sky. Cedar drags me along, both of my wrists trapped in her hands, and deposits me beside my sister.

"You've talked about that before?" I furrow a brow as I dig into the recesses of my mind and try to figure out what the hell that might be. I look to Cedar, finding no support there. I guess I'm on my own judging by the slight shake of her head. "Is that where the model shows up in whatever outfit, and that's just what the shoot becomes? No meeting the photographer, no set agenda, just show up and take pics?"

"Um … kinda."

"So what is it, then?" Another knowing look is shared between the two, except I'm certain I catch some warning behind my best friend's eyes as Aurora begins to speak again.

"It's pretty much that. Yeah," Aurora stutters out, her nod too enthusiastic in Cedar's direction.

"There will be someone else there, though, to take some photos with you," Cedar adds, her gaze cutting to Aurora.

"Because we love you," my sister blurts, and my palms slick over. "And we want you to do cool things."

She's excited, her grin lighting up the little living room we love to watch movies in, her frame near vibrating.

It's hard not to match Aurora's enthusiasm, but I can't.

Because I have no fucking idea what's going on.

"So," Cedar cuts in. "You need to pack something totally you, totally sexy, and you need to do it now." Cedar pushes me off the couch with a hand to my lower back and leads me back into the extra room I use as a closet.

"Wait, what?" Things are moving fast. So fast that I didn't get a chance to shut down the idea. Or hell, even agree to it.

"It could be good for your line, Aria," Cedar says to me, disappearing between the mobile racks full of blouses and slacks and dresses I've altered or made myself. "Y'know, once you get your head outta your ass."

I'm pretty proud of my collection. But that's not the point here …

"C …" I shake out of my stupor and move to her as she gently folds an article and settles it into the bottom of a suitcase.

She shoos me away from my own crap, and my feet follow the orders, much to my brain's protest. "You don't have much time. Grab your favorite undies and let's go."

I find my sister in the hallway holding out another smaller bag full of undergarments. Those I don't alter; I just buy a shit ton of the ones I like. I nod before my eyes and my brain catch up to the event as she snaps the thing shut, zipping it into the case Cedar has already brought out.

Was there lace in there? I'm pretty sure I saw lace.

Oh, fuck …

"This better not be a lingerie shoot," I say, cursing my sister's giggling reply.

They crowd me, pushing me out the door of my apartment and into the back seat of my car.

Slamming my suitcase into the trunk, my captors slide into the front seats and take off. When I glance at my surroundings, I realize my sister is not heading in the direction I expect.

No, we're going the way that leads *out* of town.

And what's on the edge of our city?

Maybe a new studio moved into one of the old strips—

Then I see it.

The sign for the fucking airport.

"You're both mad." I shake my head and catch Aurora's eye in the rearview mirror. "Completely insane. This is kidnapping." I massage at the tension building in the center of my chest.

I know they aren't kidnapping me.

But it sure as shit feels like it.

"You never protested," Cedar says, blowing me off with a smirk over her shoulder. "You had every option to protest, and you didn't. So … *not kidnapping*." She shrugs, nonchalant, and turns back to watch the road.

I didn't stop them.

She's right.

Dammit.

There's nothing that I wouldn't do for these two. No matter how crazy. I know deep down that I've been stuck in a lull, and maybe this is just the thing to break me out of it.

Whatever this trip actually is, it might be just what I need.

Something other than anxiety-driven fear of the unknown nags at me, though. I try to read the two of them, but I don't see anything beyond the loungewear on my best friend and the professional look donned by my sister. Not to mention the lack of bags for either of them in the trunk where mine currently lies.

We've been on trips together before. In fact, that's one of the first things that we did as a group after Chip's death. It was one of the hardest moments of my life, to lose someone so close to me, and it took months for me to get out of the house again.

I had just turned twenty-four when he started to get sick. He finally had a diagnosis the day I turned twenty-five. My husband since the age of nineteen (he was twenty), my high school sweetheart, didn't make it past twenty-six.

That's right, folks. I'm a widow at the ripe young age of twenty-nine.

The thought sobers me in the back seat of the car he gave me shit about buying. He would joke about the size. I would laugh when he tried to squeeze in the driver's seat. It's funny how he thought it was too small for us to tote kids in, considering I'm back here now. On my way to who knows where. For some shit my sister and best friend set up so that I can start moving on with life.

I have, but I haven't.

I turn my attention back to the front windshield, a tinge of worry settling into my gut as realization settles in.

They aren't coming with me.

"Neither of you are dressed to get on an airplane." They share the look that I used to enjoy seeing and now hate because it's directed around me instead of *including* me.

"I have work," Aurora squeaks.

Cedar hangs her head, then whips it back against the headrest and rolls to meet my eyes.

"We're not. You're not going to want us there." There's a light in her eyes, a levity, which begs for trust.

"You *bitches*." I slap both of their shoulders with the backs of my hands, the anxiety rearing its ugly head right in my gut.

"It was her idea," Aurora says on a laugh.

"*Traitor.*" Cedar abandons her defense from my assault only to turn her attack to our driver. Aurora laughs, swerving the car between the lines of the back roads as she bats away Cedar's hands.

"Stop hitting the driver," I say, pushing at both of them, Cedar sinking back in a sighing smile as my sister straightens out the car and clears her throat with a chuckle.

Their ease soothes me.

Maybe this isn't going to be so bad.

The night begins to take over the scenery as we drive, darkening the edges and triggering the streetlamps to illuminate our path. I sigh into my seat, an exhaustion I haven't been able to bounce back from settling into my bones, demanding a reset.

Just like this one.

Aurora checks on me in the rearview mirror, and I can't deny how the corner of my lips rise in a smile I haven't truly felt in a long time.

I guess I'm leaving on a jet plane, and I'll be all by myself.

Chapter Two

Rex

R *ING.*

The phone chirps from the poolside where I abandoned it, interrupting the peace and quiet for the hundredth time since the sun came up.

From the moment I got to the penthouse, it hasn't stopped making noise, and I'm in no mood to answer the damn thing.

It's almost three p.m.

The stereo only stopped blaring two hours ago.

Whoever is on the other side of that ring is clearly insane.

Dragging my tired and achy bones out of the leather recliner with enough pops and cracks to make me reconsider my choice, I step out into the sunlight and hiss. It's not where I'd intended on landing when I walked into the rager going on around me, but it seemed as good a place as any when the drinks never stopped flowing.

Five outa five stars, will recommend to my brother.

Speaking of, that better not be him on the still-blaring phone.

I step over and around bodies as I make my way across the patio of my penthouse in the blinding midafternoon sun. Some still cling onto consciousness, while others have been passed out despite the risk of being tea bagged or drawn on.

Toby grins at me from the concrete, an almost-empty rum bottle still firmly wrapped up in his fist, his long hair a wild mess around his head.

I kick his boot out of spite, the movement jostling the chick drooling on his arm, and flip him both birds.

Sniggering echoes behind me as I leave him on the pavement and attempt to make it to the incessant phone before a headache sets in.

I round the pool just as the noise stops and pick up the device, only to have it start right back up again.

"What." It's more of a snap than a greeting, which I hadn't intended, but you get what you get at this hour after a show night while having been on tour for the last three fucking years.

"Rex, my dear." *Shit* … Recognition of that voice has me pursing my lips and rethinking my life choices. That kind of opening to a conversation won't win me any awards with this one.

"Genevie," I soften my tone with the photographer, an old friend of mine, and scratch at the eagle tattooed on my bare chest. "What can I do for you?"

"Ahhh, that's a much better tone. Glad to see you've woken up a bit." Genevie chides in my ear as I slide my ass to the concrete and roll up my pant legs to dip my feet in the pool. "I have a proposition for you." Continuing on without a response from me, he explains a bunch of crap about the photography world.

I've spent time with this person on plenty of occasions. We've shot cover photos, layouts, calendars, merch shit for the band, and all kinds of crap.

Tour posters and billboards.

Headshots and interviews.

If I need a pic, Genevie is the person I go to. Always open, always down to do whatever.

When he needs a famous but down-to-earth subject, I'm his guy. No questions asked.

Just to be clear, I am no model.

I'm covered in tats—some of which were way before I had any coin to spend on them. Hosting a crooked nose from one too many mosh pits that didn't turn out as I had intended, along with a lion's mane of curly hair that is way harder to take care of than most people think. It's messy and it's *me*.

They love it.

I actually do, too, which is the only reason it's still weighing down my head. I'm known for it, recognized by it.

But that doesn't stop the hours needed to untangle the shit or the money spent on fucking goop to keep it *shiny for the fans.*

It's like I can hear Leo bitching at me all over again.

'They like it, Rex.'

I mock his voice, except my inner monologue version of one of my best friends is higher pitched and makes me chuckle.

'Keep it pretty for them, Rex.'

Except right now. I'm on vacation until I decide otherwise, and there are at least twelve hair bands holding this shit up from my face and neck. It's hot and sticky. Nearing a hundred fucking degrees of the sun up here on the twenty-fourth floor, and a voice I'd rather not deal with still droning on in my ear.

I've clearly stopped listening to Genevie talk some time ago. So, whatever mumbo-jumbo, special project bullshit he's got going on is going to have to wait.

For like six to eight months.

Maybe the next ninety years.

Or at least until I regain some of my composure. Get my diet under control. Kick my muse into gear and start doing something with myself again.

I have music to write and family to see and new albums to record.

Don't get me wrong, I love my career. I love being on the road, touring, singing my heart out to the fans of our music while they back me up in the most harmonious of ways. But three years is a long damn time to sleep on a bus, eat shit food, and not be stationary for more than two days.

I miss my bed. And my new recliner.

"Rex. Please don't tell me I've put you to sleep."

I chuckle into the phone as I kick my feet and splash water around the edge of the pool, soaking my ass more than I had intended. But I don't give two shits about anything right now.

"Nah, old friend. But pretty close." His grunt of displeasure pulls a laugh from deep in my chest.

"Can I count on you? I do believe you'll end up getting more out of this than me."

I allow my laughter to fizzle out into a sigh, shaking my head despite the fact that Genevie can't see me.

"Listen, I'm not up for fuck all right now." Tsks echo across the line at me before I even stop speaking. My eyes roll up to the bright sky before he retorts. I already know he'll spend the next two hours trying to talk me into it, and I'm not so sure that he won't succeed.

"Rex—"

"G, I've been on the road eating garbage and pulling all-nighters for the last three goddamn years. It's break time."

His exasperated sigh shoots static through the line and has me jerking the phone back to save what little hearing I have left.

"What if I tell you there's a woman involved?"

"Nice try, G."

His scoff travels from one ear to the other.

I'm lead vocalist for a famous rock band. I don't have issues finding willing participants in the bedroom or the dressing room or the back of a car, if you know what I mean. So, his attempt to bribe me gets him nowhere.

"Clock is ticking. I'm going to hang up when I get to three, unless you have something worth my time."

I start to count out loud to him, Genevie stuttering his proper boy bullshit into the phone.

He's got nothing, and I'm having too much fun teasing him. With a grin a little too cheeky, I pull the device from my ear, prepared to end his suffering with a thumb hovering over the end call button.

"Please."

I pause.

"Please, Rex." I hear him clear as day as if I'd flipped to speaker phone. "No one else will do except you. It *has* to be you."

"G ..." The fight has left me, the teasing gone along with the calloused fingertips that drag down my face.

"Only you."

Chapter Three

Aria

I DON'T KNOW HOW I got here. In this dungeon that's not a dungeon with a strange man who's petite enough, proper enough, and just a step beyond odd enough to safely consider him gay.

Is that judgy?

Feels judgy.

If it hadn't been for the connection to my sister, and a *very* long pep talk from her and Cedar on the drive over, I would have left so many times by now.

But here I am. With a group text that says *"Go get 'em, no one's gonna murder you"* and the scent of vanilla filling my nose.

There has to be at least a hundred candles burning on the far side of the studio, filling one entire corner with orange flickering light. The flames are almost hypnotic as they burn down into the glass holders, leaving trails of molten wax in their wake.

The place has an open floor plan, ceilings higher than my entire apartment building, and brick walls as far as I can see. There's one loft-like spot with an iron spiral staircase leading up to it where I can see a bed and some mussed sheets.

Maybe the photographer lives here … or maybe that's part of the shoot.

Fuck me.

Nerves slick my palms and nip at my heels, the voice in the back of my head screaming for me to run. Run back home where I'm safe and comfortable, and I'll die with just Chip's memory to keep me company.

Never mind this baffling idea to leap out of my comfort zone and lead a more adventurous life.

I like boring. I like safe.

Whose idea was this?

I'd rather be eating snacks in my bed than wearing one of my originals with almost nothing underneath. Donning my frame is a hand-tailored little black dress that I was saving for a huge occasion. I brought in, hemmed, and loosened all the right spots to fit my large ass and wide hips. I don't know what occasion it was supposed to be worn for, but they chose this one for me.

Dress sexy, they said. *Dress to impress*, they said. It might be fun.

Damn them both.

The strappy neck feels like the dress weighs about a million pounds around my throat. The neckline dipping low and loose around my hot skin, the silky fabric cool against my breasts. I swipe my sweaty palms on my legs again as the photographer comes through one of the only two doors in the place that I assume is some kind of office or changing area. There's a smile on his feminine face that wasn't there when I arrived.

Apparently, my counterpart was running late and we aren't a fan of tardiness.

Shame on them.

"Come now, Ms. Scarlett." Arm outstretched toward the corner with the candles, the photographer, whose name I've forgotten, gestures me to join him. There's a silk tie draped over his arm that has my stomach diving with nerves, but my feet follow him anyway.

"We're really doing the whole blindfold thing." My nerves rattle.

I must be crazy. This is how women go missing.

"I assure you, madam, I am a professional. You can trust me." I feel the color drain from my face as he spins on his wing-tipped heels, the candlelight at his back darkening his features.

It's creepy as hell.

"Holy shit, did I say that out loud?" My hand is over my mouth in shock, assessing how quickly I can run in these heels to the door.

Is this where he murders me and tells my sister I ran off into the sunset?

He chuckles lightly and steps to the side with a head shake. "No, you didn't utter a word, however I know that look. I've worked with many a clientele in the industry and even more who aren't. I honor my word as a professional that you are safe here. We can stop any time you need, for whatever the reason."

The soft smile cracks at the corner of his lips, setting some of my nerves at ease. It's not his fault it looks like the emotion hurts his tummy. I give a short nod in response, which is enough to get him going again.

"So, we are going to start out with blindfolds on you both," he says as he holds the fabric out to me.

I take the silk that matches my dress and watch as he steps away, adjusting candles so the light flickers differently on the wall. I finger the material, feeling the smoothness tame my nerves.

"Neither of you know a thing about each other, but that's the point. However," he says, spinning back to me, sending my heart into a palpitation, with his index finger held up in pause, "if you recognize the other participant, you are obliged to notify me." He steps forward, looking taller somehow, the camera hanging from his neck right in my face.

Holy shit balls, I'm about to do this.

Am I really about to fucking do this?

"This other participant is a high-profile client of mine," he says, collecting this and that.

Shit, I don't know how it works or what it's called, but I've seen my sister with similar items.

He practically levitates from one spot to the next, his steps graceful and calculated. His gaze comes back to me to make sure I'm listening.

"It is imperative that you keep your composure."

I nod, but inside, my stomach is in knots, and my pits are sweating.

Oh, my God. I can't do this.

My stomach turns, every bit of the reassurance he gave me melting away. Who the hell is the other person? Do I even want to know?

Are they like … *famous* or something?

"I certainly hope that you won't recognize him."

Oh no, it's not a chick. Why is it not a chick?

Why does that freak me out even more?

"The only thing I will need from you, Ms. Scarlett, is to act natural. You must ignore my presence wherever possible and embrace the moment."

I suck in a breath at the words, and Chip's voice echoes through my head with that very same phrase. It became his mantra when the sickness started taking its toll on his body and eventually his mind. He knew that each moment we had together was a blessing and that any could be his last. A sense of calm washes over me as goose bumps blossom across my skin.

Embrace the moment.

"Ms. Scarlett. Are you prepared?" The photographer stands in front of me, his arm open wide in an invitation.

I look from his hands to his face, fill my lungs to the point of bursting, and give him another curt nod.

I finger the silk in my grasp.

Inhale. One … Two … Three …

I lift the fabric to my face.

Exhale. One … Two … Three … Four.

And wrap it around my head.

With one knot to secure it, the lack of sight makes my skin prick and my hair rise. My hearing goes sensitive, desperate to catch anything that might give me a clue. I pick up on the photographer's fluid footsteps, which I now notice has a faint limp.

Inhale … One, two, three.

A door in the distance opens and then closes.

Exhale … Two, three, four.

Soft whispers echo across the room, but I can't quite make out what's said, which is followed by thunderous footsteps that make me jump in my skin. There's more than one set of feet traveling in my direction, several of which sound like heavy boots.

This is where I die, for sure. I know it. Chopped up in little pieces and saved for later.

"Remember to breathe, Ms. Scarlett." The photographer's voice at my ear startles me, has me jerking in that direction to see where he's come from, except I can't. A light hand brushes over my bare shoulder, startling me again. "Won't be long now, dear."

The thump of boots gets closer.

More words are whispered, a male voice that isn't the photographer traveling over my skin.

More steps approach closer to me, and my heart begins to thunder with anticipation instead of anxiety.

"Perfect, now …" The photographer trails off as the boots shuffle to a stop, and heat warms my back.

Someone is close but not close enough to touch. I hear the faint shutter of a camera and square my shoulders with the familiarity of the sound.

My lungs release, the momentum instilling strength in me to embrace this damn moment.

"Remove the blindfold, my dear." I reach up and peek under the darkness. My eyes take a second to focus on the wall in front of me, my skin prickling. "Now turn."

Dropping my arm, I spin, the silk dangling from my grasp.

And stop.

Dead.

Hair flips into my mouth from the momentum, my breath leaving me in a whoosh like I've just been sucker punched.

The eyes that stare back at me drink me in hauntingly, curiously, as they sweep from my head to the heels on my feet. The odd mix of green and blue in his gaze blazes its trail back up my body to settle on my breasts for a beat, then land back on my face. "Holy shit."

I flush and brush the hair from my still-open mouth.

His voice is deeper than anything I've heard in person, his tone genuinely amazed.

Amused?

His whole person is nothing like anyone I've ever met.

I gulp, my throat working to swallow down the intensity I feel.

Tattoos … so many tattoos color his skin, exposed by the crisp white button-down that screams anything but professional. It's unkempt and wrinkled on purpose, several buttons undone, the sleeves rolled up his thick forearms. Only the front is tucked into the jeans I'm certain he had made for him with the way the dark denim hugs his thick thighs and …

Holy shit is right.

The bulge suggests he's either hung like a motherfucker or already likes what he sees.

My breath hitches in my throat, my eyes unable to willingly look elsewhere, my breathing coming in short pants like a dog in heat. That is until his hand blocks the view and not so inconspicuously points an index finger upward.

"Oh, fuck." I'm redder than the thong I wear, self-consciousness settling in thick and quick as the sounds of a shudder clicking register in my brain. My head whips to the sound, guilt and embarrassment bulging my eyes out of my head.

I'm caught looking at his junk. Just put me out of my misery now.

"No worries." His low, warm tone brings my attention back to his grinning face. "I like what I see, too."

I've never melted before at just the sight or the sound of another person. But I'm fairly certain that's what's happening right now. Warmth pools all over my body, but especially low in my belly, as I take a step forward.

"So much hair."

Oh my God.

Just take me out now.

It's all the words I can muster as I focus beyond the gorgeous set of eyes and see the locks of curls falling from the crown of his head. A dark blonde on the verge of brown, the curls silhouette his face in massive amounts.

Then there's that grin. Set under a crooked nose. And hot damn, do I wanna do bad things right now.

Another step forward and I can feel the heat radiating from him, the pull of him drawing me in. His amusement feathers across my face with a minty freshness.

"I've seen people fawn before, trust." He reaches up slowly, the back of his hand caressing across my cheek. "But never like this."

Confusion furrows my brow, but the stretch of his grin into a smile has me entranced.

Where am I again?

"G's kept me in the dark on pretty much all of this." The backs of his fingers continue their dance over my reddened cheek, and his hand flips, his palm grasping my jaw tenderly. "Judging by the emotions flickering on your face, I can assume the same is true for you."

I'm leaning in, more on my toes than I would normally sustain for long without realizing, but his words bring reality crashing in.

Along with the echo of a camera shudder.

G? The photographer snaps away at our interaction, this whole thing caught on film.

I spin to him, shaking off the spell this guy's scent has drawn me into, anger beginning to bubble in my chest when it hits me.

Blind shoot. My sister's words sink into my conscious mind, connecting the dots of this interaction with the stranger.

The photographer's way of setting subjects up, adding a weird creative flair, and being able to market their work.

"Blind shoot." I wag my finger at the photographer but turn my attention back to my co-captive in this situation. "I've only heard of the term recently. It's essentially a blind date."

"Clever girl." G tsks from behind his camera, but there's more approval to the noise than guilt.

The male counterpart of this shoot just grunts, a shrug lifting his muscled shoulders, complete nonchalance permeating his aura.

"G's sneaky like that, but I still win." His hand reaches out, wraps around my waist, and tugs me against his hard body.

Whoa. What is breath? I clearly don't need it.

Is a chest supposed to be this hard?

"How so?" I breathe against his neck, my gaze taking its sweet time studying the artwork there as my hands flatten against his pecs. He smells of musk, like the kind you find around sweetened bourbon barrels, and a great fucking time waiting to happen.

"I get the chance to admire a masterpiece." Slowly, his hands slide down to my hips, leaving a trail of warmth in their wake. I meet his sparkling eyes. "Can't go wrong there."

His smile wounds me with its brilliance and lifts the corners of my lips in return. It's uncontrollable, the movement, as I drink it in and allow myself to just be here.

"What's your name?" I ask.

My co-subject leans in, a head taller than me means he's in more of a hunched position, and his hair falls around us like a curtain blocking us from the outside world. I can't help the giggle that escapes me as he closes the distance, diverting his lips to my ear at the last second, and gives me a face full of his incredible curls.

Why am I so damn giddy?

"If I told you that," he whispers, chills racking down my spine and clenching my toes. "I'd have to kill you."

Chapter Four

Rex

S HIVERS RACK HER BODY as I caress her neck with my thumb and bury my face in her hair.

I can't help myself.

She's so goddamn beautiful and willing that I have to touch her fair skin. She smells of the tropics on a summer day, a hint of coconut and warmth.

She wears her emotions on her face. I see the embarrassment redden her high cheekbones, the reservations furrow her sculpted brows, the curiosity sparkles in her green eyes. Even more than that is what I *don't* see.

Not once has recognition contorted her features when she looks at me through her thick lashes. She drinks me in like a real person, not a rockstar, and it's not until she averts her eyes in embarrassment over nerves that I realize how much I missed it.

It's not often that I can get by without being noticed, something I used to thrive on, but years in the limelight take their toll.

And this fucking dress has my dick filling the longer she's okay with pressing her warm body against me.

"Divine, you two." Genevie's low voice cuts through the little bubble we've begun to create, like a feedback scream straight to the ear drums.

Shock shoots across her face like she forgot all about him snapping photos of us, and another giggle slips out of her as she meets my eyes again.

"I haven't smiled this much in a long time." Her hand covers her mouth, but the lift of her cheeks tells me her smile doesn't fade.

"I have," I retort but shift my gaze up to recall if it felt the same. There's not anything that's ever rivaled the feeling I get on stage, when seventy thousand people sing my songs back to me and my band without missing a single beat. "But not quite like *this*."

This ... is different somehow. Genevie may have been onto something, and for that, I might owe him.

"What do you say, babe? Wanna give the artist some inspiration?" I cup her face in both palms so I can read her reaction as she reaches up for the first time and threads her fingers through my hair. I lean into the touch, so tender, yet bold, that it has my half smile amping up and my eyes closing. Sighing, I press my forehead to hers.

"Absolutely," she breathes, determination lacing her tone.

"Tell me to fuck off if it's too much," I whisper to her, raising my eyes to catch her reaction. I get the faint nod I half expected, and that's all I need.

Grabbing her hand and spinning away, I leave the flickering light of the candles in our dust and beeline straight to the spiral stairs. I pause there and lean against the railing with one arm around her shoulders, her hand still in mine, and the other running up the cool metal.

Click, click.

She's already looking at me when I check on her.

Click. Click. Click.

Satisfied with the look I get, I pull her closer and plant a gentle kiss to the center of her forehead.

This stunning woman melts into my hands, her body leaning impossibly close and her breath leaving her on a slow sigh.

Chuckling, I slide down her side into a crouch and wrap a hand around her ankle. When she pauses, I look up in question to find a smirk on her face and her hand making its way to my shoulder for support.

Click.

She lifts one foot for me to remove the heel I know won't fare well on these stairs, then the other. Straightening up to my full height, a towering six feet and four inches, I peer down at her.

Pinning her between my arms, I press her back against the railing.

More camera shutters echo in the otherwise silent room.

The sexy smirk on her face tells me I don't need to ask for what I want next, but to be an uncharacteristic gentleman, I do anyway.

"Can I pick you up?"

Her wide eyes are stuck on me and full of wonder, and I'm caught up in the way they sparkle at my request when she nods.

Running my hands down her sides, amping her grin up the lower I go, I lean until my palms find the backs of her knees, and I pull her along the front of me with ease.

With her legs around my waist, arms around my neck, I take the steps two at a time until the bed hits my shins. Her core radiates against my groin, the way her dress slips up her hips sending my cock solid between us.

I lean slowly into kneeling on the plush bed, her legs still wrapped around my hips, and push her back into the dark sheets.

Completely aroused, my dick throbs in my jeans against her core.

My sight flicks to hers.

Click. Click. Click.

Fuck it.

Supporting my weight with one arm, I palm her jaw with the other and hover my lips over hers.

Click.

"Kiss me," she demands, her breath washing over my heated face.

Smirking when her hands find my hair, I crash my lips to hers, and it's like the heat of a thousand suns that has my mind spinning, my body aching to come home. It's like exhilaration and relaxation in one as I press my tongue to her plump lips, and she opens up to me. Our tongues slide and tease against one another, her hands slipping up the back of my shirt and pressing into my lower back. She pulls me tight against her body, melding from hip to chest, her full tits pressing into my pecs.

I'm lightheaded when I pull back, my lungs heaving, desperate to catch my breath.

"Holy shit," she whispers to me through her own labored breathing, her eyes darting between mine in search of my reaction.

"Holy shit is right."

Click, click, click.

For good measure, I dip down to meet her again, a sweet and gentle touch of her swollen lips to mine.

Fuuuuck …

We mold into several other poses on the bed, along the floor, against the overlook of the loft to the rest of the place. Genevie guides us gently back to the main floor for different backdrops and settings around the studio.

The tension left in the wake of that kiss has me ready to explore with her, except we have company, who seems to make himself known at the exact moment I would have stripped her bare.

She tells me her name while she straddles my lap, her soft fingers stroking the side of my face.

Click.

Her hands travel to the buttons on my shirt, her exploration finding its way to my inked torso.

"Aria," I whisper in her ear, and I feel her grin against the palm I have her face nestled in. "You have no idea how fitting that name is."

She barely leans back, her face just a breath from mine, her core pressing into my groin in all the right ways, heating me up and sending me insane.

"Tell me something else about you," she lilts, the look on her face screaming sex and comfort that I find I want to wrap myself in.

To tell her all about my life.

My secrets.

But I don't. Because that would mean bursting this bubble of anonymity she's unknowingly created for me.

And I'm just not ready for that.

I want whatever she's willing to give me, though.

To not discourage her from telling me about herself, I try to come up with something to say that won't give me away. Or something that could become public should she decide to tell the world she met a rock star.

If she figures out who I am.

"I've got just the one brother. He's actually my twin." Sharing that detail feels cheapened by the entire world already knowing that about me. So I add, "He's fraternal, but we often get mistaken as identical." Publicly, fans believe that we *are* identical twins; he just keeps his hair shorter than mine. The information feels less than, but she squeals with delight at my confession.

"Dear God, there are two of you?" Her eyes are wide, and her lips pull up tight. "Is he as pretty as you?"

I full-on belly laugh at her reaction, allowing it to fill me up with lightheartedness. "I suppose so. He does have the same face as me."

Aria giggles, her hand coming back up to cover the sound. "I wouldn't want to insult him, but it's just not possible."

My cock jumps at her brazenness, but I scoff in faux offense anyway. "Too late. I can feel his attitude change from here."

We share a laugh, but I can see the question in her eyes before she asks it. "Where is he?"

There's concern lacing her words and drawing her brows down, so I reach up to soften the muscles with the pad of my thumb. "He's at home. Maybe in my home. Possibly with another brother of mine." Confusion undoes the work I just did softening her brow.

"Brother?"

"Not by blood."

The muscles under my thumb soften at my words.

Click. Click.

"G," I call out, not taking my eyes off her. "We done here?"

Her face falls the moment the words leave my lips, disappointment I can feel pulling her shoulders inward.

"I suppose we can be, Rexy dear."

My head snaps in the direction of the man, pinning him with my gaze through the camera lens he's yet to sit down. He lowers the device from his face as realization sets in.

"Rexy?"

I'd managed not to tell her my name this whole time, but the sound of the stupid pet name coming from her rosy lips does tingly shit to my spine. I side-eye her for a moment but return my blazing gaze back on our photographer.

"Not my name," I correct, colder than I intended and not taking my eyes off him.

Genevie lowers the camera completely and returns my invisible daggers with a look of his own. It screams a half-assed apology but to also get the hell over it.

I'm so caught up in my own shit that I don't notice the demeanor change until Aria pulls away from me to get up. She's been in my lap or against my body so long that I feel the absence of her the instant she breaks contact. The void of warmth.

She's already walking away from me when I push to my feet.

"Aria?" I question softly, reaching a hand out to her.

She glances at me, but there's already a shutout starting, her dismissal digging straight into my chest. "It's not fair, *you*." She scoffs, tossing pillows around in search of something.

"It's not," I admit on a half shrug that has her spinning on me with squared shoulders and hands firmly on her hips.

"What's your name, then?"

I can see she doesn't think I'm going to answer. I should because it's the only fair thing to do but instead, I ask the only other thing I can think of. "What music do you listen to?"

Aria jolts at my words, a mix of attitude and confusion radiating from her, another scoff pursing her lips. "That has nothing to do with anything." She spins away with a shake of her head and begins searching again. "Why would I tell him that if he can't tell me his name?" She directs her comments to the man behind the lens, but he backs away slowly with his hands up.

"I am not at liberty to say, Ms. Scarlett."

She pins him with a look, picks up a nearby throw pillow from a pile we posed in not that long ago, and pings it off his head. He's flabbergasted, his mouth dropping open with a gasp, allowing me the chance to step toward her.

"What music, Ms. Scarlett?"

She spins on me, one shoe in her hand and somehow another pillow. "*Soul.* I like oldies, *okay?*" She grunts and wings the pillow that I dodge with a laugh. "And I don't know how you find this amusing." Aria's yelling now, which leaves me snickering at her level of emotion.

"I like soul, too, sometimes," I admit on a shrug as I step closer to her, invading her space.

She's found her other shoe and armed with yet another pillow, but I'm in her face, too close for her to throw it at me.

"So, he likes music, too, but doesn't have a name." Her chest heaves with her words, her eyes betraying her annoyance with a roll.

Stepping into the lion's den, I lean into her and wrap my arms around her waist. She pulls at me after dropping the pillow, pushing at my chest, sweat beading at her brow.

"*Babe.*" I bring my lips to her ear, pushing the hair back there to tuck it behind her ear, and I suck in a breath of everything *her.*

Either she really has no idea who I am … or it'll be on the news tomorrow.

I can see the headlines now: Rex Thompson spent the evening ravishing a female for the camera.

But I don't stop the words that tumble off my tongue and seal my fate.

"My name's Rex."

Aria's body tenses against mine, her fight long ago forgotten.

Does she know now?

Would she even believe it's me?

My name has been chanted by the thousands. My band's name screamed. Our lyrics replicated and sung and remixed.

But when Aria pulls back, meets my eyes with emotion I can't recognize, and whispers my name back to me, my rigid muscles loosen and my skin chills all over.

Goose bumps. They're called goose bumps, idiot.

She says it like she's tasting decadent chocolate or fine wine for the first time. Savoring the flavors on her palate, yet preparing to devour the treat on the next bite.

Our lips slam together with a kiss that has my dick filling and my chest swelling like nothing I've ever felt before.

"*Rex.*"

Her hands are on me, in my hair, pulling and tangling in ways that make my heart beat faster.

"Yeah?" I say against her mouth, trailing kisses and licks down her neck as my hands find her ass and squeeze.

"I like that name."

Her breath races down my throat, exhilarating me to my bones, and I growl out my response.

"*Then say it again.*"

Chapter Five

Aria

IF WISHES WERE BOTTLED and I could be spared just one, it would be that this moment never ends.

The aura of mystery around Rex is more alluring than I should allow it to be, but isn't that the whole point? To take a chance on something?

He's got the whole badass exterior, with a soft inflection that begs me to explore. To touch. To know more about him than he's willing to share with the rest of the world. That curiosity is driving this car and calling my name like the cat to its death. I'd be a liar if I thought this was going to end easily.

I'm not sure how to exit this moment with him, y'know, curiosity and all. So, instead, I steal a glance in his direction while I slip the heels back onto my feet. He's already studying me through his thick lashes as he reaches around to feed his belt through the loops with bulging arms and nimble fingers.

When did he even take that off?

Heat rises in my cheeks, and I avert my eyes back to the small buckle on my strappy heels that give me at least another four inches of height. I struggle, yet draw out, fastening the thing back on as a means to hide from the scrutiny.

Or the inevitable.

Boots fill my vision as he comes close, his scent assaulting my nose.

"I want to see you again." The words are low, spoken from the base of his vocals, and send tingles right down to my rolled-over belly.

Craning my neck, I stare up at his tall frame, my sight trailing along to find his belt hanging open at his waist and his shirt barely covering any of his broad chest.

"How about later? Or tomorrow." I speak to the rings that glint from his nipples, my mouth thinking of all the ways to play with just those.

My plane leaves tomorrow.

Why did I offer tomorrow?

Breaking my trance on his chest, I slide my gaze up to his jaw, with enough stubble to make my thighs itch with want, and meet his steely gaze.

Fuck.

"Absolutely." His clipped nod and complete lack of hesitation tug at the corners of my lips and my heartstrings.

Guess I'm driving home …

Pushing to my feet, I catch movement out of the corner of my eye. Another set of boots attached to a guy bigger than Rex approaches us, several items in his large hands that catch me off guard.

"Who the hell are you?" My fists flex with concern, my brows shooting to meet at the center of my forehead.

Rex doesn't seem alarmed by this guy, but I sure as shit am.

How long has he been here?

"Ma'am." He nods subtly to me but doesn't answer the question as he hands a phone to Rex and offers my purse to me.

Out of instinct, I snatch the clutch from his huge hands and muster my best bravado attitude.

I angrily flip through the contents to ensure nothing is missing, my fingers touching the smoothness of my wallet filled with too many items and fingering the insanely expensive makeup tubes while pinning him with daggers from my eyes.

He seems more amused than he is threatened, but I keep up my best intimidation anyway.

"Here." Rex's voice soothes the edges of my mood, pulling my attention back to his crown of curls then the extended phone in his hand.

Wait, that's my phone …

Confused, I take the device from him and look it over. Sure as shit, the red lips on the dark background of my lock screen stare back at me like a beacon in the night.

"I put my number in and sent myself a message."

The light of mischief in his demeanor has a smile forming despite the looming giant watching our interaction and the confusion hell-bent on leaving a permanent V between my brows. I give a single nod as Rex dips closer, his hair falling forward over his brow, casting shadows over his features.

I know what he wants.

It's sexy, alluring, the way his mane fills him out and begs to be touched. To be grabbed. To be used as guidance from between a set of thighs while his tongue does things I'm certain only happen in fantasies …

I lean in and plant a quick peck on his plump lips.

But for Rex, that's not good enough, no.

He grabs me with one hand on my hip, the other on the back of my neck, and pulls me into his chest until his warmth permeates my bones. His lips meet mine, fervor lacing his actions as his tongue licks at my bottom lip. I grant the access he's demanding, matching his enthusiasm with my own passionate tongue strokes and nibbles as my arms snake around his shoulders. Rex presses his groin into my stomach, his cock hard and pulsing between us. That fancy red thong underneath my dress soaks through with my arousal, nipples peaked in anticipation of what might come.

He wants to see me again.

"I'll text you." Rex pulls back, pressing his forehead to mine, his labored breathing burning down my throat in a battle to see whose air wins out.

"Okay," I pant, slowly raising my lids and catching sight of his charming pearly whites.

Before I can thoroughly fill my lungs again, he's gone from me, the warmth along with him. He disappears through the door with the boot-clad stranger on his heels and a copycat on his front.

What the hell?

Click. Click.

I whip my head around to find the photographer hiding behind his lens, still snapping pictures of me panting like a damn dog after a man I *just* met. He peeks out from behind the device with a knowing wink that both irks and settles me.

"Holy shit." Eyes wide and a hand to my chest, I feel my heart beat a thousand miles a minute. Like it's ready to burst out from behind my sternum.

"I concur, Ms. Scarlett." He nods, a ghost of a smile on his sculpted face.

"I forgot you were here," I admit on an awkward chuckle that escapes me, a flush running from the crown of my head to my chest.

"That, my dear, is the point." He snaps another pic, then lowers the camera to the pressed dress shirt covering his chest. "Now, you are welcome to stay as long as you need, but I am curious to see these results." He taps a finger to the side of the camera, then clasps his hands behind his back in wait.

Oh, right.

"Thanks." I nod, dumbfounded and probably in shock.

I stumble in these stupid heels that I will never look at the same way, in the direction of the door Rex just left through. I clutch my purse, holding the thing to my chest as if it might stop the beating organ in there from escaping my body and leaving me for dead.

I'm outside even though I don't remember opening a door. My phone buzzes in my hand, my sister's picture flashing across the previously blank screen. I barely feel my shaking hands as they swipe to answer the call and bring the device to my ear.

"Ari?" my sister calls through the phone, filling my eardrum with echoes and static as my brain tries to catch up.

I'm a jumbled mess as I walk on ankles that threaten to give out in these shoes, and I breathe in the fresh air that helps settle my pulse and my racing thoughts.

Inhale ... one ... two ... three ...

Hold.

Exhale ... one .... two ... three ... four.

"Holy shit." It's all I can muster in this moment as my heels click against the pavement, my feet propelling me toward the rental car I parked in the lot a block down.

I pass others on their journeys as I walk with my sister's voice in my ear, and it's as if they have no idea that a feeling like this can exist.

I don't blame them. I wouldn't have believed it either.

She's asking me questions rapid fire, too excited to hear what happened, so I allow her the time to calm her shit while I work through calming mine.

Breathe, one ... two ... three ...

"Okay." She blows static through the phone with the word as I beep the car open and slip into the seat without flashing the world my soaked panties. "Okay, so. I totally went off. How was it?"

Chuckling, I lock myself in the car and flop back into the seat. "Oh. My. God."

She squeals, I squeal. My hands shake, and I do a little dance in my seat.

"I can't believe I did it. I can't believe how hot it was ... *he was*. I am in shock and awe."

Fuuuuck.

My heart still races, my thoughts running over every detail of what happened as if I can live the moment all over again.

"Hot damn, Ari. I didn't think you'd have it in you. I never should have doubted you."

I put the car in drive as we laugh and swoon while I recount the events with my sister all the way to the hotel and up the elevator to my floor. Tapping the card against the lock, I let myself into the place I'm calling home for the night, allowing the door to penetrate the otherwise silence with a heavy *thunk* behind me.

We continue to chat about my counterpart and Genevie, the photographer, as I meander about the room, checking out the small snack selection and the minibar. I select a bag of M&M's and a soda as I venture around the room to the bed and toe off the shoes, then flop onto the fluffed mattress.

She tells me of her day and that she worried sick about me, whether I would go through with it or not. Apparently, Cedar called her twenty times to see if I'd checked in. I think she's full of shit, but it might be close.

My sister still managed to get her infant shoot done for the day because she is a damn rock star at her job.

Aurora patches in my best friend once it's time for her shift to end, and I get to recall the whole thing again, with pleasure.

"It's the most intimidating, fun, bullshit, anxiety-ridden thing I've done in a long time." I admit to them through an achy face and a levity in my chest that I swear hadn't graced me with its presence in a long time. It makes me feel like more *is* possible.

Like if I can do that, then what else can I do?

The adrenaline still pumping through my veins gives motivation to my dreams and sparks my muse to rear her enthusiasm for creation. I'm so deep in sharing the things, embracing the day, and feeling my feels that I almost don't catch the beep that sounds through the tiny speaker.

Gotta be an email or something.

I spare a glance at the screen but bring the thing back to my ear before the words in the notification can register in my poor riddled brain.

Oh my God.

I yank the device back into my sight.

Ohmy—

One unread message highlights my lock screen like a beacon.

Falling silent, I stare.

The name sitting there in my phone, clear as the harvest moon in the night sky.

"Oh my fucking God," I squeak, my eyes growing wide and my heart stopping in its tracks.

"What?" Cedar snaps.

"*Whatwhatwhat?*" Aurora chants.

I just gape and try to remember to breathe as I read and reread the message.

> *SexyMane: Hey, babe. Whatcha doin'?*

It's almost as if I hear him speak the words directly to me, not through a message, and my thong loses the battle to yet another flood.

The contact name has giggles bubbling up my chest and my brain confirming the thought.

Sexy indeed.

I'm suddenly very aware of the soft, silky satin against my heated skin, thanks to the dress I've yet to change out of, and the wetness collecting between my thighs. Goose bumps blossom across my body at the thought of his hands on my hips and his hair feathering over my bare skin.

"WOMAN, what ARE you DOING?" Aurora enunciates through the phone speaker loud enough to pull me out of the trance I've fallen into.

"He fucking texted me."

Crickets fill the line for a moment, and I just *know* the two of them are sharing that knowing look with each other without being able to see them at all. The silence lasts for only a millisecond once my statement sinks in for these two to lose their minds.

"What did he say?"

"Are you going to text him back?"

"*Tell us.*"

I shake my head at the barrage of questions but can't help the grin that pulls my lips up farther than they already were. "Of course I am, guys. How could I not?"

One of them screams while the other whistles from high to low.

"How could you not?" Aurora agrees.

They continue to gab with each other over the line despite being in the same place—I can hear the echo of one when the other speaks—as if I'm not even on the phone. So, I open the message with hovering thumbs and prepare to respond.

Me: Chilling in my room. You?

I hit send and take a breath with the intent to break up the conversation happening between the women without me, but my phone beeps again with another notification before my brain can catch up with their commentary.

SexyMane: Thinking of you.

Oh, Lord have mercy on me.

The line falls into a heady silence, and I realize that one of them may have asked me a question I clearly didn't hear while I stared at the screen. I let them sit for a second, though, as I type and send my next response.

Does he really mean it that *way?*

Me: That's cute.

The reply is almost instant.

SexyMane: My thoughts are not cute.

The winky face emoji that appears on my screen next sends me into a fit of breathless giggles I don't even bother to dampen.

"Girl, you better spill what's going on. Like right now," Cedar drawls over the line, and I can't help but chuckle more.

"He's thinking of me, and I'm hanging up." A barking laugh and a *whoaaaaa-ho-hooo* from my sister and best friend bring warmth to my chest. "Love you, bitches."

"Love you," Aurora singsongs.

"Love you more," Cedar returns, and the line goes dead.

Chapter Six

Rex

The ghost of her lips on mine, her hands in my hair and on my chest, still lingers. The spots tingle like she's still there, but they're colder now that she's not. Despite the hours that have passed since I left her in the studio with Genevie, all I've gotten are a few text messages.

I've already called him for more information about her, but in true Genevie fashion, he won't divulge shit.

Mysterious bastard.

I gotta respect the client's privacy, though. He does the same for me.

My twin brother pulls for my attention as he takes up the entire length of my couch with his bullshit and stank-ass feet.

As I suspected, Mac was here when I got home, raiding the fully stocked fridge like he lives here and flicking through streaming services.

Can't exactly ask Aria over if his ass won't leave simply because I feel like she wouldn't be down to have company like that.

And being a famous person means being in public brings too many sets of eyes and cameras. There's just too much risk of her finding out about who I am if she meets my brother.

So I've resorted to true childish behavior by sitting at the bar off the kitchen counter and pelting ice cubes at Mac's head from the bucket I have next to me.

"*Ow*, you turdscicle," he yells at me from across the room.

I laugh as I watch the cube bounce from his noggin to the floor and skid into a corner somewhere for me to find with my socks later. "Know where no one throws ice at you?" I grab another, my palm freezing with the melting ice, my fingers long ago numb.

"In hell because it's too hot to have ice." He brushes off the drops of water left behind by my assault just in time for me to wail him with another. "You fucking heathen."

"Get out of my house," I shout, throwing another. This one he retrieves and tosses back in my direction without leaving the couch. I dodge the projectile as my phone vibrates along the counter.

"*Never.*"

> **Aria:** You're doing what now?

> **Me:** Throwing literal ice cubes at his head.

> **Me:** He still won't leave.

She returns with a laughing emoji that has me grinning like a fool and not paying enough attention to my surroundings. I hear the cascade of falling ice before I feel it and shoot to my feet with boiling rage at my sibling. The bucket I had stashed next me, now empty, its contents scattered down my body, in my hair, and along my floor.

For the second time tonight, I send a message with numb fingers, asking for a moment to deal with my twin. The last time took me way too long to return to her.

"Macaroni, you fart knuckle."

I pocket my phone as I lunge at him.

"Don't call me that." He takes off, sliding along the wet floor and only barely skidding around the corner without eating tile.

I chase him again, sidestepping the slippery spots and clearing the distance quicker than he expected.

"Oh, shit," Mac says on a laugh, skirting around the pool table in the game hall instead of over it like I do.

I hook him with an arm around his big head as my feet hit the floor, pulling him to a stop and tucking him into my side.

Two, three jabs to my ribs in a feeble attempt to break loose, but my grip is solid around his forehead.

Noogie time.

I viciously rub my knuckles over the top of my twin's head, mussing up his treasured hair and loosening the bandana he wears like a headband all the time. It's purple today. I watch as it flops to the floor while he grunts and squirms against my assault.

"You *asshat.*" Mac wraps his arms around my sweatpants-clad thigh and yanks until I'm off balance, then we're falling on the ground.

We roll. I pin him, he pins me.

Being twins, in this case, means we're built pretty close to the same stature. I work out to maintain an image while my brother is the drummer of our band and, therefore, has the stamina plus the strength to give me a run for my money. Every set is basically a four-hour workout for him.

Threads pop as we both try anything and everything to get the upper hand, including grabbing clothes and taking cheap shots near the treasured bits or vulnerable coverage.

He's the cause of times two and three that I've broken my nose. Ma was not happy with either time.

"Call it," Mac grunts, his thigh pinning my neck to the floor with enough force to knock me out cold if I don't break it. "Say *uncle.*"

I suck in what little air I can, then bridge his ass, ripping my shirt in the process, and lock him with an armbar.

"Call truce and leave." I pull his wrist tight. "Or call uncle." He fights it, tries to slip out on a frustrated growl, but stops.

"Truce."

I release my hold and tap his forehead for good measure as I roll away in search of the phone that slipped from my pocket some time ago. Finding it face down in a puddle of melted ice, I wipe the screen on my pants, plant my ass on the floor, and pray that the water didn't seep into any of the ports.

Thankfully, the screen lights up, a text sitting unread from twenty minutes ago. I open the message and kick my foot out to trip my twin as he rolls on past. He returns with a thump to my bicep and keeps walking.

> **Aria: What's good to eat around here? I'm starving.**

Shit. That was an opening.

I type back quickly with an apology and an inquiry on whether she'd found something yet. She's quick to respond.

> **Aria: No, I finally got through to someplace called Pop's, but it's an hour wait for delivery.**

It's almost like I can hear the defeated sigh I suspect comes off her lips. I take a moment to connect the dots on whether she's home or from out of town and take a leap.

> **Me: Does your hotel have an outside chill spot? Firepit kinda thing?**

If I can't get Mac to leave so that she can come here, maybe I can manage to go there. There's normally a place in the back of the building that's semiprivate. The security company we pay good money for should be able to cover the rest. I tap my phone to my chin in thought as I await her reply.

> Aria: Yeah, I actually just walked down here to check it out.

> Me: Alright, you want Pop's? I'll bring you Pop's.

I'm up and changing before she responds with the hotel's address, my phone to my ear, calling in a favor to my favorite diner.

A fresh pair of jeans and an old-school band tee later, I'm in the parking garage on a sprint to my shimmering midnight-blue Audi with two security agents on my heels doing their jobs. One slips into the passenger seat of my car, the other behind the wheel of a blacked-out SUV.

It's not too late for dinner time, despite the dark, but that doesn't deter the paps from collecting at the exit to my building.

They know I live here.

They know I'm home now that the tour is over, and they've been camping on my street for the last three days, waiting to get a good shot of me or one of my brothers.

Anything to make the headlines.

The security vehicle in front clears the path for me to jet out like a bat out of hell and drift onto the main road with more ease than I had expected. I jog the car into town, pass my destination to make sure no one's tailed me, and circle back around.

I'm at Pop's with a call in to let them know I'm outside in less than fifteen. Georgie, a former classmate of mine and fellow band geek, steps out with the bag and pizza box before I can even hang up the phone. Perks of not only knowing the owner but helping him get his restaurant off the ground means I get priority when I call in for food.

He's even offered to shut the place down for me at a discounted price so that I can have a meal in peace. Nice enough, but not worth him losing the business.

"Georgie, I heard business is good tonight." I speak across the car to the owner as he hands the items through the passenger window to my bodyguard.

Georgie grunts his response as Ian checks the food for accuracy and tampering. With a nod of security approval, I wave to Georgie, roll up the window, and back the car out of the space.

Getting to the hotel proves not as easy though. Paparazzi pin my car on the main road before the security SUV has a chance to cut them off. They hang out of the moving vehicles with cameras flashing, the lights placing spots in my vision.

Ian, who already dons aviators, passes a pair to me as I tap the brakes and avoid smacking the ass end of the pap's shitty car in front of me. He rolls the window down and sticks his entire arm out, flipping them the bird. More flashing, some yelling.

"Sharp left," Ian directs, holding the bag up to block the view of me from the side.

Anything for a stupid money shot, these bastards.

I follow his directions and barely decelerate to take the next left. Brake lights fill the rearview as the pap cars skid to a stop but don't make the turn like I did. Security pulls up behind me, closer than any normal car, and rides my ass to keep out the riffraff until I circle back to the final destination.

I kill the headlights before I pull into the lot and inch across the pavement to ensure I don't hit anybody on accident. I slow at the edge of the building to let Ian out of the slowly rolling car so that he can do the other parts of his job like scope the scene. Coasting again, I find the little spot around the back of the building, as I suspected, and park the car.

Pause … observe …

No one jumps out of the bushes that protect the gathering area armed with a camera, or worse, so I hop out and let myself in through the privacy gate with grub in hand.

A small, paved pathway leads into an opening with a firepit front and center. It's surrounded by stone seating with plush colored cushions that's encased by a stone wall to mid-chest and bushes extending the height beyond that.

Nodding, I walk around the blazing flames to find Aria sitting at the head of it all with stars in her eyes and a pile of firewood at her feet.

She's sexy like that in tight-ass bright red high-waisted pants and an oversized cutoff hoodie.

"Babe." I match her smile with one of my own as she stands and meets me halfway.

I open my arms, one filled with the food containers, and she easily steps into me. One hand to my forearm, the other on my chest, she leans in for a peck on my desperate lips.

Still not good enough.

The smell of her perfume, accentuated by the scent of rich smoke, fuels me as I wrap my free arm around her waist and pull her against my chest to deepen the kiss.

"Rex," she breathes against my lips, her body warm and fusing to mine.

Fuck, she's perfect.

The sound of Aria's stomach growling rumbles over the roar of the fire, interrupting my deep inhale, and I can't help but burst into laughter.

"Let's eat." I smack another quick kiss on her lips and spin her around in the direction of her seat.

"It smells *amazing*," she groans with hands to her cheeks, her thick ass settling into the cushion.

I've never been jealous of a fucking cushion before.

I plant my ass in the seat next to her and plop the pizza box right in her lap.

"So do you."

Chapter Seven

I F HUMAN NATURE HADN'T taken over, I would have him in my room already.

But the smell of pizza and fresh garlic bread fills the air around the fire more than the burning wood, and I down a slice before Rex even gets the bag open.

Oops.

I lick my fingers clean, not missing the side-eye from him as he observes me without trying to be obvious. It's not judgment I catch in his gaze but admiration.

I haven't eaten more than sugar since yesterday.

Doesn't stop the negative Nancy in my head, though, from labeling the look as slight disgust.

As if able to hear my thoughts, Rex pops the lid off the garlic bread—*I knew I smelled it*—and shoves an entire piece in his mouth with reckless abandon. Grease smears across his cheek and cheese molds to his lips as he attempts to chew around the massive carb ball in his jaw.

I laugh.

"It's fucking great." He speaks around the mouthful, crumbs falling to his chest. "Isn't it?"

I nearly snort as I nod my response.

Why am I so comfortable around him?

There's no nagging voice in the back of my head, screaming that garlic breath is bad for a first date. Nothing telling me that meeting a stranger in a place I've never been is a terrible idea. Only mild concern that he'll realize I'm lame and want to leave, but I have his attention right now.

In this moment.

That he chose to share with me when he could've been *anywhere* else.

I can appreciate that, so I lean in and take a piece of garlic bread for myself as he dives in for a slice from the box still in my lap. My cheeks redden at the closeness of our faces, the heat from him and the fire. Rex's sexy half grin notches up, though, setting me more at ease. He sneaks a quick peck on my lips, then settles back to eat his pizza in two bites. I giggle and shake my head.

"What?" he asks, his attention half on the fire, the other half on me.

"Nothing." I shake my head but amend myself with a reminder that I don't want to parse my words. *We're embracing this shit.* "I just didn't expect adorable to be so sexy."

He nods with understanding, light dancing across his features from the flames burning between us.

There's mirth there in his eyes, and I enjoy it a little too much.

"I called my brother a fart knuckle earlier." Straight-ass face, speaking into the fire, Rex's words don't sink in at first.

"A ... what?" My brow furrows, and my nose flares in question at the randomness and confusing statement.

"A fart knuckle," he answers, face still dead serious as he turns to look at me.

I can't help the outburst that ensues. Doubling over with full-on belly laughs, I hold the pizzas out from being smooshed by said belly and mull over the words in my head.

"Why would you do *that?*"

He snickers with a shake of his head. "Thought you might want to take me a little less seriously." He shrugs. "Besides, he started it."

"And what did your brother start it with?" I hold my abdomen, my guts threatening to evacuate my body with the cackling that racks through me.

"He called me a turdscicle."

Blinking, I chew on the words, the scene playing out in my head in real time, when it smacks me like the knowledge finally makes sense.

I howl.

I'm overcome, noise no longer leaving my body, my lungs seized with hilarity. The cushion next to me receives a few slaps in an attempt to force air back into my body.

"You're joking." I guffaw, tears leaking from my eyes.

He shakes his head. "Nah. We're weird like that."

As if I didn't just fall into this fit of laughter that he pushed me toward, he snags another slice and folds the thing in half. Except, it's not in the way New Yorkers eat their pizza, no. He flips up the edge where all the toppings are to the crust and begins to eat it like a sandwich as if proving he defies all logic with comedic flair.

"Jesus, you are too much." Hand to my chest, I try to regulate my breathing back to a semi-normal state, but his incessant pizza eating has me giggling all over again.

"Try it, makes the shit taste better." He shrugs but can't help the smile that tugs up his lips.

"Doubtful, but why the hell not?" I follow his lead and bite into a pizza sandwich with lightness in my chest. It doesn't taste different to me, but it changes the experience to something more adventurous. And that's enough for me to embrace.

"So, Ms. Soul. Who's your favorite artist?"

My eyes bug out of my skull, and I look away with my hand to my mouth to cover how full it is. Redness heats my face more than the flames have already.

He remembered that little tidbit about me?

"You remember that? Sheesh." I think about it, index finger to my chin as I stare into the flames and try my best to tuck the embarrassment into the burning logs. "I like a lot actually, but I would say my favorites are Sam Cooke, the Temptations, and Otis Redding."

Turning to him, I catch his rapt attention on my features as the light from the fire dances across his face, reflecting in his eyes.

He nods, a slow close of the eyes, and begins to hum. Rex keeps time with his thumb against the Styrofoam on his thighs, and then his hand waves about, his head swaying to the beat.

I don't recognize the song at first, but when it sinks in, I find a vibration to my vocal cords sounding along with his. Breathy at first, almost a whisper, the lyrics of a Bill Withers song begin to leave my lips.

See, I don't sing in front of others, except my sister and best friend, but they don't count.

However … I love soul because I love the melody, the tune, the words I can replicate with a carelessness that no other genre can produce.

Lyrics sang from the chest, time kept with a heart.

So, I sing, belting the notes higher and longer than that of the original, creating my own mix of the song I almost wish I was recording to play back later. I feel Rex's gaze on me as he slips the box from my person, sets the bag on the ground, then pulls me to my feet.

Rex's hips meet mine, his hand landing just above my ass and leading me into a sway to the beat we produce. Fire snaps beside us, warming my bare hands and kissing my cheeks, the heat battling to be felt over that which is coming from Rex.

He's struck a chord I'm not willing to cut off just yet.

My chest expands, my vocal cords in tune more than they've ever been.

In reality, I am basking in this moment where I feel truly alive, singing along to a true classic about women and sunshine around a fire I created next to a man who feels comforting.

Almost feels like home.

His hums bring the song around to the last set, the final lyrics already off my breath. I still, allowing myself to absorb the fuzzy feeling settling behind my breastbone, a soft smile playing on my lips.

"Damn, Aria."

I chuckle at his breathy tone, nerves snaking their way up my spine and begging to settle into the base of my skull where I keep all the tension anxiety brings me.

Rex doesn't let me sit in my head too long, though. His fingers find mine, bringing my hand to his upturned lips, and he places a gentle kiss to each knuckle. "That was fucking beautiful."

I flush, but Rex doesn't stop at my knuckles. His lips trail up my palm to my wrist and down my covered forearm. He cups my jaw, bringing those soft, plump lips to mine. The Italian on his breath tastes heavenly, his tongue slipping along mine, his hand migrating to my neck. The heat builds between us, the intensity making our moves harsher, more desperate, as I sneak a hand into his hair and grip the hem of his shirt at his waist.

Pop.

The noise has me breaking our contact, jerking my head toward the fire to investigate the cause. Watching on, I catch the tail end of a large ember floating off into the night sky, then extinguishing into mere ash.

"It's just the fire," Rex says and leans back into my neck, trailing kisses and nibbles over my flesh.

I shiver at his advances, my hands finding themselves back in his hair. I grip him, and I hiss as he touches the right spots, turning me on like a light switch that gives no fucks about the public nature or the popcorn in the fire.

"Mmmm …" I hum for him when his hands knead my ass and his teeth sink into the base of my neck.

Rustling settles into my arousal-fueled brain. Branches and brush swiping over each other and something else. It takes a moment to register the noise, but when Rex freezes, I'm on alert. Gaze darting, I try to see beyond the fire, but my eyes won't focus past the flickering flames, and my heart aches to ignore it all.

"*Quiet*," Rex whispers in my ear so low I almost don't catch the words.

He's got a phone in his hand, typing without looking, his sight trained on the shit around us as he pulls me in tight against him.

"I don't hear it anymore," I try to whisper back, but Rex snaps a hand over my mouth, cutting me off from saying anything else.

"Not an animal." He tries to seem nonchalant, his words suggesting anything but.

If it's not an animal, then what is it?

I grab onto his arm as it falls away from me to get his attention. My face falls when he glances back at me, but he just shrugs.

The rustling sounds again. I grab onto him and try to get him to move, but I'm struck paralyzed when sounds become extended, then progress into thudding.

Is that grunting?

Like fucking human *grunting?*

His arm bars me in place from getting us out of there, slowly pushing me back behind him until my knees hit the seat and I bend to sit.

"Rex," I whisper louder than intended, tugging on his arm. "We should get out of here." I fight against his hold, but it doesn't matter.

The bushes to our left burst forward, a mass falling off the barrier with a thud and hitting the cement walkway. I jerk back, the fire illuminating the heap as a person—or maybe two?—rolling around on the ground. Rex is in my face, ushering me away, pulling me to the exit before I recognize what's happening.

What the fuck?

I look back and catch sight of two men grappling as we round the corner to the gate that I assume leads out of this little sanctuary. A fist lands with a sickening crack, the shattering of glass and plastic skittering across the walkway as we pass.

Was that a camera?

The taller, bigger of the two stands with a device in his hands that he bashes into the wall at his side, the guy from the bottom watching on through a bloodied nose and swollen eye. Rex tugs me along with a large hand wrapped around my wrist, away from the mess, and tucks me into the passenger seat of a car.

We're on the road, peeling rubber out of the lot before I can blink.

"Rex, what the fuck?"

I grip my seat belt as the vehicle in front of us slams its brakes, the red lights illuminating the interior of the car, my face screwing up as if we've already hit them. He yanks the wheel to avoid the collision and cuts off another car that blares its horn at us. "Holy shit."

I just met this man.

Oh my God, this is how the kidnapping happens.

My palms dampen with nerves the longer Rex chooses not to answer my question. Or say any damn thing.

Panic settles into my tight chest as I watch headlights that shoot by at an unnatural speed. The scenery around us flies thanks to the high number on the speedometer I refuse to look at.

My stomach rolls with fresh waves of nausea, threatening to empty itself if this race Rex thinks we're in continues.

He glances at me periodically but keeps his white-knuckle grip on the wheel and main focus on shifting from the traffic in front of us to the rearview mirror that lights up his face with the reflection I swear I'm imagining.

I take a chance and turn in my seat to look behind us.

Oh.

I gulp down the lump desperate to choke me out.

There's a vehicle so close to our tail that I can't tell what it is.

Oh my God.

"It's gonna be alright." He's speaking to me but keeps his focus on the view before us.

I brace myself on the dash with one hand, keeping a death grip on the seat belt with the other as he whips the car away from yet another collision. I peek behind us and don't feel any better.

The tail is still so close to the back of the car, and I swear I feel it bump us. It's been joined by a shitty van to our left, and more cars try to pack in front of us.

"Get your head down," Rex shouts, one hand leaving the steering wheel to grasp the back of my neck and push me forward too fast.

My seat belt catches. I choke and swing before I can think things through. My fist makes contact with something hard, and I yank back as pain barely settles into my adrenaline-filled brain.

Oh my God, I'm gonna die here.

My knuckles scream when I slip the belt and end up nearly inside the panel of my door. I cradle my injured hand to my chest and duck under Rex's hold.

"Stop *pushing* me."

What did I hit?

With my mind racing and my body slinked down into the seat, I try to take in the shit around me, but I feel like I'm seeing stars. Lights flash across my vision from the slam into the seat belt and the pain in my hand.

Was it really that hard?

I slide farther down the seat and try to block the lights with my hand. The pressure of my palm against my face makes me feel better, the lights in my eyes fading to colored spots almost immediately. I breathe for a moment, the sound of the roaring engine lulling me back to earth.

"Aria, *are you okay?*" The intensity in his voice snaps me back. It's filled with concern, his hand on my shoulder. "Oh, shit."

The car jerks again, and I slide into the door with a little more force than I'd prefer. The move jolts me, the panel of the door jamming into my bicep and bruising another part of my body.

"Jesus, Rex." I try to push up from the seat, only to be stopped again.

"Aria, you have to stay down."

I shoot him a look he doesn't see because his focus is back on the road again, shifting from the rearview to the front every few seconds. Then back again.

"And you have to tell me what the fuck is going on," I yell, mustering my best attitude despite the amount of overwhelm and fear that's coursing through my veins. It comes out sounding better than I thought despite the numbness taking up space in my fingertips and the fear threatening to stop my heart.

Rex grunts his response more than he speaks, and the air between us deadens. "I can't."

"The fuck you mean you can't?" I snap. There's more venom in my voice, more intensity. I sit up tall despite his grabby hands attempting to keep me down.

I'm in a vehicle, with a man I just met, breaking all kinds of traffic laws.

He winces. "I mean I can't."

Oh, hell no.

Chapter Eight

Rex

I CAN'T TELL HER.

The words bounce around in my skull as I speed past another pap van in an attempt to shake them.

She'll never look at me the same again.

They haven't stopped for miles, tailing and leaning out of the vehicles to get a money shot.

Especially since I have someone in the damn car with me.

I swerve the car in and out of traffic, taking sharp turns and slamming Aria around like a damn rag doll. I hate that she has to brace herself anytime I grip the wheel. I hate even more that she's stopped demanding shit from me and, in turn, has chosen to remain silent.

I'm also worried about what the fuck to tell her when she looks at me like I just killed her mother. I see the betrayal in her eyes as she shoots daggers through her gaze, pinning me to the seat while the car burns in a fiery crash around me. She doesn't even have to tell me the vision.

She repeats herself again, each word a knife through my heart.

"What is going on?" It's quiet, so quiet.

She can't know the truth.

Nerves have sweat beading on my brow, my hands aching from the death grip I keep on the wheel.

I ease back on the throttle and cut sharp into oncoming traffic to catch the left turn at the last second. I narrowly miss smashing the front end into a pickup and damn near swipe a pedestrian.

"*Rex.*"

The way she says my name still sends chills down my spine as I ride down the narrow alleyway and give my best effort not to hit anything. The tires bump against the brick roadway, vibrating the car and traveling up my ass to rattle my brain.

"*Rex.*" She slides up the seat, the death glare heavy in my direction.

"Aria, babe. I can't tell you. I'm sorry."

I speed out of the alley and pray there's nothing in my path as I pull the e-brake and skid onto another main road, going the opposite direction we just came. I risk a glance over at her like I have been since this whole thing started, only to find her staring blankly out of the windshield.

"I'm in a moving car with you, breaking so many speed limits …" I've broken more than speed limits tonight, but the name of this game happens to be the less she knows, the better. "And you don't think I deserve to know why the hell I feel like I can't let go of the dashboard?"

Shit. She's got me.

I shake my head on a sigh as I settle back into my seat, some of the adrenaline coming down. I peel my fingers from the steering wheel and shake out a trembling, aching hand.

"I *do* think you deserve to know," I rebut because that's not the point.

She deserves the world at her fingertips, not her picture plastered all over every social media outlet and tabloid, thanks to me. She doesn't know it, but I'm protecting her.

"Then what *the fuck?*" The last words come off on a shriek that pierces my ears and makes me cringe at the pain shooting through my eardrums and down my spine.

She's damn persistent.

Wouldn't you be, too, you fucking schmuck?

I coast into traffic and blend in as much as I can with the public.

"How's your hand?" I try, true concern eating at me as I watch her flex the thing for the hundredth time.

"It's fine," Aria deadpans, her gaze going straight to the window.

"Your shoulder?" Again, I try to redirect the focus onto the concern tightening my chest at the abuse her beautiful body has taken because of me.

"It's my damn arm, Rex. What the hell do you want from me?" She turns in the seat, pulling a cocked knee into the cradle with her, and I have a feeling that if she could, her hands would be firmly planted on her hips.

Or around my neck. I'm not sure which is more likely.

She's cute, and it pulls a smile at the corners of my lips.

"I want a lot from you." I flash her my best grin, the one I've used to charm the panties off women in the past, and reach over the center console to clasp her knee.

She scoffs but doesn't push me away. "That doesn't answer my question at all, Rex. You won't answer *any* of my questions."

I half shrug—she's not wrong—and pull the car off onto a side street with less traffic. A check in the rearview confirms that Ian is back on my tail with just enough space between us to not cause any more questions.

"Maybe I like being mysterious," I defend lightheartedly.

I have to bring her back down.

"Maybe this is how women go missing," she shoots back at me like a shot to the chest.

"Whoa, hey…" I grab her hand, concern furrowing my brow again. "I'm not trying anything weird."

"Sure as hell seems like it." She snatches her hand back and crosses her arms over her full chest. "The only reason I'm still in this car is because you're still going way over the fucking speed limit and you're somehow connected to my sister."

Her sister?

Confusion settles in, and I do a double take of Aria after a quick check of the speedometer.

I must be missing the point or something as I ease back on the accelerator again.

I've never met anyone that looks or acts like her; I'd remember that shit if I did.

She's too damn alluring to forget.

"Aria. Listen …" I steal back her hand, thread my fingers with hers and give a little shake for attention as I switch mine between her and the road. "All I'm really asking for is trust. Just as I am giving you." It's not untrue. I still don't know for sure if she recognizes me. I don't know what she knows, if she knows anything.

I haven't asked her to sign any NDAs other than whatever Genevie had her fill out, and I know that people will go to insane lengths to get shit from people like me.

To get fame, even if it's only their thirty seconds.

Whether it's a pap with money shots that get them the big bucks on the headlines. Or a girl falling in love with a celebrity to get a baby and money from him.

I don't feel any of that to be true with Aria. The look in her eye is pure of heart and her mannerisms scream reserved.

Well, unless you're me and manage to piss her off.

"Fuck, I guess that's true." Aria ponders for a moment, the tension lessening in her shoulders. She's still pissed at me, still concerned, but I think I finally broke down the wall. "You've trusted me, a complete stranger, so far."

At least maybe a little bit.

"Exactly," I start with a grin in her direction. "You could be trying to kidnap me. Maybe these cars are here for you, not me," I tease.

The air shifts, though, and she stiffens, her grip tightening on my hand. My eyes are on her, trying to gauge her reaction, trying my damnedest to understand her moving lips where no words come out.

I feel the force before I ever see it coming.

White smoke fills my vision as I watch the horror crossing Aria's face.

Her airbag deploys, slamming her back into the seat.

The car jerks and skids, and I can feel the tires lift from the ground with a terrible screech of metal on metal that deafens me.

The white becomes black for a moment as my body jostles around the inside of the car-themed pinball machine. My head bounces off the headrest, smashes into the window, and begins pouring blood into my eyes.

"*Rex!*" Aria's scream pierces my eardrums more than the wail of a guitar ever has.

I try to reach for her as the concrete jungle outside the car spins around and around.

"Aria …" We finally connect hands as the car comes to a sudden stop with a slam that has glass raining down over her head. "Fuck, babe." I search her with my hands and my eyes, which have gone blurry, trying to assess the injuries. "Are you hurt?"

"Oh God, your head."

She's kneeling on the seat despite the shards embedded in the leather and in her knees and reaching out for me. I swipe the blood from my eye and bump into her hands as she tries to make work of the fluid running from my head. I feel the warmth seeping where it shouldn't be, running down my brow and dripping into my lap.

"It'll be fine. Head wounds always bleed a shit ton." I swipe again. "But how are you? Are you okay?"

"I'm fine." She pushes my advances to check on her and instead pushes a finger into what feels like a gaping hole in my head. "You on the other hand …"

"No stars. At least as long as I'm not looking at you." Aria rolls her eyes but continues her poking, which causes stars to taint my vision despite my words. "Okay, you can stop that," I respond with a chuckle but grunt as the door is yanked open, and hands start pulling at us from both sides of the car.

"*Rex*," Aria screeches.

God, I hope it's Ian or Lugh.

"I'm okay," I shout back as beefy arms I recognize lift me out of the accident and set me on the pavement outside.

"You good, Rex?" Lugh is in my face, waving a finger to test for a concussion.

I slap the thing away when he takes too long and look around me.

"I'm fine, Lugh. But the crowd is fucking not." He looks over his shoulder at the growing mass and curses under his breath. "Who's with her?"

"We got it, Rex." He ushers me up but keeps a hand on my head, forcing my face down and away from the crowd. He tucks me in so close I'm almost in his armpit as we walk, pain shooting up my knee and throbbing in my head with each step I take.

Lugh pushes me into the back seat of Ian's SUV and slams the door closed in my face. I'm looking for her, but I don't see her. Sirens wail in the distance, red and blue lights begin reflecting off the surrounding buildings as the seconds tick by, and Aria isn't stuffed into the back with me.

I look around the seat to find her securely under the arm of another security agent I don't recognize. He walks her to the other side of the car and opens the door. I slink back so that I can't be seen from the outside, but I'm damn near in her lap the second we're closed in.

"Aria. Baby." I palm her pale jaw in my hands and search her wild eyes for pain, anything that's causing her discomfort. I know I'll find it there if she fibs about it. "Are you okay?"

"Holy shit, Rex." She's got a death grip on my shirt, the favorite one I'm certain is now ruined, but I don't care right now. She's in my arms, and she seems physically okay.

"Tell me you're alright," I demand again as tears begin to flood her eyes and spill over.

"Hoooooly shiiiiiiit." She sniffs and weaves a hand between mine to wipe her nose. "I'm pretty sure I'm in shock," she states with a watery chuckle that lacks all the humor of a normal one.

She's way too pale. Way too stiff in my arms.

"Probably. Shit, I'm so fucking sorry." I press my forehead to hers and rub the pads of my thumbs across her cheeks. Gentle and steady, I hold her head in my hands and soothe as much as I can in the confines of a car while her erratic breath bathes over my face.

I'm still not convinced she's unscathed from this.

I'm not.

I've got a throbbing knee and a leaking head to show for it.

She begins sobbing, the sounds breaking my heart into a thousand little shards, and I hold her as she crumbles in my grasp. I pull her into my lap, wrap her up in my arms, and rock her gently.

Aria weeps into my chest, her fists clenched between us.

"Shhh ..." I cradle her head, massaging the base of her skull. "You're safe now, baby. I've got you."

Eventually, the tears stop, and she returns my soothing rubs on her back with ones on my neck. I know that the cops are going to need to speak with us about what happened, even though I don't know, but they're going to have to wait. I didn't see a damn thing anyway.

"Rex, we almost died tonight."

"I know." I stroke her hair and push loose strands out of her face as she sits back and looks me in the eye. "But we didn't." I try to smile for her, but the desperation that meets me is debilitating.

"You need a hospital." She wears her worry in her tense shoulders and in the way her eyes shift between mine and the cut on my head.

I shake my head, but the movement has spots filling my vision.

My damn knee is throbbing, and my head is pounding inside my skull. *She's right. I'm fucked up.*

"I can't do that, either." I stroke her hair and focus my weary gaze on her. Aria's irritated with my comment, but she doesn't push anymore. "Did you see what happened?"

"Here comes a cop now." She nods to the side of the car and slides off my lap.

He raps his knuckles on the window of the driver's seat despite it being empty. Before I can make a move to answer him, Aria is already climbing over the center console and rolling the window down.

"Evening."

"Sir," she greets, earning her a smile from the officer, who's probably about my age and wears his uniform well.

I see how this is gonna go.

"Want to fill me in on what happened, ma'am?" His voice is deeper now, like somehow that's going to make him more attractive.

I roll my eyes but keep my ass in the seat.

I'm pretty sure rolling your eyes is not supposed to make you nauseous.

I try to listen as Aria fills him in on the details of what happened. She reports where we were hit, the color and make of the car, and the license plate number of the perpetrator. I barely heard her talk about how the other driver ran the second our car stopped spinning. The longer they talk, the more I start to fade in and out.

Definitely a concussion.

Shit.

I pull out my phone, but the screen is a blur.

Double shit.

"Aria," I say, catching her eyes in the rearview mirror. She's quick to dismiss the cop by rolling the window up and climbs back to me.

"Rex," she tries, but I hand her my unlocked phone.

"Call Ian. I'm crashing." My words slur like I've been pounding the old-fashioneds, and the world fades out.

Chapter Nine

BREAKING.

YOU HEARD IT HERE first.

It's rumored that a car chase took place around the town in an effort to detain local rock star, Rex Thompson, only moments ago.

Keep watching WDTZ for your local news and updates on this ongoing story.

Chapter Ten

Aria

"**G**OTTA STAY AWAKE, REX."

Ring, ring. A voice connects before I recognize the ringing has stopped.

"Rex? What's wrong?"

I'm flush. I don't know who the hell this is or why I'm not calling his brother, but here we are.

Wait … is Ian his brother's name?

"It's Aria," I say with a shake of my head. "Rex has got a concussion, I think, and needs a hospital."

Curses fill the line, but then it goes dead on me.

Miffed, I look at the screen that lights back up as if the call never happened.

"Babe …" He's slurring pretty badly.

I grab his hand and give him a little jostle to keep him alert.

"I'm here," I say, leaning closer to him. "What's your name?"

It comes out sounding more like *Wex* than Rex, but I'll take it.

I nod him on and dare to ask another question. "When's your birth-day?"

"May third."

I can't confirm whether he's right when he answers me, but now I know a smidge more about this mystery man. Too bad it took a stupid car wreck to make it happen.

I sigh. At the situation and at myself. What would Chip be thinking of me right now? How crazy I am to still be next to this guy, even though he almost got me killed?

He almost died, too.

"Rex, stay awake." I shake him, and his head rolls to the window, then back to me.

Keeping an eye on him, I also eye the phone in my hand. I swipe every few seconds to keep the screen lit up in case I need to call someone else—I'm on the verge of calling for a damn ambulance—but I also can't lie and say that the picture in the background doesn't intrigue me.

"Tell me your name," I demand.

He gives me the right answer, so my eyes wander back down to the picture.

It's one of Rex, a man that *has* to be the twin he told me about with how much they look alike, and a few others. There are neon signs plastered behind them, confetti sprinkled over their heads.

I'm about to ask him about the picture when the driver's door swings open, then slams shut, rocking us with its force.

"Ian?" I ask as the large man puts the SUV in drive and maneuvers out of the growing group of gawkers.

"Jesus." He shakes his head, our eyes locking through the rearview mirror. "You've got a lot to learn, miss."

My brow furrows. His size is intimidating behind the wheel, the thing dwarfed in his hand.

"Be nice, Ian," Rex speaks clearly, a bite to his words.

Do I trust his judgment right now?

I look from Rex to the back of the driver's head. We were just in a hit and run. And before that, we were being fucking *chased*. My brain launches into hyperdrive with overanalyzing the situation and how bad this shit is.

Shit like *What if this isn't Ian?* plagues me.

Why the hell were we being chased?

Who is Ian anyway?

Ian—at least I'll call him that for now, until I can prove that he isn't Ian—eases the car into a turn and floors it.

"Just doing my job, Rex," he rebuts, changing lanes, then straightening again. "Which you apparently love making fucking difficult."

My stomach lurches at the excessive speed Ian chooses to drive, but I swallow the lump building in my throat to get my nerves at bay. We are trying to rush to a hospital, after all.

"Gotta live life." Rex slurs again, his eyes locking on me for a long beat.

I'm not sure if it's because he's trying to find something to focus on so his head stops spinning or if it's a message to me.

It feels like a damned message.

I shake off his heady stare and turn back to the driver, who I now notice is equipped with a cord running down from his ear into the collar of his shirt. He's dressed nice for a large man. Someone you'd expect to find in the gym, not behind the wheel of a nice-ass SUV, donning a button-down and slacks.

"And what exactly is your job, Ian?" I ask. Curiosity leaves a rock in my gut, telling me I need to know but that I'm not going to like the answer I get.

"Hang on," Ian suggests, pulling the wheel hard into a turn and passing the hospital's emergency entrance.

The rock that curiosity left in my stomach?

Yeah, it just dropped through my asshole and out the bottom of the car.

Nerves coat my palms as I risk a glance at Rex. He doesn't seem fazed at all, but I still don't trust how cognizant he really is. He *needs* medical attention.

Ian, the man who's about to receive a new crater in the back of his head courtesy of my shoe, pulls the wheel again. The car bounces into a back entrance I'm certain the public is not supposed to use, as it appears to be meant for large deliveries and semis, not patients in need of care.

"What the fu—" My words are cut off as a bay door opens, and Ian flies through the opening without a care.

Rex's door is swarmed with people in smocks. They pull him out and have his ass on a gurney before I can get out and around the car to his side.

I have to run to catch up.

"Ma'am, you can't be back here," a nurse tells me as we burst through a set of double doors.

"She's with me." Rex reaches out to me, yanks on my waist, and has my ass on the gurney next to him as the staff continues to wheel us along.

The nurse grumbles a response but doesn't force me off the moving bed.

Sterile paint, clean floors, and that ever-present scent of rubbing alcohol overwhelm my senses.

I hate hospitals.

Deep breaths help keep the panic at bay as more doors are passed until we're in an exam room, surrounded by white coats and more blue smocks.

"I'm gonna be alright," Rex whispers in my ear, his arm still around my waist, holding me against him.

His warmth is nice against the chill in the air. His scent is a reminder that this is not the same as the last time I joined someone in the hospital.

They poke and prod him, ask a thousand questions.

"What's your name?" *Rex Thompson.*

"What's your birthday?" *May effing third.*

"What happened? What's your pain level?" And all those other medical questions they ask to ensure the diagnosis is proper.

"Mild concussion, adrenaline crash," Rex answers.

"And the thing on your head?" a nurse asks him, only to receive a shrug.

"Butterfly should do."

It's not until I try to roll out of their way with a wince that a nurse begins asking me the very same Rolodex of crap that I dismiss.

I'm not sure how, but I managed only a few minor scrapes and some bruising. Rex is the one who needs the attention, not me.

Somehow … he's assessed, tested, treated, and back on his way out the door with not much more than a bandage on his forehead and a pain med prescription.

They rushed his ass around, mentioned not being secured enough to keep him, and got him priority release once they established that Ian would be staying with him.

What the fuck?

With a slight hitch to his step, Rex's melodious voice carries us through the halls as we walk back in the same direction we came. Or at least I think we are. This place is a labyrinth, but the only thing that seems to keep my attention is Rex.

He sings a song I don't know, but he knows well, the lyrics melancholy in nature. His words seem sad with low tones, but the smile on his face is a complete contradiction. The warmth of his body against mine when he sings of cold nights alone sends tingles down my spine.

When we emerge into the dock area, Ian comes into view as he leans casually against the SUV.

"Rex." He comes forward slowly as if it hasn't been hours since we last saw him. "You good?"

He's answered with a sincere nod that he returns.

I witness the relief wash over Ian's face as he follows us around the car and opens the door for us to climb in. I get in first and scoot across the leather seats. Rex smacks my ass before I land, eliciting a snicker from me.

"*Is that Rex Thompson?*" The excitable question cuts through the air just before Ian can slam the door closed and make his way into the driver's seat.

"No," he answers abruptly and slams himself in.

We're moving through the open bay door when I catch sight of a female in smocks being held back by another much larger nurse as she reaches out in our direction.

Okay, that's weird.

"Where to, boss?" Ian asks as if we didn't just shake off a crazy lady who somehow knew who the hell Rex was. Knew his full fucking name by just a glimpse.

Nobody gets a reception like this.

The tidbits begin to float around in my subconscious, even as Rex grips my hand.

Stalked on an outside date.

"Take us home, Ian."

Car chase.

"Alright. I'll drop her off first."

Car wreck. Where the at fault runs.

"No. She comes, too."

Secret hospital entrance and rapid treatment.

"Rex, I don't think that's a good idea."

Now, a lady screaming his name.

"I wasn't asking for your permission."

Who the hell is this man?

"She'll have to sign, Rex."

He's gotta have a wealthy family or something.

"Ian, it's fine."

I feel the scrape of calloused fingers touching my jaw, bringing my gaze away from the passing landscape I wasn't watching anyway to the wild curls framing a handsomely bandaged face.

I scrutinize what I see—the crooked nose, the light freckles dusting his cheeks, the intrigue and touch of playfulness lighting up his eyes, his grin that ratches up the longer I stare—and the things that run through my mind just don't seem right.

No way he's in the mob. He's too pretty, which would be too much attention to get away with shit.

Hitmen live in the dark, right? Except they don't have homes nearby, and they never stick to one place. Can't be that.

Lawyers definitely don't get in car chases. Right?

How am I still alive?

Is it witness protection?

"Babe." Those rough fingers caress my chin from one side to the other as I have a silent existential crisis. "Can I take you home?"

I stare longer, my palms giving away the anxiety eating away at me.

He asked for trust.

This is stupid.

So, so stupid.

Embrace the moment. Chip's voice enters my mind with his infamous catchphrase that has me questioning my sanity.

I've lost it, and this is all a hallucination.

"Yes," I whisper. Just as I did at the photo shoot, I pick up my big girl panties and do what my gut is screaming for me to do. "Yeah."

His character—the badass with hard glances who only smiles halfway at a time—breaks into an all-out, megawatt grin that softens his eyes.

The kiss that comes next, I wasn't prepared for.

It's feverish but sweet. Tender, yet demanding. He grips my jaw with both hands and slides his tongue along mine in a way that has my panties ready to make a run for it.

"Fuck." He pulls back with the curse and leans his forehead against mine, his breathing labored just like mine. "You're … goddamn." He flops back against the seat and groans. His eyes roll as he sucks in a breath, one hand still firmly planted in my hair.

"I'm what?" Call me a cat, go ahead. Like anyone else wouldn't want to know what the hell he's talking about right now.

The eyes that meet mine again are dangerous. Hungry. Darkened with desire and a primal need. And I swear my thong just ran away on its own. It already knows it's going to get torn to shreds the moment we're alone.

Clearly I've lost my mind.

"You're a babe, Aria." He leans in again as darkness blankets the car's interior and nips at my ear lobe. "A fucking ten." His hands are on me, trailing down my sides to grip the part of my ass the seat will allow him to reach, his mouth teasing the sensitive flesh on my neck with nips and licks.

My skin breaks out in goose bumps, his touches pulling gasps from me.

"Oh," I whisper, not wanting any of it to stop, but very aware that Ian is still in the SUV with us.

He groans against my neck and slides his hands between me and the leather to lift me up. He sits me firmly on his lap, knees on either side of his hips. I gasp when his very hard and very restricted erection lands against my covered core. The subtle movement of the car has me leaning farther into him, gripping the back of the seat for dear life.

"Say my name," he demands, a hand snaking into the hair at the base of my neck and tugging.

"Rex," I whisper-moan, shifting my grip from the seat to his broad shoulders as his other hand finds its way to my hip and urges me to move against him.

I grind down against him, his cock rubbing me in all the right ways. It pulls another groan from his lips that find mine again.

He devours me, his scent intoxicating, and has me throwing my head back in a full-on moan.

Why was I holding that back?

"God, yes, Aria." Rex thrusts up to meet me, the friction between us growing.

"*Ahem.* Not in the damned car, Rex." The male voice that is not from the hottie I'm currently dry humping breaks through my desire-fueled brain and has my movement halting like a deer in the headlights of the very same vehicle.

Shit.

"Don't be a dick." Rex clears the gravel from his throat, his words coming in deeper than before.

Why is that voice so hot?

He leans around me and taps the back of the driver's seat, then turns his attention back to me.

"*Fuck*" is all he says as he looks me up and down.

I snigger but slide into the seat next to him. He flings the door open and hops out with his dick proudly standing as much as the denim will allow.

Jesus, I didn't even know we'd stopped.

"Babe." He crooks a finger at me, demanding I come forward, and I don't hesitate.

Rex's hands are behind my knees before I can climb down, wrapping my legs around his waist. He moves us through the parking garage until I hear the ding of an elevator.

I don't bother to look at or analyze anything. I just lock my lips with his and trust.

Chapter Eleven

BREAKING NEWS

LEAD SINGER OF BELOVED band As Above, Rex Thompson, seen receiving medical treatment after news of a car accident occurring with him in the vehicle.

How's our rock star faring? What was he treated for? So many questions with not enough answers.

Will Rex give an exclusive?

As more information is pouring in, MegaCeleb is doing our best to give you the most accurate and up-to-date information.

Stay tuned.

Chapter Twelve

Rex

THE ELEVATOR RIDE IS too short, but it doesn't stop me from exploring her skin with my mouth. When the ding announces our arrival on my floor, the top floor, it's near impossible to tear my lips from her neck, but I do.

Picking her up again, her legs firmly around my waist, each step pushes the head of my cock against her warmth. Her peach ass warms my palms, which I knead the flesh there as I kick the front door closed behind us. She does damage to my neck and shoulders, leaving me groaning every other step. Each nibble distracts me further from the aches taking up space in my body and, instead, center them right in my balls.

I come around the short hall into the main living space, and I can feel my twin is still here almost as solidly as I feel this beauty in my arms.

"Hey, shithead—" His words cut off when my only response is to release a hand I can flip him the bird with, and I keep walking.

Aria switches sides and starts working her way to a spot I know is gonna make my knees buckle with its responsiveness. I make quick work of kicking the bedroom door closed and stepping out of my boots on the way to my bed.

"Fuck," I moan and drop us onto the black sheets as her lips find that stupid erogenous spot I normally try to avoid.

Her teeth graze it, and my cock leaps behind my zipper, the fabric rubbing my head just right to have my hips jutting forward in search of more friction.

She grips me, legs wrapping around me as I lean over her, and bites down hard enough to have my eyes rolling and my head shooting back to release another moan.

"Aria," I rasp in warning.

She fucking giggles.

"You're going to pay for th—*ah.*"

Her jaw hammers the spot again with a clamping of her teeth that has me solid on top of her. My hips slam forward in response, every ounce of my blood filling my cock to the point of pain.

With shaking hands and flaring nostrils, I fumble with the buttons on her pants, but there are too many on the sexy red coverings.

Through labored breathing, I growl, "Get them off before I rip them off."

"Fuck, okay," she moans, her hands making quick work of the fasteners keeping her from me.

I lean back and tear the things down her legs.

She follows me, sitting up to tug my shirt over my head. When the shirt is gone and I toss her pants somewhere, I'm struck paralyzed by the sight of her. I'm pleasantly greeted by the sight of her labored breathing beneath her cropped hoodie and her soaking wet cherry-red panties.

"Baaaabe," I groan, sucking in a desperate breath and filling my lungs with her sweet scent.

"I could say the same." Aria's fingertips dart out to trace some of my tattoos, circle around my nipple rings, then trail down my stomach to grip the waistband of my jeans.

I groan when she pops the button and lets my cock free.

She squeaks, her wide eyes shooting to meet mine. "Is that a … ?"

I nod and grin, the cool air chilling the silver ring that glints back at her.

Aria's nostrils flare as her gaze shoots back down my body to the piercing through the head of my cock.

Her hands come up but pause before touching me, the warmth radiating from her closeness. Once she's worked through it in her head that she doesn't need permission from me, ever, she touches the ring with curiosity, fingering and spinning the thing through the cylinder of skin. Chills shoot all over me, my balls tightening with need.

"*Aria.*" My voice is deeper, more demanding than I intend, but her curiosity is driving me insane.

In fact, I haven't felt sane at all since I set eyes on her in that sexy black number at the photo shoot.

"Nightstand," I demand on a growl.

She nods in understanding and flips over to crawl up the bed. The sight of her on all fours in my bed, that glorious ass on display, has me grabbing her hips and pulling her back to me. I plant a firm smack on one cheek that pulls another squeak from her, then grind my hips against her. My cock slips between her spread legs, creating friction on the outside of her pussy, and comes back slicked with her need.

"*Rex,*" she moans, gripping the sheets in her fists, her back arching into me.

God, she's so sexy.

My erection throbs as I run the shaft against her wet core, the lacy thing adding that extra little bit of a teasing scrape over my skin.

"Do you want it?" I ask, a hand fisting in her hair and pulling until she's upright, her back flush against my chest. I reach around and run a finger up the inside of her thigh until I reach her groin. Her body tenses in anticipation, but I pause before I apply any pressure to her sensitivity. "Words, baby. Tell me yes, tell me no."

"*Yes,*" she moans, nodding feverishly. "Yes, Rex."

I'm already pushing her panties aside, my fingertips finding her clit and circling.

She cries out, so wet that my fingertip slides right over her, and my head spins. Aria reaches out, her hands coming to mine where I tease her, and hugs onto my arm like she needs the tether. The notion has my hips moving again, my knuckles brushing against the head of my cock that's still between her legs, sending chills down my spine.

Pure need blinds me as I nibble her ear, her vocal pleasure driving me closer to the brink. Releasing her hair, I push at her shoulders until she's back on all fours. I need more friction, need to be inside her, but I still don't have a rubber.

"Pill?" It's all I can manage to ask as I pull my hand from her core and lick the delicious wetness clean. I curse when she response with a shake of the head.

Smacking her ass, I demand that she not move as I slip off the bed and make my way to the stash I have in the nightstand. She doesn't listen, though. Instead, Aria rolls onto her back and dips a hand into her panties as she watches me retrieve a foil pack and tear it open with my teeth.

I groan at the sight of her touching herself on my bed, her eyes glued to my movements. I roll the rubber on, careful of the extra equipment. The friction and the show have me pulling my top lip between my teeth. I bite down as a distraction to keep from blowing already.

No way am I wasting this one.

My eyes roll back when she makes herself moan but says *my* name.

I love the way it sounds coming from her kissable lips. Love it even more that I see how genuine she is.

Her eyes scream *fuck me* when her hand switches position and she slides a finger inside herself. She thrusts, her head falling back with a gasp, then slips another digit inside.

She fucking undoes me.

I rush the bed, over the show that is now permanently etched in my spank bank, and hook my forearms around her legs. I haul her farther back onto the bed and kneel between her wide-open knees.

"I've never wanted to be inside someone so fucking bad," I say as I push her panties aside and rub the head of my cock against her clit.

She's warm and inviting. But when she plants a palm on my hip, halting forward movement, I freeze.

"Slow," she half moans, half demands from beneath me. "It's been a while."

Relief washes over me, her words answering all unknowns that began to run through my head.

I sigh and give a chuckle to release the nerves that racked up.

She nods, though I'm not sure what she's agreeing to, and trails her hand from my hip to my cock. Chills rise when she grips me, guiding me to her opening. I take the invitation and push inside, slow and gentle.

"Oh my *God.*" Her gasp of pleasure and her warm wetness tight around my cock have stars dotting my vision, my resolve breaking down quicker than I anticipated.

I pull back, then thrust forward, slipping farther inside. The heat grips me, and I fall forward onto braced arms, thrusting into her. Aria moans as I hike one leg up onto my hip, her neck arching back into the mattress.

Sliding forward into her wetness, I'm about halfway there. I can't stop the groan into her ear but force myself to pause.

"Talk to me, baby." I strain, body tense.

The only thing keeping me grounded is the softness of her body under me. The heat of her pussy wrapping me up.

"*So good,*" she moans for me, her hands finding my back, nails digging in as she encourages me to move. "God, yes."

"Yes, *what?*" My words are demanding, harsh even, but I can't wait any longer to pound into her.

If any more blood fills my erection, I might pass out. Or it might burst. I'm not sure, and I really don't want to find out.

"*Fuck me.*"

My hips begin moving on their own at her words, grunts coming from me as I try to at least slow the movement for her. Except she doesn't seem to mind, her hands finding and gripping my hair.

"*Fuck yes, yes. Yes.*" The deeper I slide, the more she begins chanting affirmations. I take the invitation for what it is and let my body go.

Drawing back, I slam home, over and over.

I grip her leg to keep the position, but the harder she moans, the harder my hips drive into her.

Sweat glistens on her skin, her body sliding up the bed with each thrust until she's tensing under me.

Her back arches up, her mouth frozen open in a silent scream.

"*Rex.*" Aria bursts open, her orgasm shaking the foundation of the fucking building. She grips me, her nails breaking skin on my back and shoulder.

She vibrates and clenches me.

Two more thrusts have me tipping over the very same edge, my cock exploding inside her as I watch the pure ecstasy unfold before me.

Her name leaves my lips, much softer, as the last bit of climax is pulled from me.

"Babe," I breathe, my lungs struggling to catch up, stars tainting my vision of her. Still, I lean so that I can brush strands of hair that stick to her face despite mine falling all around us, my grin threatening to split my face in two.

"Umm…" She blinks, her brain slowly coming back down, her gorgeous eyes meeting mine as I bring my lips to hers in a gentle kiss.

"Next time, the panties aren't surviving." I trail kisses down her jaw to her neck and inhale the glorious scent of post-sex Aria. I groan at the tropical paradise with the added tinge of *her* musk that greets me. "And I'm definitely gonna taste you."

"God, yes." The shivers that rack over her body at my words are enough of a response, but I like hearing the words, too.

"Glad you agree." I chuckle and slip my hands under her ass.

I tuck and roll us until she's on top of me, my raging boner still buried deep inside her. She moans at the change in position but snuggles into my chest and lets out a sigh big enough to settle us both.

Wrapping her up in my arms, I pepper kisses to the top of her head as she fingers the light smattering of hair on my chest. I know I should clean up, dispose of the cum-filled condom before it leaks, and show her the bathroom, but the contentment I feel has me opting to not move an inch unless it's to touch Aria.

I'm damn near zonked when she whispers to me a question I have to ask her to repeat. It's been too long since I felt this much at peace.

She did this to me.

"Are you in witness protection?"

The inquiry makes me chuckle, the sound a deep contrast to her softness.

"No." I run a hand down her face, using my thumb to prop her jaw up so that I can meet her gaze. "I'm just a regular guy." I leave out the part about it only being with her, but that doesn't make it untrue.

I'm a regular guy who sings in a band. Nothing crazy about that.

"So you're not in the mob?" she asks plain as day, no longer whispering, and I bark out a laugh at the outlandishness of it.

"Hell, no." I chuckle and plant a juicy kiss on her lips.

She returns the sentiment, my cock pulsing against her heat. Aria groans in response, her hips moving against me.

"Oh?" She breaks the kiss. "Will you tell me the truth," she starts, burying her face in my neck, "if I do this?"

Without any further warning, she latches onto the tender spot in between my shoulder, where my neck meets the rest of my body. My hips buck up in reply, my cock solid, a growl slipping from the base of my throat.

Thick cock ready to go again, I grab her hips and prepare to show her what that does to me.

I thrust up from the bottom, pulling her down onto me, grinding my hips into her clit with each stroke.

She gasps and loosens her assault on me, but I don't let up.

I fuck her from under her, forcing her to brace herself on my chest or risk being tossed off. She's slick, sensitive, and swollen around me as I push up to be farther inside her pussy.

"Rex," she groans, moving her hips against mine to increase the friction. Leaning back, Aria braces on my stomach with one hand and rides me. I reach up to push her top up and expose her tits that I've yet to see. She obliges, ripping the thing over her head and snapping her bra off.

The clothes get tossed to the side, and I admire the goddess she is in just her pushed-aside panties and my cock buried deep.

My O races forward, faster than any other second orgasm, as I watch her back arch and her hands come up to feel her tits. I need her closer because I'm further than she is, so I dip a thumb into the mix of her rotating hips and circle her clit. Shuddering, she moans for me and grinds harder against me.

"I'm gonna cum." Aria leans back, hands to my thighs, her nails digging in.

"That's it, babe." I apply a little more pressure to her clit, tighten the circles, and she shoots off. "Give it to me."

I join her in her climax as her pussy clenches around me, milking out everything I have.

Aria comes forward, gasping for air as her racing heart pounds through her chest, matching mine. I pull her down to me, our sweat-slicked skin sticking together, chests expanding desperately for air.

"I'm not in the fucking mob."

Chapter Thirteen

Aria

WE HAD SEX … *fucking* twice.

Rex's breath settles under me, his hard dick still firmly planted inside me, and I look around the room through heavy lids.

Okay, so he's not in the mob. No witness protection.

All I can see in the dim light are dark-colored walls, a painting or something on the wall, and double glass doors that I think lead outside. But it's so dark out that might just be the bathroom.

My brain fritzes, eyes closing slowly, but I force them back open.

Where am I?

What the hell happened tonight?

As his breath finally evens, his dick finally softens. I really should find a bathroom, but I'm nervous to wake him up again. Rex is supposed to have been resting, not fucking, but here we are, two orgasms down, and I wouldn't be mad about a third one.

That should feel more wrong than it does, I'm sure of it.

Rolling my own eyes at myself, I squint to see the other side of the double doors, but they're just black like the rest of the place. The faint glow is coming from lights set into the crown molding around the ceiling like a fancy-pants person would have, but that information doesn't give away a single thing. I sigh, somehow both exasperated and content with my current position, and let my tired eyes rest.

What if he is just a regular guy? With some extra money? And a dick piercing?

That's not a bad thing to run into. Certainly helped hit all the right spots.

Oh my God, his dick is pierced.

I let the thought bounce around in my head as I settle into Rex's chest. It brings a goofy smile to my face.

Just a regular guy… with a dick ring. Normal guys can have dick rings, too.

I doze off in the quiet of the room, Rex's even breathing lulling me into a peaceful rest.

What feels like only moments later, I wake enough to be semi-aware of being rolled over and noises sounding in the distance. I feel cool air on my skin, but it doesn't last long.

Rex's scent fills my nose as his rough fingers glide down my thigh and grasp my knee to pull my legs apart. Warmth radiates against my core, replacing the panties I once wore, pulling a sated moan from my lips. A gentle swipe, then another, is all I can focus on, but my eyes are too heavy to open, so I give a subtle arch to my back and mold myself to his body heat. I hear his chuckle as he pulls back the towel from my aching core, only to replace it again, settling my legs back together to hold it in place.

I respond with a disgruntled groan, but it has no teeth to it. I hear the humor in his tone as he groans back but settles in behind me.

"A little later, baby. You're swollen." His hot breath washes over my ear, causing goose bumps on contact. He wraps an arm over my ribs and across my chest, tucking me into his chest, my ass molding to his groin.

I can feel his hard-on pressing into my ass cheek, but he lays his head on the pillow we're sharing, his chin resting on the top of my head.

It's a simple gesture, sweet in nature, and has me grinning as sleep takes back over.

Chapter Fourteen

This just in.

L OCAL REBEL, REX THOMPSON, was caught causing havoc into the wee hours of the morning.

After only an hour in town, the lead singer of As Above is rumored to have led local authorities on a dangerous car chase during the early morning hours.

What could this riffraff be teaching our children?

You heard it here, folks.

Tune in to tomorrow for more information.

Chapter Fifteen

Rex

I SWEAR I'M A normal person.

I just have a career and a passion that put me in front of everyone else for the scrutiny and judgment of others.

Except when I'm at home, the only person who judges me here is an asshole who looks just like me, so he has no room to talk.

One thing I didn't think about when I woke up at three this morning, my cock still inside a goddess, my body cracking and aching like a glow stick, was what she would think of a man wearing a shower cap.

I'd gotten up to dispose of the used rubber, took a piss, cleaned Aria up as best I could without waking her, and wrapped my hair so that the curls didn't turn into a tangled mess while I slept. Having been on the road so long, the shit had nearly turned itself into dreads despite having someone's attempt to care for it to keep up the public image. It took me over four and a half hours to get it almost normal again.

One thing they don't keep much of a standard on, though, is how rough a rock star really looks. It's part of the image, the dynamic, to show up looking like a dung pile and still perform without a hitch.

It's rugged, they say. *Rough,* they say.

So here I am, donning a zebra-printed silk cap because, of course, the only one Ian could find was feminine, and preparing to face the judgment of Aria.

That's right, I lie here next to this sleeping *beauty* with the intention of fucking her awake while wearing a shower cap meant for women.

Like I'll let that shit stop me.

Despite the possibility of her judgment, I don't take the thing off.

Instead, I trace small patterns on the thigh she has draped over my hip, my cock fully aware of her closeness that occurred throughout the last few hours.

The heat from her core beckons me as it radiates along the length of the hard-on tucked between her legs, wanting and waiting. Her head lies on my bicep, her arms tucked into her chest, covering her full tits but exposing her soft belly. I ease my palm up her thigh, tease a finger along her hip to her ribs, and watch as her eyes start to flutter.

Aria's brow furrows, then softens as I continue to leave light touches over her skin.

A faint groan comes from her throat, and she rolls over onto her back but doesn't fully come to.

"Aria," I groan, the sight of her naked glory, sleepy and sated, has my cock jumping.

She responds by throwing an arm over her eyes, her propped knee falling to the side.

Fuck me, that looks like an invitation if I've seen one.

She's open and beautiful, her swollen and wet pussy on full display for me to take in. Which I do, despite my cock aching, begging for another release. Testing her, I run my fingertips along the inside of her thigh, onto her hip, and across the thatch of short hair she has there.

"Mmmm …" is all I get from her, but she doesn't swat me away, so I slide farther down the bed and continue tracing across her lower half. Still, she only responds with faint noises, so I push forward.

"Babe," I try, her chest rising and falling in an even, slow rhythm. Aria lets her arm fall to the side but still only gives me sleepy grunts, her eyelids firmly in place.

Farther still, but not too fast, I edge my touches to find the slickness between her thighs. She becomes a little more audible, her lips parting with a groan, her breath quickening.

"Aria."

Again, nothing seems to be disturbing her, so I push farther by slipping my fingers between her pussy lips and circling her clit.

She moans for me, her eyes dancing behind her eyelids.

"Aria," I try again, repositioning myself to kneel in front of her, circling her slickness as I maneuver. I lie flat on my chest, my cock digging into the mattress, and dip a finger inside her heat.

She moans deeper this time, her hips rotating to the movement.

A second finger pulls another moan from her as I pump them slow and easy inside her. She's wet. Wet enough that I can't help but lean in and taste her arousal. She gasps, her hands balling the sheets in her fists, so I dive in and lick.

Aria moans as I flatten my tongue against her clit and flip it from side to side. I watch up her body, her chest catching with her breath, her lips parting and closing with each moan. She races to the edge and dives right off into an orgasm that has her riding and soaking my face.

"Babe," I groan, my eyes rolling to the ceiling as my hips follow their own rhythm, seeking any kind of friction, even if it's just the sheets. "That was hot." I dip in again and help myself to another lick. She squeals and scoots up the bed against the headboard to escape me, laughing and crossing her legs. My face lands in the sheets in her absence, the sound of her laughter making the face full of fabric totally worth it. "Baaaabe." I crawl after her, snagging her ankle and dragging her back down beneath me. She howls with laughter, pushes at my chest, but wraps her bare legs around my hips.

Leaning to the side, I snag another rubber from the bedside drawer and use my teeth to tear into the foil packet.

"What—" Aria stops, her head literally tilting, her brow furrowing. "The fuck?" She reaches up and fingers the cap that has somehow still hung on for dear life. Her face reddens, and she pulls her lips between her teeth, which does nothing to prevent the burst of laughter that rushes air across my face and chest. "What is this?" she howls, pulling the silk from my head and fisting it in both hands.

"It's a cap." I chuckle at her response and roll the condom down my shaft as my curls cascade around us. "It's for my hair."

"But—" Aria stutters, tears rolling down her temples. "But why, though?"

"So it doesn't get all tangled at night." Her humor fills my chest and expands my lungs, despite it being at my expense. The curls of which we speak fall around us, humor leaking from her features as the strands caress her shoulders, and my cock twitches against her core. She bites that plump bottom lip and eyes my bare chest. Her hands find my skin, the cap long forgotten as Aria's fingers trail up my back, tickle across my ribs, and flatten on the spread eagle over my pecs.

"How many do you have?"

I think for a moment but come up blank considering most of my body is covered in ink. "A lot."

She rolls her eyes at my response, her attention shifting to my shoulders. "Do they mean something?"

I smirk at her curiosity and lean down to nuzzle at her neck, planting soft kisses there, her scent filling my nose.

My cock jumps again, pulling a gasp from her lips.

"Of course they do," I whisper against Aria's ear, eliciting shivers from her body. "A man doesn't make a commitment to brand his skin for the rest of his life unless it means something." My words pull a gasp from her, and I lean back to see the severity in her wide eyes, her parted lips. Stars sparkle there, the low light of the room giving away the emotion she feels at my admission.

"Rex." Aria's hands find themselves in my hair, tugging me closer. She presses her lips to mine gently, sweetly, her palm coming down to cup my face. I return the kiss, matching her pace when she opens up to me and caresses my soul through her tongue to mine.

"Aria." I break away, my breath labored as I rest my forehead against hers. My heart fills as she looks up at me, her hands trailing back down my body to grab my ass and pull me until the head of my cock sits at her opening.

"I want to feel you," she breathes.

I'm too drunk on adrenaline and emotion to stop her hips from gliding up, pushing the head of my cock into her sweet heat. I groan as she envelops me, taking me from the bottom, her pelvis meeting mine before retreating.

The cold that takes up her absence has my body answering before my brain can. I rock forward, slow and sensual, burying my cock deep inside her.

She moans, her nails scoring my lower back with each thrust.

My heart pounds a different rhythm, urging me to push deeper inside her when her legs wrap tighter around my hips.

Aria moans for me, deep sensual sounds that permanently etch themselves into my eardrums for the rest of time. And the way she moans my name has my heart melting and my balls ready to burst.

"*Rex …*"

There's no rushing this time. No race to finish. So, I slide my knees back and angle my hips for more of an upward thrust. The piercing through the head of my dick caresses across her G-spot on the way out and strokes back over it on the way back in.

Her eyes roll back in response.

Her mouth falls open, and her head tilts back in pure ecstasy.

Just the sight of her has my balls tightening, my cock engorging, my O racing forward to throw me off the edge of the cliff. I beat it back with sheer determination, the effort causing a sheen of sweat to cover my skin.

"*Aria.*"

My own groans roll off my tongue, uncontrollable when her legs slip off and open her up to me. I push deeper, my hands finding hers and pulling them up above her head, our fingers entwining together against the sheets. Leaning in, I kiss her with a fervor I've never felt before, and she matches me, pace for pace.

"I need …" Aria rasps around another low hum of pleasure that cuts off her words. She gasps as I slide my cock home, another moan cutting off her chance to tell me.

Except I know exactly what my girl needs. I feel it as her pussy clamps around me on every intake of my cock but loosens around me when I pull back.

"Tell me," I breathe into her neck, using what's left of my willpower to keep the pace I'm at.

When she mewls instead of answering, I give her just a taste.

Arching back, I slam my cock into her, the force pushing her up the mattress. She lets out a choked yelp, the sound guttural and pleasured.

"*Yes,*" she screams, her hips falling back into the slow, soft rhythm where we began. She meets my thrusts from the bottom, increasing the pressure when my cock disappears inside her. "Oh my God."

"Tell me what you need, baby," I breathe through a clenched jaw. "I'll give it to you."

Our pace quickens, the slap of skin on skin echoing as much as the sounds falling from her O-shaped lips.

"Harder." Her hands fist mine as I shift to hold both her palms with one of mine and grab onto her hip with the other. I thrust again, giving her what she wants. "That's it—*Oh God.* Right there," she pleads, her high-pitched gasps piercing my subconscious and digging down into the primal need that rips a growl from my chest.

"Fuck."

Growling, I hold her steady and hammer my cock into her until she shatters into a million orgasmic pieces beneath me. Her pussy clamps on for dear life as she screams, threatening to break my rigid and needy cock in two if I stop, so I don't. I don't stop hammering my hips until just before my cock explodes inside her.

Yanking back, I rip off the rubber and aim for her thigh, my cum shooting across her hip while stars burst behind my eyes.

"Aria."

Chapter Sixteen

Back at it again.

LOCAL STAR SEEN CAUSING havoc all across town last night, ending in a trip to the hospital. Is rehab in the near future for this fame boy?

Catch it here before those other guys.

Chapter Seventeen

Aria

Rex lies on top of me, laboring to catch his breath almost as much as I try to catch mine. His chest is crushing me, making the intake of air more difficult than it needs to be, but I don't dare move him.

I can't.

"Holy shit." My voice is hoarse, throat raw, as I drag air into my lungs and try my best to tame my racing heart. Rex's only response is a breathy chuckle as he props himself up on his shaky elbows and looks down at me with wild eyes.

The lack of restriction on my chest has me sucking in air like I've been drowning, my poor heart beginning to slow.

"That was …" I trail off, at a loss for words. My body refuses to do much other than focus on the aftershocks that rack through me and keep up with the vital life functions.

Is this how I die? This is a great way to go.

"Phenomenal," Rex finishes for me, his own breath beginning to slow, a smile wider than a mile plastered to his face. I smirk and lean up to plant a kiss on the corner of his mouth.

"Right," I rasp, falling back to the bed with a grunt. Rex follows my lead and rolls over to flop on the bed beside me. We lie still for a moment, his touch finding me with gentle movements across my skin. I relish the peace and the silence, my thoughts tame for the first time in what seems like a century.

It's not until my stomach rumbles, loud and obnoxious in the quiet, that I look over at him with shock. Only a little embarrassment. But he blinks at me, then bursts into a contagious laughter that has me no longer fearing his judgment.

"I could go for a bite, too." He chuckles and, smacking a kiss to my lips, rolls to throw his legs over the edge of the bed. He stands, all six foot something, and provides me the most glorious view of his tatted backside. I groan, pleased with the sight, and fan myself as Rex stretches, his arms reaching up high. His back arches, popping his ass out even more, making the ink there dance with each muscle he moves.

How did I end up with someone so fucking hot? The girls are going to freak.

"You comin', babe?" Rex looks over his shoulder at me, and I nearly die. Whether from the embarrassment of him catching me fanning myself or the pure sex god of a look on his face, I'm not sure.

Either way, I'm going happy.

I nod, snicker, and crawl to the edge of the gigantic bed, accepting the hand towel he presents to me when I stand. I do a quick cleanup as I mentally squeal and toss the towel into a nearby hamper.

Spotting the en suite bathroom, I sneak in like Rex isn't watching me. *Spoiler alert, he totally is.* Closing the door, I do my business. As I exit, I'm met with another item he's offering to me that I gladly accept.

Rex could probably hand me a burlap sack right now, and I'd willingly take it with a smile on my face.

Even if it was filled with dildos.

Why dildos? No clue.

"What's this?"

He watches me closely as I unfold the fabric in my hands, an overly large printed gray T-shirt hanging from my grip.

It's a band tee, I think? Cedar wears these sometimes, which totally fits her aesthetic. The whole emo band thing.

Is that what it's called? Did I do it right?

I turn it to face him, holding the thing up to my chest. It reaches almost to my knees. "Your favorite band?" I inquire, but he just grins and shakes his head, spinning away from me.

"You're gorgeous," he says over his shoulder. His glorious ass disappears out of the doorway in nothing but low-riding basketball shorts.

Lord, have mercy on my soul.

I stuff my arms and head through the shirt as I kick my ass in gear to find my underwear and follow Rex out into the apartment.

It's expansive. The short hall ends and opens to a wide floor plan, dark colors meeting dark marble where the living space bleeds into the kitchen. Only a breakfast bar separates the two.

Another hall leads farther around the U-shaped apartment that's a little too nice to be considered an apartment, but I don't venture past the living room.

No, I'm struck paralyzed by the sight of what has to be Rex's twin passed out on the leather sofa.

"Um … Rex?"

I don't take my eyes off the curly-haired *guest*, little snores escaping from his wide-open mouth. He's got a bandana, which I think is meant to be a headband, askew on his forehead and a sock missing from his foot.

How long has he been here?

Fuck, he looks just *like Rex.*

"Yeah, babe?" I meet his eyes across the space.

Seems he's made it all the way to the kitchen without batting an eye.

Okayyyy.

"Umm?" I gesture to the sleeping man on the couch, only a short distance from where we were just having sex. Embarrassment seeps in, my face burning red hot.

"Is there a turd nugget on my couch?" Rex asks, completely unbothered by the fact that his brother could have heard us, as he moves about the kitchen collecting various things. "His name's Mac. He won't bite you. You're not his type." I roll my eyes at his response and tentatively move forward into the room.

The damage is done at this point. He must have heard.

The thought doesn't stop the flames I feel licking at my face as I pass the couch, more conscious of the shortness of the not-dress Rex has me wearing.

"Why is he on your couch?" I shouldn't judge him, but my words come out that way. I'm not really, but I can't help but be flustered and defensive.

Rex pauses, one hand halfway to his mouth with a bite of something and a whisk in the other as I come up to the opposite side of the bar.

"You got an issue with my brother, Aria?" He points the whisk at me with a squint of his eyes. There's a hint of humor in his gaze, but I can tell that his twin is a sore subject.

"Uh, no." *Shit, fuck.* "I didn't mean..." I stutter, irritated with myself, but pull it back together with a deep breath.

"That's cute."

My brow furrows as the voice that spoke came from neither me nor Rex.

I feel my eyes widen as I spin slowly and come face to face with a chest clad in the same shirt I'm currently wearing. Except the sleeves have been ripped out, exposing the skin on his sides.

"Um ..." From his chest to his tatted throat, a jawline just like Rex's, a set of eyes greener than his brother's, my sight lands on the headband around a head full of sandy curls trimmed close on the sides and long on top. "Shit."

"She stutters when she's nervous," Mac says on a grin and leans around me into the bar to speak to his brother. "What are you making, fart breath?"

Breathe …

I spin just in time to catch Rex's whisk wielding to turn on his brother. "You watch yourself, turd muffin."

Mac lounges, his forearms against the marble, and gets closer to his brother.

What the fuck kinda name is that? Jesus Christ, what is happening?

"I can't physically watch *myself*, barf burrito." Mac snorts.

Rex rolls his eyes but shoots daggers at his brother. "Why are you here?" He echoes my question, and I feel a little less stupid but barely. I watch the interaction of these two, Rex attempting to intimidate and Mac completely unfazed.

"Why not?" Mac challenges, picking an apple from the fruit basket next to him and shining the fruit on his shirt. He takes a large bite, the crisp of it so loud it breaks the silence. Juice dribbles between his teeth that he doesn't even try to stop.

"Because you watched me bring a girl in here last night, doofus. That's not an invitation to stay on my couch," Rex snaps but turns his attention back to the bowl and cutting board in front of him.

Wait. Last night? Oh, God …

Mac takes another bite, speaking through the way he chews it. "Wasn't an ejection either." He pulls a stool out and straddles the thing like he isn't pushing every one of his brother's buttons.

I can see the flush rise on Rex's chest as anger sets in, but he doesn't push any further. He just shrugs.

The silence stretches, the only sounds coming from Mac chomping on his fruit and Rex preparing breakfast.

Seriously? The elephant is gigantic.

"What the fuck?" I can't help it. It's out before I can stop the words from tumbling from my lips. "Why would you keep hanging out?" I turn my anger and confusion on Mac first. I just met his brother, and I don't know either of them that well, but here I am, now pointing an exasperated finger at Rex when I get no answer from Mac. "And why aren't you doing anything about it?"

"Cuz it's what we do, lady," Mac answers, unaffected by my outburst. But his words only bring more confusion.

What have I gotten myself into?

"Look," I placate and turn to Rex, who watches with amusement sparkling that only serves to make me angrier. "If this is some sort of freaky twin sex thing, I'm not interested." I start backing away to collect my things with raised hands, preparing to get the fuck out of dodge. "This is why we can't have nice things."

I knew better than to sleep with a stranger, yet here I am.

Good going, Ari.

"Whoa, *no*." Rex rushes around the bar, meeting me in the middle of the living space and pulling me to a stop. "No weird twi—" Rex fakes a gag. "No. No weird shit, babe. Just you and me."

"*This* is weird." It's all I can muster as Rex palms my shoulders. He rubs my biceps in an attempt to console me but nods in understanding.

"I can see where it might be … different. We just …" He shrugs as he thinks of the words. "We've lived a different life than most." Satisfied with his choice of explanation, he continues. "He's been by my side every day since we were born. He already knows shit before I tell him. We just never shied away from it. Privacy barely exists for us."

"We just embrace it." I turn to see Mac has joined us, his ass planted back on the couch with that stupid apple and a knee pulled up to his chest. He nods to me, but his gaze drifts to his brother. "She doesn't know?"

"Know what?"

They share a look between them. One that reminds me of my sister and best friend.

Oh, shit. I haven't checked in with them.

"Where we come from," Mac says, but I'm not listening to them anymore. I push away from Rex in search of my phone as panic begins settling in. There's probably already a search party on its way with my name all over it.

"Oh God. How could I be so reckless?" I search the main area, dash back into the bedroom, and tear the bed apart looking for the device, but it's eluding me.

Rex emerges in the open doorway as I toss the last pillow back on the bed and dash back out into the main area past him. Maybe I missed it in my frenzied search the first time?

"You looking for this?" Mac holds up a phone from his seat on the couch, the thing pinched between his thumb and forefinger as he waves it about. I dive across the room and snag it from him to unlock and observe the damage. "It was going nuts when Ian brought it up. So, I answered."

I wade through the missed calls and messages as he speaks, but his words sink in when I go to dial one of the two.

"You answered my phone?" I furrow a brow at him as some of the texts begin to make more sense, things like how *hot the dude sounds* …

"Yeah, your sister was calling and wouldn't stop." He shrugs like he didn't just save my life. "So, I answered and let them listen to you 'get it' from my brother." He air quotes, and I'm disgusted, so I throw a nearby pillow at his face. It does nothing but incite laughter, deep and gravelly, from him, but I still feel like I won that round.

"Can we have breakfast now? I'm starved." Mac tucks the pillow behind his head and kicks his feet up like he's planning to hang around. I roll my eyes but flop down next to him and send a quick message to the group chat.

> Me: I'm alive. Yes, there's a brother. Just one, though.

> Me: I didn't make the flight home. I'll figure that out later.

> Me: It's breakfast time.

Yep, I've definitely lost all semblance of sanity.

Chapter Eighteen

Rex

I ADMIRE THE WAY Aria just seems to *fit* into the insanity of my life.
She's been exposed to so much over the last few hours without batting
an eye.

I still feel like a normal human with her.

Aria hasn't freaked, recognized either of us, or demanded shit to keep
our secret safe.

Even Mac has given up trying to stump her as she sits in my lap on my
couch and plays him in some stupid card game that he made up. My hand
is on her bare thigh—yeah, that's right, she's still wearing only my band's
shirt. She leans forward to lay a card on the center cushion between us
and her opponent. He matches her as I lean in to whisper in her ear how
hot she is.

She smiles and turns to wink at me but focuses back on the game.

Goddamn, she's got me.

Aria manages to win the match in an imaginary game my twin thought
up, intending to kick ass in, which makes her victory even better. Mac
accuses me of cheating, but his words don't last long when she reminds
him of the origin story he spent twenty minutes explaining.

Now, she stands, smacks a kiss to my lips, and sways her delicious ass into my room to find her pants. I follow, putting on a high-collar peacoat and throwing my hair up into a ball cap to help hide it. Simple black jeans and a button-down underneath, inconspicuous enough to seem unapproachable but not a sore thumb in public.

"I gotta head back." She emerges, still clad in my shirt that's been tied at the side to fit her hourglass figure, the print of the tee popping against the brightness of her pants.

It's like the damn thing was made for her.

"Can I?" I hold my phone up and snap a few pics when she nods. I send them to her before I close my phone and wrap an arm around her waist.

Ian drives us the long way back to her hotel. It's still light out, so when we come to a stop at the side entrance, I pop my collar and slide out of the car to open her door. I follow closely up the walkway as she taps the keycard to allow us in.

The elevator trip and the hallway to her room are way too short, too quiet after the night we had. And when she lets me into her room, it hits me.

I don't want to go back to a life without Aria.

To the stage lights. Where I have to pretend like Aria didn't just make me feel like the luckiest man alive.

I want her with me.

But I know better.

She has no idea the life I lead, the lack of privacy, the hiding in public, paying others to get groceries and shit because it's safer. Not sitting outside around a fucking fire because paps might be hiding in the bushes taking pictures. Or worse.

I should have never exposed her to that.

The sinking feeling in my gut just gets heavier when I watch her spin to me and smile.

"It's not a fancy penthouse, but it's a nice room." She's comparing this to what I have, but she has no idea that I'd take this in a heartbeat. I'd leave it all if it meant I could feel more of her.

"It's perfect." I force a smile for her despite the tension in my chest, and I hold a hand out for her. She easily steps into my embrace, snaking her arms beneath the coat hanging like lead from my shoulders.

Aria's closeness lifts some of the weight from my shoulders when I press a tender kiss to the crown of her head. Her chin rests against my chest, her brilliant smile coming into view.

"Don't look at me like that," I mutter to the sparkle in her eyes.

"Like what?" She feigns an innocence that I know damn well she doesn't have and bats her lashes at me.

"Like I'm the one leaving when you're the one who has girls you need to get back to before they call the authorities on me."

Aria snorts and spins out of my arms to start putting her shit back in a bag.

"You're not wrong." She shakes her head with a lift to the corner of her mouth, but the more she shoves stuff into her bag, the more her smile fades. Falters.

Flattens.

"Babe …" I snag her hands when they shake and pull her to my chest.

"This is stupid. We just met." Her voice shakes, her lip quivers, but she stands steady.

She's resolute and strong, and for that, I envy her.

"It's not stupid." Normally, I would prepare a whole speech.

The *It's not you, it's me* bullshit people like me have to say to shake the groupies that want to hang on for dear life.

If she were anyone else, I would have told her it's silly. That catching feelings so fast was never the intention. That it was all a great time, but that our time has come to an end.

I certainly wouldn't have brought her back to her hotel, let alone walked her all the way to the door to be caught inside.

I open my mouth, trying to shake off the melancholy settling into my chest, but I can't.

I'm speechless for the first time in a long time, so I snap my lips shut.

I don't know what to do, but I do know that she deserves better than me. She deserves someone who can be honest with her from the grip, someone who can keep her to themselves. Someone who can keep her *safe*.

That's just not fucking me.

Aria watches me flounder and takes it in a way that I don't mean.

My stomach sinks when she physically pushes against my tightened sternum to return to packing her things into a purple suitcase.

I can't take it, watching her leave like this, but I have to.

It's the only way to keep her life separate from mine.

She can walk away from this without losing something most people take for granted.

Privacy.

Aria will be able to find someone else to love her and be with her in a way that she can maintain her life. Her sense of self. Her sanity. Her safety.

The thought of her ever being with anyone else turns my stomach, but I ignore it.

One more time, I wrap my arms around her waist.

With the press of a kiss to her temple, I allow the scent of tropical paradise to fill my lungs one last time.

"Text me when you think of me," I whisper to Aria with a final kiss to the soft flesh behind her ear, and I slip away.

Out of her room without a backward glance.

Away from the hotel and into the car.

Somewhere around the third circle back to the penthouse, I lose the coat and the hat as heat takes over me.

On the way out of town, when we couldn't get back into the garage, I have Ian pull over. My stomach evacuates in the loose gravel of a back country road, unable to handle the nerves that scream to turn around.

Then we drive some more.

We lose daylight, making it easier to lose a tail, but I can't go back to my apartment without feeling that pulsing ache in my chest. My thoughts won't stop drifting back to the memories of Aria spread out on my sheets and eating breakfast on my couch.

It's the ordinary shit that's twisting me up.

Instead, I tell Ian to take me to the only other place that brings me peace.

Pulling up to the warehouse district, Ian pauses the car long enough to punch a code in the hidden panel that slides a rackety gate to the side and grants us passage. He drives us along a wide road, one big enough to house semis on both sides, until we get to the dead end.

Another hidden panel and the dead end opens up to a separate drive. This one curves and winds, barely big enough for the SUV to fit through the arched trees until we reach the destination about a bumpy mile back.

Set in a forest of green for privacy and protection is my band's state-of-the-art recording studio.

My home away from home that is, in fact, equipped to be a refuge and a practice venue.

Here, As Above has spent many nights cramming for records, recording all-nighters, and creating content and shorts for social media. We bought the land when our first record went gold, planned the new build when our second and third went platinum, and have recorded each record here since. We even rereleased the first ones from this studio.

The walls are lined with plaques, posters from each world tour, photographs of magazine covers, and stage shots that only a pro can get.

All of our accomplishments are on display for us to see, to admire and remember what we've managed to do over the last few years.

When I come here, I usually feel satisfied. Sated. *Fulfilled.*

I feel our childhood dream alive with each step through the place.

It's inspiring, empowering even, to know that my legacy will go on living long after I'm gone.

But tonight …

Tonight, my heart hangs too heavy in my chest.

My mouth is dry, hands tingling with nerves as I slink down the hall to the studio. Locking myself into the soundproof room with knots in my stomach, I grab the control tablet to block out the rest of the world, and I scream.

Hitting record on the tablet, I let loose the heavy, unclean vocals weighing on my chest.

I rasp and I sing, screaming guttural lyrics into the covered microphone until my throat aches and the beginning of a heartbreak album forms.

Emotion fuels me to keep going, to push past the pain and just *feel it.*

Adding snippets of unused riffs and instrumentals my band has recorded, the first songs come together easier than expected, the next only interrupted when my phone rings.

Is it her?

Unable to resist, I sprint across the room where I left it in hopes that it's Aria, except it's not.

In fact, there's nothing from her at all.

Instead, my twin's face pops up on the screen as his name scrolls. I decline the call and head back to my stool, my notebooks, my work.

I pass the empty drum set, the untouched guitar stands filled with bass and six strings.

I'm tempted to set up at any one of them—I can play almost anything—but I keep with my most powerful means instead.

My vocals.

Tap, tap, tap.

I pause mid-step, pinching the bridge of my nose before I swing my hard gaze to the window that was dimly lit before.

Now, it's bright, illuminating my entire band standing with stony faces lined up on the other side.

Shit.

I'm not ready for them. To explain anything. To make this realer than real.

Mac ignores my subtle dismissal and speaks into the mic on his side. When it doesn't come through to me, I hold the tablet up to show I've restricted the outside world, but he overrides it.

"Play back that last one."

I sigh but nod.

He's giving me the chance to work it through with him at a distance.

I throw my hair up into a better knot and adjust the mic closer to my mouth.

Starting out slow with sensual lyrics, just like it did with Aria, I watch as Mac pokes buttons, then signals to keep going.

Headphones slid on, I sing my heart out.

Passionate to desperate, the lyrics tumble from me as I vocalize the anguish I'm feeling in my bones.

I release harsh vocals about how love can't survive the bright lights of the stage. I growl out about dreams that have turned into nightmares and stolen the one thing I didn't know I even wanted. Needed.

I'm not sure when Finland joined me in the studio, but he's added a guitar melody to my vocals in the places where scraps won't fill in, minding his own business and just playing. He's jumped from the drums for a beat that Mac repeats for background, strung together a gorgeous guitar riff that makes my chest hurt, and added his own assisting snarls.

By the time my voice gives out, we've recorded a full album's worth of material.

"One more," I rasp, my voice shot. Mac tries to shake his head, but I shoot him a look. This is what the last one needs. The rawness and the passion. The broken vocals.

I adjust the headphones so that only one ear is covered, and I sing with almost no voice.

"Can you relate? What's been taken from you?"

I take another shot of whiskey from the bottle that's been sitting next to me since Fin came in, the liquid burning all the way down.

"Who do you want there with you when the world comes crashing down?"

A ballad is born, a love song to rival the classics built on rock and roll foundations, sung with a twinge of rasped soul that reminds me of *her*.

"If it all tumbles down tonight, it's you I want by my side. Cuz there's no sun left in your brilliance."

With the final chorus off my lips, I pop the headphones from my head and walk out without another glance to anyone else in the room.

I've got nothing left to give.

Chapter Nineteen

Rex

"Rex, it's been three weeks."

I yank at the blanket to pull it tight over my head to block out the sunlight my brother insists on letting in before it pierces my skull.

"Don't care." My voice is a graveled mess thanks to the bottle sitting on the nightstand next to me that I'm pretty sure I drained last night, maybe even this morning.

Was it two bottles?

I can feel his eye roll more than I hear his scoff with his next words. "That's all you've said. That you don't care." I shrug to myself under the comforter, but it gets enough of the message across.

Fishing a hand out of the mess of blankets, I reach for the glass I know will help numb the ache, only to feel my twin swipe it from my grasp.

"Bro, you're killing me." There's no sarcasm to his words like Mac generally has, even when it's not the time for it. "At least come to the arcade. Play a game with me."

It's like we're thirteen all over again, and I just want to chase girls and sing my heart out while my brother just wants the bullying to stop.

Except the girl I want … I let go of, and he's older now, able to stick up for himself.

Not that he couldn't then either.

Explaining the black eyes and busted knuckles to our mother, though, was a whole other story.

"No." Harsh, my words send a lancing of pain through my own chest at the rejection of my own brother.

I don't want to see the world; I want to be left alone. I have nothing left to give to the people outside this room, considering I've already given up just about every damned thing else.

Like my fucking privacy.

My heart.

"Archie wants to see you about the record." Mac's words are hopeful as he shares something I used to get excited about, but all it does is add to the rocks sinking in my gut that settle next to the other ones I'm tired of carrying.

I tighten the blanket around my head and leave his comments unanswered.

"He thinks it's a hit. The whole damn thing."

Course they do. Because it is.

"Great," I mumble into the fabric, unimpressed with the news I never intended to reach Archie and the boys at the record label.

It was about having a fucking moment. Not selling another part of my soul.

"I know it's about her," Mac rebuts, yanking at the covers and succeeding in pulling the corner from my grasp. "Isn't that what makes it good art? It's got a piece of your soul in it?" He yanks, I tug, hair flings then sticks in my face, and now I'm up fighting to get the comfort back. "Isn't that what all artists do?"

Face to face with my twin, my breath huffs out in frustration. I was just fine in my little hole of existence all by myself.

"Macaroni," I growl, spinning and wrapping my body up in the strung-out material between us so that his grip loosens. He lets go of the blanket but hugs me tight around my chest, trapping my arms at my sides.

I'm pinned in and tangled before I can blink, my brain foggier than I'd like to admit. In a feeble attempt to break free, I launch my whole body back to the couch.

Mac doesn't break loose like I expect him to.

Instead, he lands on my chest with a grunt and pulls the blanket tight to hold me down.

"You gotta get up, Rex." Desperation laces his spent words when I fight against his hold.

"I can't if your ass is holding me down," I growl.

Like magic, he springs off the couch, releasing me with hands held up in surrender.

I lie there for a long moment with a pumping chest, Mac standing over me as I huff and blow hair all over. It's in my face, stuck to my now sweating forehead.

"Rex …" My brother's tone is full of warning. "Don't make me call Mom."

Shit.

"You *wouldn't*," I challenge, my position unwavering, my eyes narrowing to slits.

Until he pulls out his phone, that is. He punches at the screen, and I sit up, throwing my twisted-up lower half over the side of the couch.

"Don't you dare, Mac."

I snap an arm out, trying to steal the phone from him, but I'm too slow.

"Get in the fucking shower. You need sunlight."

He pockets the device but stands guard over me like he doesn't trust that I won't just flop back into my refuge.

He's not wrong … I have no intention of getting up.

"Fuck you, bro." I scoff and scrunch my nose.

"Love you, turkey brains. Now go." He nods in the direction of the bathroom, arms crossing over his torso, determination and concern steeling his brow.

I hate that look.

"I hate you right now." Defeated, I unravel from the covers and leave them in a heap on the floor as I defiantly pad down the hall.

Steam billows from the shower when I turn on the tap, fogging up the glass door and the mirror. I swipe away the moisture to get a look at myself for the first time in weeks.

Jesus, I look as hungover as I feel.

My throat aches from all the alcohol over the last few days, well, weeks. My eyes are dry and bloodshot from too much focus on the tiny screen of my phone, while my voice still hasn't entirely recovered from the scream session that apparently landed us a hit album.

Eyes highlighted by dark circles. Collarbones protruding more than I recall.

Even the eagle inked into my chest stares back lackluster.

My beliefs have been shaken down to the very foundation, leaving behind a messed-up head and a broken heart.

Why am I doing this?

I should probably see a shrink about that, and maybe I will one day, but for right now, all I care about is sinking into the tile of the bathroom.

Leaning over the sink, I snag the toothbrush there and begin scrubbing.

What else do you do when your dream has become a nightmare?

I can't even be in a car accident—which wasn't a damn accident, by the way—without the public accusing me of evading police.

Running from the cops.

Yeah, that's right. I saw the articles the day after Aria left for home. I went searching, trying to make sure she was still safe, that her name or face hadn't tipped the public, and found the tabloids exploiting that night for the clicks.

Even how I ended up in the hospital.

Those same magazines and news outlets that commended me for building animal shelters and rescuing tornado victims.

Aria was right there with me in the wreck. Too close to destroying her anonymity, to ruining her life. To stealing the one thing I wish I had right now.

Privacy.

So instead, I've taken to becoming the next hermit and sending one of the Sentry Security guys to look out for Aria while I admire the one picture I took of her with the hope that she'll eventually text me.

She hasn't.

She won't.

The way I left it with her ensured that. It was a forever kind of goodbye that still gnaws at me.

I take one last look at my reflection before stripping and walking into the scalding spray coming from the showerhead.

The pressure beats against my back as I slide down to the cold tile, and I let it melt my skin and burn me until I'm a prune of a man.

Even my tattoos threaten to seep out of my skin.

Still, I ignore the knock on the door.

"Rex," Mac calls out to me, the water now cooling. "I don't smell any fucking soap, you turd. Tell Mom *hi.*"

Fucking fuck.

"*Alright*," I shout back, reaching up to snag a bottle of something from the ledge and squirting some into my trembling palm.

Shit, that's conditioner.

I smear the shit into my hair anyway to help with the tangles and feel for another bottle. Landing on soap this time, I use my sponge to lather my pits and my chest and work my way down my body.

The eagle, spread wide across my chest and pecs, taunts me a second time when I lean to wash one of my tattooed feet.

I shake my head at the symbolism behind the ink and lean over to wash the other foot.

Sliding back under the spray again, letting the frigid water rejuvenate me, the conditioner slicks the tile under my thighs. I feel around for the shampoo, squeeze out way more than a dime-sized amount and push the shit around in my hair until white foam covers my head. Reaching up, I adjust the temp to force more warmth through the pipes, grateful when the water responds and goes lukewarm again.

Rinsing the lather, I use more conditioner. A knee up to my chest, I prop an arm there while I wait for the oil to soak in and read the letters scripted on my forearm.

The font faces me so that it can easily be read in times like this, a reminder to myself.

It was the first tattoo I ever got.

A muscle pulls at the corner of my lips, the action foreign after weeks of nonuse. I breathe in for what feels like the first time in a long time, my chest expanding with the scent of coconut from the hair shit.

It reminds me of her, my muse, and I rise to stand fully beneath the spray.

Mac's right. It's been too long.

The reminder jolts me with a renewed sense of energy.

The contract was up the moment we got home.

Archie and the boys have no business fucking with my songs anymore.

I have an out.

A weight feels like it has lifted from my chest when I wrap the towel around my waist and exit the bathroom in search of my twin.

"Macaroni."

Perched on the kitchen counter with a steaming pot held under his chin as he shovels fresh mac and cheese into his mouth with a serving spoon, Mac's eyes light up the moment he sees me.

"Don't judge me," he starts, pointing at me from across the room with a growing grin.

"And I won't judge you," I finish, the statement a reminder of all the shit we've been through together.

We promised each other from the moment we could conceptualize loyalty that we'd have each other's back, no matter how stupid or crazy.

And this might be fucking insane.

It's gotten us pretty far already.

"I have some ridiculous shit I need to do." I hop up on the counter next to him and steal the spoon from his grip to shovel a bite into my own mouth. "You got me?"

He grins and holds out a fist for me to bump.

"Fuckin' always, bro." I meet his glassy gaze. "Glad to have you back, Rex."

Chapter Twenty

Rex

Cigar smoke fills the room—as if it hasn't left the mob scene since the seventies—from the occupant more than filling out the leather high-back chair situated at the head of the obnoxious desk.

Ornate fixtures adorn the large pillars filling out the space, faint lights illuminating only every other one, the surfaces collecting enough dust to start their own fire if you breathe on it wrong.

What used to be dark green colored panels between the pillars are now a brown shade of puke, thanks to the years of nicotine buildup. Only three of them are filled in with handmade wooden frames, donning platinum records boasting one million copies sold.

And all three frames belong to As Above.

I used to think this shit was cool. That it meant money and loyalty.

It doesn't.

"My boy."

"Archie," I say, amused when the rotund man finally releases his ass from the chair on the third try, his loose jowls shaking with each thunderous step toward us.

His manicured yellowed nails, from too many years of sitting in cloudy rooms like this, dig into my shoulders when the old man pulls me into a half hug. The mix of stale and fresh tobacco fills my nostrils and coats my already aching sinuses.

I paste on my best charming smile and pat the guy's back for a half a second because if I don't, I know it'll make this shit worse.

"I hear you wanted to speak with me, son. Come." He gestures to the cracked leather chair in front of his desk. "Sit and have a smoke."

Fat hands shoo away his guards who stand sentry beside his chair, which severely protests his flop of weight, then busy themselves with lighting another stogie despite the guards' refusal to stand down. They merely take a step aside.

Of course they do.

Because Ian's here.

I learned a thing or two about my bodyguard last time. Maybe they did, too.

"I cannot believe the feedback from your new recordings, son." Archie puffs on the stogie, pushing more smoke into the air from the turd pinched between his fingers. "Once we switch a few things, I think we might have another award-winning album on our hands." He chuckles to himself, completely unaware of my rolling eyes because he can never be bothered with anyone beyond his own greed.

We do have an album already. It's As Above's sound and my fucking heart.

I shoot a glance back at Ian, who cocks a brow at the man behind the desk.

"That's exactly what I want to talk about, Arch," I amend, effectively cutting him off from his own daydream and finding his startled expression searching for my meaning.

"Son?" he questions, but his face reddens with anger radiating from him across the room, its path only broken up by the seat I refuse to take.

"The contract is up, Arch."

I lean in to brace on the back of the empty chair and stare down at the man I thought would give us, my brothers and I, the world one day.

And I do it with a smile on my face knowing that Archie did not give us the world at all, but instead, taught us a valuable lesson.

Never trust a salesman.

That every bit of As Above's marketing came from me, my guys, and our small team that's grown over the years. Each stream pushed by *our* hard work. Every record doubled off *our* backs.

That he *profited from.*

His fist slams into the wood between us, ashes flittering from the lit cigar tucked between his thick fingers and landing among the piles of papers he'll probably never file or scan.

"It's up when I say it's up, *boy*," he growls at me, leaning menacingly into the desk, except what he doesn't realize is that his intimidation game is over with me. He doesn't get far, thanks to all the extra baggage around his midsection, his balding head catching the light and reflecting back at me.

"Now," I say with a lightness I barely feel as I push off the chair and step around the furniture to walk by his stale-nicotine-covered desk. I swipe a finger over the top, leaving a trail in my wake, and come back around to glance in Ian's direction.

I tuck my elbow in to inspect the pads of my fingers and thumb, only to find they turn orange the longer I rub them together.

"You have two options, Arch." I spin back to confront the raging old man with pointed fingers. "Either you delete any recent recordings you've manipulated of *my* new album, or we can take it to court." I shrug, arms dropping to my sides, and feel Ian step up to flank me as if on cue. "If you make it that far, that is."

The guards standing on either side of the old man flex at my words, hands finding handles of guns, awaiting the command to take us out.

"I'll beg your fucking pardon?" Archie's angry spittle flies from his shaking lips and lands on the dark desk, his voice rattling off the orangish-tinged walls. "You wouldn't have your little fucking band if it wasn't for me. *World tours?* Who got you *those?*"

I shrug, nonchalant and uncaring of his words.

"And you have the fucking nerve to threaten me?" Archie stands from his desk, making it to his feet with only one try this time, his fat sausage fingers aimed right at me.

"Not a threat." I glance back at Ian, who shoots me a look that suggests I should fix myself. "Just a statement of fact. Smoking is such a filthy habit and a deadly one, too."

"You wouldn't be the face of music if it weren't for me, *boy,*" Archie seethes, pitching forward, bracing his fists on the desk.

He's not wrong. We wouldn't be where we are if it weren't for him. *We'd be much further.*

"You can spit your hate all you want, Arch." I shake my head, a humorless chuckle escaping my lips. "See, I'm smarter now than I was then. Stealthier." I make a show of my hands, waving them down my body as if I'm the showcase prize. "More mature." I wink and smirk right in his ragey fucking face with outstretched arms. "But we both know you changed my shit without my permission outside of the contract. You *assumed* we'd eventually draw up a new one."

Archie freezes at my words, proving my theory right in the process.

"And then you shared it with others. Didn't you." It's not a question because I already know the answer, one that he won't share as he stutters around a response that never comes. I drop my arms to my side and deliver my final blow. "I'm out, Archie. We're *done.*"

"You don't know what you're doing," Archie comments after a tension-filled beat of silence that's not actually quiet thanks to his labored breathing, pulling a scoff from my throat and an eye roll I don't hide from him for once.

"Except I do this time, Arch. The band's obligations were up the second the plane landed. We even threw a party." I shake my head and turn to address Ian. "We're done here."

A tight jut of his chin is all I need to follow my bodyguard to the door.

"And by the way." I pause at the open threshold. The knob in my hand, a foot out the door. "My name's not *boy* or *son*."

"I'm telling you, you're—"

"It's *Rex,* motherfucker."

I raise my hands and flip both middle fingers to someone I once idolized until Ian is shoving me out into the hall.

"Just had to take it that far, didn't you?"

"Have you met me, Ian?"

His heavy sigh is the only response I get on the matter, accompanied by our echoing boot steps thumping over the worn puke-green flooring.

You'd think a record tycoon would replace his damn carpet.

Thumps echo behind us, papers flittering out into the hall from Archie's office like delayed confetti.

Sounds like Archie is big mad in there.

"What are you going to do now?" Ian asks, smashing the elevator call button and stepping to the side so that his back is to the wall and mine is covered.

"Leo set up this whole 'road trip' tour." I shrug and watch the numbers tick down on the elevator. "I owe them the final ride."

My phone chirps for my attention, and I pull the thing out to find a message from my twin. I send him a quick confirmation of my safety and dismiss the messaging app to pause on my background photo.

"And what about that?" Ian taps the screen with a meaty finger, nearly knocking my phone out of my hand as he pushes past me to take up most of the elevator car. I juggle for a moment but keep the device from skittering to the floor and step into the cramped lift.

"What's it to you?" It's a rhetorical question, his interest pissing me off more than I'd like to admit.

But he grunts his response anyway. "Just fucking call her."

Chapter Twenty-One

Aria

Six hours in the car after a night like the one with Rex had me screaming at the windshield like it was the car's fault that my heart hurt, my nether regions ached, and my eyes wouldn't stop leaking.

That's a hell of a combination to feel.

I came home a mess to Cedar and Aurora, who helped me pick up the broken pieces of my pitiful heart. They theorized and fantasized about Rex's untimely death, as any good sister and best friend would, but their anger only fueled the urge I'd felt deep in my soul for a long time.

Not to kill anyone, per se.

But to let go. Of the old me, the past.

The survival me.

The stuck version of me.

So, over the third pint of ice cream and buried under a blanket fort we made to get my mind off He Who Shall Not Be Named, I made up my mind.

That I'm an upcycling fashion designer at heart and a marketing wiz at best, and my craft needed to be shared with the world. It's time to live my dream, like my sister lives hers. Like Cedar lives hers.

"Ari."

I pull myself from my thoughts and turn to find my sister buried behind the lens of a camera aimed right at me.

"Let me call G," Aurora says.

I smile at her and shake my head. "It has to be you, sis."

We stand in Aurora's recently rented studio as movers parade in through the door with boxes of costumes and different props she's used in the past. It's on the darker side, so we'll have to have more lighting set up for her, but it's the perfect venue for both of us.

"But he has more of a following than me," she almost whines as she snaps pics of the move, one subject in particular catching her attention more than she'll admit.

"And you being mentioned on my site will help you with getting more exposure, too. We gotta start somewhere, right?" She glances back at me over her shoulder when her subject has trailed off.

Honestly ... I'm hoping to avoid G as long as possible. I currently have an unopened email from him with the pictures he took that day that I've yet to look at. I can't. I won't. And I don't think he'll understand that. Nor would my sister.

"Would it be wrong to ask him?" Aurora interrupts my internal struggle once again.

I scoff when her question brings me back to the *him* carrying in another box of decor, and I busy my hands unpacking a nearby tote. "Considering he's followed you around for the last four weeks, I don't think he'd mind."

The guy's name is Jonathon, who happens to be a local jack-of-all-trades, I guess. Which somehow includes amateur modeling or something like that. He showed up when we called for maintenance at the last studio about a month ago, and he came back a few days later to bring a comp card with his name and number on it. Amazing how he found ways to weasel in around my sister ever since.

"Just tell him to come with us." I nod at Jonathon when he traipses in with another heavy load that flexes his arms and sends my sister's jaw to the floor.

His eyes find her over the box, a slight flush darkening his cheeks.

It's cute how endearing he is. He's shy but definitely interested in Aurora. It helps that he's hot, over six feet tall, built like a stallion, and displays a few tattoos.

"Oh, whatever," she says to me, rolling her eyes. She pretends like she doesn't already know how into her he is and moves on to snap pics of something else. Her lack of acknowledgment sends Jonathon's shoulders drooping, but his gaze comes to mine.

"You need anything, Ms. Aria?" Jon's eyes leave mine for a beat, going to the opening door, only to dismiss Cedar's entrance and come back to me.

"I'm good, Jon. You don't have to keep checking in." I give him a small smile when he nods and turns on his heels to fetch another box from the moving truck outside.

"I still can't believe you guys are going to be right next door." Cedar waltzes in like she owns the place, donning one of my originals. She looks good, my recent designs having improved a thousand times, and comes right up to me to throw her arms around my shoulders.

"I know, I'm stoked," I respond with aching cheeks.

We share a quick squeal, a longer squeeze with her cheek smashing into mine, and Aurora snaps a pic of us.

"So," Cedar leans back to address Aurora, "I've got a client finishing in about an hour. I need you there for photos." Aurora nods her agreement and takes off to prep. "I gotta get back, I just took a quick break to come see you assholes." She grins at my exasperation, smacks a red-stained kiss to my cheek, and wanders off as quickly as she came in.

By client, she means a tattoo. And by photos, she means that my sister is taking all the pics for her tattoo shop to post online with credits to Aurora, too.

We've interwoven all of our passions to create a monster career for each of us, and I've never been happier.

Mostly.

I check the tablet in my hand, the screen showing we're ahead of schedule for the move, and I post to social media, commenting to the following we've gained over the last few weeks.

Once we open the doors, Aurora will be booked for the next three weeks straight. Cedar has clients lined up longer than that, and my site where we sell my creations has exploded.

It's been a long six weeks, but we're making waves.

After Cedar's appointment is finished tonight, we're going out to celebrate. We allowed a game of Rock, Paper, Scissors to decide who got to choose how we would honor the occasion. Unfortunately, Cedar won, landing us tickets to a concert in the next city over.

Wandering back to the office I share with Aurora, my face buried in my tablet so I can scroll socials and share content for each of our pages, my ass lands in a chair that wasn't there twenty minutes ago.

"Who are we seeing tonight?" I huff, asking my sister without looking up.

She clicks her tongue as she packs things into a case to carry over next door. "As Above. One of C's many favorites." I nod at my sister's words and purse my lips. The name rings a bell, but I can't recall from where.

Must just be how Cedar talks about them.

"You know I tune her out when she talks," I jest but post a final status for the night about joining us at the show and put the tablet to sleep.

"I know it's not as much your thing, but it'll be a great time," Aurora comments, as if she can sense some kind of worry from me.

She's not entirely wrong.

"I know it will be. Any time I spend with you bitches is always fun."

It's just the nagging anxiety that presents itself in a time of stress.

Y'know, like a time when you're opening a new studio to display your creative pieces along with the people you spend all your time with. And if it fails miserably, you let down your sister and your best friend and your lifelong dream.

No pressure or anything.

I shake off the nagging thoughts and smile for my sister. "We got this, right?" It's the picking of my nails that I can't shake off, though, and my smile that doesn't last.

"Absolutely." She nods enthusiastically, flips the flap over her camera bag, and throws the thing on her shoulder. "You should start getting ready." With another squeezy hug, she takes off out of the room to do her job on the other side of the wall.

I shake my head at the mess I've gladly stepped into and grab the garment bags filled with pieces for tonight, along with the makeup bag. As I head for the bathroom, Jonathon stops me for a moment to sign off on some paperwork for the move.

"Aurora said you guys are going out tonight?" he casually asks while I read the paper I'm preparing to sign.

"Yeah, something at a bar called NightOwls. We're seeing a band or something," I answer distractedly, scribbling on the clipboard once I agree to the terms of the shit there. "I've never been."

Businesses require so much fucking paperwork.

"Oh, no shit? As Above's there tonight." Jonathon beams at the knowledge and accepts the clipboard. "They put on a great show. I've seen them a time or two."

As Above bounces around in my skull like it's a clue that I'm missing the mark on, but I smile for Jonathon and keep moving.

"You should come," I throw over my shoulder as I walk.

"Yeah, maybe I will," he shouts back before I slip into the bathroom and close the rest of the world out.

Getting ready proves to take longer than I expected, so by the time I'm finishing up my hair, Aurora and Cedar have joined me again.

I adjust the black sequined crop top I'm wearing around my ribs so that my tits don't pop out the bottom when I reach up, and then I pull the long sleeves back so that the adornments don't catch in my hair. Mussing the strands, I give myself the messy wave look and apply hairspray to keep it in place.

With another glance in the floor-length mirrors, I approve of the exposed midsection I've only recently become comfortable with showing. My softer belly has slimmed a bit over the last few weeks with all this extra work, but I've learned to accept that I'm just a curvy girl.

The black skinny jeans I wear help tone down the sparkle from the top, but the silver boots round out the grungy look I'm going for.

Aurora wears more sequins, her top a loose-fitting V-neck tank that came from the same garment as mine. Her hair hangs loose and straight around her shoulders, but her destroyed jeans hug tight to her hips and taper down to boyfriend-cut ankles that show off her strappy heels.

Cedar, on the other hand, bursts out of the stall with a reconstructed As Above T-shirt, holey black skinnies we destroyed together, and Chucks. She wraps an old flannel around her hips and ties it snugly there. Her bright red lipstick on her plump lips makes her look like a pin-up girl.

"I'm so fucking excited, ladies." She grins at us, runs a hand through her black hair, and tosses most of it over one side while she swipes a coat of mascara on her lashes.

"Well, shit." I stare at the women in the mirror and have to breathe to keep the emotions at bay. I spent too much time perfecting these cat eyes to ruin them with tears. "You ladies look amazing." I fan my face when Aurora wraps me up in a hug.

"Thanks to you," she singsongs in my ear and spins away to smear glitter on her face and grab her camera.

We capture our appearances with a few poses, both together and separately, then post to social media for the content. Then we're ready to load our asses into the car with giggles that bring tears to my eyes in a good-emotional way.

I drive this time, and every time since they kidnapped me all those weeks ago. Sure, it led me to an existential crisis that brought me here, but I'm not putting my life in their hands like that ever again.

Piloting the vehicle onto the highway, Cedar explains that this venue is a smaller setting than normal. It's a cozier experience, less crowded, less chaotic, and perfect for someone's first concert.

My first.

I don't know how or why, maybe because I listen to older music, but I've never been to a show before, and that was reason number two for Cedar picking tonight as our celebration.

We listen to a few of As Above's newer songs along the drive, and I can't say that I hate them.

It's got more of a soul base than an *in your face* beat that I expected.

The excitement begins to build as we pull into the parking garage a block from the bar and unload from the car.

Cedar gets us in the door easily, between the tickets on her phone and the bouncer definitely flirting with her and my sister. I follow their lead as nerves cause a sheen of sweat on my palms.

"Get us some drinks," Cedar shouts to Aurora, who nods in response and drags me to the bar along the back wall of the venue. She orders something for us, and Cedar pops back up next to me before the bartender can finish.

"Fuck is that?" I ask, flipping the shirt that now hangs over her shoulder.

"What? It's tradition." She holds onto the material, leaning away from me to get the thing out of my grasp. "No touchy. I get one from every show I go to."

My eyes widen. "Jesus, that must mean your closet is full."

"You're not wrong." She laughs and nods to the bartender, who offers up colored shots to each of us.

We shoot the drinks as the next round is made, now sipping drinks, and make our way into the crowd in search of our seats that I know aren't really seats. The floor in front of the stage is mostly open, only a few standing tables around the edge of the space. Cedar leads us up front to one of the tables when a familiar voice calls out.

"Hey, ladies." Jonathon pushes through the growing crowd and meets us at our table.

"Hey," Aurora says quicker than the rest of us but shakes it off with a dazzling smile.

"Glad you could make it." I shoot my sister a look when she mean mugs me, but she throws up a smile for Jonathon.

He says something to her that makes her giggle and touch his arm, but he quickly addresses us. "You guys ready to hear Wonderer?"

I scrunch up my nose and turn to Cedar, who rolls her eyes and shakes her head.

"Opener for As Above," she explains to just me but plays nice with him. "I'm definitely curious," Cedar shouts over the music that begins. The lights dim so only a single beam illuminates the small stage.

Wonderer is just a guy with a deep voice and a saxophone. The music he plays is smooth, reminiscent of older tunes, and has me spending the time swaying to the beat with my eyes closed.

I eat up the melodies, even more so when he covers a song I know will get some noise from the crowd.

Elated, I sip my drink and pull out my phone to take pictures. I turn the lens on Aurora and Cedar as one pretends not to flirt with the new guy and the other sways to the beat. She'd never admit it, but she likes this kind of music almost as much as I do.

It's calming …

"So, I want to give a quick thank-you to As Above," the guy says at the end of his set. The crowd goes wild at the mention of the headliner, so much so that he has to pause with a chuckle. "I've been a fan since day one, it's a true pleasure to meet these guys and play for them." Again, the crowd cheers. I clap in agreeance, the aura in the place contagious. "Without further ado …" He pauses, gesturing to the side stage. "AS ABOVE!"

Lights drop, stage black, a single chord is played out as the floor fills in with even more people.

The noise becomes almost deafening, including the two women at my table who lose their ever-loving minds. I shake my head with a smile but turn my phone camera back on them. I'd rather see their reactions in a moment like this.

I've never seen Cedar so alive.

I'm not disappointed when the lights come back up and the girls are bathed in green. They scream, hop, and clap in excitement, all of which I capture on video. My chest expands with pride and excitement for these two, my face aching from all the smiles as the note carries out and slams into the beginning of a song.

"Good morning," a deep voice booms into the mic. "We're As Above." Cedar turns to me and pulls a face I capture, then she shakes me with a squeal.

"You *gotta* watch," she shouts as the music picks up, wrapping an arm around me. I oblige her and turn my sight to the stage as lyrics begin pouring out of a voice that strikes a chord of recognition in the back of my mind.

The platform is much bigger than it appeared when it was just one guy, screens illuminated on either side of the stage, lights flashing and highlighting each member of the band.

My eyes wander, taking in the sight of a guitarist on our side of the stage, playing to the crowd, singing along to the song. He holds the instrument up, banging his head to the beat and just vibing along.

The euphoria spreads like wildfire across the room, not a single stilled soul in the crowd, including me. I bob to the beat, Cedar dancing against me making it impossible not to move along with her.

But when the camera pans, my sight moves back to the screens, and my heart stops.

"Oh my God."

I freeze, my eyes lying to me right now as clearly as the singer screams into the microphone.

"I know, right?" Cedar mistakes my words as unbelievably entertained instead of just plain fucking *shocked*.

My breath seizes in my chest when the lead singer of As Above pauses in his part so that the crowd can sing the song back to him, his head banging to the beat.

I stare, shell-shocked, at the screen displaying wildly whipping curly hair, beads of sweat trailing down a crooked nose, and blue-green eyes that sparkle in the limelight.

For the second time in my life, my breath leaves my body like I've been struck directly in the chest.

"*OhmyGod.*"

Chapter Twenty-Two

I'VE ALWAYS HAD A propensity for gore, passion, and horror.

Morticia Gomez is my role model.

An artist at heart, the macabre has called to me since I was little. So much so that my parents have had me in therapy since I was young.

Some call it waking up and choosing violence.

Which I do.

It helps wing my liner and keep the douchebags away.

Well, most of them, if you know what I mean.

Can I say that I'm wrong for that? *Nope.*

It also helps justify my attitude because, let's face it, I could kill and bury the body, then help the next of kin search for the missing person.

No one wants to chance that shit when I get all feisty.

Like right fucking now as I watch my soul-loving best friend unable to breathe while watching my favorite band. As if they would be her speed.

Judging by the complete lack of color on her face, it's even less her thing than I thought.

"Ari, what's going on? Do you hate it that much?"

She stands stock-still next to me.

She was just getting into the blaring music. Her hips were actually moving along with the music, her head bobbing to the beat. Not entirely a first, but never have I seen her act like this in public where people other than myself and her younger sister can see her.

Now ... she's clutching at her chest and keeps repeating praise to a deity that I know she doesn't believe in.

"*Ari.*" I'm a little more forceful in my attempts to get her attention, mine no longer giving any fucks about the men on stage singing out my favorite As Above classic.

"Oh my God."

I catch the questioning brow from Aurora, only to answer with a shake of the head. She ditches her boy toy and comes around to my side of the smaller table, snapping her fingers in front of her sister's face.

"Oh my fucking God."

No change in Aria with the first snap, so Aurora steps into her face and blocks her view of anything beyond her blonde hair.

"Ari, what's going on?" I hold her close when Aria shakes, her wavy sex hair falling around her shoulders. Purely distraught when she looks from me to Aurora, lashes nearly touching her brows, her breathing speeding up like she's on the verge of a panic attack.

She whispers something I don't hear because the place is so damn loud, Jonathon screaming in excitement right next to us. It's a complete contrast to what I feel right now.

"What?" her sister and I both ask.

We exchange a worried look when it takes her a second to repeat it.

"It's fucking him."

"What?"

Wait ...

I must wear my confusion as much as Aurora when I look between the two for answers I know she doesn't have.

Finally, I drag my eyes to the stage behind Aurora, catching sight of the lead singer belting out a record-worthy note when it clicks.

Rex.

Rex motherfucking Thompson.

Son of a bitch.

Blinding, red-hot rage fills me as I watch on. I grip my best friend to my side and seethe in her honor since I know she won't.

"Like *him* him?" Aurora asks, her own panic setting in at seeing her sister's reaction.

Not to mention the damn *guilt.*

I see it cross Aurora's features as much as I feel it in my own chest. She looks to me with a pulsing chest and a wild look when Aria confirms the suspicion, her gaze locked back on the stage when the song changes.

"Yeah. *Him* him. Rex."

Hearing the name alone has my spine tingling and my fists clenching.

This fucker rocked my girl's world for a night, which she loved. We heard how much thanks to the brother answering our desperate phone calls when she went radio silent for too long.

Then, the next day, Rex destroyed everything.

Left her just like an abandoned fry dropped between the seats in the car during a rushed meal that finds its way into the tiniest nook, never to be seen again. To turn crusty and hard, only to be found ten years later when the car gets cleaned out before it's sold.

Motherfucking fucker.

"I'm okay," Aria claims, her voice stronger as she turns away from the stage, the lights highlighting her face. But she wasn't okay the last time she saw this guy. And she's not okay now, no matter how much she pretends to be.

I saw her battle the illness right alongside Chip. Watched it destroy everything she knew.

Right now? She looks fucking worse.

Music stops, and Rex's voice fills the venue, echoing off the walls and drilling into my brain through my ears like the lobotomy I would rather be getting.

Chapter Twenty-Three

Rex

"WE'VE GOT SOME NEW shit for ya."

I speak into the wireless mic, my enthusiasm uncontainable as I bounce around the stage. From left to right, I pace and jump and flex for the crowd that screams for As Above.

My twin pounds out a beat for me, background noise he'll turn into the next song the moment he gets the feel from me that we're ready.

The crowd hums with excitement at my words, a power you can feel radiating from them to us.

"We got some new shit," I repeat as I make my way back to center stage and run a hand through my hair to get it out of the sweat dripping down my face.

"*Woohoo*," Finland encourages into his mic with a grin, his strums matching Mac's beat.

"But let's talk for a minute." A roar returns in agreement, so I pause with a smirk and place my fists on my hips.

These are the moments I savor.

The ones where I could say anything on my heart, and thousands of people would agree or cheer for us. I could share my woes, and I know someone out there right now would understand.

I could make a funny, and they'll laugh as if I made their day.

That's part of why I do this. Why I share these pieces of myself with the strangers on the street. Because once you share something like this … are you really strangers anymore?

When I can relate to thousands of people for just a moment, and all I have to do is be raw. Honest. *Myself.* It makes these memories even better.

"So," I say with the grille of the mic against my lip, and I look around for the stool I know was nearby when we started. I locate it while they wait, still borderline deafening, and drag the thing back to the center for me to plant my ass in it. "I recently went through a thing," I start, unsure of how much I care to share but knowing that deep down, this is what I'm meant to do.

Share my talent.

Open my heart.

A few awws are audible through the barely dampened noise, encouraging to the emotions that bubble up in my chest.

"Have you ever …"

Chapter Twenty-Four

Cedar

THE PLACE EXPLODES WITH noise, something I would have joined in on five minutes ago, before I knew Rex Thompson was the one who broke my bestie's heart.

I hate that I hate him right now.

But girl code suggests I should demand a refund on my tickets and leave right now.

Maybe go egg his stupid fancy car and TP his house.

Set alight a bag of dookie right on his fucking porch.

His comments command the attention of the room, including the hotheaded me and my tribe.

"You ever meet someone? And they just …" His pause hangs in the air like hope, dangling there for anyone to reach up and pray he's talking about them. "Change your fucking *life*?"

"*Nope.*" I wrap up my enthralled bestie and her distracted sister in my arms, pulling them to the nearest exit to cut off the heartbreak before it gets any worse.

Last time, it took weeks to get Aria back. She wasn't the same when she returned from the photo shoot we'd intended on being a beacon of hope, only to turn into a mess.

She eventually came out better than ever, taking a chance with her passion and all, but I'd rather *not* have her go through more bullshit to keep it.

She deserves better than a lie.

Aria opened her own damn online boutique with her fashion creations, even if she refuses to acknowledge her designs that way. Because of Aria, her sister moved into a bigger studio right next door to my parlor.

I'm not sure what that jackoff said to her, did to her to make her feel so fucking low, but I refuse to let him yank her around again. I'm not gonna let him hurt my bestie ever again.

"Hey." They both chastise me when we make it into the damp alley at the side of the building, Aria smacking my bicep, Aurora huffing with her hands on her hips.

"What?" I snap more than I'd intended, knowing that what came out of Rex's mouth next was not going to go well. I can hear it now; he met a girl, fell in love, is getting married.

Or some other heartbreaking bullshit.

Blah, blah, blah.

I know it's not my bestie, and I'm not going to let her get her heart broken all over again.

"What the hell, C," Aurora whines.

I scoff but corral the two ladies closer to the opening of the alleyway and to the public, farther away from the company we've found ourselves in.

Dark alley outside a bar during a rock show is not a good place for pretty girls like them. I didn't think that part through when I dragged them out here.

I was focused on getting out before Rex fucking Thompson broke my best friend.

Again.

The ratty-looking group of guys drifts closer, but when we edge to the busy sidewalk, they fall back into the shadows where they came from.

Thank fuck.

"Let's go somewhere else," I respond as if that'll appease them, but all I get back is arches in their sculpted brows and popped hips.

"What are you talking about?"

"Hell no, you love As Above."

I'm not quite sure why Aurora is rejecting the idea. I suspect she wants the comments to be about her sister. Or maybe she was looking forward to grinding on Jonathon.

We'll never know, though, because we're not going back.

"No readmittance, ladies."

With a firm grip on their wrists, I start dragging them down the road in hopes of catching a cab or coming across another bar. We wade through people selling band merch, loitering at a chance to buy or sell scalped tickets, and make it to the next block over before neon signs start illuminating through the crowd.

"Cedar, stop."

Aria yanks her wrist from my grip as we approach the next crosswalk with a hundred other people following us. We jam up the foot traffic, but I don't much care about them and their dirty looks.

"What's the deal?" Aria asks with a toss of her hands.

I shake my head but push us off to the side when one too many shoulders brush against me, the heavy double bass from the show still vibrating the street.

Knowing I made the right call, I look up at the brick wall next to me, barely registering the wall of windows exposing the storefront inside, and try to work through in my head how to answer the questions.

"Cedar." Aurora shakes herself from my grasp, which I didn't realize we were still connected, and rubs at my forearm. She means well, I know she does, but it doesn't stop me from snapping again.

"None of us would have benefited from hearing what the fuck he had to say." I shake my head when heads whip to me from passersby and lean against the wide window with a foot cocked up on the glass.

Somebody's gonna have to clean that tomorrow.

"You're right," Aria concedes and lounges next to me. "I know you like them, though. Not fair to you to miss out on a show because of me."

"Don't fall on your sword, Ari."

She shrugs, her doe eyes meeting mine in apology. I muss her already messy hair to break the tension building between us, pressure in my chest beginning its descent.

"What the *hell*?" Aurora blisters, throwing her arms out. "What if he *was* talking about Ari?"

Dammit. She just went there.

I hang my head at her outburst, her naivety showing.

This is exactly what I was trying to avoid.

"Doesn't matter," I mutter and face Aurora head-on. "It doesn't fucking matter. He did her dirty. Drop it."

"No, it's okay." Aria supports me with a quick squeeze but addresses her sibling. "We've got a good life. You bitches are all I need." She smiles, though I know deep down she wishes Aurora was right.

I can feel her desperation in my fucking bones.

Who wouldn't after what she told us about him?

I think back on the excited texts she'd sent, the joy in her tone when we talked on the phone that night.

She deserves that excitement again.

Fucking hell.

"Y'know what?" I pop away from the wall and start walking. They're grown-ass women who can follow or not. "Let's get trashed."

"Wait." I hear the rushed click of heels behind me. "Where, though?"

With no response, I just slip into the next doorway illuminated with a bar sign and find the nearest empty booth. The aesthetic screams eighties diner rather than a bar, but fuck it, I'll take a burger right now, too.

As long as there's booze somewhere.

"Okay then," Aurora drawls skeptically.

My tribe settles in around me as a busty waitress approaches to take our orders.

"Hey there, ladies." She flips her big hair and her notepad cover with the flair I endorse and talks on. "Kitchen closes in twenty, I leave in thirty, but the bar is open later." She pops her gum and poises her pen to take the order. "What can I get ya?"

As promised, Ms. Big Hair brings out our burgers and fruity cocktails in less than ten and is gone for the night, leaving us to drag our asses to the bar for refills.

Aria makes the first trip, taking way longer because she's too damn polite, and Aurora tries her hand next to see if she can beat her sister's time.

We drink and laugh and reminisce.

Even better, we plan and forget all about Rex Thompson and his stupid band.

Somewhere around the third round, I switched to water cuz one of us has to be responsible, and after the fourth round, a spot for all three of us opens up at the bar.

Sitting here is not a great idea since I have the *fuck with me and I'll fuck you up* aura most bartenders find … tempting. Which means we get drinks easier, and these two are already on the verge of being cut off before I can stop them from getting another.

Well, Aurora is.

She turns into a sappy drunk, spreading her love and kindness all over unwilling victims, including me.

I love her, don't get me wrong, but she clings to me now, her sweaty pits swiping across my shoulders, her hair flinging in my face.

At least I know she showered today …

Even if it was over twelve hours ago.

"I'll order an Uber." Aria waves her phone in my direction, and I nod, appreciative of the rescue.

Aurora rests her head in the crook of my neck and whispers shit about how good I smell and how pretty I am.

"Thanks, Squirt," I whisper back and press a kiss to her temple.

"Fifteen minutes," Aria confirms, then excuses herself to the bathroom. Normally, we'd all go, but Aurora will need to be carried to the car, let alone the bathroom.

I hold my intoxicated best friend to keep her pretty hair off the sticky bar and watch as my other best friend enters the bathroom okay.

Wait … does this make me the mom friend?

Chapter Twenty-Five

Rex

I LOOK OUT INTO the crowd that boos and awws at once, but the lights blind me.

Some scream their undying love for me, my band.

Others request procreation despite the emotional roller coaster I'm trying to take them on.

Normally, I'd laugh at that, grin at the thought of someone in the crowd prepping to be my baby momma, or baby daddy, just for the simple fact that I'm Rex Thompson and I sing some good songs.

But I don't, not this time.

My hand finds my hair again, pushing the shit back out of my face when it clings to my forehead.

"I met someone," I start again, my words accompanied by my pointed index finger. "And she rocked the foundation on which I built my entire life in just *one* fucking night."

I jump to my feet and kick the stool back when rage and hurt puff my chest, the thing skidding somewhere behind me.

Mac picks up the beat like my heart rate, Fin falling in sync, Toby's low strings ever present.

"This song," I continue, perusing the stage, then stalking about as my need builds up. "This song's for her. Fuck, this whole damn *album's* for her."

My tone is desperate, my grip tight on the mic as my stomach dips, but my chest swells with the need to release this emotion.

To share my story with the world.

If I don't, I might die of heartbreak.

Pure adrenaline spikes when the band fills in the tune, and I engage the first verse. I have to shove the earpiece back in when the place gets too loud for me to keep time, the deafening explosion of sound drowning out the tempo enough that not even high-tech shit can keep them out.

Lights flash across the stage, dark blues to red, then teal burst in my eyes, highlighting our performance in time to the beat.

The words leave my lips, visions of Aria fill my mind like flashbacks, feelings of hope filling my soul, and I swear I can see her on stage right watching out over me.

Where I wish she was, but she's not.

The chorus comes in, Fin leads me in on time with his axe, and I leave no part of the stage untouched. I sing to the crowd, to my brothers, to the ceiling about the ache in my chest and the heartbreak of limelight.

The loneliness that comes when you want something you shouldn't have.

Pounding my chest with my free hand, sweat soaking my brow, I look out at the people here for us and pause, letting the music fill the void. The overwhelming encouragement I get in return nearly paralyzes me with admiration as my lungs struggle to catch up.

A smile pulls at the corner of my lips, but it's not enough.

Never enough.

Not since I met her.

Leaning down with arms outstretched, I let the emotion wash over me. Bringing the mic back to my mouth, I vocalize the next verse and prepare myself for the hook.

Stalking back to my brother, taking up the drums like a damn pro, I lead the crowd into a clap that they pick up.

I climb up on Mac's platform, my back to the masses, smacking the cymbal when the beat allows.

Silence fills the void as the tempo begins the descent for a drop, only the high hat ringing out.

Four … Three … Two …

I push off from the platform and fling my legs up over my head, landing a backflip on time with the tempo coming back to life with a thump I feel right down to my fucking soul.

The audience becomes a mob in that moment, boisterous roaring piercing my eardrums over the sound of the music.

My head spins, chest heaving, but the song is coming up to the final bit and I have to be ready.

I have to destroy my voice on this exit so that the next song has the rawness it deserves.

Dragging in a deep breath and stalking to center stage, I engage a guttural scream I pull from my diaphragm and fill the fucking venue.

The sound reverberates off the walls, echoing back the anguish I dish out and threatening to silence my vocals with its force.

I manifest all my rage, all my passion, every ounce of my hurt.

All my disappointment wrapped up tight in one harsh sound.

I miss her.

The front rows go still as I double over to keep the note going as long as possible, the tempo lengthening several beats longer than the recorded version that's yet to be released.

Throat screaming in pain, I go another beat with my forehead pressed to the floor. Fading the noise out on a cry as the stage goes dark just as practiced, I desperately blink back the prickling behind my eyes. A few errant tears escape anyway when I lean back on my haunches and search for my brother.

I catch his reassuring nod to me from behind his set, his arms pounding the sticks against the drums to pull attention.

Eyes dried on my bare biceps, I spring to my feet with my focus still on Mac.

Mic grille back to my lips, I ask the patrons for some love for my brother with a garbled sentence I'm surprised they understand.

And like he was born for this, he smashes the drums in a short solo for the love he gets, a grin on his face, but his eyes meet mine every few beats. I see the concern in them, but I just nod.

I'm okay, I mouth, some semblance of reassurance, except I know he feels me and that I really can't lie.

The last few weeks have been hell. Still, I find myself wondering about her, wanting to share it all with her, feeling her absence to my core.

That's gotta mean something, right?

A final nod to my twin, stronger this time, and the band leads me into the final song of the show.

The pièce de résistance of the album.

The track set to hit the top one hundred charts all over the world.

And with broken vocals, I sing of love and passion. Of a night to challenge the status quo. The one that changed my life.

I sing of the night that broke me.

And in between my hoarse lyrics, I offer words of encouragement to those who might find themselves in the same place as me.

I don't know what's next.

But I know I have to try.

"Can you relate? What's been taken from you?" I rasp as best as my aching voice will allow.

"Who do you want there with you when the world comes crashing down? For me, it's you and only you." The crowd sways with the calmer beat as I serenade each side of the stage.

"If it all tumbles down tonight, it's you I want by my side." I pause center stage and deeply breathe in the buzz of the audience.

Lights cut. The music stops.

"Cuz there's no sun left in your brilliance."

I drop the microphone and walk off the stage.

Past the VIP section armed with outstretched hands hoping for a high five or an autograph.

Through the green room filled with team members who make this whole shit show go round.

Straight to Ian who holds my phone, which I take and pull up the text app and engage Aria's name.

The thread we shared over a month ago illuminates my face as I move about backstage, my thumbs typing, then deleting and retyping.

None of it seems good enough. None of it conveys any of the shit I want to tell her.

Or how much I miss someone I barely know.

Except I do know her.

Because she shared a piece of her heart with me that night around the fire.

So, I delete the text field again and settle on simple instead.

> Me: I'll be at Moonman Arcade until they kick me out tonight. If you're nearby, come find me.

Smiling, I push my hair back from my forehead and snap a selfie.

> Me: In case you forgot what I look like.

I press send on the pic with the caption and slide the device into my pocket as my gaze settles on Ian's questioning brow.

"Let's go."

Fuck, I hope this works.

Chapter Twenty-Six

Cedar

A flash of light catches my attention; Aria's phone is lit up with a notification I don't recognize, so I pick the thing up off the bar, hopeful that the Uber is coming sooner than anticipated.

"Son of a *bitch*."

"Wha?" Aurora slurs into my collarbone but leans into me, not away to see anything.

I read and reread the notification with heat bubbling under my skin. My scalp feels tight against my skull as I open the text message and the words register.

Then a photo populates in the thread, and the red-hot rage from earlier ascends on me again.

My hands shake with unbridled anger as I catch sight of Aria leaving the bathroom and heading back our way. I react, deleting the messages and the picture. Open the Uber app and refresh the page as if I'd been checking the status all along.

"Is it on its way?" I flash her the screen, void of any communication from a douche, and hike Aurora up to start the trek to the sidewalk.

"Not yet, but she could prob use some air before getting in a car." Voice calmer than I feel, I push the emotion down and begin plotting in my head as Aria grabs Aurora's other side and helps me get her to the curb.

"Good call."

We make it to the hotel room we were planning on staying in tonight without much fuss.

I tuck Aurora into bed with seething hands I force to still. Makeup still intact, Aria collapses to the bed they're sharing, her hair flying around her head and closing her off from the world.

And when I'm certain they're both out, I snag Aria's phone again to check for any messages I missed.

No others sit unopened on the screen.

I place it back on the nightstand in the center of the double room, charger engaged, and plop my burning ass into the only chair present. It squeaks with wear as I fumble to get the old remote to turn the TV on for suitable background noise.

News channels fill the silence of the room, which only fill me with more rage, so I hurriedly switch to some sappy romcom that's almost always on in every hotel room I've ever been in.

I try to calm my nerves, soothe my anger and frustration, think through shit logically.

The chair creaks when I shift to ease my racing heart. I blow a breath out that does nothing to bring me down, so I stand and find my feet carrying me to the door.

Guiding the door closed behind me so that it doesn't wake the girls, I strut down the hallway, a metaphorical baseball bat twirling in my hands.

That motherfucker messed with the wrong girl. Broke the wrong heart.

Names don't matter. Bands don't matter. Fame doesn't matter.

I punch the elevator call button and step back to wait the short ride out until I can get out to a taxi.

"Hey." A rando passes me with the greeting as I stride for the exit, but I don't have time for them. They get a head nod response, and I keep walking.

Songs fill the void in my head as I envision all the versions of how I'm about to deal with this asshole. Most angry and violent. Only some methods verging on petty.

Like leaving a heel print in his balls.

That's not petty at all. That's psycho shit.

I smile, hail a cab, and settle into the first one that pulls to my side of the street.

The drive is a blur, getting to the front door is a little harder, but I'm at Moonman Arcade before I realize where I've told the driver to go, and I've managed to bypass security with more ease than I'd anticipated.

The arcade is huge. Multilevel, lit up in colored lights and crazy carpet, the gaming systems take up the entire first floor and part of the second, which can be seen through the loft-style setup.

People cheer, games alarm with negative whomps and positive rings, lights flashing as laughter fills the air.

If I were here for any other reason, I might enjoy myself.

But none of that slows my stride right to the entrance that leads to the second floor with only one thing standing in my way.

"No admittance, ma'am."

Built like a brick shit house, a man I'll call Tiny stands with beefy arms crossed over a thick chest I kinda wanna lick. The way they stretch his black tee tight across his muscles has me nearly drooling. He's blocking the door that leads to the stairs, in my way, but looking down his very crooked nose at me through narrowed eyes like I can be intimidated.

That's cute.

"Serious?" I scoff as a way to play into the disguised attitude I throw his way. Add in some hand gestures, and I see the questions begin to form behind his eyes. "How are you here right now? In my fucking way?"

"I …" His demeanor breaks, arms loosening, eyes darting around for the right answer.

"Do you not know who I am? *Pffft.*" I roll my eyes and pull out my phone. "Toby is definitely going to hear about this."

Thank the gods I know the band members' names.

It makes this facade so much easier to break the security guard with.

I make a show of working my jaw and stabbing at the screen until Tiny finally huffs.

"My apologies, miss." He steps to the side and opens the door, flashing an earpiece wire down the side of his corded neck.

With a flourish, I whip my hair in his direction and take the opening. "Fucking *thank* you."

I know with that little walkie hidden on him and all the other security guys I spot on this floor, I won't have much time to escape once I cause the scene I'm fully prepared to unleash …

Gotta make it quick.

Act like a roadie. Looking for a known hookup …

And don't get caught.

Beelining it to the bar, I order a drink that comes quickly and without request for payment—for the second time tonight—and smash the thing in one gulp as I try to read the room.

If I were a rock douche, where would I hide?

My eyes land on the far corner where another smaller bar sits, a little more private than this one, surrounded by booths that are filled with skanks and tatted assholes. That's when I catch sight of him, Rex motherfucking Thompson, slipping out of a ring of what could barely be classified as ladies and heading my way.

Fucking shit.

I can't lie and say that some part of me isn't fucking excited right now to meet the person I've idolized to some degree.

I hate that part of me right now.

Focusing on retribution, I force myself to recall the night Aria returned home to us. Distraught and confused, she contemplated calling or texting him, fighting herself on it for hours until she finally cried herself to sleep.

I sat with her through all of that.

Don't get me wrong … I know we also played a part in this mess of shit that tilted Aria's axis off balance. Aurora and I put her in that position. But I know what came out of it was a fucking warrior, and that beautiful soul needs to be avenged.

"How's it going?" Deep and raspy, Rex settles in the stool next to mine and flags the bartender.

I click my tongue and shrug in response as I prop my elbows on the bar and lean back. I pretend that my heart isn't racing to smack this dick back into next week and aim my focus on the crowd around us.

Distance, nonchalance, I repeat to myself.

Play coy.

Wouldn't want to feed that ego.

"Sounds about as good as my night." I catch sight of him nodding thanks to the bartender who places a drink in his hand. He sounds genuine, which catches me off guard, but he sips his amber liquid with a smirk that has me questioning him.

Back to the surroundings, I chew on my next step, knowing that the window is closing fast.

"How the hell could yours suck?" That stupid smirk against the whiskey tumbler loses its playful nature, his eyes meeting mine for the first time.

There's anger there, furrowing his brow, but something else lurks underneath.

Makes me want to punch him in his stupid curved nose.

Hello, violence.

"You ever got what you wanted and not want it anymore?" he genuinely asks me like he doesn't ruin lives every single day with his chiseled jaw and perfect goddamn voice. "All this …" He pauses, spinning his stool to gesture out at the milling people and chiming games with his tumbler hand, the alcohol sloshing around the glass. "All this doesn't fucking matter."

Mimicking my stance, Rex turns fully to prop himself up on the bar but misses an elbow. More whiskey sloshes, breaching the surface of the glass and running down his arm.

Is he drunk?

"Oops." Rex turns to catch the bartender's attention, but he's too late. "Shit." Towel is already in hand and offered to the celebrity, who responds with a sighed "Thanks."

As if it's a hardship to get preferential treatment.

"Yeah, it's so terrible." I'm being a sarcastic asshole, coupled with an eye roll and all.

Rex snorts and wipes away at the shit running down his arm and pant leg.

"How dare the famous one express any woes." Tossing the towel back to the bar, he snorts again and shoots back the remainder of his drink. He slams the glass to the bar and spins his stool to me, his eyes getting lost in the crowd. "Couldn't be that I'm still a person behind the vocals."

"So the fuck are your one-night stands."

The opening is too perfect to pass it up. Too perfect to hold back my rage.

Color drains from his face, his gaze whipping so fast to me that I think he makes himself dizzy. I watch as the gears turn at my words, his narrowed eyes darting between mine in search of an answer he's not going to get from me.

"You?" he questions after a moment, a fresh drink in his hand.

Scoffing is my best response.

"Why am I not surprised there's enough that you've started to forget."

He hangs his head.

"So many that you don't remember the names." My words grow louder with each syllable from my lips. "Or maybe you don't even ask for names anymore." My bravado erupts the longer his head hangs in defeat. I stand to face him straight on. "*Look* at me, Rex."

Haunted.

Defeated.

"You *don't* deserve her," I snarl.

His pale face encasing distant eyes come to meet my drilling gaze. His jaw ticks, his lips flattened against the words he utters.

"I'm sorry."

Fury rips through me, and I act before I think, the glass in my hand flying to the floor between us and shattering into a million tiny pieces. Shards kick up and nick my exposed skin, raining down on Rex's boots.

"*You should be,*" I snarl. Finger cocked and loaded, aiming right in his face like a drill instructor, I lunge closer to him. "Guys like you are *shit.*"

I can already feel the thick arm wrapping around my waist to haul me out of this place, my feet leaving the ground.

That was longer than I thought it'd be.

"You don't deserve any of this," I yell in his direction just before I'm carted off the floor. "Toxic fucking *prick.*"

"That's enough of that." The words boom in my ears as I'm carted into a secluded part of the venue—maybe someone's office—and tossed into a chair. I haul my own load of oxygen into my lungs when I flop back and grip the arms to keep from flying off the handle.

"Oh, hey, Tiny," I rasp after a loaded moment, licking my dried lips and heaving more air into my chest.

"You played me."

A half shrug is all I muster for the brick shit house blocking yet another door looking beyond intimidating this time. Even to me.

"You fell for it." I don't succumb to the act, though, I bet this guy is actually a teddy bear, which is why he let me pass before.

"Yeah, thanks for pointing that out." His hands go to his head in exasperation, sighing out a breath. "I'm so screwed."

"Welp." I settle back into the chair and cross my legs. "Sounds like you should be better at your job."

"Wow, that's rude." His arms fall to the side, his attention diverting away from me. It's silent for a beat, then he touches the breast pocket on his tee and speaks again. "Affirmative, threat contained."

"Oh, am I the threat?" My attempt at charming my way out of this situation is dismissed with a hand wave that only causes me to giggle.

I didn't assault anyone. They don't have anything on me.

Maybe trespassing since I wasn't invited.

"Let's go, lady." Fingers wrap around my bicep. I'm manhandled out of the chair and out into the hall. "You are a pain in the ass." Tiny pushes us through another crowd of people on the main floor and back out the main entrance, right past the spot I fooled him, his post taken up by someone else.

Someone bigger and scarier with hawk eyes that follow us out the door.

"*You're* a fucking pain in the ass," I repeat, jerking my limb from his grasp, my hair flying and the movement causing me to stumble across the sidewalk.

"Oh, c'mon. *Me?*" He points to his swollen pecs. "Get the fuck out of here." Tiny throws his arm in the opposite direction of the arcade, emphasizing his words and showing me the direction he really wishes I would go.

But I don't.

Why, you ask?

Because fuck you. That's why.

I woke up and chose violence today. Welcome to the shit show.

"Poor baby get yelled at?" I back up a foot when he steps toward me in a sad attempt at intimidation.

It's just too fun to know how far under his skin I am.

"No." He grinds his teeth, preparing to snap at me with literal teeth to skin. "Docked my pay." He steps in close, his chest to my nose, his beefy arm stiffly reminding me where to fuck off to.

Oh. Shit. They can do that?

"Wait. Doesn't the band pay for you? *They* docked it?" Tiny hangs his head and lets out a heady, annoyed-with-me breath.

"None of your business, lady. Now, off you go." Palms to my shoulders, Tiny spins me away from him and pushes at my shoulders until I stumble forward.

"Rex is a dick to do that to you," I shout over my shoulder.

"Wasn't him," Tiny shouts back, but by the time I spin around to question him, he's gone.

I watch as his broad shoulders disappear into the sea of people that part for him, making way for his girth and leaving a gaping hole in his wake.

But I wasn't prepared for what Tiny exposed.

Left in his trail stands Finland "Fin" Montgomery among the masses.

Over six and a half feet of tall, dark, and handsome, Fin sticks out like a sore fucking thumb.

Greatest guitarist of all time. Hall of Fame inductee. Former high school crush of mine.

Fuck. Me.

His eyes latch onto mine, his stony expression boring into my very soul and cementing me in place.

All boldness leaves me, shock taking its place as I drink in the sight of him.

The years have done him well, Fin's body more filled in than I recall. Ripped and too perfect.

The void begins closing in around him, a wave of bodies blocking the view, but not before I catch the smirk forming on his smug face.

Fucking fuck.

Chapter Twenty-Seven

Aria

"WHERE THE HELL IS Cedar?" Aurora asks for what feels like the thirtieth time in the last hour.

"Still no answer." I stare at my phone, the screen long ago gone dark, and wonder what Cedar has gotten herself into now.

While I also contemplate why in the *hell* I suddenly have a new message waiting in my text threads that's from Rex.

Did he know I was there?

Shit … does he think I was looking for him?

I don't want to be labeled a stalker. Or a crazed fan.

Shit.

My sister rambles because she's nervous, but I'm too sucked into my own thoughts to register what she's saying. Her voice bounces around in my skull like the mumblings of a cartoon teacher and jumbles my thoughts even more.

Do I even care what he thinks?

Shaking my head, I do my best to let go of the assumed booty call sitting on my phone.

Aurora and I woke up, still tipsy, to a silently spinning room. She puked twice, and I took a cold shower before we bothered to notice Cedar's been

AWOL for at least that long. With no response to cell communications since I started texting her an hour ago.

I gave her a few minutes, thinking she ran to the snack shack for a candy bar or to get some ice, but then she still didn't come back. Aurora freaked and started blowing up her phone.

And judging by the sender of the unopened text, I would suggest I know exactly what she's been doing.

I just don't know where to find her *now*.

"You seriously mean you two don't have Find My Device set up for each other?" My sister is in near hysterics like this isn't normal behavior for Cedar, screeching shit in my ear when she thinks I'm not listening.

Jokes on her, though. I haven't heard more than two words she's said.

Benefit of being older, I guess. You have more practice tuning shit out.

"Jesus Christ, Ari. I'm going to go find her." Aurora stomps across the room like a toddler and snatches up a jacket that's not even hers.

"And how are you going to do that?" I deadpan from the same spot on the bed I settled into when I realized Cedar was gone. Not to return before dawn, at least.

"I don't know." She throws her hands up, tossing the coat into the air on accident. Still a little drunk and running on a whole lot of adrenaline, my sister huffs heavily and flops onto the bed opposite me.

Drama queen.

"C does this, sis." My attention diverts from her distraught face when my phone vibrates in my hand. I glance at the screen to see Rex's faux name fill the notification box, a snippet of his message available to read, but it's longer than the box allows.

Dammit. I don't think I want to know what's going on.

I blank out the screen with a tap of the power button and roll over onto my side.

"She gets a burr up her ass about something, and she'll show up when she's ready with a new tattoo or some weird cuisine she found. Possibly drunk. Possibly with a guy. Maybe even a chick." I punch my pillow, done with tonight and it's messed up way of celebrating, and slam my head into the stuffing.

I'm tired, still a little buzzed just like Aurora, and trying my best to avoid the infamous booty call at four in the morning with a rock star that I know I'll regret in the actual morning when I wake back up.

Maybe it's just a nightmare, and I'm actually about to wake up?

My lids get heavy, my brain turning to foggy mush.

What if he was talking about me? Why else would he text me now, after all this time?

Consciousness slips, darkness taking over me, but not enough to block out the room. Not nearly enough to stop the words floating around through the air.

The TV blares obnoxious crap from a newscast, my sleep-filtered brain only picking up certain words.

"Rock star attacked."

"Crazed fan outburst."

"Thrown glass."

"What. The. Hell." At my sister's tone, I open an eye to see the flat screen filled with wild hair whipping as a whiskey tumbler is tossed at Rex Thompson's feet.

Hardly an attack, but okay.

He probably deserved it.

Showing again, the video from another fan's perspective loops to show black hair cascading down a back clad in a tour shirt to an ass covered by a flannel that looks pretty goddamn close to the one I found for Cedar.

"No …" I'm up, no longer foggy, snatching the remote from my sister and turning the volume up. "No way."

"*Reports suggest the fan started out at the bar alone and coerced beloved rock star, Rex Thompson, to join her. It was then that words were exchanged, and the glass was thrown.*" The screen pans back to showing a shocked reporter and her sidekick. "*The audacity of some people …*" Head shakes and a segue into the next bit, my dropped jaw meets my sister's like I'm looking in a mirror.

"She didn't."

"No way."

We both jump up and slip shoes on. We're out the door in a minute, both phones engaged to reach Cedar.

She fucking confronted him.

Holy shit, that's why he's texting me now.

Whoa …

What the fuck.

I flag a cab when we make it to the street, still no contact from my best friend, and flop into the back seat when one finally pulls over for us.

"What's the effing plan, Ari?" Aurora asks as she thumbs away like crazy at her phone. "I'm texting Jon to see if he's seen her."

"Okay. I'll try her again."

No answer.

No damn answer.

"She could have been arrested," Aurora so helpfully adds, and I sigh.

Wouldn't be the first time.

I direct our driver to drop us at the arcade mentioned on the news.

As we take off into the minuscule traffic, a thought interrupts the chaos in my head. A thought that twists my stomach and hurts my brain almost as much as my poor little heart.

I have to text Rex. He would know what happened.

Shit.

Nerves send my knee bouncing, and my sister misunderstands my sudden interest in the passing landscape as concern for Cedar. I see it in the way her hand steadies against my knee and her kind eyes meet mine.

She's not completely wrong.

How do I tell her Rex already tried to reach out?

"It's C. I know she'll be fine." I pat my sister's knuckles to reassure her but turn my body so that I can open my phone without her reading over my shoulder.

Tapping into the two-month-old text thread, I scan for Cedar's name and see nothing mentioning her.

He doesn't know her name, dummy.

Or did they talk enough that he's not going to press charges?

She threw shit at him.

Dammit, Cedar.

I shake my head at myself and start at the beginning to read the messages all the way through.

> *SexyMane: Tonight has been fucking insane, like most nights for me, but for some reason, this one is even worse than normal. I know you ignored my last texts, and I don't blame you, but I think I have some shit I should have said long ago that I need you to know.*

Last texts?

I scroll back up but only see the things we sent weeks ago. Nothing new. Nothing missed or ignored.

I dismiss the comment and keep reading.

> *SexyMane: My life is mostly made up of stupid shit, bad decisions, traveling, and living on a bus. But it's also a good kind of crazy I never got to tell you about.*

My brow furrows deeper the more I read; something's just not adding up.

> *SexyMane: I mean … someone called me out on my shit tonight, and it really put some things in perspective. Nothing I didn't already know deep down. I just don't think I was ready to accept it.*

> *SexyMane: I'd love to see you again. That's what I'm really trying to say with all this. And that it's been a weird fucking night that I just don't want to share with anyone else.*

He's not wrong about how off this entire night-turned-morning has been. Five a.m. is a weird time to text someone unless you're only looking for the next few hours of your time to be filled.

To be filled…

I snicker at my own innuendo but hide my face when Aurora looks over to me.

> *SexyMane: I know it's cliche as fuck to tell you all this now, but it's the truth.*

> *SexyMane: I just hope you decide to believe me.*

Our cab jerks to a stop, the driver yelling shit in another language as people mill about outside the car. He inches us forward a little more but then slams the car into park.

"Close now." He points to the tall building standing over the giant gathering. "No closer." I nod, seeing the people taking over the street and sidewalk around the building, throw some cash on the front seat, and dive out of the back. My sister follows suit, her hand clasping mine to prevent getting lost as I wonder how in the fuck we're going to make it past all these bodies.

Packed in and dripping with bad news, people surround the arcade like a messiah resides inside and all they need for redemption is to party it out until blessings come.

A mere sighting of the all great one will do.

"Oh, *c'mon*." Aurora tries her best to push us closer to the arcade, but it's not working.

As Above band tees float all around us, packing us in tight. Some dance while some hop in place and play music from speakers. Others smoke or make out.

Some might be secretly making sacrifices around the barrel that's been set alight.

All fans trying their best to get a glimpse of a rock star so they can go back to their lives tomorrow and know they were close to someone famous.

Something to talk about.

To gloat about.

To see the powerful redeemer.

It knots my stomach to know that all these people would much rather steal a touch than respect someone as a fellow human being. As evidenced by the hands that grab at me, the unwanted skin that touches mine, the chanting of different names and phrases I'd rather never hear again.

Signs. Some handwritten. Some professionally done. All professing some form of love for Rex, for Mac, for the band. Wishes for marriage or just a night.

Some company made and sold that shit.

All for the sake of being able to say they were here. They were this close. Maybe this time the band will pick one of them.

Gross.

"God dammit. *Move*." I take over, pulling Aurora behind me, and bulldoze forward with as much care as I've been shown. I knock shoulders, taking an elbow to the ribs in my tirade. Sweat that's not mine and doesn't make sense in the cool air slicks across my skin, rising bile to the back of my throat.

We make up some ground, the entrance to the arcade getting closer by the second, only for me to see a rather large guard standing there, no one going in or coming out. "Shit."

"Another door?" Aurora whisper-yells into my ear, and I nod my response.

There has to be some kind of emergency exit or something, right? Employees only thing?

We push, then pull, and with enough effort to have me gasping for breath like I ran a marathon, we make it out of the crowd and into an alley at the side of the building with only minimal battle scars.

One of my sleeves has ripped, my hair a hot mess. Aurora's makeup is smeared across her face, her top twisted around her torso, hair sticking out like a halo around her pretty head.

"Jesus."

So glad I changed.

"Right." Aurora sucks in a shaky breath, hands to her hips. "There's no way they let C stay in there." She gestures around with a limp hand, her chest heaving.

"Doubtful, but this is the last place she was." I pull out my phone to see no new messages with a quick glance. "Anything?"

"Nope." Aurora shakes her head and pockets her device with a hand through her hair. "What now?"

"I don't know." I look around the brick walls surrounding us and spot a steel door blocked by yet another obstacle.

No way we're getting past him with all this chaos.

I need to text Rex.

Cedar could be anywhere by now.

I whip out my phone but match my sister's look over the device.

"I have to message him." Backing up, I plaster myself to the cool cement wall and poise my thumbs over the open text thread.

"Fuck you mean," my sister demands, following my actions to keep close, "text him?"

A nod is all she gets as my thumbs fly over the screen.

Me: Where is she?

Almost instantly, the message kicks back as undelivered.

Fuck.

Service is shot with all these people trying to use data in such a concentrated area. I tap the thing to my forehead in frustration.

Think, think.

What now?

"Welp," I say out loud. "I guess it's plan W." I push off from the wall in the direction of the guarded door as Aurora hangs her head.

"Plan W is what gets us into these messes. Text him, *who*?" she scoffs out, whines almost, but follows my lead anyway.

Aurora's heels tap on the concrete beneath us, announcing our arrival way before we're within earshot of the gargoyle perched at the secret entrance.

"Nothing back here for you, ladies." A rather large man with arms bigger around than my head tightens his stance against the steel, staring straight ahead.

"I really need to get a message to Rex." I attempt to plead my case, but the guard doesn't budge.

"You and fifty thousand others, ma'am." Arms tight across his chest, biceps flex with palpable irritation.

"I'm serious." I flash him the texts from Rex. "He's asked to see me." The guard's eyes flash to the screen, then go right back to staring through the wall across from us.

"Could be anyone." He's monotone, over our shit already and prepared to keep this shit up until we get tired and leave or fuck up enough that he can make us leave.

Shit.

"Wait, what?" My sister's knuckles slap against my shoulder, but I don't divert my attention from him. I need him to let me in.

"Right. Convenient, I suppose." I sigh at my sister's assault. "Who wouldn't try that shit to get to someone like him." Hand to my forehead, I feel dizziness settle in thanks to the nerves and the several-hours-old alcohol.

Shit.

I step back and lean into the brick across from the only door that doesn't seem to be infested with people.

Why is no one over here?

"Ari, you good?"

"Ladies, I'm going to need you to move along." Gargoyle booms from his spot, Aurora spinning on him like a rabid dog.

"Can't you see she isn't feeling right?" She fires back, standing between me and the meathead like she has a chance to take him in a fight.

She doesn't.

Still, he doesn't encroach on us, his entrance a station he's refusing to leave. Bulky frame looms, though, his brow furrowing the more agitated he gets with our interaction.

"Ari, you good?" Aurora turns her back to the guy and palms my face, forcing me to look in her eyes.

"I'm alright." I breathe, terrified my mouth reeks of old cocktails and last night's food, but I know it can't be much worse than the fire she breathes heavily into my face.

"Then what do you mean by texting him? Why didn't you say something?" Her eyes search mine, emotion pricking at the back of hers.

"I didn't want to make something out of nothing." I pause for a moment, then decide it's best I let her in on the shit anyway. "He sent me a message after the incident with C. He's asking to see me again. I need him to tell us where she went or if they arrested her."

"Oh ..." my sister breathes and steps back from me, hands falling from my face. "Okay, then."

"*Fuck.*" The curse rings out from across the way. "Serious, ladies. You need to fucking beat it." He steps in our direction, arms out in an attempt to herd us back to the throng of people we came from.

He's too late, though.

The steel door swings open, and out comes a group of muscle men dressed just like him in a seemingly coordinated fashion. Two step out together, block the door, then move forward as one unit, the two behind them following the same.

It's not until the group descends on the alleyway as a whole that I catch a glimpse of wild curls hidden in the middle of it all.

"*Rex,*" I yell, but gargoyle man steps to us, blocking us from moving forward. "Rex."

How does that make me any different than any other fan trying to get his attention?

Shit.

My sister tries to call after him as well, but security corrals us together and blocks my view of the famous rock star. She jumps, and I try to peek around, but he's not budging.

Double shit.

Wait …

I look over at my sister, who is going nuts against the bodyguard, then trail my gaze back to the meathead keeping us steady when it hits me.

Something he called his brother …

"Fart something …" I think out loud and turn away from our bouncer and my sister's antics.

"What?" she asks me, unaware of my thoughts taking me down memory lane to having pizza on our first official date.

Our only date.

I taste the Italian on the tip of my desperate tongue as vividly as I see Rex's curls tenting around us from his position on top, blocking out the rest of the planet.

I spin back to the bouncer a few steps away and watch the backs of the large men getting farther away from us, taking Rex to the back of the building and away from the chaos.

Away from me.

I breathe deep, prepare myself to make my voice carry, open my chest, and yell with hands cupped around my mouth.

Chapter Twenty-Eight

Rex

"**H**EY, FART KNUCKLE."

I stop dead in my tracks, causing a domino of other gents to ram into me from behind and the group in front of me to pull away.

"No fucking way." I turn to look, but all I see is a wall of bodyguards clad in black shit and headsets, prepared to do the jobs that the band's manager hired them for.

"Rex, you need to keep it moving." Ian's hands fall heavy and demanding on my shoulders, trying to turn me back to fall in line with the group.

I can't do that.

"It's her, Ian." I shrug off his hands, knowing he knows exactly who I'm talking about, but this prick plays dumb.

"Her?" His brow quirks up in question. "Doesn't matter, Rex. Keep moving." He pushes again, harder this time, and I stumble into another body like a damn rag doll.

This is the kinda shit I'm fucking sick of.

"No, Ian." I push back, jerking my arm free of the grasp another guard tries to have on me. "I can't do that." More hands land on me, try and direct me. They push and pull, nearly lifting the soles of my boots from the pavement.

But the more they insist, the more I fight back.

"You're gonna make me do this, aren't you?" Ian shakes his head with a heady breath of constant frustration, his hand going to the mic button I know he has hidden in his left breast pocket. "Bring the girls."

Relief washes over me, contentment loosening my joints, and I'm spinning back to the group, where I fall in line with the exit plan like nothing ever happened.

There's a car waiting on the other side of the upcoming fence, hidden away from the public to keep my leaving private.

We left Toby and Fin back inside to shut the place down. I was supposed to be the distraction so they could exit, but I guess I wasn't in on the plan change since there's no massive hoard descending on us as we move.

I wouldn't change a thing, though.

My girl is here after all.

The fence opens up in front of us, and another synchronized-swim thing occurs with the guys covering my front, opening up the way for me to enter—exit?—into the second clear alley. Behind me, they do a similar thing as we pile into several blacked-out SUVs, some of which will stay behind to collect my bandmates and brother.

Nerves eat at my stomach as I settle into the seat. The car rocks with Ian's slam of the door at the driver's position, Lugh taking up point on the passenger side, but no one else enters the vehicle.

"Where is she?" I ask from the middle of the back seat with a little too much enthusiasm. Partly to get on Ian's nerves but mostly because I'm nervous and I don't want her hurt.

Physically or otherwise.

No one can see that she just came with us.

No one can find out that she knows me.

"They're coming with," Ian grumbles to the window as he peers over his shoulder, steering us out onto the road and into traffic along with two other SUVs.

They?

I furrow my brow and look behind us to see if I can see anything.

Blacked-out SUV, stupid. Nice try.

I huff but flop back with my arms crossed.

"I only heard Aria." Pushing my hair out of my face, I catch Ian's rolling light blues in the rearview. "Who's with her?"

"Ian to Sentry, confirm our guests."

Guests … Plural …

Silence falls over the cab of the car as chatter sounds from both men's earpieces, Lugh making no effort to engage in any of my antics or the conversation going on next to his head.

"Two females identified as Aria and Aurora Scarlett. In the third car back." Ian eases the car into a turn as he conveys the information, eyes to the road then flicking to the rearview for sight of the vehicles behind us.

"Why isn't she in the middle car, Ian?" My nerves dive for a different reason this time. My question, more of a statement of *what the actual fuck,* comes out clipped.

Doing this as much as I have, I know that the payload is supposed to be in the middle car to prevent tails or pins by suspicious vehicles.

So why the hell am I in the front, and she's all the way back there?

"We have two payloads, Rex. Now shut up and enjoy the ride." Lugh gives an approving grunt like my questions are getting on his nerves, too, but taps his earpiece like he's trying to hear better.

"Boss …"

"I fucking heard." Ian veers off, taking a sudden turn down a side street and then another that doesn't seem to have been part of the plan.

"What's going on?" My question goes unanswered as Lugh taps Ian's arm and makes a signal with his hand that I don't get, but Ian acknowledges it and speeds up. "Guys?"

I snap my seat belt in place when Ian takes another corner like Mario Andretti and nearly has me slamming into the door from the center seat.

"Jesus." Ian thinks he speaks under his breath, but his words are audible enough to send me into a panic.

"What the hell is going on?" Another sigh, another look passes between the two in the front without any indication to me that they know I'm fucking back here.

God dammit.

"She better not be hurt, you numb nuts." I grip the seat to keep from flying around the back despite my restraints as Ian floors the car, the engine roaring to life.

"She'll be fine," Lugh grunts, Ian meeting my gaze in the rearview again. He knows better than to keep me out of the loop.

"Mac had to jump in the car with her. Now they've got a tail."

"Circle back," I demand, fishing my phone out of the pants I wear that are too fucking tight for this shit. Dialing my brother, I have the thing to my ear before Ian responds.

"Already on it, Rex."

The car whips left again, taking us in a giant circle. Engine roaring to life, we propel forward as the call rings out.

"Shit." I smash buttons with shaky thumbs and try to call again. "C'mon, turd munch. Fucking answer."

"Hey, dick." Relief washes over me at the sound of his voice, calm as ever, filling the line.

"Hey, prick," I respond, the car whipping around another corner, wheels squealing in protest of the move. "Is she good?"

I need to hear it.

"Serious? You're not going to ask me at all?" I hear his exaggerated huff over the line. "Thanks, bro. I guess I'm good."

"Great, smart-ass. I know that twin shit works, now how about Aria?" I can feel his nerves, minor as they are, but he's fine enough. Just like me.

"All good here," Mac answers, a seriousness to his tone that eases the edge. I release the death grip I had on the phone along with a breath. "Routine shit, bro."

"Thank fuck," I growl into the speaker. "Let me talk to her."

"Not a good call," Mac cuts in, piquing confusion and a little bit of a twinge in my chest.

"What's that supposed to mean?" I growl, my blood reaching a high temp at the anger that incites.

I know he's not keeping her from me, so why does it feel like that?

"Nothing, bro. Just that there's a lot of emotion here." His voice carries gently over the line as I see the back of his SUV come into view, a minivan wedged firmly in the ass.

No pun intended.

"Let me talk to her." I need to talk to her. She wouldn't be where she is if it weren't for me, and I feel responsible.

I should have left it alone.

The thought creeps in, tearing my chest into a million pieces, but it's too late now. I asked her here. And I'm watching on as a pap gets way too close to the people that I love most.

I'm not okay with that.

"Hold on," I tell my brother as I unsnap my seat belt and scoot to the passenger window, engaging the button to roll the tinted glass out of my way.

"*Rex,*" Ian says my name like a reprimand but gets my intention and maneuvers until the pap vehicles—that's right, as we get closer, I realize it's more than one boxing them in—are nearly trading paint with our SUV.

Lugh says shit into his mic that I don't catch, but I don't stop. As soon as the window is no longer blocking the outside world, I lean out past the threshold with hair whipping in the wind until I can be seen.

On full display, I raise both middle fingers to the driver of a passenger car, who snaps a photo with a camera that's bigger than his head.

Dissatisfied, Ian swerves, shifting the car in a maneuver that has the driver backing off enough for us to squeeze between Mac and the minivan.

It barely keeps up, but the person inside is hell-bent on pushing the engine of the damn minivan to the limit and taps the bumper of our SUV.

"Dammit." Lugh rolls down his window, leaning out enough to try and ward off the final danger. "Piss off," he yells and waves them off.

They're persistent, as always.

"Rex." Ian peeks back at me. "You good?"

I nod, take the cue, and lean until the upper half of my body is hanging outside the window. Arms waving like a total dick, hair flying about like I'm in a tornado, the minivan veers to get the shot of me in time for Ian to slam the brakes.

I slam into the frame of the door, smashing my knee and nearly falling the fuck out.

"Fuck, Ian." I pry myself back, Lugh's hold of my belt releasing as I slam back into the rushing wind. The window goes up like my heart rate, but the car slows despite my hyperventilation. "Holy shit."

"You alright?" Ian speaks over his shoulder but doesn't take his eyes off the road.

"Yeah, I'm good," I heave, my chest tightening around my ribs, making breath hard to get into my lungs.

Shit.

Hand to my pecs, I focus on the image I know is underneath the band tee I wear and suck in oxygen like I need life.

Breathe, one … two … three.

It slows, the hyperventilation, the shake in my hands calming.

"Shit, where's my phone." I feel around with trembling limbs and locate the thing on the floor, the call still engaged. "Mac? *Mac?*"

"Still alive. Thanks for that." He's sincere, almost undisturbed. He's also sarcastic as hell, considering the rapid breathing I hear over the line.

Twin shit.

Either my brother felt my response to nearly flying out the window, or he saw and freaked out.

"I know you love me," I breathe back to him, fuck his sarcasm and calmness.

"Absolutely." I hear the nod, feel it even, as I focus on the vehicle in front of us. "Here. Aria wants to cuss you out a little bit." Shuffling sounds over the phone as I cement it to my ear, my heart racing for a different reason.

"Aria?" I sense her before she speaks, a tranquility falling around me despite all the events that just happened. "You okay?"

She can be mad at me. I don't care. As long as she's safe.

"God dammit, Rex." Her tone suggests I shouldn't feel relaxed at the sound.

I am.

"I am *really* glad to hear the sound of your voice, babe." Instead of just thinking it, I say it outright. Something I realized she needs if this is ever gonna have some semblance of a chance to work.

I'm met with a sigh over the phone, one I know is more of agreeance than irritation. I tuck the device between my shoulder and ear so I can lean back in the seat and buckle the seat belt.

"I really want to say so many things to you, you jackass." She pauses, her frustration with me evident in her forced words. "That was fucking stupid."

"I know. Not sure if you've gotten it yet, but I do a lot of stupid shit." I try to dampen the chuckle that bubbles out of my chest, but it sounds anyway.

"Clearly." The word is laced with an eye roll I can hear through the phone and my chuckle turns into a laugh I'm so glad I can have in this moment. That I can share with her.

"Fuck, I never thought I'd hear from you again." I rub my chin, the stubble scratching against my palm that then lands on the back of my neck.

"And I certainly never thought I'd have to chase your ass down to find my best friend, but here we are," Aria retorts, her words furrowing my brow, the ache in my chest returning.

Did I read it wrong?

Shit.

"Where is Cedar?" she challenges, the bite in her tone has me snapping up in my seat.

"I don't know who you're talking about." I tap the front seat for Ian's attention, and he signals that we're two minutes out from the rendezvous.

"Bullshit. Did you have her tossed in jail for assault?" *Huh?* "Or did you just kick her to the curb?"

The jab of her accusation hits right in the gut, sinking my stomach and hanging my pounding head on tight shoulders.

"I don't know who Cedar is, but I'll help find her," I offer with a heavy heart and a weight bowing my shoulders.

"The fuck you mean you don't know her? You know enough to piss her off." I hear her growl back, like I'm some kind of kidnapper and she's Liam Neeson preparing to find me and take me out.

"The tussle with the dark–haired chick is viral, Rex." Ian cuts in from the front. "Her name was Cedar. Cedar Jones."

Oh, fuck.

I'm transported back, as if Cedar is in front of me now, her words bouncing around my skull like stuck lyrics.

You don't deserve her.

Toxic prick.

The words bring a slow nod of recognition. Cedar wasn't just someone I found on the road, nor was her friend or whoever she was defending. The numbness that conversation brought forth in me melts away and leaves lumps of guilt building in my throat.

The whole thing was about Aria.

Fucking … fuck.

She's right.

Chapter Twenty-Nine

Aria

THE LINE IS SILENT, but my heart refuses to stop pounding its drums in my ears.

Flexing my fists, I try to release the energy, the emotion, but it sticks in my throat like broken glass.

I'm angry. I'm frustrated. Worried about my best friend.

Mostly … I feel hurt.

I know I shouldn't. It's even more evident that he wouldn't want to be with me now that I know he's a *rock star*, with groupies falling all over him and all. But I can't help feeling like I deserved to know that and so much more from the fucking beginning.

God, how many people has he been with? Do I even want to know?

I feel the color draining from my face the longer the line sits quiet. I snapped, and I'm not sure I won't snap again.

Shaking hand to my forehead, I rub my temple in a sad attempt to self-soothe while also doing my best to avoid making eye contact with his damn twin.

Twin.

The one I'm not mad at but looks so much like him that I'm near blows. My elbow is awfully close to making his nose match his brother's.

Lord, help me.

Universe, send good vibes ...

Any damn thing right now.

"Where the fuck is Cedar, Rex?" I whisper-growl through a cupped hand over the phone's mic. I try to dampen the emotion I feel, but my tone suggests I'm not doing a very good job of it.

I hear voices over the line that I can't make out, thanks to the drummer boy in my head and the man next to me tapping his leg as if his bouncing knee wasn't enough.

"Babe." That sultry, gravelly, deeply worn voice caresses my eardrums and shoots straight to my panties.

Shit.

"One of the security team escorted her out of Moonman two hours ago. Ian's radioing for more info now." He pauses, a scratching sound coming from his end, but continues. "We'll find her. She was more than okay when I saw her last." The sincerity in his deep tone, the concern laced in his words, have my shoulders starting to pull away from my temples.

"Thank you," I breathe out.

"We'll be pulling in right up here." I hear rustling as if he's gesturing ahead of us even though I can't see him.

"Okay," I almost whisper, my words less like daggers, my muscles relaxing at the sound of his voice.

"You sound better," he acknowledges. "How are you doing now?"

I don't answer him though. Our SUV bumps along into a lot, swerving and swinging around small pathways next to a large building that looks familiar but not, at the same time.

We pull up to an open lot surrounded by more cars like this one, several people wandering around with passes or cameras dangling from their necks, and a huge RV. I look around, eyes taking in both sides of the car as I turn my head, the phone going with me.

Cars parked, doors open.

Mac steps out his side as Aurora dips out the other, leaving both doors open for me to be free of this death trap.

Still not a fan after the last time we rode in one of these.

The soles of my shoes hit the pavement as my eyes settle on a mess of sandy blonde and windblown hair.

"Babe."

His grin hits me almost as quickly as his body does. A bear hug that he wraps me in has my arms restricted to my sides and my brain struggling to process the fact that I'm still holding the phone to my ear.

"Could you—"

Another quick squeeze before he sets me back on my feet, but he leans into me, pressing my back against the cool surface of the car. He steals the phone from my grip, slipping it into his pocket, his cheek meeting my temple and his hands landing on my hips.

I hear his deep inhale, clouding my judgment, and his exhale rings around my brain like sparklers in the nighttime.

"Fuck, I missed how you smell." Deep, sultry words only for me have my lips parting, my tongue poking out to dampen them.

"Really?" I attempt skeptical, but my words come out on a sigh. More like a hopeful romantic with a bleeding heart, less like a hardened female tired of this man's shit.

Shit, shit.

"Mm-hmm," he hums in my ear, chills running down my spine. "And the way you taste." Rex dips in to nibble my earlobe, trailing kisses down my neck. His palm finds my jaw, cupping my face tenderly. "Then there's the way you feel …" His grip on my hip tightens, pulling me flush against his pelvis.

Is he hard?

"Oh God …" I don't plan on saying the words aloud, but I do. The smile, then the chuckle I feel more than see from him, uplifts me, even when I know it shouldn't.

"Not God, but pretty close," Rex smarts, earning him a slap to his bare bicep. The skin-on-skin contact sends more chills down my spine than I'd like to admit.

But that laugh, though …

He's leaned back now, staring down at me with smiling eyes, our hips still pressed intimately together.

"You have a lot to explain if you want to keep touching me like this," I hiss, making his features falter, his jokes a crumbling defense.

He nods his understanding, though he keeps a smile firmly planted on his newly pierced lip.

"Fair enough," Rex responds softly. "I owe you that."

"DooDoo brains." I hear Mac call for his brother.

Rex's hand slips confidently into mine and tugs me away from the SUV. He doesn't take his eyes off me until the last second, his middle finger already up in the air in the direction of his twin's voice.

"That's a new one." I snicker.

"He's taken creative liberties recently," Rex says with an eye roll as he leads in the direction of the massive RV we passed on the way in.

The familiar click of camera shutters echoes around us as we pass people milling about. Flashes point in our direction, slowing my speed, my arm extending to the point of nearly breaking our interlocked fingers. My vision splinters, lights dancing around in my head and making me nauseous.

"Rex?" I come to a complete stop, anxiety cementing my feet to the ground despite my utter desire to turn and run.

I don't like the spotlight.

I'm not a fan of being violated, and this feels like a violation. All I see are lenses pointed in my direction, photo after photo taken without my permission.

Without *Rex's* permission.

"Hey." Rex wraps his arms around my shoulders, holding me close to his chest. Our feet are moving, but I don't see where we're going. I hear rustling as Rex shuffles us up a few small stairs, keeping my face and ears away from the onslaught of cameras. "Ian, confiscate all the cameras."

More shuffling, and a slam has me jumping out of my skin. Today has been too much, and it's only just begun. I try to remember how to breathe, how to be a human, but my chest constricts.

Cedar is still missing.

I don't even know if I'm up for this shit with Rex, whatever it happens to be.

Where is my sister?

My nails dig into flesh, what part of Rex's body I can't be sure, as I try to understand the wave of emotion I feel.

More shuffling, more stepping.

Another slam nearly sends me through the roof.

I'm in sensory overload with all the lights and noises, not to mention the firm body plastered to my side, slicking my skin with sweat that doesn't belong to me. My thighs hit something velvety soft, and I fall back, relishing in the smoothness against my palms.

"Babe," Rex whispers gently from somewhere in front of me, but my eyes are squeezed shut in an attempt to keep the rest of the world out. Reduce the senses. Stop the flashing lights from blinding me while I focus on my breathing.

"Anxiety," I mutter, then pause to focus on my inhale, pushing evenly out more than what I just took in. "It'll pass."

Breathe, one … two … three … four.

Exhale, one … two … three … four … five.

"Got it." Rex's warmth leaves me shivering from its absence. The light filtering through my eyelids goes dark, easing the tension in my head and relaxing the muscles in my face.

Softness envelops me. The same velvety fur-like texture drapes around my shoulders, nuzzling into my cheeks.

I tuck the blanket around me, tight to my racing heart, as the bed dips behind me. I smell his scent before I feel his warmth wrap from my ass to my shoulders, his legs spread along either side of my thighs. Rex's arms lie loose around my belly, holding me, the body heat from his chest warming my back through the blanket.

My body slows as I allow myself to focus on how he feels against me, bringing me back from the brink quicker than any self-soothing technique I've learned.

More focused breathing has my eyes fluttering open to take in the dark bedroom, the quiet that I break.

"Thank you," I whisper, leaning my head back onto his shoulder.

"Nah," he breathes into my ear. "Thank you. For trusting me."

Shit, he's right. I did.

A small smile pulls at the corner of my lips.

"Are you ready for twenty-one questions?" My voice is soft, like the blanket I'm wrapped in, his chiseled jaw against my temple.

I want to know more about him. I want a distraction from the outside world while someone else tries to find my best friend, and I subconsciously decide if I'm okay with this.

Whatever this really is.

Relationship? What is this?

We slept together once. Hardly constitutes a relationship.

Shit. Overthinking it again.

Technically, it was more than once.

"As long as you're ready. I'm not in any hurry, babe." His tenderness pulls at my heartstrings, and I allow myself to sink farther back into his warmth.

"Why the lip ring?"

Don't ask me; it's the first thing that came to my mind.

He laughs, deep and perfect in my ear.

"Jesus, I was not expecting that." Rex's chuckle simmers down into a sigh of contentment that blows across my ear. "It's one I wanted, had at one point but took out. I got it redone before the tour." He tucks hair behind my ear and presses his scratchy jaw against my head. "What else you got?"

I pet the fur of the blanket against my chest as I contemplate the things I want to know and ask. There are so many, and yet all I want is to just be right here, without ruining it, in this moment.

I sigh, partly from contentment but also a little frustration with myself—and him.

"I was supposed to be mad at you." This time, I opt for honesty instead of a question. It's what feels most right to say.

"Does that mean you aren't anymore?" I hear the hope in his words, the tension building in his chest as he holds his breath.

"No, I am. I just can't bring myself to show you how upset I really am," I admit, tilting my head back and searching his face in the dark. I catch a glint of that familiar sparkle in his eyes and a crooked grin.

"You should. Be mad at me, that is." He tears his gaze away from me. "It wasn't fair. I have my reasons, but that wasn't up to me to choose for you."

"It wasn't up to you to judge yourself for me." My hand finds its way through the blanket and to his face to bring his eyes back to mine. "But what were your reasons?"

Rex's face lifts in a charming half smile, the look on his face conveying his intensity with its softness.

"You didn't ask for a selfie the moment you set eyes on me. Or an autograph. Or to have my babies." The last one comes out on a chuckle from him, a flush set around wide eyes for me. My look doesn't stop his words, though. He continues on with the same emotion. "You didn't beg for my fame, my name, or my songs, Aria." My name falling off his lips sends chills despite the blanket as he leans back to look at me straight on. "You made me feel like I was normal again." He cups my face with one hand, his other arm supporting me around my shoulders. "You looked at me like you didn't know me."

Emotion swells in my chest, my breath catching in my throat.

Rex's lips are on mine before I can respond.

Red-hot passion explodes between us. Tongue and teeth battle as much as our hands fight the blanket barrier to feel each other's skin. I push at his shoulders until his back hits the mattress.

I follow, unwilling to break the contact, and straddle his hips. His hands grip my ass and pull me against his groin as his tongue teases mine. Groans and grunts slip out between our sealed lips, the fervor too heady to stop for oxygen. Hands to his pecs, I feel the rings beneath his barely there shirt, and I pinch at his nipples just to see what he'll do.

Rex chuckles and cups the back of my neck, his tongue flicking against mine in ways that have my panties slicking and my core clenching.

God, is this even real?

Don't wake me if it's a dream.

It's gotta be a dream. No way Rex Thompson feels normal because of me—
Wham!

I've been startled before by loud noises, but not like this.

My heart leaps into my throat at the thunderous whack, and complete-ly, involuntarily, I shoot farther up the bed, the rock star trapped beneath my legs.

"Got ya." I hear Aurora through my adrenaline-fueled heartbeat in my ears, twisting my torso in my newfound crouch over Rex's head to stare daggers in the direction of the source. "Sis bags a rock star."

"*Aurora*," I snap, but I'm already alone on the mattress, my ass hitting the cushion as Rex shoots to his feet and blocks her camera flash from my view. "What the fuck is wrong with you?" I crawl over to stand between them, pushing her lens out of Rex's heaving chest and angling the camera down so that the strap digs into the back of her neck.

"Aw, c'mon," Aurora whines. "You let G take your pics together." I scoff at her jealousy and push her out into the tiny hallway, away from Rex's seething.

He says nothing, just breathes heavily. Which I'm not sure is a good thing, considering he doesn't follow us either.

Double Dutch shit.

Chapter Thirty

Rex

FUCKING HELL.

It's hard as hell to go from intimate vulnerability to *intimacy*, only to have her sister's fucking camera in our faces.

The adrenaline spike has me ready to fight the third world war, to protect her, to keep her safe.

But my logic is screaming at me to remember how to breathe because it's just her sister. Not the stupid paps.

You need to oxygen somehow, dumbass.

The door has swung closed in my face, the thin wooden panel blocking Aria from my view, and I have yet to move. I'm pretty sure if I do, I might smash something.

Dramatic, I know.

Still standing where she left me, hands laced at the top of my head, I force a box breathing to even out my lungs. Expanding my chest with deep inhales and slow exhales.

Sweat sheens on my skin, heat radiating from my body, hair sticking to my lips as I suck life back into my vibrating lungs.

I was ready to kill for her. Pissed that my security let someone past them, but ready to act for her.

She's worth jail time.

"What the fuck are you thinking?" I hear my girl yell through the thin door. Her sister yammers some shit I can't make out. All I know is that Aria's kinda scary, and I am here for it.

"Don't be like them, you asshat. He deserves some fucking respect."

Wait. He?

She's defending me?

My arms fall to my sides, my chest swelling for a different reason this time. Emotions I'm a little scared to name but have been waiting for knock at my ribcage and have me questioning my sanity level.

I wrote an album for this woman.

Of course my heart begs for her.

I reach out and crack the door open at Aria's back. Her head bobs, her hair longer than I remember swaying around her shoulders, as she melts the face off her sister. The sister catches sight of me with watery eyes and a trembling bottom lip.

"I'm sorry, Rex." She speaks between Aria's harsh words, drawing the attention over her sister's shoulder. Green eyes, shining with emotion I recognize in my own heart, meet mine and bring a pull to the corner of my lips.

"You don't have to apologize to me." I meet her sister's blotchy face with sincerity. "Having cameras in my face is what I do." I wink because someone needs to bring it down a little bit in here, and I step closer to the woman whose eyes haven't left my profile since I stepped out of the door.

My next move … It makes a statement. For the whole bus to see.

I wrap my arms around Aria's waist and pull her flush against my body, pressing a kiss to her temple as she watches in horrified embarrassment.

Then she melts into me.

Thank God.

"I just don't want to violate Aria's privacy." I speak to her sister while focused on Aria, taking pride in the flush that rises across her chest when I cup her face in my hand. Her cheeks deepen in color when I press my hard dick against her.

"Rex," Aria breathes. "Shit isn't that fucking easy."

Knowingly, I bob my head and prepare my rebuttal. I've been trying to practice what I'd say if she ever gave me the chance again. Trying to find the words that match how she makes me feel every goddamned day since the moment I met her.

But now? I feel too many eyes on me, on us, and I realize that a lot could have changed in the last few months.

What if she's with someone else?

What if she isn't?

I shake my head but smile for her. I know I have to try despite the stage fright that sets in and threatens to paralyze me in this spot.

She has been my undoing since the photo shoot.

"I know it's not going to be that easy. Trust." Pressing my forehead to hers, I close my eyes and let her scent fill me up with resolve. "But I've been a songwriter as long as I can remember. For *decades*." I pause and meet her gaze through my lashes without leaning back. "And I've never written an album about anyone like I did with this one, about *us*. About *you*. That means a fuck load to me."

"Damn you," she whispers to me, her anger deflated like the shoulders that relax into my hold.

"I want you. I want a life outside of the stage lights. I want all my work to be *worth* something." Palming her jaw, I look her dead in the eye and admit shit I haven't said out loud to anyone before. "I'm fucking great at lyrics but terrible at this." I chuckle but continue with itching eyes.

"You had me since 'holy shit' crossed those lips because of what those words meant." I press a kiss to the tip of her reddened nose. "You didn't recognize me as the front man of a famous band." Another peck to her forehead. "*You saw me as a man.*"

I see the soul she bares to me through her irises despite the gulping bob I catch in her throat.

The bus falls silent, making me furrow my brow.

My lungs falter when all she does is continue to stare at me, blinking slowly.

I feel the air being sucked from the room. Astonishment and concern weigh heavy around us like the newsroom before presenting worse than normal news.

"Aria?" My brow furrows further, my eyes flicking between hers, searching for what her silence means.

"I … Uh, *wow.*" Her arms tighten around me when she stumbles over her words. "Jesus, I'm… fuck." The concern threatening to etch itself in my ribs loosens when tears well in her beautiful eyes and spill over. "Dammit, I missed the shit out of you, too, Rex." She sniffles, and it's enough for me.

I smash my lips to hers, claiming the win in front of my people. She meets me with as much force as I give, her hands finding and fisting my hair to hold me in place, tugging me closer.

I'm reluctant when I pull back, but I need to read her face.

"You still have nineteen questions to answer," she pants her words out through a smile I'm so fucking glad to see.

"Of course." My grin matches hers. "I'll give you *thousands* of questions to ask me just so I can answer all of them." Another peck to her reddened lips and I'm walking us back into the small bedroom at the back of the bus.

I kick the door closed, leaving our family on the other side, and essentially take my girl to bed. Arms around her waist, hers around my neck, I lift her onto the mattress and settle in beside her.

She sighs, her body nestling into the fur blanket beneath her and my warmth at her side.

"Has anyone heard anything from Cedar yet?" she asks, looking up at me and catching me take in the sight of her.

"Ian'll find her. She seemed pretty scrappy when I saw her." Aria's chuckle lightens the load on my shoulders even more.

"That she is." She pauses, fiddling with the hem of my shirt. "I can fix this, if you'd like."

I follow her gaze to where the worn shirt has popped threads, the edge of the material rolling freely.

"It's actually weird to see you in this." Another snicker leaves Aria's lips, and I'm certain she's recalling the first day we met.

I opted for dress clothes that day.

First impressions matter.

"But somehow they both suit you," she says. My face aches, my hand finding its way to her bent knee, my other arm wrapping around so that her head rests on my bicep. "Versatile. I like that."

"Right back at cha." I press a gentle kiss to the top of her head. "Now stop giving me compliments and give me the real shit."

She snorts, legit snorts, and throws an arched brow in my direction.

"I know you're a rock star and all, but that was a statement of what I like," she jabs. "Not a compliment." Laughter overtakes me, my hand coming to my chest to tend to my feigned bleeding heart.

"You *wound* me."

She rolls her sweet mossy eyes. "Fine … Tell me why you left my hotel room. Why you never called me?"

I suck in a sharp breath, my stomach knotting before the words finish leaving her lips. "Damn, we're going straight there." I nod, knowing I asked for it, and rest my hand on her exposed stomach. "I thought it would be the best thing for you." Tracing little circles on her belly, I feel goose bumps rise in my wake. "How stupid that was."

"Very." Her nod vibrates the bed, encouraging me.

"I didn't want you to get caught up in the media if you weren't prepared for that. Thought maybe you'd find someone who wanted a minivan and a white fence." She snorts at me again for that one. "It's true." I chuckle at the thought of myself behind the wheel of a minivan, tattoos and all. "Someone else could give you a life you can keep private. With me ..." I pause, the moment bearing enough weight between us to change her mind. "With me, your name's gonna be trending on social media. Pictures are no longer just for your immediate friends to take. People will kill to get a money shot of me. Even more so if they catch me *with* you." My voice cracks. "Your life isn't just yours anymore."

I have to stop myself. I'm almost talking myself out of all the shit I've been working toward. All the plans Ian and I have put together to make shit possible.

I know I can't protect her from everything. There will be attention from the public. It's inevitable, especially at the beginning.

But maybe I can control it.

For her, I'll try anything.

As long as she's willing to stick by my side.

"If you thought I'd be better with someone else, then why now?" Her words are spoken softly, concern rounding out the edges of her tone, echoed by the tension I feel in her muscles. "Was it Cedar? How did she even find you?"

My brow furrows, my hand pausing its trek across her delicate skin, as realization settles in.

"I texted you well before she showed up at Moonman. In fact, I sent my location to you, thinking maybe you'd be nearby and might come. It was a shot I took in the dark."

Her mouth forms a cute little O shape, her eyes widening at my words.

"Yeah," I drawl. "I didn't know who she was, just some girl at the bar with a vendetta that I probably earned." I shrug. "Maybe I was crazy to try and reach out to you." I lean my head down to press my forehead against hers, but I don't miss the tears that prick her eyes. "But I had to anyway."

"Rex," Aria whispers, my name both a gift and a curse in that tone on her lips. "I can't be in the spotlight like you. I can't be center stage." I kiss her forehead to soothe her worries and inhale that sweet tropical scent that is Aria.

Hell, maybe it's to soothe my own anxiousness still swirling in my gut.

"I don't expect you to be." Sitting back, I hold her jaw in my hands and look her dead in the eye. "After this tour, I'm out."

All the color drains from her face, her lids popping open in shock.

She pushes to sit up, propping herself up on an arm and running a hand through her hair.

"What do you mean, *out?*" she asks over her shoulder, her words barely above a whisper. As if speaking any louder will break the little bubble we've created here.

"I mean out. Out of the band. Out of the spotlight." Aria blinks at me slowly, absorbing the emotion behind my words. "I don't need it like I once did. I'd rather take my chances with you." I grab her wrist and tug until her torso meets mine. "If you'll have me, that is."

"That's stupid as hell," she blurts, the color and her attitude returning full bore.

Holy shit, that's hot.

Aria pushes up and kneels beside me, armed with a cocked brow and a pillow. I barely get my arm up and a laugh out before she launches into an attack on my face and upper body.

"You"—she thumps me with the pillow, and I snort—"can't let"—*thump, thump*, straight to my aching gut—"your fucking brothers down." *Thump.*

I howl at her assault. The pillow's material spreads static like wildfire with each point of contact, tugging at my hair, shoving the shit over my face and into my mouth.

Heaving, she sits back on her haunches, still fisting one corner of her fluffed weapon, and pushes back her mussed hair with the other.

"That was the first real thing you ever told me. About them," she reminds me, as if they weren't a heavy factor in making that decision. In every decision since the beginning.

They were the biggest thing aside from her, actually.

Mac was the first person to support my decision, though reluctantly, as always.

But the others? They were just as important.

Fin's sat at my Ma's dinner table on more than one occasion, gobbling up her famous cobbler just like the rest of us did as kids. He didn't find us until later, but I was glad as hell to have been in the presence of a guitar god for this long. To have him write and play with us was more than I'd ever hoped for after so long with just the three of us.

In fact, the end of this tour leads right to an award show with Fin as the nominee.

I mean, winner.

Toby learned bass in my garage at thirteen, giving As Above the first beat we ever wrote a song to.

And Leo? Even though we tried our best, he never could learn an instrument. So you know what he did? He went out and got a goddamn business degree to help us manage the band.

I admire my crew, the motley bunch of 'em, and I'm touched by her response.

"Babe." I snicker, my heart full and my hands finding her skin like a moth to the flame. "We've sold millions of records, played in thousands of cities across the world. Had some of the finest meals and slept on a bus for a really long goddamn time. I'm not letting them down at all."

I claim her lips with mine, hot and ready. Slowly, I ease her back until her spine meets the mattress, and my body covers hers.

I'm ready to finish what we started. To explore her curves and sample her skin.

To fuck her like I love her.

And then make love to her like I missed her.

So, I do.

Chapter Thirty-One

Aurora

I'M SPENT.

Grumpy as all get out and ready to fade off into the sweet oblivion of sleep.

But can I?

Nooooo …

Thanks to my sister and her newfound rock star lover, I'm stuck on this bus, unable to leave, and alone until they come out.

Coming, alright.

And I suppose it doesn't count as newfound *either … right?*

The RV shakes despite the shock system I know is attached to a machine like this, which means my sister is getting it good.

I roll my eyes for what feels like the thousandth time tonight and peep back on my phone for yet another multiplicity of times. Cedar finally texts me, but I didn't tell them she did.

I just want to go home.

Tonight was supposed to be a celebration of *our* accomplishments, but I'm spending more time with strangers than my own sister and best friend.

Assholes. Both of them.

Like I said … I'm grumpy. Sleep deprived. And hungry again.

I chew on my thumbnail despite it being down to the quick already and sigh back into the plush leather chair I've been perched on since we got here. Mostly.

It is pretty nice in here.

It's the exact opposite of what I'd suspect a rock group to travel in—creams and beige colors line the walls. One TV, modestly sized, hung on the wall and hid behind a secret compartment toward the front of the bus. The living quarters lead right into a full kitchen—one bigger than my apartment—with an entire set of full-sized appliances. Beyond that are the bunks that line the wall, three stacked on each side, with curtains available to slide into place for privacy. Most are open now, the beds inside clearly slept in.

Much like the one on the far side from the bathroom, which happens to be the only thing separating the bunks from the primary bedroom.

The outside door opens, drawing my attention, but my jaw drops down to the shiny marbled floor.

Jonathon walks up the few stairs and into the cabin like he owns the place, and I watch every move he makes.

His ass flexes with each step. His gait is strong, but one side has the slightest limp you probably wouldn't notice if you weren't creepy little me.

And his back muscles, highlighted perfectly by the black tee he wears? Delicious looking.

Lord, have mercy.

Forgive me, Father, for this man wants me to sin. Over and over again.

That is, until my eyes land on the giant white neon sign across the back of his shirt.

"Ian," he greets the other meathead, who stands at Jonathon's entrance and accepts the clipboard he's handed. "She's all checked out, boss."

"Good, thanks." Ian looks over the paperwork, then nods his acceptance slash dismissal to Jonathon, who spins on his heels like a good little soldier right in my damn direction.

Shit.

Jonathon echoes my thought, except his is out loud and directed right at me.

Handyman, my ass.

That bitch is labeled as SECURITY.

"What the hell?" I'm monotone, too exhausted to express any more emotion, but clearly confused by this man's intent in my damn life.

He legitimately grimaces, his hands coming together in front of him in a nervous tick, one nail picking under the other.

"Hey, Aurora …" He's almost sheepish, his eyes softening on me.

I must look like total garbage. My hangover is hungover.

And maybe still a little under the influence.

"So you just take any job that shows up?" I ask with a flick of the wrist, my tone betraying how I feel. All it earns me is a sigh from Jonathon, though, which pisses me off even more.

This guy has been hanging around, all sweet and helpful. So why is he checking into Rex Thompson's band's RV like he works for them, wearing the same damned shirt as the meathead, but has spent the last few weeks trying to get into my pants?

"Are you even qualified for half the shit you do?" I poke, my mood in the shitter and dragging everyone with me.

"Wow, okay." Jonathon scoffs at my attitude and slides into the plush leather recliner across from me. He takes up the whole damn thing and then some with his shoulders hunched toward me, elbows resting on his knees. "I was asked to hang around. That's it. The rest was on me."

As if that excuses showing up at our door with motive.

"I don't even care what that means." I turn in my seat, facing the window shade I'm not allowed to move, and do my best ice queen impression. "Apparently, you're all a bunch of liars." He jerks back like I decked him, his spine snapping straight, eyes narrowing.

"Not sure who you're talking about, but it ain't fucking me." He pats his own knee and pushes to his feet. Jonathon towers over me, not intending to be menacing, and I feel like he might be, were I someone else. "You need some caffeine before you piss off the wrong person."

"Like you?" I whip my gaze to match the fire I see burning behind his eyes. "I'd ask you since I can't leave this hellhole without my sister, apparently, but who knows where you'd end up." I shrug and feign nonchalance, turning away from him to admire my nails like they're more interesting than he is. "Maybe fixing some chick's drain or some shit." I give a quick sniffle and pick at a cuticle while he scoffs at me.

"Aurora." It's all he says. Soft and yet curt, I can hear the shake of his head. It's Jonathon's way of saying goodbye as he spins away from me and walks out the door like he still owns the bus we're on.

Fuck him.

Liar pants. Must be a fire somewhere.

The door slams in his wake, drawing Ian's attention but making me roll my eyes.

"Drama king," I accuse out loud, sneering in his direction.

"I really don't think the drama came from him." Ian's deep timbre reverberates across the space between us, commanding. Almost like a correction to me. Like a dad might speak to a kid who's acting out.

"Fuck you, too, Ian. You *meathead*," I spit the words in his direction.

Who is he to *correct* me?

Who does he think he is?

I did just insult the hell out of one of his guys, though ...

I recognize I could have handled that better. I do.

I'm just sick of the sneaky bullshit, the lying, the *waiting*.

"You're rude as hell, Aurora." Ian drops the bomb on me, then just walks away from me to the other end of the RV, his back staying to me, even when he sits in another seat.

Ian straight-up adjusts the seat until he's facing completely away from me.

What a cock.

I shake my head, steadfast in my attitude, and send another message to Cedar.

> Me: Rescue me. Bring loads of caffeine. Pretty please.

> Me: I def just pissed in Jon's Wheaties. How the hell is he involved in all this shit?

> C: Can't get there, they won't let riffraff like me in. You're fine. Quit being an ass. X

Minutes tick by with no further responses. I don't blame her. She's probably passing out in our fancy hotel beds without us, just like I would still be had I not been stuck here.

Or out looking for her ass.

"*Aria*," I call out with a stomp to the wall near my hanging feet, trying my best to ruin her sexcapades, but no one answers me.

Dammit, I want to go home.

"Ian," I try, but he just ignores me like a prison guard avoids speaking to the inmates.

I would try running for the door again, but that didn't work out so well the last time. Which was like two hours ago.

No, this time, Mac and his bodyguard are stationed outside for privacy reasons. I can still see the silhouette of Mac's hair through the shade in the small window set into the door.

They're assholes, too.

Fuck everybody.

Chapter Thirty-Two

Aria

BIG BADASS REX THOMPSON is lying on my bare chest in the bed of his tour bus as we ride into the next city for yet another show.

It puts us within twenty minutes of home for me, where I intend to get my ass back into the studio to prep for opening tomorrow.

Aurora is pissed at me, and Cedar chose to head home already for an early appointment I know she's regretting making. She's never been a morning person, but apparently it's a big client she had to work into her schedule.

Cedar never did share where the hell she ended up for most of the night after she addressed Rex—we'll call it that, anyway—but she'd messaged Aurora to let us know she was safe and back at the hotel.

I think she's pissed at me, too, but I'm having a hard time finding it in me to care too much as I stroke Rex's golden brown curls and listen to him breathe deeply against my chest like he hasn't slept in ages.

His tattoos pop colorfully on his bare skin, drawing my attention to more than his sculpted body.

This man … Jesus, he's willing to give up his career, his passion for a chance at a life with me.

How the fuck did this become my life?

That's the question I can't answer, and I know all too well not to ask too hard or the universe might jerk it away from me.

I make *Rex Thompson* feel like a man. Like a normal human being.

Which everyone deserves.

I caress his muscled bicep gently with the back of my fingers that went numb long ago as I wonder about my sister.

I know Aurora feels left out a lot. She's clung to Cedar as her best friend because she could never find one in her grade that clicked as well. I love that they get along and care about each other. It makes hanging out so much easier.

Makes my life easier.

But does it make hers easier?

Another question I can't answer, and I'm not sure I'm supposed to anymore. I think it's up to her to figure out what she wants out of this life.

Maybe Jonathon would be good for her …

"Aria," Rex drones, his sleep-ridden and raspy voice even deeper than normal, the timbre sliding over my skin and landing straight in my groin.

I bite my lip, keeping my voice low. "Yeah?" I'm not sure if he's awake or if he's checking on me again like he has throughout the morning.

I think he's still in disbelief, too.

"Would it be weird for someone to bring us breakfast in bed?" His question brings a laugh bubbling out of my lips, jostling his head against my chest and making his unshaven jaw prick into my skin.

"Rex, it's well past time for breakfast. It's almost dinnertime," I inform him, lighting up my phone to show him the time. He responds by snuggling in closer to me, his arm tightening around my stomach and his leg crossing over my thighs.

"Never too late for breakfast," he mumbles, his breath tickling my skin. The sensation makes me shiver, almost as much as his hard-on does bouncing against my thigh with his movement. I clear my throat to distract myself from his utterly sexy nakedness and opt for more questions.

"What's your favorite breakfast?" I ask, my arm gaining some feeling back, enough for me to use it to trail feather touches down his ribs. Goose bumps blossom across his skin at my touch, bringing a smile to my face.

"Chilaquiles," he answers without hesitation, the words some shit I've never heard of.

"Umm …" My brow furrows. "What the fuck is that?"

Rex snorts, which turns into a deep-as-shit chuckle I absolutely love hearing.

"It's a breakfast served in Mexico. Fried tortilla dipped in salsa or salsa verde with crème, feta, and a fried egg. No dippy eggs for me. Raw shit is gross."

Did he just call them dippy eggs?

"Okay, then." I laugh. "I was not expecting that. Here I was thinking I'd hear you say French toast over pancakes or something." I shake my head with a slight eye roll at myself for assuming this cultured and well-traveled man would prefer plain old eggs and bacon. All Rex does is look up at me without removing his cheek from me, the hair there scraping across my heart and leaving delicious red splotches behind.

Physically … And metaphorically …

Fuck, those eyes are gorgeous.

The way he's looking at me leaves me breathless, distracted, and ready to go another round in the ring of this bed. Maybe the bathroom.

I'm game with both.

My cheeks heat with the thoughts, the memories, of him fucking me until well past morning light and into a sleep deeper than anything I've ever experienced before.

Is it supposed to be that good?

I rack my brain for the moments I shared with Chip, nothing coming close to this intense, and wonder if I'd done it all wrong. I remember a lot, but most of our time together is a blur, drowned out by hospital stays and appointments. Doctors with shitty news and medications.

So many damn meds. IVs. Tubes and wires.

It's because of those things that I've not gotten close with anyone else since his death. And guilt floods me, even now.

I'd promised Chip everything and couldn't deliver.

"Babe, what's wrong?" Rex's words are laced with concern as he sits up, propped on his arm, and looks down at me.

I feel like total shit.

Tears prick my eyes, my chest tightening at how much Rex and I don't know about each other. I don't know if I can do this again. A relationship. The emotions, joy and contentment, I felt over the last few hours flee like a criminal just passed the barrier of their prison.

Still, that look in his eye causes me pause, makes my heart skip a beat, as it bears down on me in all my naked glory.

I'm exposed. More than I've ever been.

"Aria …?" His deep voice catches with nerves I can feel, palpable at such a close distance and accompanied by a furrowed brow line that makes my stomach knot.

"I—um." I don't know how to say the words I need to say, but I know that if I'm ever going to make anything work ever again, I'll need to just say it.

No one else will ever be my first love.

"You, what?" He leans down to me and caresses my face with such gentleness that the tears spill over.

"I guess it's my turn to answer some questions." A watery, half laugh spills out of me like my emotions. I try to sniffle them back, but Rex catches the tears on his fingertips and wipes them away.

"You can tell me what's going on. No judgment."

Rex does not share in my attempt at humor. Instead, he looks at me like I'm about to run away and he's wondering how he can catch me. If he *could*.

I inhale a deep and filling breath, his scent filling my nose and encouraging me to press forward. He needs to know now, not later.

"I was married," I blurt, my voice shaky as I meet his widening eyes. "High school sweethearts." I try to get the words to tumble from my lips, but the longer I take, the more I see Rex retreating. His eyes hardening, his breath coming in short spurts, as he searches my face for answers to the questions I know he's assuming.

"Babe," he breathes, then shakes his head as if catching himself. "Fuck, can I even call you that?" Rex falls back and sits on the bed next to me, his forearm propped up on his knee, effectively cutting himself off from me. "Shit, I've done some questionable shit, but never …" He clears his throat, his hands running through his hair in exasperation. "Never on purpose."

I'm messing this up. I'm a mess. I shouldn't be here.

"Rex. I was married. *Was.*" I nearly choke on the words as I, too, sit up and pull the sheets up to cover myself.

"Aria," he starts, speaking with a deep resolve, words I know are going to hurt, so I do what I can to muster my emotions and cut him off with an outstretched hand.

"*Rex.*" I demand his attention; I need him to look at me.

When he finally bites his bottom lip and flares his nostrils but swings his gaze my way, I grab his tense bicep and unload myself all over him.

"He died, Rex. I married my high school sweetheart, and he *died.*"

The fallen look I see next is one that I'm used to seeing. One I try to avoid at all costs when I meet anyone new. It's one that even my sister and best friend looked at me with for way too long, and I burst into tears when I see the pity, the pure empathy, shine across his face.

It's that look people give you when they say they're sorry for your loss, even though they have no idea what it's like. They have no idea how to be sorry enough. Or how it feels to bury your husband who was supposed to be in the prime of his fucking life. Who had promised to be there through sickness and health for me, too.

But he wasn't.

I hate the things that I think and that I feel for my past. Especially the guilt for trying to move on after five years.

To me … five years has seemed like a lifetime ago, yet just yesterday. Too long yet too short for moving on.

But it's exactly what I've been trying to do.

As Rex holds me now, absorbs my sobs and takes my burdens like they're his to carry, I no longer feel the guilt or worry about the reaction to my choice to be with him. I welcome his hold on me with arms that snake around his naked and tattooed torso. I welcome the sweet words he whispers in my ear that begin to calm my soul and bring the tears to a gentle flow instead of a whitewater rapid.

His hair sticks to my lips and blocks out the rest of the world until all falls quiet.

Rex holds me—no, he cradles me—pulling me in his lap and rocking. His hand encases my face, keeping me against his pec as he rains kisses along the top of my head.

"I'm so sorry, babe," he whispers to me. "I know that doesn't mean shit, but I can't even imagine what you went through. What you're going through now." He kisses me between words. My head, my face. My lips. "Jesus, please tell me it wasn't like two days ago." He sighs but kisses me again anyway. I roll my eyes but answer against his lips as they meet mine again.

"Five years," I whisper, meeting his eyes, searching them for the fear, for the emotion, for the reason he runs from me like most others have in the past.

"God." He exhales slowly, encasing my face in his hands. "You've carried this for five fucking years?" When I nod, he presses his forehead to mine, his lids fluttering closed. "My chest aches for you, Aria."

I … I love that he isn't asking a thousand questions about it. I also love that he isn't pushing from me like I'm damaged goods with too much baggage to carry.

He's empathetic in a good way, so much so that I feel warmth flooding in my own aching chest. I feel shit I haven't felt since Chip was taken from me. Not until Rex stumbled into my life and crooked an inked finger in my direction.

Rex admits something most others don't …

That he's unable to compare it to his own experiences. He doesn't diminish how I feel with retellings of his own losses.

Dogs, great-grandmothers …

You'd be surprised how people try to relate.

I know they mean well, mean no ill intentions. It just …

It doesn't help.

"Thank you," I whisper.

I don't want this to change or to end. The tenderness he shares with me speaks to the cracks in my soul and brings life back into me.

"That's a huge share." He grabs my hand and kisses the backs of my knuckles. "Thank you for trusting me with it." His eyes shine with emotion, connection I've been dying for since Chip got sick.

I reach up, cup his face in my hands, and bring his lips to mine. It's gentle at first, soft and sweet. The longer we stay connected, though, the more intense it feels. He presses harder into me, his tongue probing my lips, asking for access that I grant.

Rex tilts my head back and ravishes me with such fervor that I'm breathless.

With a heaving chest, he pulls back and does a once-over of my nakedness that I'd long forgotten about.

It's amazing how he undoes me, distracts me, makes me feel *full*.

"Babe." His voice is almost a groan. "I need to feed you," he breathes, the air washing over my face with his closeness. "And then I need to fuck you."

God, yes, please.

Chapter Thirty-Three

Rex

I FEED MY GIRL egg whites and fruit pieces Ian managed to find for us and deliver straight to the room at her request.

I wanted to feed her a damn burger. Fries. Burritos. Something, anything, to comfort her.

I answered the door naked while Aria giggled behind me with the comforter tight to her chest, the sound music to my ears. Which was almost as good to hear as the moans she let out as she came on my fingers not but a few moments before.

Ian paid me no mind, though. He's used to the rock star life.

Which means sometimes someone is naked.

Okay, most of the time.

Hand-fed and rehydrated, Aria lies sprawled on the bed like one of my French girls, and I sit back to admire her beauty.

"What?" She squirms under my gaze, clearly unused to being as seen as she is when she's with me. But she doesn't cover herself. Doesn't move away from me.

And I fucking *love* that.

"You're absolutely beautiful." I smirk and trail my fingertips down her side, leaving goose bumps in my wake. My cock twitches when she smiles, insatiable and hardening again. She scoots closer to me, her chest pressing into mine and her legs wrapping me up.

"So, we've checked eating off the list …" She returns my soft touches with some of her own, her hands trailing along the dragon on my back and kneading my ass.

I hiss when her nails dig into the flesh there, my cock filling despite now digging into the mattress.

"Absolutely. And I'm a man of my word." I roll us until I'm on top of her, nestled between her gorgeously soft legs, thick and ready to wrap around me.

Which she does.

Fucking perfect.

Kissing her plump lips, I prop myself on one arm over her head so that I can feel her tits with the other. Tits I have not spent nearly enough time touching, worshipping.

She purrs beneath me, those nails latching onto my shoulders and holding onto me like she might float away if she doesn't.

Or maybe she's more worried about me floating away.

The thought hurts me to my core, that people have left this goddess of a woman with feelings of inadequacy in her pain. *I* left her, too. Despite my good intentions, I hurt her.

She deserves security.

So, I kiss her with enough passion to set the room on fire. I know I can't make up for the past, but I can show her what it's like to love and be loved. Show her consistency. That I'm not going anywhere.

That's all that matters now.

My fingers tease her nipple, pulling it taut and hard as I caress her chest. I move from one tit to the other, keeping my lips sealed to hers.

Aria moans when I sweep my hand over her stomach, making my way down to where my cock sits across her soft belly. I dive down the middle of us, slipping my thumb between her swollen, wet lips and rubbing the pad against her clit. She bucks against me with a gasp, slamming my wrist up into my pelvis. I hiss at the pain but settle into the pleasure it brings her when I touch her.

My lips release hers for air and drag along her jaw to her ear.

"*Rex,*" she moans as I rotate my thumb against her, and I can't help how my cock throbs at my name on her lips.

"I want to feel you," I whisper into her ear, my voice gravelly, and she shivers out another moan for me.

"*Yes,*" Aria responds, her breath washing over the side of my face. "I need you," she groans. "I need your cock."

Yes, motherfucking, please.

I arch my hips back, lining up with her wet entrance.

With my face buried in the nape of Aria's neck, I fist the base of my cock and slip the head around her clit for friction. She moans when my ring passes over her, sending shivers across her already vibrating body.

"You ready for me?"

I already know the answer. I can feel it radiating from her like heat from the sun.

She breathes, and then she nods.

"Yes, yes, please. I need to feel you," she whispers to me.

"Anything for you, babe." I grab her hip with my free hand and slip just inside her. I groan at the heat, the pressure of her bare walls around me.

"Yes," she gasps, panting like she's already run a marathon. "More. I wanna feel all of you."

"Fuck."

My cock twitches, needy and begging for more of her, too.

Leaning back, I look at her face when I move. She bites her lip as she looks back up at me through thick lashes.

She undoes me.

My hips move forward, pressing into her with such a slow anticipation that I'm already about to cum.

Aria moans as I go deeper, gasping when I finally bottom out. My pelvis meets hers, her pussy tight around my cock, swollen from all the play we've done since she got on this bus.

I wouldn't have it any other way.

"Aria," I moan when her walls twitch around me, begging for movement, for friction. "Goddamn, baby."

I gasp when I slide out of her and slip right back in where I belong.

"Fuck," she groans, her eyes rolling and her mouth falling open, desperate for air. Her pussy pulling me deeper into her body with each thrust. "Yes …"

"Babe," I mutter. "You feel so fucking *good*." I lean down to press my forehead to hers as I thrust, keeping a slow, measured tempo.

She looks up at me, and I swear if I wasn't in love with her before, I fucking am now.

Emerald gems stare back at me with such passion and admiration it stops my heart and tingles my spine.

Her arms wrapped around my shoulders, fisting the hair at the nape of my neck.

"You're perfect, Aria." I grind my pelvis against her clit, her wetness slicking … well …

Everything.

Her legs fall to the sides of me, opening herself up even more as I bury myself inside her. She inches slowly up the bed, soft mewls and moans falling from her lips with every move I make, and that's when it dawns on me.

I've always been too afraid to go bare with anyone. Until now.

She's a first for me.

I'm raw-doggin' my girl.

"Rex," she moans into my ear when I wrap my forearm under her neck to hold us closer together, part of my weight pressing into her.

"Babe," I groan back and angle myself so that the ring through the head of my cock slides along her G-spot.

"Fuck, *yes.*" Aria wails under me and sinks her teeth into my shoulder to stifle her moans. She's close, I can tell.

So the fuck am I.

I speed my thrusting up, driving harder into her wetness, pulling a moan from my own lips.

"I've never been bare with anyone, Aria," I admit breathlessly into her ear, her teeth sunk into the sweet spot on my shoulder.

Her only response is another sound that can only be described as pure ecstasy as her pussy walls clamp around me with her orgasm.

"Yes," she screams as her nails score my back, holding me for dear life, and she cums on my cock.

"*Fuuuuck.*" It pushes me over the edge, and I make it mostly out of her before my cum shoots from me. I ride out the wave against her hip, her skin rubbing the bottom of me in all the right ways as I finish all over her lower stomach.

"Jesus, that was—" She heaves under me, breathless, but still rubbing her palms up and down my back.

"Fucking fantastic?" I finish for her with a deep rasp to my voice. I try to lean back, to lift my weight from her chest, but she's like a magnet I'm too powerless to break away from.

"Yeah, that."

I feel her nod as I turn my face to see her. She's beautifully flush, her lips swollen and parted with stars in her eyes and a slight flare to her nose.

I grin. Goofy and spent, I press my lips to hers.

"Aria"—I'm smiling, too joyous to connect my emotions to my words—"I'm not sure I got completely out of you."

I'm sighing, too content when I should be panicking.

I'm pretty sure part of my load went into her.

But she doesn't freak out like that little voice in the back of my mind is poking at me over. She doesn't panic like my brain says that I should be.

Shouldn't I be?

"I know," she whispers to me, her own contentment written all over her face. "What happens, happens, Rex."

Dear ... God. I'm in fucking love.

"We met by chance," she continues, her gaze boring into mine. "Found each other again by another chance." I stare at her in complete awe of this stunning woman who has done nothing but see me for me. As a man. A man who could be her lover, her partner, even if that involves another life.

Aria can have my balls.

Carry them in her purse, I don't care.

As long as she touches them like this all the time.

"By chance, huh?" I ask as I arch my hips back and line my cum-covered hard-on with her slick, needy pussy. I meet her eyes, wait for her answer to my silent question, and when she fucking nods for me, I slide back home.

My length penetrates her heat once again, spreading my seed all over her, in her.

"God, *fuck*." Aria's head tilts back, her eyes rolling again as I rock against her. The sight alone has my second O rushing forward, the connection driving me even closer.

I've never felt like this before. She's so goddamn perfect.

"I am so in love with you, Aria." I moan for her when she brings her eyes back to meet mine. I thrust, deep and certain, into her pussy, as if my action can drive my point deep into her body, deep into her fucking soul. "I love you."

"Oh God, Rex," she groans. "I—" I suck the words from her chest with a kiss hotter than anything I've ever felt before, and I grind my cock deeper into her.

I want more.

I want everything.

Leaning back from our kiss, I drag breath into my lungs.

The sight of her beneath me, taking me raw without any protection, sends me fucking wild with a need I've never felt before.

Keeping my cock buried in her, I pull her legs up between us so that her calves rest on my shoulders. Aria moans at the change in angle, my cock sliding into her slick wetness and going as deep as I'll ever get into her body.

"*Rex*," Aria calls out and squirms against me, increasing the friction our bodies are creating in a delicious amount of pleasure that drives down my spine into my balls.

I groan.

I'm ready.

"*Aria.*"

It's like a promise on my lips as my piercing smashes her G-spot, edging her right up to the brink of her orgasm. She grabs at me, at anything to hold her steady, as the waves crash over her.

"I love you."

Aria explodes with that sentiment, gripping my cock so tight that I shoot off my own cliff.

Right off and into the certainty of a life with my gorgeous goddess.

This time, I don't pull out of her. I thrust deep and short, keeping my cock buried inside my girl as I unload everything I have.

Even when I finish, I let her legs slide to the sides of me, but I don't pull out of her. I want my cum to stay right where the fuck it is.

She's mine.

"I know there's still a lot to figure out," I admit as I caress her flushed and smiling face. She nods in agreement, but nothing removes the glow emitting from her. "But I want this. Every bit of it."

"I want a life I can share with you, too," she whispers so quietly in the silence of this tour bus bedroom.

"Absolutely." I match her grin with mine and kiss the tip of her nose. "Anything for you." She scrunches her face up at the contact but giggles into a sigh.

"As much as I … *love* … you. And this." She nods to our still connected bodies, clearing the thickness from her voice. "You have a show, and I have work to do." Aria moves to push me off, but I return the favor by grinding my perpetually hard cock into her again.

She moans for me, and I smirk.

"I'm sorry, what were you saying?"

She sighs and brings her hips up to meet mine, pulling a groan from my lips this time.

"We have work, Rex." She smacks a kiss to my lips. "And I have a ton to tell the girls."

I roll my eyes, knowing that I'm about to be the star in their conversations, which some I feel might not be all that great, but I still can't keep the grin from spreading my lips wider than I have Aria's legs.

With one last thrust into her wet pussy to go home with, I roll off my girl and help her stand on shaky legs.

"I love you, babe," I say as I wrap my arms around her very naked body, her tits pressing into my swelling chest.

"I fucking love you, Rex."

Chapter Thirty-Four

Aria

I
T TAKES WHAT FEELS like hours of lectures on what not to post.

Or say.

Or do.

Boss man Ian sends Aurora and me on our way, but not before Rex gets ahold of me in the back office of my studio, which they just so happen to park behind, and leaves me with yet another kiss that lights my soul on fire. The kind where asses are pawed and legs are wrapped around waists.

"You're hella gross." Aurora scoffs at me as she leans over the counter, waiting for the coffee to percolate like it's a life force she can't go on without. Her eyes don't leave the brown elixir as if looking away might mean missing the secret to living forever.

"*You're* gross." It's all I've got right now as I slump into the plush chair and thank fuck it's padded.

After a night like last, I'm amazed I can walk.

I let him cum in me.

The thought permeates my brain as my phone pings with a text, and Aurora stares daggers at the machine that doesn't produce her life force fast enough.

Holy shit. I need to tell them everything.

But there's almost no time. We're *way* behind schedule, and I have to make sure that Aurora can keep her damn eyes open for the rest of the day.

"You're all vibrant and shit." My sister slumps onto the counter, mug held pathetically in hand as the machine spurts and drips, its brew taking a lifetime to produce. "Glowy and stupid," she mutters into the countertop, officially draped over the kitchenette like her life is dependent on the shit in the pot.

Ping.

"Aurora," I snap to get her attention, but she just slowly melts into the counter.

I should just say it.

"I'm so mad at you," Aurora whines, tapping the ceramic against the marble.

"I love him, Aurora," I admit on a loaded breath, quiet enough to be drowned out by the spewing coffee machine. I know it's crazy and that she might have me admitted for saying it, but I can't help that I feel the same way about Rex as she feels about her precious coffee.

Mental note: time for a new one of those.

It's not in the budget, but I can make do. Aurora deserves to get her coffee.

"I *know*," she sighs. "You're gonna run off into the sunset with him now, and all I get is to marry this broke-ass coffee machine." She scoffs and steals the pot from the machine while it attempts to pause its brewing but drips away into a sizzle on the hotplate beneath.

"Hey, I'm not going anywhere." I adjust my hips on the seat to ease the tension building in my aching muscles and shake my head.

I need a bath and a nap.

"We were supposed to celebrate *us*." She casts stones at me with her words as she pours her brown life force into the mug and sips like it doesn't burn the holy shit out of her.

No, I think she's used to the burn. The coffee is far from the pain in this room.

"We were supposed to do this life together. Honor *our* accomplishments," she emphasizes, spinning to raise an eyebrow at me. "Not some *man's*."

My jaw drops as pain sears across my heart.

"Aurora," I chastise, her words bringing me to my feet. "What the hell?"

She downs her mug and steals the carafe again without looking at me. The coffee drips from the spigot, sizzling away into mist on the base of the machine. It's the only sound in the room other than the speeding heart pounding in my ears, and my poor, old, overthinking mind starts to whirl. The room spins with Aurora as she takes to her heels and hair flips her way out into the studio.

The silence in her wake is deafening.

Even the stupid coffee pot has stopped sputtering shit in my direction, leaving me breathless and pained.

Am I making a mistake?

My ass meets the padding again, my head in my hands, tears threatening to spill over my eyes.

Ping.

The stupid phone breaks the silence with what feels like an explosion, demanding I check it.

Anything to get my mind off my grumpy-ass sister.

And her words that are not untrue.

Ping.

I address my phone with more attitude than it deserves, smacking my lips at its presence in my hand when it begins ringing.

My heart melts a little bit at the name that flashes across the screen

SexyMane: Incoming video call.

I slide my thumb over the device to answer the call and startle myself when my own face populates the screen.

Shit. I didn't realize it was video.

I sniffle and smile as Rex's gorgeous curls fill my screen. He's beaming at me, a smile wider than anything I've ever seen, and I'm grateful to see it right now.

"Hey, babe."

His words are like a salve to the aches in my heart and my body. His voice like a warm blanket wrapping me up and hugging me tight.

"Aurora's mad at me," I blurt without greeting him, my aching heart bleeding through my love for him.

"What?" Rex's brow furrows, his smile fading. "Why is she mad at you?" His concern softens his deep voice as it reverberates over the small phone speaker.

I shrug, recite her words to me, and pout into the phone.

I don't like that she's mad at me. I don't like not knowing where Cedar is on this, either. All of which I share with Rex as more tears prick my eyes and spill over.

"I'm sorry," he says into the phone, his eyes darting to the knock I hear over the line. "Two minutes," he calls out to whoever is bothering him, but I catch the door opening anyway.

Slamming open, actually.

"Too fucking bad, turdnado." Mac's voice carries over the line like a damn wrecking ball, making me wince and pull the phone away from my face. Noise fills the void, then cuts off with another slam of the door. "Is that her? Already, man?"

"Fuck you," Rex tells his brother, his eyes staring over the camera. "I wanted to share with her, but she's having a thing." I scoff and roll my teary eyes, which I try to dry with the back of my hand.

The knowledge that everything about me is going to be shared with Rex's damn twin for the rest of my life settles into my chest.

The rest of my life ...

"What?" The phone jostles, the screen whipping back and forth. "A thing?" Mac's face fills the screen, albeit violently shaking with what I can only imagine is Rex attempting to take the phone back.

The screen jerks, and the full length of Mac's arm becomes visible as he holds the thing out of Rex's reach.

I laugh at the exchange when Mac bends to keep Rex back, my response causing Mac to look over the thing at his brother.

"She's laughing. Looks okay to me." He brings the phone back to his face, giving me a close-up of his eye that pulls more laughter from me.

"Fuck off, eggnog," Rex curses his brother, and there's more movement, but Mac's eye stays steady on the screen. "Stop making my girl laugh."

"*Ow.*"

I giggle, my free hand coming up to cover my mouth, pretending not to swipe away tears from my chin.

"Hm." Mac backs off the screen, bringing back his whole face. "There *is* evidence of waterworks. What's up, baby girl?" Mac's brow furrows in concern as his eyes search mine.

"*Bro.*" I can feel Rex seethe somewhere in the background, his chastising tone aimed at his unreceptive brother.

And because I know that the twin will find out anyway, I share what happened with him, too.

"Hmmm." He runs a rough hand down his even rougher jaw. "I know Jon was pissed, too," Mac comments and looks at his brother over the phone. I watch as unspoken words pass between the two over Mac's face, a communication coupled with a flexed jaw and squinted eyes.

"Babe." Rex's face squeezes into the frame along with his brother, the two nearly cheek to cheek.

I'm not blind. The love and concern and emotion on their faces speaks volumes to my aching chest.

That's ... that's all for me.

So I take a screenshot of the two of them.

"Just give her some time," Rex soothes.

"And she'll come around," Mac adds, equally as comforting.

"A lot has happened in the last few hours," Rex continues, his eyes searching mine in the phone.

"Yeah," Mac starts, "you went from hating Bam Bam here"—he eyes his brother, who keeps watching me—"to banging him."

There's a fist. That's all I catch as the phone skitters onto the floor, and the ceiling comes into view.

Scuffling, thudding, and grunting echoes over the line, shit I can't see but hear.

"Watch your fucking mouth." Rex lays down the law, his face filling the phone again as he picks me up off the floor, flared nostrils filling the screen.

"Fuck you, Bam Bam."

"Rex," I drawl. "He's not wrong." I shake my head at the accuracy of his words and wonder how I would feel if I were in my sister's shoes.

Or Cedar's.

I'd be pissed, too.

Actually ... I'd be worried. Upset. Concerned for them.

And it would come out like anger.

Realization hits me as I stare into Rex's eyes. His temper is gone and replaced with his love for me as he stares right back.

"You deserve more respect than that." Rex runs a hand through his tousled hair to push it back from his face, making it look another level of sexy messy.

"You didn't hurt him, did you?" I ask, but Rex shrugs and flips the screen to show Mac flipping him off from the floor of the dressing room.

He's fine.

"She cares about me, bro. She knows I mean no disrespect."

Rex flips the cam back to his face in time for me to catch his eye roll.

"Seriously, though," Rex amends, bringing the conversation back. "Give her some time, and she'll come around. Not gonna lie, I'd be upset if it were Mac. I wouldn't trust me either."

There's an awkward clearing of the throat. Rex looks over the phone, and more unspoken shit is communicated between the brothers that leaves Rex with an empathetic look on his face.

I don't know how to decipher it, and I'm about to ask when another knock sounds on their side of the phone.

"Five-minute warning, boys." Another male voice booms into the space, Rex nodding to the owner of the deep timbre.

"Thanks, Tob."

The door slams closed, and Rex looks back to me. "I gotta go, babe." He smiles gently for me, contagious and adorable.

"He'll sing of you," I hear Mac call, and I return the smile I see lighting up my screen.

"I will. And the crowd will love you as much as I do." Rex winks.

He fucking *winks*.

Why is that hot? Since when do I like that?

Because it's Rex. That's why.

"I love you, too, *Rexy*."

He chuckles and shakes his head at me. "Why do I love that name when you say it?"

I laugh and blow a kiss that he catches and smears across his face like a totally adorable weirdo.

"Call soon," I demand.

"Of course."

We end the call with shared smiles that only kinda make me wanna puke from how damn cute it is, while the voice in the back of my mind is worried that I'll watch him disappear again.

He's not going anywhere.

I breathe in the resolve I begin to feel.

Rex and Mac are right. I need to give Aurora some space to learn and absorb the newness that I'm not even used to yet.

Is this even real?

There's still so much to figure out.

But right now? All I have to do is show up for myself and my studio and my sister.

Which I'm officially late for.

Crap.

Chapter Thirty-Five

Rex

Life on the road used to be a blast.

Meeting fans, new and old, who lived for As Above as we lived for them.

The parties, the perks.

The girls, the drugs, the booze.

Hearing our songs blaring from radios, sung back to us by the tens of thousands in venues bigger than football stadiums.

VIP treatment at well-established businesses. Clubs, bars, restaurants.

You name it.

Seeing new cities, some familiar states. Traveling to places I didn't even know existed.

Watching as my brothers live a life full of mischief and fun. Complete disregard for normal, for rules.

Creating art to share with the world.

It doesn't seem so big, the world, when you're trying to share your experiences. Finding others to make us feel less alone or odd.

Odd.

The word bounces around in my mind, muddling the things I used to enjoy about being on the road.

Funny how the meaning changes when your eyes open to all the things you didn't know you were sleeping on.

Now?

I sit with a bent leg and an elbow propped on my knee as I lean against the wall and stare out at the passing landscape. There's a bottle I've barely touched held steady between me and the back of the seat.

Deep greens fly by and bleed into dark skies and asphalt roads as we travel down a lesser-known path to our next destination. A trip that takes me farther away from my girl and leaves funky shit weighing down my chest.

Odd.

The feeling has made a home deep in my chest since the night we left Aria's hometown.

We called, texted, videoed throughout the day when she wasn't busy trying to mend her relationship with her sister and best friend, and open a fucking studio all on her own. Except every time we hung up, I had to fight the urge to hijack this bus and turn us around to go back home.

Her home. Not mine.

So, I lean into the side of the bus with my notepad in my lap and hope that lyrics come to me.

Instead, my mind wanders to everything else.

That As Above has a contract to keep, a schedule to follow, and at the end of this trek is a fucking award for Fin. Which he deserves more than anyone.

How my girl is fighting with the women she calls family and running a business of her own.

She's disappointed that I'm gone even though she won't admit it. I know that.

Just like I am.

I should be writing more songs for the band to use without me when I step back, prepping for them to find the next lead singer for the band. Leaving them with enough material to last while I disappear into the night with my girl.

She might need me, and I'm not there.

That last one is like a rock sunk deep in my gut, leaving me breathless more often than not as the miles add up between us.

I miss her.

I send her another text, knowing that the last two have gone unanswered thanks to her busy schedule and definitely not helped by the time difference.

I'm officially on the other side of the country from her, and it's already late as balls here.

I can't sleep. I tried that remedy. There's only so much shut-eye you can catch on a moving bus with a bunch of motherfuckers.

Those jerks are loud as hell.

The amount of whiskey and women that boarded this bus in the past is something I've become ashamed to witness.

Keeping groupies on board for the sheer pleasure of it.

The drugs that laced my brothers' veins to keep them up or keep them down, whichever they chose for the night. The alcohol causing too many slurred words and fist fights.

It all feels odd now.

Wrong almost, as I watch Toby make out with a girl he met at the last show over six hours away from where we are now. It's the second one today.

I don't even know her name.

I've never known their names. That's Ian's job.

Or to see Mac with a joint permanently hanging from his lips, his perpetually reddened and baggy eyes I never noticed before.

That's cuz it's new.

The musky smell permeates the tour bus, leaving us all with a contact high of sorts. Something I used to not give a shit about, but for some reason, it's really getting to me tonight.

Drugs were never my forte. Too many variables in kinds and where you got it from.

It was much easier to send Ian to the local liquor store and pick up a bottle of something smooth that went down easily. A bottle of which is wedged between me and the seat cushion now to keep from sloshing all over the floor of the bus.

Several swigs are missing from the amber, but it doesn't hold my attention anymore like I thought it might.

No, the only two things I give a fuck about are my family, which includes my girl, and my songwriting.

There's one in particular who's got my attention more than anyone else. When his eyes meet mine, I feel pain sear across my chest.

I've been so focused on my shit that I haven't noticed his.

He looks at me now like he's haunted.

An orange glow lights up his darkened features as he inhales off the joint still lingering on his lips. He holds my gaze with sunken eyes, telling me without saying a single word as he blows smoke out of the side of his mouth.

And when his eyes sweep the bus, landing on one of the guys from Sentry, the feeling sinks in my gut.

I know exactly what's going on with my twin.

He's in love.

His face, however, portrays anything but rainbows when his uncharacteristically flat eyes come back to me, then shoot to the floor. A gloved hand rests on his heart, the heel kneading into the muscle there in hopes of easing some of the ache.

He's in pain.

I drop my bare feet to the floor and ditch the bottle next to Toby, who accepts it without looking, drinking without removing his eyes from the chest of the chick in his lap.

I head to the back, tucking my notebook under my arm, and almost regret my decision when I flick on the lights, illuminating the very bed I made love to Aria on, which takes up most of the room.

I miss her even more.

Just as I flop down on the soft mattress, Mac's frame fills the doorway. His shoulders are slumped, his eyes are red and puffy, his whole demeanor is way off.

I don't like this.

My phone finally pings in my pocket, but I don't take my eyes off my brother.

Mac quietly shuts the door behind him but doesn't sit.

Instead, he leans back against the panel and plucks the roach from his lips, his head falling back with a thunk I feel in my own skull.

"I fucked up, bro." His words are aimed at the ceiling that rain down on me like anvils from the sky.

To anyone else, he looks normal.

Mac's signature bandana is wrapped around his forehead—it's yellow today—his much shorter sandy curls falling out of the top but into his eyes. A muscle shirt covers most of his chest, black shorts hanging from his waist.

What I see, though, is the downturn of his normally grinning face. I see the weight pushing his shoulders down and making him seem shorter. His chest, normally proud and full, is sunk into his body like it would much rather spend time with his spine than out in the open.

"What happened." It's a demand more than a question as I rub my palm across my own breastbone in order to ease the ache burrowing its way into my organs.

Mac just shakes his head, returning the joint to his mouth for an inhale, and slides down the door to sink into the floor of the bus. Knees to his chest as he exhales the smoke, he wraps his arms around himself, his eyes refusing to open and fucking look at me.

"Macaroni," I try. "Talk to me."

The heel of his palms dig into his eyes and rub, the roach dangerously close to burning the fingers it's pinched between or setting his goddamn hair on fire.

I sit for a moment. Allow my brother the space to feel without judgment and watch closely as the ember burns down enough that I'm certain it's heating up his skin.

Licking my fingers, I steal the thing from him and put it out with spit. I roll it to make sure it's not burning anymore, then flick it onto the floor, where I know one of us will clean up later.

That's when my twin's chest collapses, and tight sobs squeeze out from his thinly pressed lips.

"I fucked way the hell up, Rex," Mac tells me through a tear-streaked face that finally swings my way.

I squeeze onto the floor beside him, the small room not leaving much space down here, and wrap up my usually levelheaded brother in a sideways hug.

The calm one. The *I won't let the water around me in to sink me* one.

The one who doesn't panic when crowds rush us or when security slips.

He sobs quietly into my chest, his body shaking, his hands fisting my shirt.

"I'm sure it's not that bad, Mac."

I try to soothe him, but the shaking doesn't stop. We sit still for a while, long enough for me to lose track of time and my phone to ping again.

"You should answer her." Mac leans back from me and sniffles, using the back of his hand to wipe at his nose.

"She'll understand, bro." I don't move to get up and get the phone from the bed, so he does. Mac snatches the thing and drops it into my lap and flops back down beside me on the floor.

I look at him, trying to gauge him, he rolls his red eyes and steals the phone back to open the message himself.

"You might not wanna do that," I warn, but he's already got the thing open, eyes darting back and forth as he reads the screen. "If you see a nude, it's your own fault."

He only scoffs at my attempt at humor and turns the screen to face me.

"She misses your cock more."

He's monotone when he recites the message out loud, and I burst into laughter.

"Told ya." I was trying for fun when I sent it to her, something to make her blush and smile so that when I called her later, seeing her reaction would lighten my dark-as-hell mood.

It worked sooner than anticipated.

A ghost of a smile tips Mac's lips as he brings the phone back to his face and types something to her. "You could just text her yourself."

I try to snatch the phone from him, but he manages to evade my grasp.

"Don't want security in my phone," he speaks as he types, then locks the thing and throws it back onto the bed.

It's worth being able to talk to her. Even if all of Sentry has to see the message. Make sure it's safe for her and for the band.

"So what's going on, bro?" Wrapping an arm around his shoulder, I tuck him back in. He resists at first but leans in and rests his head on my shoulder.

"I fucked up," he repeats with a hoarse, hushed tone.

"I heard that part." I jostle him a bit, trying to get him to open up. "C'mon, man. You have been with me at my worst. I saw the look." I meet his gaze and ask the real question I need the answer to. "Who is he?"

Because I swear if he hurt my brother for the sake of fame or some sick gain from someone famous, I'll have him take a swim.

I'm sure my twin can feel my afterthought that I dare not speak, but he doesn't bring it up. Only shakes his head with watery eyes that he diverts back to the floor where his hands pick at his nails.

"Who do you want there with you when the world comes crashing down?" Mac whispers the lyrics into the room, his tears sliding down his face and splatting on my leg.

It's almost like code. His way of telling me that he's right where I was not that long ago.

"What'd he do?" I ask my brother, stern and demanding.

I need to know. Cuz that motherfucker is going to lose something tonight.

And the severity will depend solely on what my brother says next.

"I messed up, bro," he chokes on the emotion, balls his fists against the ache I feel in his chest.

"Mac …"

"I fell for a straight man."

My head swims. Heart falls. My gut wrenches up so badly that I'm certain I'll need medical assistance to untangle it.

I think my phone pings again, but I can't hear it over the pressure building in me. The buzzing in my ears.

"What."

It comes out harsher than I mean, but I can't help how protective I feel for my brother in this moment. Or how I'm already planning this guy's demise.

Did he lead Mac on?

It's a requirement that security knows Mac's gay.

And they have to be okay with that.

So why did the bodyguard let my brother get so close?

I have so many questions I feel like I need immediate answers to, but I cap my bullshit when Mac turns into me and fucking full-on sobs.

"I thought, maybe …" He sucks in a breath that heaves right back out of him. "I don't fucking know, I just … It happened, and I-I don't *know*—"

I hold my brother, even as my chest splits in two and his heart bleeds out onto the floor.

"Macaroni …"

"I straight up fell in love with someone I can't have. He's fucking straight."

Chapter Thirty-Six

Aria

CEDAR HAS MANAGED TO evade me for way too long.

It's been weeks of pure tension from the woman I have called my sister for years, my best friend for longer than that.

Aurora is talking to me, but I can feel the strain from her every time my phone rings.

The studio is full of clients for my sister and walk-ins looking for a unique piece.

It's also been equipped with a round-the-clock guard supplied by the security agency that Rex uses, so a scary-looking stranger is perched at my door more often than not.

We're booked weeks out still, and my website has blown up.

My hands ache from all the alterations, but it's been worth it for every smile that walks out of this building and every positive review online.

Still, I miss Rex.

He's been virtually by my side for the whole deal whenever he's not singing on stage or practicing. Sending so many reminders of how much he loves me, asking if I've remembered to eat when I've been particularly busy and tend to forget.

The only thing that would make it better is him physically here.

I know I can't ask that. I'm sure there are people and things riding on this tour, so I just have to deal with him being gone for now.

He'll be home soon.

Except we don't share a home.

More shit to figure out ... which I don't have time to overthink right now.

My phone pings with a response from him as I stalk my happy ass—that isn't all that fucking happy—over to the tenant next door.

Aurora is hot on my heels as I slam the door open to the tattoo parlor and walk right past the dropped jaw of the e-girl at the front desk.

Seems fitting ...

I stalk across the open floor plan and pass several occupied chairs, but I don't care. Not even about the chick with her cooch hanging out in the open air while she gets more ink in her bathing suit area.

Cedar is in my sights, and we need to have a little *chat* about her being absent lately.

I'm tired of the bullshit act. Tired of her avoidance.

"Seriously?" I challenge as I come right up to Cedar as she focuses on the ink and tools on her workbench. She doesn't meet my eyes in the mirror but glances at Aurora instead.

"What."

It's not a question.

Like I'm just an annoyance to her, she keeps working on the shit in front of her.

"You get to ghost me? That's how this shit is going to go?"

Aurora tries to grab my arm, but I yank from her and bump into Cedar. She whips around with a sneer aimed right at me, pieces of a tattoo machine strangled in her threatening fist.

"This ain't about you. Not every fucking thing is," Cedar growls at me like an animal, her eyes darting to Aurora for a split second only for her to turn back around like I'm not still there.

"What the fuck is going on with you two?" I step back and bring both of them into my sights, my anger speeding my heart and seething from me.

"I have a client." Cedar is even-keeled in her dismissal.

"Don't mind me, ladies." The burly guy says from her chair. "I love a good catfight." The fucker has the balls to actually wink at me when I meet his eyes.

I roll mine.

What a douche.

"C ..." I run my hand through my hair, something I've seen Rex do a million times, and try to breathe through the frustration.

It doesn't work this time.

I've been the levelheaded one for far too long. I've been the steady one, the safe one. Giving them their space to be okay with the pretty damn good hand life has dealt us.

Fuck it.

"You both are *assholes*." I point an accusatory finger from my sister to my best friend. "It's fucking funny how you two can have your shit, your moods, but the second I get something good going, you *both* turn on me like I'm heading for the hills. Like I'm not even here." I suck in a breath when Burly's shocked look catches my attention, then darts to Cedar's back, but I don't stop. "I wouldn't even be with him if it weren't for you two." I point to my sister and drive the nail in the coffin of my relationship with both of them. "Why can't you let me enjoy this? Why can't you be happy for me? I thought that's what you wanted."

I spin on my thrift shop heels, dropping my venomous words to the floor behind me, whip my hair in their faces, and leave every dropped jaw in my dust.

Just for good measure, I flip off the goth behind the receptionist's desk, slamming my way out into the fresh air of freedom.

I've tried to call movie nights with them.

Brought in dinners and snacks, only for Aurora to snag then run and Cedar to not even show her face.

I hand out business cards for both of them, run their damn websites in what little free time I have.

If they want in this life with me, they're going to have to make some strides to fucking meet me.

I have a man to love, a shop to run.

A life to live.

As I blow past pedestrians on the sidewalk, I whip my phone out and open the text app.

Fingers flying over the screen, I type a message to Rex, my ass meeting the glass of my shop door, only for it to disappear and for me to nearly fall backward.

"My bad."

A calloused hand on my bicep steadies me on my feet, and I look up to meet a set of familiar eyes.

"I thought I'd get it in time," Jonathon says.

"Shit." It's off my lips before I can catch it. "Draw the short stick this week?" I stare up and wonder how pissed my sister is going to be.

"You could call it that," he says with a slight smile as he returns to his perch near the front door. "Maybe I'm just a glutton."

"Clearly," I say, nodding. I press send on the message to Rex and shake my head for Jonathon. "She's in a shit mood, too. My fault." I raise a hand with a mocked hiss.

"Think she'll ever get over it?" Jonathon cocks a knowing eyebrow at me.

Maybe there's more there than I thought.

"I couldn't fucking tell ya, Jonathon. She's always pissed about something these days." I shrug and glance at my phone when it pings for an alert.

The socials are going nuts again.

"Right," he affirms, his attention going back to the front window, out of which he scans the street and sidewalks.

Security shit I'm still not used to.

I've seen the look a thousand times. Sometimes I wonder, terrifyingly so, if someone was actually out there, preparing to take my head for sleeping with their beloved rock star.

It's intimidating as hell to have a bulky-looking muscleman stationed like a bouncer at my store.

Recently, though, I've become accustomed to them being here around the clock.

Someone is here when I come down in the morning.

Someone else relieves them around noon, and the next guy comes in around midnight.

It's become a sort of comfort. Like a piece of Rex is here despite the distance.

I know it's crazy, but they wouldn't be here if it weren't for him.

"Good luck." I nod to the storm brewing as she waltzes by the window, heading for the front door poor Jon is guarding.

"Thanks," he says, almost defeated, as I disappear into the back to read through some of the comments online. I don't want to be present for that shit show, but at least Aurora has twenty minutes to get her panties untwisted for her next appointment.

Sinking into my cushy office chair, I slide a stack of designs to the side and power up my laptop when my phone rings.

Music blasts from the speaker the second I slide the answer button across the screen, and I wince at the noise.

"Baby?" Rex shouts into the phone. "Can you hear me?"

As Above's number one hit plays over the speaker, Rex's voice filling my chest and settling in to warm my heart.

"Yes," I answer. "And a million other things." I chuckle as I drop the volume and tuck the thing between my shoulder and my head.

"Hang on. It's too fucking loud," he shouts, a slam echoing across the line, the music becoming muted.

"Aw, I like that song," I tease.

"Yeah?" He chuckles, then accompanies the recorded version of himself and sings the next few lines to me.

I love it when he does that.

"Nailed it," I say when he stops singing and lets the music take back over.

"Thanks." He snickers. "*Anyway.* I didn't call just to sing to you. I will if you want, though." My smile splits open my face and my mood.

"Of course you would." I suck in a breath like a weight has lifted from me.

It feels good to feel good.

"I miss you. Like fucking crazy."

I flop back into my chair and let out a sigh. "Miss you, too, Rex." My words are soft but still manage to pull a chuckle from him. "How was the show?"

"Well," he starts, his scoff blowing across the speaker and causing static. "It was great for a rock show. Not so good for me. Or Toby." He snickers.

"What's that supposed to mean?" My brow furrows at his response, but the line goes dead, and almost as soon as I look at the thing to see the call ended, a video call begs for my answer.

I accept.

And what shows on my screen is not at all what I was expecting to see, making my eyes flare wide.

Rex already has his hair pulled up, his face filling the screen. But it's not the hair that catches my attention.

It's the black eye forming—wait, both eyes are purpling—and the crusted blood around the edges of Rex's nostrils.

"What the fuck?" My eyes are wide, my free hand to my mouth.

"Good news is I get the weekend off. Bad news is that my fall is viral right now." He's grinning when I feel like he shouldn't be, considering the hint of red coating his normally white teeth.

"Rex," I sigh and prop the phone up so I can search on my computer.

Within seconds of hitting enter, my screen is filled with hundreds of videos of Rex Thompson taking a nosedive off the stage.

Memes have already begun to fly, parody videos mixing in with real-life accounts. All of which I spin the phone to show him.

"I know." He snickers again but scrunches up his face as if the action hurts him. "I tripped over a cord I exposed while I was jumping around like an asshat and smashed my face. Ain't it pretty, babe?"

I roll my eyes, and he laughs.

"You're gorgeous," I say and shake my head at his carelessness replaying on my screen. "So graceful. You know you're supposed to at least *try* to catch yourself?"

"I did." He smirks. "Just with my face."

I laugh, his gaiety contagious across the phone screen.

"So you mentioned the weekend off?" I ask, and I'm met with an enthusiastic nod before the words finish leaving my mouth.

"Yep. Ian's getting the jet ready right now. I'm coming home, baby." He flips his screen and shows an empty airport terminal and a lone suitcase.

"Jesus, that was quick."

"You were pretty engrossed in those videos." Rex's smile fills the screen again, and I can't help the excitement that bubbles up from the depths of my soul and splits my face wide open. I even do a little happy jiggle.

"You're coming home for the whole weekend?" He nods, the corner of his lip pulled up in a sexy half smile. I squeal and hug the phone to my chest.

"Babe …" Rex's voice vibrates off my ribcage, muffled by the fabric of my top. I pull the thing back to see a glint in his eye and his brows bouncing. "Do that again, just without the shirt."

"You perv." I giggle, my flush reaching my cheeks.

"I'll get you naked on screen eventually," he promises despite my shaking head. "And you'll be screaming my name." He winks into the camera, the action pooling wetness between my legs.

"When you get here," I tease back, my ears on fire either from embarrassment or arousal, I'm not entirely sure. Probably both.

"*Ian*," Rex barks, the screen jostling with his sudden movement. "Ian, we must go now."

"What's your deal?" I hear Ian's gruff voice in the distance.

He always sounds like he's over Rex's shit, and it's hilarious, considering he's mild compared to how I've seen Mac act.

"She's gonna—"

"You better not tell him that—" I cut him off, yelling into the mic with as much fire as I feel burning at my face.

"But"—Rex's gaze meets mine—"how else will he understand how serious it is to leave right *now*."

"Right now? When the fucking plane has no fuel yet, you twit? Go sit your ass down." Ian's stern comments remind me of a dad who's had enough shit for today, and it has me shaking my head.

"Dad's mad," Rex confirms with a laugh and settles back into a seat closer to the gate.

"Don't do that. It's weird," Ian chastises, Rex's eyes looking over the phone at his bodyguard.

"You're weird," Rex refutes but brings his attention back to me. "I'm coming home soon." He smiles for me, bright and full of love.

"You'll stay with me?" I ask, hope surging in my chest.

Not only would I have Rex in my bed, but maybe ... maybe the girls could see how good Rex really is, as a person and a partner. Maybe they could get to know him and understand why I love him.

They don't even have to love him back. They just need to accept that I do.

"Absolutely." He's resolute in his answer. "Every second you'll have me, babe."

"I love you," I breathe into the phone.

"I fucking love you."

Chapter Thirty-Seven

Rex

The airport sucks.

It takes forever to get anywhere, and there are always too many people inhibiting forward progress.

Paparazzi hold us up as they demand my attention and try desperately to snap pics of my bruised face, asking questions like they didn't see all the videos online.

I'm surrounded by security, but it doesn't stop the assault of questions and bodies.

"Why are you leaving?"

"Did your brother hit you?"

"Are you in a fight with Toby?"

"Did you knock up someone else's girl?"

"Who did you piss off? Is there a band feud going on?"

Ian's front is pressed to my back with way more intimacy than I'd prefer to have with my bodyguard, his arms around me to ward off headshots and his hands firmly grasping the shoulders of the guard in front of me.

He's in the same position as me, intimately familiar with how my front feels pressed into his back.

Poor bastard.

However, he's doing a decent job of making a path for us, including pushing people to the side, some of whom flop onto the ground like he's Hulk smashing his way through this shit.

Never mind the fact that I want to ring his neck.

The entire band decided to come back with me since we had to cancel the shows for this weekend.

I'm under strict orders to rest due to too many past concussions.

Even though I don't have one now.

Which means that Lugh is with Mac and the others as they attempt to leave the same airport from another extraction point while we push through this bullshit at the front where people expect you to leave the airport.

Forever the distraction.

Since I held my sobbing twin, I've learned a thing or two about the man in front of me.

Jordan Kauffman.

The guard newest to Sentry Security, who only has a job as long as Mac continues to vouch for him.

He volunteered for this particular situation, which I'm convinced is a way to get away from my twin, considering the two of them have been practically inseparable since Jordan joined our crew.

He's known since he accepted the position that my brother is gay. There's no way he doesn't know.

"Rex. Look here."

I tuck my shoulders and press my nose to Jordan's shoulder, effectively hiding my face.

A pap falls into Jordan's front, staggering us back and putting a painful amount of pressure on my aching nose.

"*Fuck,*" I curse, then regain my footing thanks to Ian's wall of a chest pressing me forward.

"Sorry, boss," Jordan says over his shoulder.

"Do better or don't volunteer." My words are harsh and direct to his ear. So much so that he clamps his mouth shut, gives a short nod, and presses onward.

We clear the rest of the sidewalk to the waiting car in half the time it took to get through the handsy press, and I'm shoved into the back seat alone.

Jordan's back slams into the glass as he pushes at people to keep them away from the car.

Ian slips into the passenger seat and clips his belt in place.

Fists tap on the car, a desperate attempt to get my attention for a money shot.

"Let's go." Ian speaks to the driver, someone I've not met before.

I pull out my phone as we lap three streets over from Aria's for the fifth time to make sure there's no tail and type up a message.

Me: Be there in a few, babe.

There's a response before I can even lock the phone.

Aria: Fuck, yes.

My lips stretch wide.

Me: You'll definitely be saying that out loud.

Aria: The girls are here.

Me: I'll be on my best behavior. Maybe.

Aria: I want them to accept us, believe that this is real.

> *Aria: You are real, right?*

> *Me: I'll show you real, baby*

My dick thickens behind my zipper.

"Just up here," Ian instructs the guy behind the wheel, who turns and comes to a slow stop at the back entrance of Aria's studio.

I'm out of the car and throwing open the door before Ian can even unclip his belt and clear the area.

Too slow.

"*Babe*," I call down the long hallway, sprinting toward the light I see in the studio at the end. There's a soft glow to the room I emerge in, the light even more muted against the brick walls. "Aria."

I hear the squeal before I feel the impact, catch the legs that wrap around my waist and relish the kisses that rain down on my face.

Her warmth almost feels unreal, dreamlike, as I cup Aria's ass with one hand for support and her face with the other. Our lips crash in a feverish kiss that sets my blood on fire and wakes up my sleeping cock.

Teeth clang together, and tongues battle in desperation to be closer. To make up for all the missed opportunities.

Busted lip and broken nose be damned; I feel no pain now that I'm with her.

My hand moves from her jaw to the base of her neck, where I grab a fistful of her hair and pull until I can get her neck between my teeth.

I inhale deeply, taking in her tropical scent, and I'm transported to the ocean with her beside me, coconut cocktails in hands as I make love to her on the beach.

"Rex," she moans softly as she rubs her hips against my hard cock.

"Goddamn, I missed you," I groan into her flesh.

"Fuck, I missed you."

"Ahem."

It's quiet at first, but when I pull my face away from Aria's flesh, I see nothing but daggers staring back at me.

"Hey," I start as I slide Aria's body down mine until her feet hit the floor, but her body is tucked into mine. I wrap an arm around her shoulders and face the two most important ladies in my girl's life. "Cedar, it's good to see you again. Aurora."

"You don't deserve her." It's Cedar who speaks first, her raging gaze focused on me.

"Cedar—" Aria tries to interject.

"Not even a little bit," Aurora confirms, as if one angry sister isn't enough.

As if Cedar's words aren't loud enough.

"You're right." I wet my drying lips, the bottom one still aching, and I spare a glance at a shaking Aria under my arm. "I don't deserve someone as perfect as Aria, but for some reason, she chose to forgive me." I tear away from Aria's shining eyes and meet the strong gazes of the women that love her. "And as long as she does, I'm going to do everything I can to *be* deserving."

"What a damn *romantic*," Aurora mocks with rolled eyes, acid in her words, and a shake of the head.

"Jesus," someone mutters from the front of the shop. A voice I've heard and know well.

Jonathon.

"You left her heartbroken, doubting herself all over again, when you just walked away. What makes us believe you won't do that again?"

Drawing in a deep breath of tropical paradise, I run a thumb along Aria's shoulder when she grips the shirt covering my lower back. "I can't make you believe anything you don't want to, Aurora." I ignore the way my chest pings with regret at the mention of leaving Aria at that hotel. "But I don't plan on doing *anything* to hurt your sister. Not ever again."

My girl turns into me, her hand finding the shirt covering my abs, her gaze heating up the side of my face.

"Fine." Cedar stuns the room with her words, Aurora spinning to her with her jaw on the tile beneath us.

Aria fists the fabric covering my abdomen. "Cedar?" Aria questions, stepping in front of me like shit might go to blows, and *I'm* the one who needs protecting.

"Prove it. Prove that you choose her." Cedar's steadfast, unmoving. Her eyes challenge me, refusing to leave mine as she crosses her arms over her chest. "You'll do anything to prove it, right?"

"Name it," I agree, my own steadiness driving my words, my actions.

My girl needs her family for when I'm not here. They need to get on board with us.

Whatever it takes.

"Then you'll let me ink you."

It's a challenge. Enough of one that Cedar squares her shoulders against Aurora's shaking assault. "Why would you put your art on this asshole?"

"Cedar, stop." Aria steps up to Cedar, hands to her biceps, but she doesn't remove her striking blue eyes from me.

"When?" I ask, meeting her stare with my own, accepting her challenge proudly, knowing that I'll be at a complete disadvantage once I get in Cedar's chair.

I don't know her work, if she's heavy handed, or what she's going to permanently ink in my skin.

Maybe she's trying for a dick on my face.

"No, *Rex*." Aria is back at my chest, tapping at my pec.

"Right now." Cedar tilts her head, her grin spreading across her face like a demon who's just got their last soul contract needed to retire.

"Nothing on the face."

We're walking to the front of the shop before Aria can protest more, but it doesn't stop Aurora from pulling at Cedar's elbow.

"Stop. Don't give him your art, C."

"Aurora." Cedar halts at the glass door and grabs Aurora's shoulders. "You *have* to stop. I know exactly what I'm doing."

Without another word, they push out into the night air and disappear.

"Rex, you don't have to appease her." Aria's hands are on my stomach, pulling my attention back to her beautifully lined eyes and cute nose.

"I know. But if it's going to make her feel better, fix this rift of shit between you guys, then I'm okay with it." I wrap Aria up and slip out into the night air with her, passing Jon with a nod of acknowledgment, to find the new guy perched across the street on watch. "Besides." I lean down to whisper in Aria's ear. "The faster I can get this over with, the faster I can be inside you."

She squeaks, heat radiating from her as we step into the tattoo parlor next door.

It's after hours, so the shop is dark except for the light at Cedar's chair in the back corner of the open floor.

Artwork adorns every inch of the walls, ranging styles and colors over toned designs.

Canvases hang over each chair we pass as if the artist there gets a small part of the space to highlight some of their work.

The ceilings are tall, painted black to hide the ductwork and wires that cross it. Makes it appear more open.

"What do you have in mind?" It's Aria that gets the question out before I do when my ass meets the wrapped leather of Cedar's workstation.

"Your name," she says plainly over a shoulder, her hands already inside a pair of black gloves, pouring and mixing small caps of color on her toolbox.

"Hell, no." Aria stands directly behind her best friend, arms crossed in defiance of the shit about to go down.

"Okay," I say to Cedar's back, completely content with having Aria's branding on my skin for the rest of my life.

"It's bad luck, Rex," she interjects, throwing her arms up in protest. "You can't do that."

"It's only bad luck if you believe it to be." I shrug and meet Aria's wary eyes.

"We don't need to test the universe, Rex." She shakes her head at me, but Cedar doesn't stop her prep for my next tattoo.

"If it's meant to be, then it doesn't matter," Cedar offers, spinning from her workstation with a tattoo machine in her hand.

She fixes a small piece on the equipment, tests the pedal that brings the buzzing noise to life, and sets it on the small table next to me.

"No amount of bad luck will make a difference. But"—she straddles the stool near my knee, pulling at her gloves to seat them better on her hands—"if it doesn't work out, then he's gotta live with the reminder for the rest of his life."

The rest of my life ...

I'm in.

"Where do I sign?" I'm smiling, but I'm as serious as I've ever been.

Aria's concerned features meet mine as she wrings her hands in front of her. "Fuck, I think I might be sick."

"Aurora, get her a chair. She needs to watch," Cedar demands, and Aurora is on the move to push a wheely chair across the hardwood.

"C, you know I hate the needles and shit ..."

"You'll be fine," Cedar mumbles.

I meet my girl's pale face and hold out a hand as Cedar, armed with a disposable razor, aims for the only blank space she can see without removing any clothes.

The base of my neck.

"I've never watched before," Aria admits, flinching when Cedar cleans up the space, then grips her tattoo machine and presses the pedal, bringing the room to life with its all too familiar buzzing.

"I have a feeling this one is going to hurt." I meet Cedar's hardened gaze as she stands over me, adjusting the chair until I'm lying flat, my head pushed all the way back, exposing my neck.

"Oh my God," Aria whimpers when the needle makes contact, and Cedar begins to freehand letters on my skin.

To my surprise, she's not too heavy with the hand.

But the shit hurts like a bitch. Which is why that space was empty.

Needles penetrate my skin, and I squeeze my eyes shut, the flesh there firing with each stroke of Cedar's hand.

I breathe as deep as I can to distract myself from the ache building, focusing on the death grip Aria has on my hand as if *she's* the one in pain.

Keeping my eyes on her face, I see how my pain has become hers.

Swipes of paper towel across the overworked skin nearly bring tears to my eyes, but I refuse to show weakness.

Aria needs to know. The world needs to know.

I'm in for life.

My jaw is clenched so hard that when Cedar pulls back, I have a hard time moving the stiff joint. She wipes away the excess blood and ink from me and cleans up the wound with a little solution.

"Fucking done." She snaps her gloves off and tosses the things away.

I sit up slowly, looking first to Aria's distraught features, and stretch my neck from side to side.

"That bad?" I ask her with a grin as she watches the fresh ink move with me, but she just shakes her head and points to the mirror.

"It's goddamn breathtaking." Her hand covers her mouth, tears building in her eyes.

I turn to catch a glimpse in the mirror over Cedar's station and nearly lose my breath.

Right there across the base of my neck, in bold vines constructed of vibrant greens, teals, and yellows that stand out among the other colors already there, is my girl's name.

"*Fuck,*" I breathe.

"You'll regret having anyone else ink you ever again." Cedar's hand is on my shoulder, her grip tight and sure, as I admire her handiwork. She leans down to whisper into my ear. "And if you hurt my best friend ever again, a neck tat will be the *least* of your worries."

Chapter Thirty-Eight

Aria

I STARE DOWN AT the clear patch covering my name across Rex's fucking neck.

Vines, styled like graffiti, with brilliant earthy colors.

Greens and yellows and a little orange and teal mixed into the shading, making it seem more plant-like than bold lettering.

I think that was the point.

Golden curls fan over my mint-green pillowcase as he lies beneath me, hands on my hips, a seductive grin on his gorgeous face.

He's between my legs as I straddle his hips, his cock buried deep inside me for the third time—maybe the fourth.

"I can't believe you let her do that," I breathe and rotate my hips, creating friction between us. Rex groans his response, his bottom lip sucking between his teeth.

"I honestly thought I was getting a dick tatted on me somewhere," he breathes and sits up to press his chest to mine, his hand finding the hair at the base of my neck. "Speaking of getting dick …" He fists the hair there and tugs, exposing my neck.

"Mmmm …" It's all I can muster in my foggy brain as Rex grinds his hips up against me, rubbing my clit and my G-spot in one go.

His piercing is phenomenal.

Wetness floods between us for what feels like the thousandth time, and yet the first all in one.

"I want the world to know you're mine, babe."

I grab onto his shoulders to hang on when his hips speed up and his words rock me to my core.

"And that I'm yours," he breathes.

I groan at the friction his cock causes, my toes tingling and my spine arching into him willingly.

"You've already got the branding." My thumb grazes the tape holding the plastic in place, and shivers rack down my spine. My belly clenches, my pussy throbbing for release.

"I won't show it until you're ready." Rex's breathing increases with his movement, his thrusting punctuating his words.

A promise.

I moan when he flips back, his hands finding my hips again and rotating them for me.

"Ride me out, babe," he breathes into a groan. "I wanna watch you."

I'm close, so I lean forward to brace myself on his solid chest. Gasping, I rise from his groin and drop back down with enough pleasure building that I almost burst.

"Fuck, Rex."

I shudder as I slide back down on his cock, rocking myself closer and closer to that delicious edge.

"That's it, baby," he coaches, hands helping to keep the rhythm when I falter.

I'm so wet and ready that when he slips a hand between us and his thumb touches my clit, I explode like he triggered the detonate button on my body.

"*Yes.*" I scream out my orgasm, Rex's fingers gripping me tightly as I ride him until he's cumming beneath me.

Inside me. Again.

What a test of the universe.

"You're so beautiful, Aria." His words are healing to my soul, his voice deepened by the sex and the admiration.

"I love you," I whisper, blinking my vision back into focus thanks to the sex-crazed fog and the tears that well there.

"I love you."

He slips out of me with a smirk, and I flip to the bed beside him with not much care for how awkwardly I land.

Arm crooked, ass up. Face smashed into the pillow

Rex slaps the exposed skin of my rear and laughs.

"Had enough yet?"

"Never."

Rex could touch me for days, and I wouldn't bat an eye. Just as he grazes me now, the tips of his fingers teasing my wide ass and up my back.

"You ever thought of getting ink?" I turn my head so that I can see him through a screen of my wild hair. He's beautiful as he lies there beside me, a knee bent, his torso propped up on an elbow.

His eyes are both black from his fall, only the edges just barely yellowing with any healing.

"Never really thought much about it," I admit, rolling so that I share his level of exposure and comfort. "The needles and things kinda freak me out." His hands find their way to my breasts, toying around my nipples, trailing down my ribs to circle my belly button.

"Ever thought of …" He pauses, his gaze rising from my body to my face. There's something hidden in his face, some kind of need or desperation that seems almost primal when his eyes lock on mine and his palm flattens against my stomach.

The longer his words hang in the silence, though, the more my anxiety decides to make a comeback.

"Thought of what, Rex?" I rush out, my heart racing and running laps around the hand he presses to me.

"Having a family?" He tilts his head, that same look turning the corners of his lips up. "You've let me in. Quite a few times now, and we haven't talked much about it."

"There's a lot we haven't talked about," I squeak out, my throat tight with emotion as my mind plays on my feelings and spins my head around with so many questions.

What if he doesn't want to?

What if he's never home?

Do I have the mind for this?

Holy shit, what did I do?

My mind runs with all the bad things.

All the shit that could be wrong. Could be wrong.

But when his hand grasps my chin and brings my gaze to meet his, I see the softness in his eyes. The sparkle. The wonder.

"There's not a damn thing we couldn't figure out, Aria." His grasp leaves my skin feeling tingly and cool in place of his warmth as his fingertips pick at the tape around his fresh tattoo. "The good and the bad. Whatever comes."

Rex peels the plastic-wrap-looking shit back, unveiling my name across his neck.

My sight shoots to it, my breath leaving my body like it did the first time I saw it.

"I'm in it, Aria. I've got your brand." He sits up, wads the shit from his ink and tosses it to the nightstand. "I want it all with you, whatever you want. Hell, a picket fence if you want it," he promises, his hands finding my face again and tilting me so that he can stare into my soul. "But I need to know you feel that way, too."

"Okay," I whisper. "I do, too."

I'm overcome with emotion. Overwhelmed with the feeling this man brings out in me, the things he makes seem possible and easy even when they shouldn't be.

Rex leans in and kisses me. His lips are soft and swollen, warm against mine as he leans all in and shows me tenderness. He shows me caring and effort. He shows me his love. The kind that leaves me breathless when he pulls away, tears pricking my eyes.

"I want it all. Every bit you're willing to give me," I breathe the words. "I miss you so damn much when you're not here."

"Fuck, I never knew someone could feel *this* good." He grins, big and toothy, the love shining in his gaze on my naked body as he leans in to kiss me. "Now, let me give you what we *both* want."

Chapter Thirty-Nine

Aria

BY THE TIME REX is done ravishing me, it's morning.

We haven't slept a wink.

The sun peeks over the horizon through my window in this small apartment above the studio and paints the sky brilliant purples and blues and pinks. I watch on as the colors bleed into reds and oranges in just a few moments.

"I love it when the light touches your skin," Rex whispers to me.

He's got his head propped up on his elbow to see over me, his body spooning his warmth into my back, his perpetually hard dick tucked between my still slick thighs.

I smile, content and satisfied.

"I love it when *you* touch my skin," I add, and Rex sighs into my hair, his hands gripping my hip.

"That, too," he agrees, the breath of his words caressing my ear and blossoming goose bumps across my neck. "So, you wanna have my little tatted babies, Aria?"

I snort into a belly laugh.

"I don't think babies come out *tatted*, Rex." I roll my eyes at the thought.

"Damn."

I lean back to catch his smiling eyes on me, tucking my body farther into him.

"I do want a family, though," I say. "I mean, who the hell wouldn't want *Rex Thompson's* babies?"

I snicker when his expression falls and his hands find my ribs.

"Are you throwing shade at me, Aria?" He tickles me, his fingertips grazing my skin just enough to elicit uncontrollable giggles and goose bumps all at once.

I thrash to get away from his assault with laughing tears streaking down my face. The sheets end up in the air, tossed around in an attempt to dismantle the attack, pillows sliding to the floor.

His laugh, deep and throaty, echoes through the room, slicing right through my chest and settling in the crevices in my heart.

Goddamn …

My ass hits the floor with a thud, and I end up snorting. Rex follows me to the hardwood, his nakedness straddling my thighs to keep me from kicking him away from my sensitive rib cage.

"Okay, okay," I yell through my giggles and snorting, my hands doing their best to push him away.

"Okay, what?" Rex laughs and pushes forward again, overpowering me and catching my skin again, using only one hand to pin my wrists together.

"It wasn't shade. It wasn't."

My jaw hurts, my cheeks aching from the smile stretching across my face.

"I want your tatted babies, Rex. Because I love *you*."

He stops, grip loosening, that look of admiration returning to his eyes.

"Do you wanna get married again?" Seriousness crosses his features and catches me off guard.

"This is a hell of a way to propose, Rex." My brow furrows with questions when he shakes his head of wild curls.

"No. I'm not asking you. Yet."

Yet.

His eyes meet mine when the *t* clicks off his talented tongue and he pins my wrists against the floor above my head. "I mean do you want to after what happened. Is that a thing for you?"

I shrug with what little room my shoulders have to move in the cramped space between my bed and the wall. "Never thought I'd be close enough to anyone to make it happen again, but I guess. Yeah. I hope to get married again one day."

The look that greets that answer has my own smile spreading.

My own chest expanding as Rex leans down to nuzzle his nose against mine. His hair falling around us like a little curtain of privacy just like that first night together.

"You have no idea how happy that makes me."

I catch his wince when our noses bump more than rub, but he pulls back to smack a kiss on my lips.

"Doesn't that hurt?" I ask, following his lead and sitting up, watching his naked body stand in all its glory in front of me.

What a great view ...

"Fuck, yes." He chuckles and offers a hand to help me up. "C'mon. We have a lot of work to do."

"Work?" I question as he pulls me to my feet and over to my dresser.

"Yeah, work." Rex opens the drawers and starts picking things out; panties, socks, a lacy bra he inspects before draping it over my shoulder.

The knickknacks on top of the wood shake as he rumbles through, opening and closing things with one hand, keeping mine in his other.

"What are you doing?" I giggle as he tosses a pair of jeans at my face.

"You gotta put clothes on to work. No one else should see you naked but me." His side-eye that I barely catch is demanding, fun, but dead serious.

"Well I don't just walk around naked, Rex." I roll my eyes but hold the items anyway. "I also need a shower." He's pulling me in the direction of the bathroom before I even get the words out.

We pass boxes I've yet to unpack because the studio has been priority number one since I moved into the building.

Well, this half anyway.

As Rex toes a box out of the pathway to the full bath, I wonder what the hell is even in them.

Do I even need this shit anymore?

"Babe?" Rex looks at me, his mouth downturned with concern. "You okay?"

"Yeah." I shake away the boxes cluttered in the hallways of my mind and focus on his frowning face. "Why, did you say something?"

"No. I just turned around and you looked lost in your own apartment."

I shrug and let his love put a smile back on my face.

"I guess I kinda got lost in my head a little. All the boxes and shit still sitting around are embarrassing." He seems to chew on my words for a moment, his eyes narrowed with questions, but he doesn't push any further.

Instead, he bends into the tub and turns on the water. The shower kicks on, having been the last thing used, and sprinkles rain down onto his head.

"Shit." He pushes the lever to redirect the flow, but I'm already laughing my ass off.

He grips my hand once the flow is closer to the ground, droplets running down his forehead, and presses me into the single vanity, his hips pinning my ass to the cold ceramic.

"Was that funny?"

I pinch my lips between my teeth to keep from laughing, but gasp when his pelvis grinds into mine. "It was, not gonna lie," I simper, rotating my hips back into him as payback.

His eyes flutter closed, his nostrils flaring. "You got me on that one, babe," he says huskily, his hands going to the sink on either side of me, boxing me in.

Yep, that's hot.

"Now get in before I fuck you again." My clothes are removed from my grasp and my ass is slapped, pointing me in the direction of the steam now billowing from the spray.

Chapter Forty

Breaking news

Front man, Rex Thompson, of renowned rock band As Above was spotted near his mother's last known address only a day after the big fall.

While there was a rumor that Rex's mother moved from the location, does his appearance mean that was false information?

Tune in for more information.

Chapter Forty-One

Rex

T HE COUNTDOWN IS ON.

I only have a short time before I have to be back on the road, and I want to get all the important shit out of the way before we head back out.

Aria was willing to leave the studio in the care of her sister, who seemed a little more accepting when we left, but I know she'll want to get back to it well before I'm ready for her to.

My girl, freshly fucked and showered, takes my offered hand and steps out of the back seat of the car into the afternoon sun.

Ian pushes the door shut behind us and jogs around to the driver's side to pull the car away.

Large sunglasses cover half of Aria's gorgeous features, similar to mine, and when she slips them down to take in the sight in front of her, I nearly faint.

Swear, my heart just did the pitter-patter shit.

She looks at me over the dark lenses, her green irises darting from man-icured hedges and crisp green lawn to me, then back to the wrap-around porch and the all-white house.

The shock and awe in her gaze sends chills down my straightened spine when she brings it back to me.

Aria's shoulder-length hair blows in the wind, her slow smile spreading the longer she looks from me to the house, her palm warming mine.

She's wearing all the shit I picked out, her jeans tight enough to leave nothing to my imagination, her top a low-cut tank-like thing under a scuffed leather jacket I found in her closet.

And then there's the heels …

Fuck me.

She's my fucking wet dream.

What she doesn't know, though, is that there will be a reunion of sorts going on inside the picturesque home.

Pulling her hand, I lead us onto the crisp lawn of the colonial-style house under the midday sun. The grass has been cut recently, the scent still clinging to the warm air surrounding us like a special kind of welcome home I didn't know I needed.

I lead her onto the paved pathway that leads all the way across the yard, to the front of the house, with a different kind of beat in my head and a special elation to my step.

It's you and only you, I sing to myself, the inflection taking on a whole new meaning with her in my grasp.

"It's gorgeous," she breathes, allowing me to wrap an arm around her shoulders and tucking herself into my side, her palm going to my stomach.

I love the way she fits.

"So are you, babe." I grin and walk half the pathway to the house without taking my eyes off her.

"Oh, stop." She scrunches her nose and taps my stomach, but she can't hide the tinge of pink that rises on her cheeks.

"Never." I mimic her words back to her, loving the grin that they place on her face, and hit the first step up to the porch.

Commotion sounds inside, the front door flying open and Mac spilling out like a damn tornado.

"What's up, fuck nugget?" he greets wildly as he blows past us and leaps down the stairs with one step.

"*Macaroni.*" The voice that calls to him is anything but friendly. In fact, it's more of a reprimand. "Get your ass—"

"What the fuck?" Aria whispers as we step up onto the porch. She's twisted out of my grasp, our hands still intertwined, but she watches Mac's back as he disappears down the pathway.

"*Macaroni.*" It's higher pitched this time, and I know he's in trouble for whatever bullshit he managed to fuck up in the little bit of time he's been here without me.

He's always had a knack for pissing her off.

We all do.

I smirk as footsteps echo down the long hall on the other side of the foyer, the heavy footfall sounding more like an elephant as it bleeds out through the screen door.

"*We're not done talking.*"

"Who is that?" Aria is tucked back under my arm, more for safety than comfort as the footsteps get closer to us.

"It's my ma," I answer down to her with a gentle grin.

"Wha—" She cuts herself off, freezes in her spot on the porch, when my words sink in. "No way." Wide eyed and flared nostrils, she makes to take a step back but pauses midair when the screen door pushes open again.

Except this time, it's not slammed.

This time, no one flies out.

"Rexy."

Illuminated before me is my mother with her silver waves pulled back in a slick pony, and her hip popped with all the attitude I'm about to catch for Mac's wrongdoing. Her words, however, are ones that greet me like I've come home.

Comforting.

"Ma," I return with an easy grin, leaning in to kiss each of her cheeks. "You know I hate that nickname."

"Who is this, baby?" Ma asks, ignoring my comment, when I straighten and she can get a good look at my girl, standing stock-still beside me with no color left in her face.

"Ma …" I grin, tucking Aria into me again and squeezing her with as much reassurance I can transfer through my skin to hers. "This is *my* girl, Aria."

"*Aria,*" Ma breathes the name, her hand going to her chest, her eyes darting to me for confirmation. I nod proudly when Aria shakes herself from my grasp and steps forward with an outstretched hand.

"Yes, ma'am." They shake, gentle and quick, Aria stepping back into my embrace. "I must apologize for my initial response." She looks up at me, gives me the stink eye, but returns a gentle look to my mother's curious gaze. "Your son didn't tell me I was meeting his *mother* today."

"I said we were working," I retort, gaining myself a discreet pinch to the ribs. "*Ow.*"

"And neither of our work has anything to do with meeting *family*," she tosses out the words at me with a scrunched nose.

"Ooh, I like her." Ma beams, waving a nonchalant hand to the lawn Mac disappeared across. "Come, come. Dinner is soon. I hope you came hungry." She ushers us into the house with a reassuring hand on Aria's shoulder.

"I'm starving," Aria admits as we slip into the sitting room.

"Why aren't you feeding her, Rex?" Ma chastises, swatting the back of my head as she passes behind the couch we sink into.

"*Ow.*" My hand goes to the ache, my scowl aimed at the back of Ma's head.

"Don't give me that look, Rex." She disappears into the kitchen without actually seeing me give her the fucking look. "And what's wrong with Macaroni?" she calls from the kitchen, clangs and bangs punctuating her words.

"Dunno, Ma," I call back, my arm sliding around the back of the couch, anything to be as close as I can to Aria.

"Why the hell didn't you tell me?" she whisper-hisses between Ma's loud cooking.

"So you wouldn't freak out." I shrug because, to me, it makes sense. Aria is an overthinker and does best when she doesn't have time to obsess about shit.

"But I look like a hooker. Not the girl next door you bring home to your *mother.*" She's still hissing at me, smacking at my chest, when Ma comes back around the corner with a tray of sweet tea in hand.

"Thirsty, kids?" Ma offers the tray to us and I snag a fresh glass of sun tea and down the shit in one go.

"Fuck, I missed that." I wipe my mouth on the back of my hand and set the empty glass on the table before Ma can even leave the room again.

"*Mouth.*"

"You realize I scream *fuck* into a mic for a living, right?" I respond with a roll to my eyes.

"Not you, baby." Her head pops around the corner. "I gave up trying to fix your manners *decades* ago." She's armed with a wooden spoon aimed right at my girl, the deadly *Mom* stare directed next to me. "I heard that bullshit you said about yourself, and I'm not having any of that in this house. Do you understand me, young lady?"

Aria straightens under my arm, her nod quick. "Yes, ma'am."

"You're gorgeous." Ma's head disappears along with her wooden spoon, and Aria relaxes under my arm. "And clearly my boy loves you. That's enough for me," she continues from somewhere in the kitchen.

"Whoa," Aria whispers beside me, and I tear my sight from the doorway to find her hand against her forehead.

"Babe?" I turn in my seat and pull the appendage from her face, concern furrowing my brow.

Maybe it was too much to bring her.

"I'm okay." She smiles at me, but something keeps it from reaching her eyes. "It's just … she's great."

I grin at her and place a gentle kiss on the tip of her nose.

Ma comes back into the room, places the tray of biscuits, more than likely made from scratch, on the coffee table next to my empty glass. "Got used to these boys coming and going as they please, but none of them ever brought someone home."

Aria nods, tucking her feet under her, as she searches my face for something I can't name, but she comes up with a matching smile.

"I'm certain my babies weren't trying to set you up, dear." Ma settles in the matching floral chaise across from us and crosses her legs like she's some kind of proper lady.

She can be polite when she needs to be.

"But he also should have told you *first*."

She's also savage as fuck.

"I don't mean to think ill of your son." Aria pauses to take me in for a moment before returning Ma's gaze.

"Don't worry about it." Ma waves a hand around. "I think ill of them all the time," Ma finishes with a knowing nod that makes me snort. She taps her knee and goes to stand.

"Thanks, Ma."

"You're welcome, baby." She turns back into the kitchen, pausing with a hand on the door. "When will the rest of your brothers get here?"

There's so much hope in her voice that I almost forget how long it's been since we've been back to visit.

"Soon, Mama," I say gently, the corner of my lips turned up in a soft smile for the woman I've admired my whole life.

"Brothers?" Aria hisses, gaining me another backhand to the pec. "As in, plural? And not the one that just hauled ass across the lawn?" She looks over her shoulder to the large bay window overlooking the front of the house. "I think I'll just fuck off to where he went." Worry creases her brow as she longingly stares at the green grass.

"*Ma*," I call out, making Aria jump. "We're gonna go find Mac." I tug Aria to her feet with me and rub reassuring hands over her arms.

"Okay, baby," Ma yells back.

"You're gonna be fine," I say to my girl as I plant kisses on her face, venturing to her neck. "I love you. They already love you."

"I hate you for this," she groans but sighs and melts into my touch.

"I know." I chuckle, reluctantly pulling back from her delicious skin and walking us back out into the sunny day with hands held and smiles shared.

"There's a trail right over here." I nod my head to the tree line on the far side of the property.

Birds chirp out a melody I remember from my younger years of spending time here, cicadas accentuating the tune with their vibrations, and before I realize it, I'm humming.

"You really are talented, Rex." Aria's words are quiet as we step into the shade of the trees, pushing branches and brush out of our way.

Damn, my heart.

"Thanks." I wrap an arm over her shoulders and pull her in to kiss the top of her head.

"So it's really the rest of the band coming? All of them?" We step over fallen logs and roots, dip under branches and vines.

"Yes," I answer, clearing the tree line and coming into an open space with only one tree left in the center.

And a treehouse built right into the sturdy trunk.

"*Oh my God,*" Aria squeals and takes off at a dead sprint for the latter despite the heeled shoes she wears.

Yeah, my girl can handle herself.

"You better not have brought Ma," Mac shouts, poking his head out of the open window, past the worn drapes.

Well, they weren't originally drapes.

One's a blanket Ma hasn't noticed that we took and the other is a fitted sheet from Mac's old bed.

Aria flies up the ladder without any issue, pushing the trap door open and disappearing inside.

"Babe," I call out on a laugh and take off after her.

"You let the cooties in, Rex," Mac whines as soon as my head breaches the surface of the treehouse.

"Oh, *whatever.*" Aria snags a throw pillow, kicking up all kinds of dust, and tosses it at Mac's face. He gags when he catches the pillow, but not the cloud that assaults him as a result.

"That was mean, baby girl." Mac works his mouth, desperate to rid himself of the dry filth coating his tongue.

"You said I had cooties," Aria defends, throwing her hands up. "You deserved that shit."

"That's raw." I chuckle at my brother, who attempts to dust himself off, a gentle coating of gray all over the front of him despite his brushing hands. I roll my eyes and flop into the sun-bleached beanbag, kicking up another cloud. "What are you gonna tell Ma?"

"*Fuuuuck*," he groans, leaning into a lawn chair before sitting to make sure it doesn't cave under his weight. "I don't fucking know. He'll be *here* with Toby."

"*Shit,*" I sigh, feeling Aria's gaze burn a hole in the side of my head as she whips from me to my twin. "Just say the word, Mac. And he's gone."

"No." Mac shakes his head, dust flying from his hair. "I don't want anyone to lose their jobs," he says into his hands that reach his temples.

Aria finally cracks. "What the hell is going on, guys?"

Chapter Forty-Two

Uh-oh.

DRUMMER FOR AS ABOVE found his way back home to his mommy early this morning.

Mac Thompson was said to have been traveling alone back to his family in the Hills.

Without his bodyguard?

Could spell out trouble for As Above.

Is this it for our number one band in the US?

Keep BSTD up to date with all of your celeb sightings.

Chapter Forty-Three

Aria

Scrolling through the social media accounts for the studio, a shared post about As Above catches my attention. The article I click flashes a picture of the band, most seated around me now, on stage with confetti and streamers highlighting their perfect grins and sparkling eyes, encased by sweat-slicked brows.

They stand together, arms woven around each other, and pose for the picture. It's clear it was a great night for them. They even look younger despite the tag in the photo suggesting it was from only about a week ago.

Looking over my phone from my spot on the couch, I catch Mac's desperate eyes set on his brother, who sits next to me and stares daggers at one of the security guys their mother convinced to stay.

Which means Toby is around somewhere, according to what the guys said in the treehouse, but I've yet to be introduced.

The other guy wandering around with his phone plastered to his head is Leo, band manager and brains of the operation.

He sits in the corner and scours over his phone, similar to me, except he's donning a three-piece suit and looks nothing like the type to hang with Rex, the walking canvas.

All business versus straight-up artist.

Mac has a few pieces of ink himself but nothing compared to his brother.

Then there's Fin. The outsider who came into the band much later than the rest. He's intimidating at best, covered in ink and enough piercings to jam up a metal detector. His demeanor screams some cross of *don't fuck with me* and *I definitely know how to get away with murder.* Both terrifying in their own right, but he smiles for Rex's mom and hasn't been anything but respectful to me.

He's one of those that likes nasty shit. I feel it in my bones.

The thoughts widen my eyes that I divert back to my phone in order to tame them.

That was rude as hell, Aria.

You don't know this man.

Scrolling, the article I'd opened furrows my brow the more I read and sends my anger skyrocketing.

What the hell?

Chapter Forty-Four

What would you do if you fell, center stage, in front of the entire world?

R UN HOME TO MOM, duh.

Rex Thompson was spotted in his mother's town just this morning with the rest of the band in tow.

The stronger the bond, the weaker the man.

As Above's lead vocalist heads home to lick his wounds after viral embarrassment, making his clumsy nature the number one watched video of the last forty-eight hours.

It's a shame that rock music has stooped to this level of victimization and necessity for care.

Back in the day, Ozzy would have done a line off a whore's tit and kept singing.

Who the hell does this guy think he is muddying the genre with his weak nature?

Subscribe if you think Rex Thompson and his brother should just stay home and let Mommy take good care of them.

Pitiful.

Chapter Forty-Five

Aria

P ITIFUL?

Fucking *pitiful*?

"If anyone is fucking pitiful, it's you, sir," I seethe with a reddened face and fisting hands. "What the hell?"

"Babe?" Before I realize what's happened, I've already slapped Rex's reach away from my chin with only a slight bit of misplaced anger.

"What the hell is right," I hear Mac mutter.

"Oh, shit." I hiss at the look on Rex's face. Grabbing his arm, I flash the screen to Rex. "What is this shit? They talk about you like this all the time?"

"I told you not to click on shit," Ian snaps, stealing my phone from my grasp before I even register he's entered the room.

"It was right in my feed, Ian," I snap back and try to snatch my phone, missing by a hair when Ian evades me, his eyes scouring over the article.

"*Hmph.*"

"*Hmph?* That's all you can say to that?" I stand and stalk up to the towering bodyguard like I'm his equal and pry my phone from his grip with venom lacing my words. "He basically called my boyfriend a wimp. Fuck this guy. I'm gonna destroy him."

"Listen here, Scarlett, I told you not to read this shit," Ian snaps the phone back from my raging fists and stalks out like he's pissed at me.

I watch his thick back disappear into the kitchen, simmering, wondering what in the hell my boyfriend's security is going to do about this garbage soiling his name.

"Babe." The fingers on my wrist are light at first, gentle as his words. "Look at me."

All I see is red.

I'm angry as hell.

"*Aria.*" Stern, the grip on my wrist tightens and pulls, spinning me into a broad chest. My hands flatten against his pecs, finding the piercings under his shirt.

"It's not okay, Rex."

His soft gaze lands on me, the pad of his thumb caressing my cheek bone.

"It's not," he agrees, boxing my face in with his hands. "But it's part of the job. A lot of fucking people love us. Some others aren't impressed, it's all part of the job."

"They're just making shit up." Voice strong. Body tensed and ready to take on the world for him.

"They don't always like me, or us, because I don't do stupid shit up on stage." His arms snake around my shoulders and hold me against his warmth. "I'm not hard enough because I don't drink, smoke, or shoot up on stage. Throw shit at our fans ..." He shrugs. "I've heard it all."

"But I haven't," I snarl through gritted teeth.

"And you don't even fuck on stage. How could you have morals?" I hear Mac's eye roll in his words, his voice monotone.

"They aren't the ones I sing for. We play for." Rex shakes his loose curls. "People will talk shit. That's on them, not us. You can't let it get to you."

"But, *Rex.*"

He leans into me, his lips teasing the hairs near my temple.

"Defend my honor, babe. Go ahead." Leaning lower, his words whisper over the crest of my ear. "But you keep saying my name like that, we might have to find the nearest empty room."

Shivers rack down my body. The anger bleeds into pure, insatiable desire.

"We can't," I gasp when he presses his erection into my belly. "It's bad luck, Rex."

"So's this." His grasp finds mine and leads my fingertips to the plastics wrap taped to his neck. "But here you are."

We're already moving before I can protest further.

To the front door.

Rex pulls me back across the lawn, through the tree line, as another car pulls up in front of the house.

I don't get the chance to see who it is, though, because Rex is tugging me into the woods we just came back from, in the direction of the clearing.

I suppose the treehouse doesn't count.

Halfway there, he pauses. Spins back to me.

Rex is backing me up before I realize I'm pinned against the trunk of a large tree. His hands are on me, his lips to mine.

It's not long before his hands find the backs of my thighs and hoist me up until the bark digs into my back and my legs are firmly wrapped around his waist. His strong hips grind into me, his dick finding all the right spots even through both pairs of jeans. Lips to my neck, he bites and sucks hard enough I know there's going to be a mark left in his wake.

"Rex," I breathe, my hands tangled in his wild hair, my core clenching with need.

"I'm going to put you down." His words are muffled against my neck, but my body does not miss the vibrations his gorgeous vocal cords create. "And when I do, you're going to turn around and bend over."

My feet are on the ground before I can process his words. He expertly unsnaps my jeans and wiggles the tight material halfway down my thighs with pushy hands that spin me toward the tree he was just holding me against.

"Brace, babe." His hands are on my ass, on my hips, his cock finding its way between my thighs and slicking through my wetness. "*Fuck.*"

I barely grip the tree when Rex thrusts inside me. I stumble forward on a cry at the sudden fullness, but Rex follows me.

"Fuck," I choke out as he hammers his cock into me until I'm nearly hugging the tree from the force of it. Dipping between my legs, his fingers brush over my clit and have me moaning his name.

"That's it." My arms turn to jelly with my impending orgasm, my legs buckling under me.

Rex grabs my waist to hold me steady. To keep my face from meeting the bark.

"Cum on my cock, baby." Moaning, he drills his hips into me with a punishing rhythm that his hand matches on my clit, faster and harder.

"Oh *my God.*" My mouth is stuck open, my eyes rolling as I crest the edge and gladly dive off.

"Fuck yes, *Aria.*"

Rex doesn't just cum, no. He buries himself as deep as he can get, his growl of pleasure echoing in the woods all around us, his cock pulsing inside me with every wave of his orgasm.

"Dear God." I'm breathless when he fists my hair and tugs until my back meets his chest.

"I fucking love you, Aria." His fingers tease my clit in time with his still hardness sliding in and out of me.

"I love you, Rex."

It doesn't take much to get me worked up again, considering I feel the result of our first orgasms running down the inside of my thighs.

Along with his skilled hands and hips …

His groans fill my ears, and the softness of his breath rushing out over my skin sends me wild with the contrast.

The first one was fast and hard.

Me like.

This one … is soft and loving.

Me also like.

I hold onto the arm that snakes around my chest from my hair for dear life, Rex's hips rocking into me at a steady tempo.

"Cum again, baby." His rasps make me see stars. "Let me feel you—" His words choke off with a groan as I clamp around him, nails digging into his skin, leaving my own marks behind.

My head falls back to his shoulder, his hips pumping into me a few more times, pulling another moan from my lips.

He feels so damn good.

Rex's arms wrap around me, hugging me to his chest.

"I could do this all day."

Clearly.

As if to prove his point, he drives forward, pumping his still-hard cock inside me again.

Fuck. Me.

"We have to get back." I'm breathless, my words barely more than a whisper. My chest heaving with the post-orgasm shudders.

"Nah. Ma won't care how long we're gone if she knew we were making her some grandbabies." Rex waggles his brows at me like he doesn't give a single shit about privacy and plans to tell her every little morsel over tea.

"Jesus, you're terrible." My eye roll turns into a shiver when Rex slips his dick from me and pulls up my pants. I rebutton my jeans and turn back to find him tucking his cock back into his pants.

Pants that have a wet spot spread over the fly like he pissed himself.

Or like he wore them while we fucked.

Fuck. Me.

"Oops." A knowing shrug accompanied by a shit-eating grin is all the answer I get, and I know I'm screwed.

Cuz that's totally what you want your boyfriend's mom to think of you when you first meet.

Shit.

Chapter Forty-Six

Rex

As we hiked back to the house, I offered to take Aria's jacket, considering her perpetually red face meant she might cave and bolt at any minute should anyone notice the state of my jeans. I've been holding the leather in my lap and in front of my junk since.

She keeps checking on me, though, her eyes scouring me to make sure I'm covered up.

But she can't hide the utter desire that flickers across her beautiful features anytime her face drops to my crotch. The knowing in her gaze when she tries to re-interject herself in the conversation. The flush that seems permanent even when Ma holds her attention.

"Tell me about your store, dear." Ma sets down the final serving dish on the long dining table and takes her seat to the left of the head.

She refuses to exclude anyone or pull rank unless she has to. Including where she sits at the table.

Today, Fin takes up the head of the table, Toby seated at the foot. We had to pull extra chairs up to accommodate all the bodies present this time, placing me in a folding chair so I can squeeze in next to my girl, who's across from Ma.

Grabby hands take servings of food from Ma's table, dishes emptying faster than she anticipated, considering most of it is gone before Aria can finish her statement about the studio.

"Boy, you need to save some for others," Ma chastises Ian with a smack to the back of his hand when he tries to take the entire platter from the center of the table. He drops the shit right back where he got it with a sheepish look I've never seen on a man so big.

"Yes, ma'am."

"Good boy." Ma redirects her focus back to my girl. "So why didn't we bring the sisters along? I'd love the chance to meet them, too."

Her smile is genuine, one that meets Aria's small grin.

"I didn't know what we were doing, or I would have." Aria shoots me a look. "Honestly, I'd like that, too," she answers softly.

The part she doesn't share is how her best friend tattooed my girl's name on my body.

Something I'll have to try and hide from the public until she's ready.

Aria's hand finds my thigh, breaking my train of thought. I grin for my girl, covering her hand with mine.

Yeah, wouldn't change a thing.

"Why aren't you eating?" she asks quietly, gesturing to the full plate despite my lack of reaching for a single bite.

I guess Mac decided I needed some grub.

Shoveling food into my face like a starved man, I clean my plate in a matter of minutes just like the rest of my brothers and reach for whatever happens to be left over.

Then Ma takes off with my girl when the serving dishes are empty, leaving us guys to clean the whole thing up.

Toby tries to weasel his way out of it by wandering into the living room, Fin on his heels with his phone attached to his hand like he's got someone important to talk to.

"No socials." Leo snags the device right from Fin's grasp as he goes to pass, and points it in the direction of the kitchen. "We clean up here."

Fin scoffs in protest but follows the band manager's direction.

"You, too, Toby. You know the rules," I call from my seat as I start stacking plates and silverware together.

"*Man*, c'mon," he grumbles as he passes me, snatching random shit and carrying it into the kitchen.

"Did I hear someone complaining after a fresh homecooked meal was provided to them, free of charge?" Ma calls out from somewhere else in the house.

Toby freezes mid-step on his trip back to the kitchen with a single fucking plate.

"No, ma'am," he calls out, grabbing a handful of silverware and two more serving dishes.

"Punk ass bitch." Mac shoulder checks him as he passes.

"Fuck you," Toby hisses. "Your mom is terrifying."

"Damn right, she is," I agree, following Toby's tracks into the kitchen to find Fin set up at the sink. His sleeves are pulled up, exposing the ink there, a soapy dish rag in his hand.

What the hell is Ma doing with my girl?

I hear faint giggles in the distance, my lips pulling at the corner.

Toby mimics the sound of a goddamn whip, and when my gaze shoots to him, I see him tying a floral-printed apron around his waist.

"You really want to start with me?" My raised brow lands on the secured fabric at his waist.

"Don't judge me. The T-shirt is fucking Egyptian cotton." Toby shrugs, taking up the spot next to Fin, and starts washing.

"Yo, get your own chore," Fin protests, knocking his hip into Toby's.

With an eye roll, I set my stack of shit on the counter next to them, careful not to get too close to them jockeying for the same spot.

Just like in the band.

"*Leo.* Better come get them before they break Ma's shit." The words on the tip of my tongue come out of Mac's mouth as he saunters into the room with the rest of the dirty dishes.

"Jesus Christ." I hear Leo's curse before I see his face, reddened with anger, come around the corner on the other side of the kitchen.

The same side the living room enters from.

So much for setting the example.

"Dickhead," I say under my breath before he can pass me, catching Leo's nipple through his crisp white shirt and twisting.

"*Fucking hell, Rex.*"

He jumps back from me, his hand flying to his pec, face contorted like he's been hanging out in the living room eating lemons instead of helping us the fuck out.

He's even lost the suit jacket, his suspenders hanging loose around his hips.

"You know the rules," I remind him on a shrug, the bickering getting more intense behind me.

"That hurt. *Hey*—cut it the fuck out." He quickly diverts his attention from me to the fight about to break out when Mac saves a plate from hitting Fin in the face.

Assholes.

With a shake of the head, I wander through the house in search of my girl and my mother because the two of them together for this long can only lead to embarrassing childhood stories of me and Mac.

Not that I care all too much.

Aria already carries my soul in her smile.

I catch sight of that same smile when I lean into the open threshold to the back patio and find the two most important ladies in my life chatting over naked baby pictures and mimosas.

Ma talks of the time I flipped my thrift shop Little Tikes car over Mac's head and we both ended up in the emergency room. They giggle as Ma flips to another picture of my brother and me covered in grass stains and mud from the fair she was able to afford to take us to one year.

As they banter and laugh at my and my brother's expense, I can't help but feel completely content.

Like a weight is off my shoulders and the colors of the world show a little bit brighter.

I guess love will do that to a man.

"Shit, how long have you been there?" Aria's startled tone breaks through my daze, spreading my smile wide.

"Since before the Little Tikes story," Ma answers with a grin, her hands steadying Aria's frantic attempts to cover the super embarrassing photos spread across the coffee table between them.

"Oh …"

"Don't mind me." I gesture to the table. "I'm just admiring my Ma and my girl getting along."

I see Aria's not-so-subtle shiver at the same time I catch my Ma's wink.

"I understood the assignment." Ma picks up another stack of Polaroids from her side table. "Now tell me why you're here, interrupting girl time, when the rest of the guys are inside working hard to clean up the mess?"

It's not a question but a dismissal.

Damn.

Sighing, I hang my head. "But, Ma—"

"No but's. Just because you happened to be the one to finally bring a lovely girlfriend home doesn't mean you get to skimp out on your responsibilities." By the time she's got all the words out, she's pointing a stack of pics at me incredulously. "Get your ass."

I lean over the back of Aria's chair and plant a kiss on the top of her head.

"Tough crowd," I mutter to my girl, but Ma hears and throws *the look* in my direction.

The Mom look.

You know, the one that says you better listen, or I'm gonna light your ass up?

Yeah, that one.

I might be a grown-ass man with my own place and enough money to buy the entire city this house sits in, plus some, but if you aren't at least a little bit afraid of your ma, then she's not doing something right.

So, instead of hauling my girl up from the chair and fucking her in the woods again like I want to, I settle for tipping her chin to me for a real kiss that makes her swoon.

Sealing my fate with a wink to Aria and a middle finger to my mother, who promptly follows my actions with a throw pillow to the back of my head, I walk back into the house in search of my brothers with a grin.

Mission accomplished.

I pass Leo perched at the clean dining room table with his laptop in his face and his phone stuck between that.

"No, Anna," he grumbles into the phone to our nightmare PR rep. *She's so damn strict.* "The boys were tucked in safe last night. Get the shit off the web."

Consider my curiosity piqued …

I stop in my tracks and walk backward until I see the illuminated screen open in front of Leo.

"I don't care, Anna," Leo states a little more aggressively this time as the contents of the laptop begin to register in my brain. "Release a statement, and get this shit under wraps."

Frozen on the fuzzy screen is a guy clad in the traditional black shirt and slacks ensemble that our security team wears, lounging back in a hotel chair with a chick kneeling between his knees.

I catch fisted long black hair and my twin's signature As Above duffle he made when we first went big sitting on the bed next to them.

Except neither participants in the video are my fucking brother.

"What the fuck, Leo?"

I see red as my mind runs over a million possibilities of what I'm actually looking at. None of which make any kind of sense and certainly don't lead to anything good.

He snaps the laptop shut and spins in his chair to face my clenching fists and burning gaze.

Is my brother in the goddamn video?

"I'm taking care of it, Rex." Concern laces Leo's tone when he addresses me, suggesting that he has no idea *how* he's going to fix this.

Recognition sinks like a boulder in my gut.

Security … with access to Mac's room …

"He better not still be here." My growl is so low, so calm, it doesn't even feel like it came from my body, but the threat is more potent than if I'd screamed it. My feet are moving to find my twin before Leo can answer the question.

"Ian took him off-site for questioning. He's already gone." He pulls me to a stop with a hand on my shoulder just as I cross the threshold to Ma's living room. "It wasn't him."

The room where I know Mac is.

"I don't care. I want him gone. *Yesterday,*" I demand when I catch sight of my normally calm and collective brother balled up on the couch with stress lines marring his face.

"Mac doesn't know yet, Rex. We still have to investigate." Leo's tone is quieter, calmer than he should be, but that's probably because he doesn't know the true extent of the damage this guy is doing to my brother.

"Mac doesn't need to know. He's hurt enough. Just fucking look at him." I swing my burning sights on Leo and cement fate in my next words. "Jordan isn't good enough for As Above. He better not make a return."

Leo's hand goes through his blonde hair. "Fuck, alright."

Chapter Forty-Seven

News update:

REX THOMPSON BOARDS A jet straight back home after accusations of drug use.

Appearing tough in the spotlight doesn't mean you are.

How else would a professional performer end up nose-diving off stage?

Click here to see the fall in action.

Chapter Forty-Eight

Aria

WE SPENT ALL AFTERNOON at Rex's mother's house. It was calming once I got to know her a little bit, and even better when she gave me access to know Rex and Mac a little better, too.

But sometime after the meal and the pictures, everything changed.

The aura around the guys became odd, as if something was off but no one wanted to talk about it.

Trust me, I asked.

Now, I watch Mac sulk in the passenger seat as Ian drives us to the next location.

Shit, I didn't even ask where we were going.

I assumed it was home, but judging by the SUV coming to a stop outside of a thumping club, that was not the right answer.

"Mac, you don't have to do this." Rex reaches around the seat and squeezes his brother's shoulder.

"Thanks, shark nuts, but I need a fucking drink." He's out of the car as soon as the statement leaves his lips, Rex turning his attention to me.

"There's a bag for you in the back. Get changed. Meet me at the bar." And before I can protest, he's jumping out after his brother.

Why isn't Ian going with him?

"Ma'am." Gruff and beyond huge, a bodyguard I don't recognize clears his throat from the open door, a duffle encased in a hand big enough to make the bag look like a child's toy.

I meet Ian's sight in the rearview mirror because something just isn't sitting right with me, but when he nods approval, I accept the outstretched bear paw and plop ever so eloquently out of the tall-as-shit SUV.

Not.

"This way, ma'am." Hand to the middle of my back, the oversized polar bear leads me away from the massive crowd lined at the door to the side of the building.

Built into the brick is a stairwell guarded by yet another gargoyle who greets us with a jut of his chin and unclasps the red rope to permit us access.

Guess I could get used to no lines.

My polar bear of a companion wrenches open the large metal door and lets out the pulse of the populated club.

And by pulse, I mean the heavy thump of bass. The voices of patrons, both singing and shouting, are heard over the music.

The farther into the crowd we fade, the more the music overcomes me, vibrating off my skin and making me itch to get back to Rex.

It's alluring in a way that makes my heart race and my groin come to life.

Is that moaning I hear?

I shake my head to clear it as my body responds like I'm back at the photo shoot with Rex for the first time, and all I can think about is getting him naked.

"In here." Polar bear gives me a gentle press to my middle back, urging me to a door he's not following me through. "It's a private ladies' room. Don't set anything on the floor."

All I can do is nod because, honestly, I might have to touch myself in order to calm my shit a little bit before I emerge back into the public.

Slipping inside with a light sheen of sweat blossoming on my skin, I drape the bag over the hook and slide the lock in place.

The bathroom is … dingy at best, with cracks spiderwebbing the single mirror over the broken sink, both of which seem to be held together by stickers.

Writing spans most of the walls, different numbers to call for a good time and initials of lovers.

I shake my head and spot the seemingly clean toilet I'm still planning to hover over, thankful the floor is sticky enough to give me balance on these heels when I do.

This doesn't seem like the place for a rock star …

After a kick to flush and a quick wash of the hands, I feel around in the bag Polar bear had me bring in here and nearly shit when thin tabs brush over my fingertips.

Fucking sequins.

I'd know that feeling anywhere.

A grin plasters itself to my face when I pull out my newest creation, finished just yesterday, and a pair of strappy metallic heels that look green when you look from one side, purple or blue from another.

I squeal. I can't help it.

Because the shoes match the dress perfectly.

Ripping off the old outfit, I slide into my new dress and revel the feel of the silky material against my sensitive skin.

This one, though, has a neckline down to the navel, a nonexistent back, and a terrible tolerance for panty lines.

So I unclasp my bra and toss it into the bag like yesterday's laundry so I can secure the clear halter strap around my neck and fan the material over my breasts.

Another look at my derriere after I strap my heels in place at midcalf, and I huff at the line traveling across my ass, even in this shitty light.

Looks like those have to go, too.

I clench my thighs together to ease the throbbing for a moment, but the thought of going completely commando does nothing but drive me to find Rex faster.

Maybe if I call him here now …

I swipe the thin material from under my dress and toss them into the bag, too.

Cannot say that the idea of touching myself before I leave this room is off the table, but when Polar bear knocks on the door to check on me, I quickly nix that idea.

Seems wrong when he's right outside.

"Just a minute."

The song pumping over the speakers switches to one I've heard before but don't know the words to as I fish around in the bag one last time and celebrate when I find my travel makeup case tucked inside.

I wing my liner like Cedar taught me, dark and thick over a smokey eye that I compile with vibrant greens and blues that match my dress. Finishing up, I swipe away any fallout and apply a purple so dark to my lips that it looks almost black in this light.

I don't know who the hell put this bag together or what Rex has planned, but I'm fucking ready.

One last wink to myself and a tousle of my hair in the mirror, I strut out of the shitty bathroom like I own the place.

"Oh. *Shit*," Polar bear greets me with a dropped jaw and wide eyes as I toss the bag to his chest.

The shit slides right down his body and falls to the floor before he can get a grip.

Snickering, I watch as he literally shakes himself when he bends to pick the bag up off the floor and slings it over his shoulder.

His hand hovers over my upper shoulders now, the exposed skin soaking up the heat radiating from him as he leads me down a set of stairs and onto the main floor of the pulsing club.

We pass hordes of people, some dancing, some humping, some gyrating to the heavy rock beats. The tempo of the bodies has me bobbing my head along as we wade through the masses.

Halfway around the dance floor, a wolf whistle rings out in my direction from the private tables lining the wall. My head whips to the sound, glad to find Mac as the patron instead of some of the other creepy gawkers I catch eyeballing me as we move.

"Total knockout, baby girl," he calls out to me.

Sheepishly, I nod my thanks toward Mac, my feet moving me closer to the bar.

Closer to the crown of golden locks holding a whiskey tumbler and waiting just for me.

Merely feet away, I catch Rex's gaze in the mirror behind the bar, sending him careening around with even wider eyes than Polar bear.

Smirking, Rex leans back against the bar with a cocked brow, his elbows propped against the wood. The movement stretches his button-down shirt open, exposing the spread eagle inked into his chest.

Delicious.

But it's not just how hot he is sitting there, no.

It's how his gaze racks down my body in the slowest and hottest once-over I've ever gotten in my entire life.

His eyes linger on my groin area, no doubt wanting to be inside me as much as I want him to be, then move to my chest and the bareness between.

Grinning, sly and sexy, I crook a finger at him. Rex's heavy boots meet me in two strides, his hands finding my hips, his drink left abandoned at the bar.

"God*damn*. You take my fucking breath away." A flush, rosy and hot, reaches up my chest to my cheeks when Rex's words wash over my ear and his hips meet mine. "I could fuck you right here and not give a damn who's watching."

We sway with the beat, his hard-on poking my stomach as if to illustrate his point, and slowly step back into the crowd of people on the dance floor.

"Rex," I breathe when his hands slide down to cup my ass, and our sway becomes more of a rotation set on driving me insane.

"That's it, babe. Say my *fucking* name." He grinds into me to the beat, his thigh angling between mine, the moves working the hem of my dress up higher.

Do I care?

Nope.

Not one bit.

The music's speed increases, the song building its climax as Rex builds me up to mine, and he spins me. My ass slams into his pelvis on a gasp, one arm bracing me to his chest as his hips continue their assault on my libido.

"Fuck." I shudder against him when his hand slides beneath the material and palms my breast, kneading my flesh and pinching my nipple.

I'm so close that I'm pretty sure I could bust all over this dance floor and not give a shit.

"You want to cum, don't you." His sultry voice in my ear. His hand on my tit while his bare chest heats my back. His other hand inches up my thigh, dragging the hem of my dress up along with it.

Dear God.

Rex pauses, his venture up my thigh stopping with teasing fingertips at the junction where my thigh meets my groin, and I hear a literal growl leave his fucking throat.

My core throbs with need in response.

"Are you …" He's breathless in my ear, his fingers feeling farther onto my pelvis, finding nothing stopping him from plunging inside me.

A strained groan rushes over my ear when he cups my bareness, confirming that I am, in fact, not wearing any underwear.

"*Baby.*"

I am surrounded by Rex, the pressure of him against me driving my skin to prickle. I become the vibrations that rock this building the longer he grinds against me. My head swims with pure ecstasy.

His lips find my throat, leaving kisses and nibbles down to my shoulder as the song switches to something I think I've heard before.

"Fitting," Rex mumbles against my skin, edging me closer to the end of the cliff and preparing to throw me off before he even touches my most sensitive area.

But when the familiar, velvety vocals fill the bar and Rex runs a finger down my slit, I throw my head back and completely expose myself to him.

He growls at how wet he finds me, how fucking turned on I am.

Biting down on my shoulder as the bass drops, he slips a digit inside me and pumps in time to the music.

His music.

Lyrics of heartbreak and lost love accompanied by heavy guitar and even heavier bass vibrate across my trembling body, pushing me closer, pulling a moan from my lips.

"I'm gonna fuck you, Aria, and you're gonna cum on my cock to my song." Rex adds a second finger for two pumps, then a third, readying me to do what he's asking for, my body clenching in response.

I'm gonna fucking cum.

Then he pulls out, leaving me empty and on the cusp of orgasming.

I gasp at the lack I feel, my body collapsing forward in search of more, but he holds me together.

Reaching between us, he tugs his zipper down and the back of my short dress up. Freeing his cock and my ass.

I feel all of it.

Every heartfelt word booming over the speakers as the head of his dick edges my entrance from behind.

Every inch of my pussy that Rex's piercing caresses as he slides into me.

Every breathy groan that leaves his lungs and tickles my ear as he withdraws from my heat.

Only to slip back home, and I gasp at the fullness.

Rex fucks me in time to his music.

Hips riding against my ass, sheathing his dick inside me as he rolls my nipple between his thumb and finger. I rock back, desperate to keep him inside me, trembles of need clawing at my insides, ready to explode.

And I do.

As the speaker Rex hits a high note on the song, I scream.

And I cum.

Harder and faster than any orgasm before it, my body clamps down on Rex's dick and slicks his erection with my arousal.

"Fuck, yes, baby."

Rex groans into my neck, pushing farther inside me as his cock pulses and he releases more of himself deep in me.

I reach back to grab his hip as his song fades into another one and sway us to the new beat.

My sway goes wide, though, and we jolt forward when bodies bump into us.

I bury my face in his arm that's still braced across my chest as realization sets in.

There are about a thousand people here on the dance floor, moving to the same beat as us, and we just fucked in front of all of them.

And his hand is still kneading my tit.

Red-hot embarrassment flames across my face, and I go to pull Rex out of me, but his strong grip holds me to him.

"If you move now … everyone's gonna see my cock." I shrug, like that notion doesn't bother me, but he continues into my ear with pure sex in his voice. "And you're gonna have cum running down your legs."

I shiver.

"Shit."

"So just let me dance with my sexy girl while my cock is still inside her."

So damn naughty.

Yet fucking exhilarating.

"It'll let every motherfucker here know *you're mine.*"

Chapter Forty-Nine

Rex

I'VE NEVER KNOWN LOVE and lust could feel so powerful.

So exhilarating.

I dance with my girl, my cock tucked back into my jeans about four songs ago, her dress securely around her thighs and covering her ass.

My ass.

The scent of sex still wafts between us as I grind my hips into Aria, a sheen of sweat coating our skin, smiles aching our cheeks.

This couldn't be a better moment.

Her hands are tangled in my hair, mine on her hips, and we gyrate together to the beat of a song from a band I've done shows with.

I don't feel like the front man of a famous band.

I don't feel like a rock star.

No one would believe it's me anyway, out in the open, dancing like a fiend on my girl.

I feel like a mortal man, in love and drunk on possibilities.

Bodies mingle around us, swaying just like we do, packing in closer the longer we take up prime space on the floor.

Lights flash around us, lasers shooting across the crowd and lighting up Aria's grinning face.

I don't even mind the brushes of skin that belong to someone else. The arms that tag me on accident as the music fuels the aura and creates a living, breathing pulse inside the building.

Because I know it's not about touching me to say they've touched me. It's not about screaming my name, desperate for my attention.

It's not about being Rex Thompson from As Above.

It's about living in the moment and coming *alive*.

More alive than I feel when I'm on stage.

More in tune with my body and where it meets Aria's fluid movements as the other patrons fade away from my focus.

I'm consumed by her.

How this dance with my girl makes me feel like a fucking man. A man who can love and be loved and not share a damn thing with the world out there.

Because the world is in my hands. *My world.*

Is this what euphoria feels like?

It's just me and her. Together.

"Marry me." I don't stop moving when shocked eyes meet mine.

"*What?*"

I cup her face and place a tender kiss on her swollen lips.

"Marry me." I repeat the words, less than a question, searching her starry gaze, our hips slowing to the beat of the song.

"You want ... I ..." Aria blinks rapidly, like the gears in her head are struggling to compute.

"I want to marry you, Aria." My forehead meets hers. "Come on tour," I breathe against her lips. "Spend the rest of my life with me."

"Rex." She leans back, her body going rigid, her movements freezing. "I can't do that."

My brow furrows.

My heart seizes.

The bodies around us become all too overwhelming as we stop the pulse and stand against their sway.

Sweat from skin that isn't Aria's slimes against me, and I recoil at the thought.

The scent of sex from others becomes overbearing. The lights overpowering.

And our little bubble bursts.

People around us begin hopping, jumping to the tempo, someone nearly elbowing Aria in the face.

I push them away and gather her closer to my chest.

Feet land on mine, crushing my toes despite the heavy boots I wear.

"What do you mean you can't?" I demand, nearly growling as I step us backward and bump into dancers who throw curses my way.

But I don't care. I need out of the horde. I need Aria safe.

"I—" Aria's words are cut off as I use my back as a battering ram and haul her to the edge of the dance floor. I stomp on feet as I go, but the sea parts and we emerge near the exit.

Taking my chances of being noticed, I grab Aria's hand and bust through the side exit, inhaling the fresh air deep into my lungs.

I waltz us down the building with a firm grip on Aria's wrist, turning into an alley where darkness envelops us.

My ears ring when I spin her into the brick and box her in, both of my arms pressing against the wall above her head. Her chest rises and falls in rapid succession with her breathing, her hair sticking to her forehead from the sweat that cools quickly and leaves her looking sexier than ever.

"What the fuck do you mean you can't?" My breath is labored, my tone harsh as I glance over my shoulder, eerily aware of the presence down the way.

But I need answers I can't wait for.

"Rex, I can't just give up my life for you. *Fuck*." Aria scoffs, her red-hot rage making my cock twitch.

"I'm not fucking asking you to do that."

She darts under my reach, stepping back into the light from the streetlamps overhead.

"You did. You *just* fucking did."

"No, I—"

"You need some help with that?" Snide and greasy, the voice reverberates chills down my spine and raises the hair on the back of my neck.

I watch Aria freeze, her sight darting over my shoulder to the asshole I should have known was going to be a problem.

Hands up, I glance over my shoulder slowly, a grin pulling at my lips.

Please give me a reason to knock your lights out.

"Touch her and you die, motherfucker."

The laugh that echoes from his body is sickly erratic as he steps toward me. His hair is long and disheveled—not in a good way—his torn clothes covered in dirt and oil stains.

He's either homeless and desperate or damn good at blending into the part.

And there's no way to tell if he recognizes me as Rex of As Above or if I just look like the type to have a couple hundred in my wallet.

Aria moves in my peripheral, inching back into the busy street, closer to the light.

Good girl.

She's fully illuminated when I feel it against my spine, the cold steel seeping through my shirt and chilling my bones.

"I think ... that maybe ... you're mistaken," he singsongs his words, and the undeniable click of a gun cocking echoes through the alley as if it's the only noise on this entire block.

It feels like slow motion when I meet Aria's terrified eyes and mouth for her to go.

Run.

She takes off at a dead sprint into the light and crowded street, safe from me and this shitty place I put her in.

"Aw, she didn't want to play?"

Once she's out of the trajectory, I spin on the guy.

I pin his gun-wielding hand between my arm and my ribcage when he pops off a shot, the bullet whizzing past me and crashing into the brick.

"*Fuck*," I growl as the muzzle burn singes my shirt and heats my skin to blistering.

Hauling back, I land a punch on his jaw.

Blood spurts from his mouth when I make contact, the sick fuck laughing and popping off another shot.

I don't hear where that one lands.

So, I fist his grubby shirt, my forearm crossing his throat, and slam his back into the brick building.

He laughs again when his head makes an audible crunch into the wall, his neck pinned beneath my rage.

Another shot bursts from the gun and explodes against the building. Except this one grazes my already singed side and sends white-hot pain up and down my ribs.

I pull him back and slam him again, my elbow landing on his jaw as his head makes contact.

Momentarily stunned, the bloody grin on this fucker's face fuels me to keep slamming him.

To start punching.

Until his face is covered in blood, my knuckles are busted, and the arm pinned against my body exposes his elbow.

I uppercut the joint, sending it bent in the wrong direction.

His howl of pain reverberates off the brick, his hand going limp enough to finally drop the gun.

The metal clangs to the asphalt beneath my feet, and I kick blindly until I hear it skitter away from me and this psycho.

My hand wraps around his throat and squeezes, pinning him in place.

"*Rex.*" Deep and vicious, I've never been so glad to hear my name called out.

Like a full-on bulldozer, Ian's huge body slams into me and my punching bag, knocking me back a few steps and nailing the guy to the ground.

He shouts shit I don't comprehend through the ringing in my ears, his massive frame sitting on the guy's back and wrapping his arms around his back to be cuffed with zip ties.

Once he's secured, I turn back to the mouth of the alley and wipe my freshly busted lip on the back of my hand.

Guess he landed a punch or two after all.

The pedestrians recording the event part as I pass, cameras and lights in my face. I palm an outstretched hand or two and push them out of my face as the crowd gets thicker around me, heavier and harder to wade through.

Picking up the pace, I barrel through people and cover my face with my arm to prevent some recognition, but it doesn't work.

The mob descends on me, stopping my forward progress just a few feet short of the door back into the club.

"*MOVE,*" I shout, startling the ones closest to me and making them falter enough for me to break through the wall of flesh and bone.

Wrenching the steel doors open, I stride inside with wetness trickling down my side and an absolute resolve to find my girl.

I ignore the bouncer who tries to stop me, the clubgoers who think they can do it better than the mountain of a man I already blew past.

Yanking out of gripping fingers and pushing aside grabbing arms, I scan the sea for my girl. I squint past strobing lights, my sight landing on her at the table Mac has taken up.

The tightness in my chest loosens at the sight of her.

Knowing she's safe and with my brother eases my rage a fraction.

I close the distance with laser focus, the anger subsiding into hurt the closer I get to her jittery movements.

She's nervous.

Mac's arm goes across Aria's shoulders, reassuringly rubbing her bicep. Their mouths move with a conversation I can't hear over the thumping of the music.

Her hand goes through her hair, similar to what I do when I'm frustrated.

Her focus is set on the seat across their table and not on my twin like I would expect with the type of conversation it appears that they are having.

Pushing more people out of my face on my way, brushing off hands that try and stop me, I stride up to the end of the table.

Aria's rising gaze is slow to meet my face, her wide eyes settling on mine when her hand goes to her mouth and my name chokes out past her lips.

It's then that I realize Mac is holding her tight, pinning her shoulders to the booth, stopping her from rising.

Temper flaring, I turn my fury on my twin in a gaze that burns his head off in my mind.

"What the fuck," I demand when he still doesn't let my girl go.

My brother's words are for my girl. The ones spoken out loud not coming from his mouth. "You're fucking *bleeding*, Rex."

Reassurances go to her as my brother fishes his phone out of his pocket and puts the thing to his face without removing his gaze from me.

More hands grab at me, but this time they're more calculated, covered in calluses, and closer to the blood that soaks my shirt.

I am so sick of people thinking they can fucking touch me.

I snap.

Grabbing two fingers of the hands that think they can just be on me, I twist until I pin the perpetrator against the edge of the booth.

Pushing, I warp his spine over the back of the seat and wrap a hand around his fucking neck.

"Shit," Aria screams, her voice breaking into my subconscious, the table jarring in my direction as the lights illuminate the face of my handsy victim.

Jordan goddamned Kauffman.

Red-tinted tunnel vision sinks in, and I add to the force I have around his throat.

"Why are you here?" I demand.

Jordan's hands peel at mine but don't make great progress on removing my grasp from his windpipe.

I slam him against the booth when he doesn't answer.

"Rex. Stop."

Forever the Maverick, hell-bent on testing the waters of the universe and begging to get knocked the fuck out, Mac's grasp on my arm tugs at me and pulls us upright.

Jordan's eyes are for my brother as my grip loosens and oxygen makes its way back into his system.

"There were gunshots. They called everybody back," Jordan comments under my grip, only fueling my rage more.

"Being back and being *here* are two very different things that I don't think you comprehend, jackass." I punctuate my words with a tightening of my hand around his neck. His clenched fist holds my wrist, making no real move to stop me in my tirade.

Weak-ass bitch.

"You don't understand, Rex," Jordan wheezes under my hold, his bulging eyes filled with some kind of misplaced resolve on mine.

"No, *you* don't understand," I jerk his ass into my face and spit my next words, "Stay the fuck away from my brother."

"Rex," my twin begs. "Fucking *don't—*"

Too late.

I'm already hauling back, my fist connecting with Jordan's nose.

Chapter Fifty

BLOOD SPRAYS.

All over the table, the booth …

Me.

My mind reels as if I'm still there, watching as Rex's side blossoms in red and Jordan's nose busts all over the place from his fist.

I stand at the sink of my boyfriend's mother's kitchen with a soft bristle toothbrush and Woolite.

My focus is on softly scrubbing red stains out of my one-of-a-kind dress with tears streaming down my face.

I ruined it—

No, he ruined it.

I grunt in frustration and drop the shit in the sink for the third damn soak. I swipe angrily at my cheeks and eyes, the betrayers, with the backs of my hands and waltz my ass back into the living room.

Wiping the shit on the sweatpants and tank top Rex's mom was gracious enough to loan me, I stuff my feet into someone's boots and storm out onto the illuminated front porch.

My clomping footsteps echo around me as I cross the wooden surface, only dampening a smidge when the soles hit the grass of the perfect lawn, darkened in the night sky.

Guided by memory alone, I walk the path, tripping over hidden roots and branches along the way. I stumble into the clearing and find the treehouse lit up, Mac leaning out of the opening used as a window with smoke plumes puffing out of his mouth.

"Baby girl." His previously chipper attitude is gone from the words, his eyes glazed over as he leans a little far out of the treehouse. "You look about as good as I feel."

Probably not the best to be with his brother right now.

What if he's mad at me, too?

"Yeah, thanks." I shake my head but climb up anyway.

Breaching the surface of the floor through the trap door, I poke my head into the cleaner wooden box built by a young Mac and Rex and admire the weathering this place has withstood.

The beanbag no longer sends out smoke signals when I plop my ass in it, the material softer under my touch.

"Ma." Mac shakes his head, blowing a puff of smoke out of the window. "Her ass replaced all the stuff while we were gone."

"That was nice of her." I nod, my hands smoothing over the brand-new microfiber, leaving stripes of dark and light.

Fitting.

"She's a great person." Mac nods to himself, inhaling deeply and holding the smoke in his lungs.

I shake my head in refusal when he offers the thing to me with an outstretched hand.

"More for me." He shrugs, the smoke snaking from his lips. "Anyway." Mac pauses for another hit. "My mother taught us to be good people, too. You know that?"

I shrug, not really in the mood to have the conversation I think I'm having with my boyfriend's twin.

Ex-boyfriend?

I don't even know where we are anymore.

The thought chills me to the bone and sends waves of nausea through my torso.

But how the hell do you come back from a denied proposal?

He couldn't have been serious.

"My brother's a good person, Aria." Mac's statement breaks through my heavy thoughts, a fog building between us.

"He asked me to give up my life for *his*."

The words are out of my mouth before I can stop them.

The ones I shouldn't have shared with the twin who pauses with his arm halfway to ash out the window.

And when he doesn't respond with much else besides a cocked brow, as if I'm the one in the wrong, I purge my thoughts as justification for turning down his brother's marriage proposal.

"Mac, I worked my whole life for others. For my sister. For Chip. For managers and bosses I hated. I am just now starting to live my life for myself, and I'm not about to give that up just because some rock star with a great cock and an even better promise comes swooping in."

I suck in a breath but keep going despite the grin pulling at Mac's lips that doesn't reach his eyes.

"I don't need the swooping-in-and-saving-me kind of shit. I am living my dream with my girls, who happen to be dicks, too, but if I left now, everything would crumble. I love what we've built together, and I'm not going to give that up."

Huffing, I watch as Mac tucks the lit joint between his lips, squinting away the smoke and *slow claps*.

"Good for you, baby girl."

I stare in shock at my *maybe boyfriend's* twin.

How can he be so nonchalant about this?

"Mac," I scoff out skeptically and shake my head. "Your brother asked me to fucking marry him, and I said *no*."

Shining eyes pass over mine with a shrug. "I'm not worried."

"*What?*" It comes out louder than I mean, the words reverberating off the makeshift walls and old rock band posters. "How are you not mad at me right now?"

Another shrug as Mac ashes out the window and takes another puff from his pinched fingers. "He knew better than to rush it. He didn't think it through." He points at me with his joint-holding hand. "That's his own fault."

Wait …

I'm not convinced that Mac's words are entirely meant for me after what happened with Jordan.

After what happened with the mugger.

"I do love him. And I do want *more*. But if he expects me to jump on the road with him …"

Chills rack my body at the thought of Rex being hurt enough to be in his mother's bathroom getting stitched up by their security's doctor.

How much worse it could have been.

What would have happened if Rex hadn't been there …

"You deserve more than a one-sided, selfish demand. He knows that."

Another wave of nausea rolls over me, my arms going to my midsection, trying to ease the ache there.

"Baby girl." I look up at the face that looks so damn similar to Rex, tears welling in my eyes as Mac tilts my chin up to meet his bloodshot gaze. "Don't let up. He'll get it right."

A watery laugh leaks out past my lips, the humor missing from the sentiment.

"That would require him to actually talk to me." A half shrug and a crouch back to his window is the only answer I get from Mac.

Ping—

Pingpingpingping.

I fish the phone from my pocket, Mac mirroring my movements, to silence the device.

Except what's on the screen freezes me in my tracks.

"Oh, fuck." Mac is on his feet, pulling me to the trap door, the joint tucked between his lips. "We gotta go."

I follow his lead, completely dazed out of my mind.

Like I'm in a dream, the words from my screen bounce around in my head as we rush over green shit hell-bent on tripping me up.

The scenery blends together. The clearing mixes with the woods, which becomes the yard and the house, and I don't know where each thing begins or ends.

I don't know how we got to the house; I don't remember walking in the front door, but I sure as shit shake out of my stupor when we breach the living room and all eyes land on me.

All five sets.

Leo, with his phone attached to his ear, stops mid-step in his pace, words trailing off at the sight of me.

Toby's wide eyes swing from me to Ian to Leo, like someone's supposed to break the ice rolling over the room.

The ice I put there.

Fin pins me with a gaze, his hands frozen with a pocketknife to his nails.

Mac's hand falls to my shoulder and squeezes when Rex's bare footfalls pause on the plush carpet.

"Babe."

It's not the words that my attention catches on. Not the bare pecs or the stitches in his arm and his side that still looks blistered and angry as hell.

Not the rings through his nipples on full display or the one through his busted lip. Or the colored skin.

Not even Rex's mother as she comes up behind him and places a reassuring hand on his forearm.

"Babe."

It's the bob of his Adam's apple in his throat that leads my eyes right to the brilliantly colored skin covering just beneath it.

The freshly done ink underlined by his collar bones.

My fucking name.

ARIA.

The words from the breaking news article bounce around in my head, the TV vocalizing the shit in the background.

New ink, new girl.

Rex from As Above was spotted out and about with some fresh arm candy and a tattoo.

As Above front man seen manhandling a mugger—but wait. Is that a new tat?

"Looks like no one can tell what it is just yet." Leo is the first to break the silence.

He comes to me, flashing his phone with a close-up of my name on his damn neck and the tagline asking for pros to analyze the lettering for confirmation.

"Great." The word doesn't sound like me. It sounds like it comes from someone else's mouth.

"It's only a matter of time." Toby, forever helpful, comments, earning himself a slap to the chest from Rex's mom. "*Ow.*"

"Not helping," she scolds.

"Baby." Rex rushes me, wrapping his uninjured arm around my shoulders. He kisses my head and whispers apologies to me that I don't feel.

In fact, I don't feel anything right now.

I think I'm in shock.

"We could spin this into a one-night stand kind of thing," Leo drones on, back to pacing the floor. "We could blast the other shit to drown this one out."

"*No.*" Rex's words are resolute and immediate. Steadfast, he spins until he's looking at Leo over my head, my back to the room.

"Could suggest it's a longtime friend." As if Leo's comments hit play on the room, everything comes rushing around me.

"You could admit it's his girlfriend," Fin adds.

Am I?

The TV croons on, and the suggestions keep coming as phones ping and ringers alarm, the noises filling up my ears and jumbling into too much noise.

Too much contact.

Too much risk.

Everything runs together in one big mistake that heats my skin and makes my feet move for me.

I push off of a surprised Rex, knocking him back a step, and take off out the front door.

"Don't." I hear someone call as heavy footsteps begin to follow me, then pause.

I run as the headlines flash over my mind.

It's only a matter of time before they find out.

The world will know who I am and who I sleep with.

I wrench open the car door, surprised when I find the keys tucked above the visor that fall into my shaking lap.

Desperation starts the car with white knuckles on the steering wheel, only to jolt when the knock on the window scares me senseless.

"*Jesus Christ,*" I yell.

Fin rips the door open and ushers me aside. "Move over. You can't leave here alone."

Heavily tattooed hands shoo me to the passenger seat as his big ass climbs in despite my body still being in the way.

"The hell I can't," I protest, and I fight, slapping at his back and arms, getting absolutely nowhere.

"Just move." He shoves his hands beneath my ass and hauls my body over the center console like I'm a rag doll. I grunt and punch his chest when he settles into what was my seat and shifts the car into drive.

His phone is ringing before we pull away from the house, Fin engaging the call via Bluetooth.

"Don't you fucking dare, Newb." Rex's rage fills the confines of the vehicle as he shouts into the phone.

"Too late."

Fin hangs up the phone and whips the car out onto the main street, flying past camping vans and tents with camera lenses poking out. He kicks up gravel as he turns, raining rocks down on the paparazzi creeping just off the property.

"Please take me home." I grip the seat to prevent my body from slamming into the dash when Fin taps the brakes.

"You might wanna buckle up."

"No shit—" I cut myself off on a gasp, gripping the dash, as Fin weaves into a lane that has no room for us to be in, narrowly missing another car. "Jesus."

"He's not here, darlin'." He switches lanes again, speeding well beyond the speed limit, and I jerk at my belt until it frees itself enough to secure my body to the seat. "And I can't take you home."

I whip my head to Fin's profile as my stomach sinks with his words. "The hell you mean?"

He nods to the rearview and swerves the car into oncoming traffic, earning himself a scream from me.

My chest heaving, hands planted on the console between us and the door, he dips back into the right side of the road.

"What the *fuck*?" I screech, slapping his arm.

"*Hey*," he booms, blocking my attack with one hand, keeping the other secured to the wheel.

"The fuck is wrong with you?"

"*Me?*" Fin scoffs, "I'm not the one beating the driver."

He points this time to the mirror as if I'm the one who missed the point about being a safe driver, which only fuels my anger more.

"You dickweed, I see the goddamn mirror—"

"No, you fucking idiot." He cuts me off and looks over his shoulder to change the lane again. "We're being *followed*."

His statement rings around in my head more than the first as the words sink in.

Not again.

Fear, ripe and ready to stop my damn heart, grips at me and turns my insides around as I glance in my side mirror.

And there it is.

The van littered with camera lenses driving way too close to the bumper of the car.

My heart races out of my chest as memory steals my breath.

The memory of a very similar car chase.

A wreck that landed Rex in the hospital.

This can't be normal.

"We're gonna be fine."

Certain, Fin's words sink into my panicking mind, his tone bringing me back to the present.

"I'm…" I can't get the words out past my tight throat and my racing breaths.

"Having a panic attack?" Fin nods in my peripheral as I focus on the road in front of us flying by. "I can see that."

He jockeys around more traffic, cuts off down a side street, and takes another turn that puts us back in the direction we were coming from.

Once he's satisfied with the view behind us, he slows the car and places an open hand, palm up, on the center console.

"Here."

I'm already shaking, but the thought of holding another man's hand sends me into another downward spiral.

"For fuck's sake, it's not a proposition." He rolls his eyes as he eases around another turn and snatches my hand anyway.

Warmth envelops my palm as he loosely wraps his fingers around mine.

I feel small compared to his touch, the feeling grounding me so I can breathe a little better.

Calloused skin scrapes gently along my palm as the bumpy ride sends us jostling in our seats.

The feeling helps bring me down. Gives me focus.

"How'd you know to do that?" I ask with evening breaths, my free hand clenching and unclenching to steady the shake.

"It's a grounding technique," he speaks to the windshield.

"Oh." I slip out of his grasp as we slow even more through a residential area. "Thank you."

Fin nods his acknowledgment and pulls the car off to the side of the road and kills the lights.

"Where are we?" I ask, poking my head around to see the different but similar-style houses lining the street.

"Nowhere." He keeps his sight trained on the rearview. "Just a decoy."

The moment the words leave his mouth, the van that was trailing creeps around the corner two blocks back, the headlights swinging into and illuminating the interior.

Fin ducks down on the seat and I follow suit as the vehicle passes, surrounding us in darkness before the passengers can see inside.

When it's finally out of sight, Fin busts a U-turn in the dark and takes off back to the main roads.

Chapter Fifty-One

Aria

Darkness envelops us for most of the ride except for the sparsely-placed streetlamps along the way.

Trees and brush whiz past us like black blurs in the dead of the nighttime, broken up only by the occasional concrete barrier.

Despite how terrifying Fin looks, along with his fuck-all attitude, the drive has lulled me into some weird sense of calm.

My trust for the driver grew after he evaded the paparazzi without getting us killed.

Fin's presence is comforting in a way that makes him soothing so long as he doesn't speak.

I still don't know where we're going.

Right now, it doesn't matter.

What does matter is that I'm still just the widowed girl.

The woman with a past, a crap-ton of baggage, on her way to making something of herself. My girls and I are doing this shit, making a name for ourselves, and I'm not ready to give up on those dreams.

My heart, however, palpitates at the thought of not having Rex in that mix. Of not feeling loved and *seen* like he sees me.

It's taken me *years* to get here. Past the drama and through tons of mental healing. To feeling like it might be okay to love again.

Can I do this again? Lose the man I love?

I thought I was ready for the next thing.

But *this*?

The news stories and trending social media presence?

It's a whole other story.

It's got me picking at my nails, two of which have already broken and torn in a jagged mess.

Rex says that I make him feel like a man, but he makes me feel human again. Something I didn't even know I needed until he stomped in with his heavy boots and that sexy, cocked grin.

The way he touched me at the photo shoot, held me and laughed with me. The way he shared pieces of himself with me, photographed to last forever …

Pictures I haven't even had the heart to look at yet.

Reality slams into me when Fin drives up close to the only car on the road and taps his brakes a little rougher than I was prepared for.

Memories of the first car chase flood me again as my heart rate kicks up, a deep knowledge resonating that this is the life I'm going to have if I keep Rex in the picture.

Fame that isn't mine.

Paparazzi in my face, stealing private moments for their own gain.

Security around the clock at my store.

Car chases and cameras that don't belong to people I trust.

Hand to my heaving chest, I try to steady my breathing when the wave of nausea rolls over me.

"You're gonna be alright," Fin says softly from the driver's seat and switches lanes to pick up his speed in the free space.

I feel the word vomit almost as sure as I feel actual bile building in the back of my throat.

"I don't know how, Fin. I don't know how in the hell I'll still be me if I'm dragged behind him for the rest of my life." I wring my hands in my lap when the pressure does my chest no good.

"Isn't that any relationship, though?" Fin asks as he eases back into the seat with a wide spread to his legs, a single hand steering the vehicle. He's relaxed. How the hell can he be *relaxed*? "Take out the fame for a second and you get attachments. One person doesn't know where they end or begin. In the end, you both just end up dragging each other around."

"I don't believe the whole '*incomplete without you*' methodology," I mutter, huffing at the past I knew all too well, knowing the work I desperately put into making myself better after all of it. "Shouldn't both people have their *thing*? Be able to pursue the parts of themselves that exist outside of the relationship?"

Part of a relationship is give and take. But his take would engulf all of me. His bright light of fame would overshine everything.

I spent years consumed by Chip and his illness.

So many that I lost who I was along the way.

When he passed, I didn't know who I was anymore. Where I began or he ended. Or what part of me died with him.

It took the photo shoot to really start breaking the cycle after years and years of self-induced mental torment.

To start listening to myself and what I wanted. To feel like I found my true self again.

To believe I deserved something more out of this life than just being someone *else's* rock.

It only took digging myself out from under the rubble Rex left me under when he took off from my hotel room that night for me to truly embrace it.

Maybe he *was the lesson after all.*

"No one intends for that to happen, I don't think. Look," he says, rubbing his scruffy chin with his palm in contemplation, and looks over at me. "It's not easy giving up your privacy, but there are ways to take it back. You just have to figure out what parts you're okay with feeding to the sharks first."

I'm just not ready to be on the front page of the news.

I nod and return my gaze out the window.

I suppose he would know.

"Of all the bandmates I've met before all this ..." I wave a hand around in front of me. "You're the one I know the least about." I catch his nod in the darkness of the car.

"Exactly my point, Aria. I do it on purpose." His words sink into my chest and begin to settle my stomach. "I often hide in plain sight."

"So you're saying there's a way to have my cake and eat it, too?"

Fin laughs, loud and sudden, catching me off guard.

Alright, I fucking jumped. Sue me.

"Not entirely." He shrugs, swiping at his mouth. "You just trade off one for the other, then back again. That's what I'm saying."

"Oh." *Well that's not what the hell I wanted to hear.*

I sink down in the seat and hug my arms around my torso, the seat belt nearly choking me.

"It's more like understanding that with Rex, the fucking front man, everything will be public at some point. You can just do things to buy some time. Or ..." His hand snags mine from my side and grips me when my breath rises and falls faster as the panic rises back up. "Use it to your advantage."

I scoff and snap my hand back from his grasp.

"No, thank you."

"What? There's nothing wrong with using the shit to your advantage, Ms. Designer. Why the hell do you think Cedar tatted his *neck* to begin with?"

My spine snaps straight.

"*No.*"

"*Fuck, yes,*" Fin returns on a hissing laugh. "She's fucking cunning like that."

"No way Cedar would use Rex like that."

He chuckles under his breath as I shake my head, tufts of hair tickling my neck.

"Then you don't know her all that well."

I throw my hands up. "Like you know her *at all*," I snap. "You're just judging her based on the shit from broads you've known in the *past*."

Fin makes a noise in his throat that suggests I know nothing about what I'm saying, but he can suck my balls.

No one is gonna talk about my best friend like that.

"What*ever*, Fin."

He just shrugs, the movement odd coming from this massive and tatted guy.

Easing down an exit ramp, Fin takes the corner and heads into a town I don't recognize.

"Where the hell are we going?" I ask when he loops around and avoids the main street that would take us closer to civilization and farther from the creepy warehouse district that screams of a murder scene.

My question goes unanswered as we delve farther into the manufacturing park, the factories getting more prevalent with each passing block.

We come up to the end of the road, the dead-end street stopping us with warning signs to turn around, and my heart kicks up twenty notches.

"Fin."

It's more of a warning than a question as he engages the window to roll down and peeks his head out of the car.

"You're fine, priss." His fingers fly over a keypad previously hidden by the brush, and a gate swings wide, moving the greenery to the side for us to pass.

"What the *hell*, Fin?" I ratchet up in my seat, taking in my surroundings, logging all information I can so I know how to get away on foot. "Where are we?"

I'm screeching at this point, whipping about in the seat, fully prepared to see the torture chairs littering the yard and the bouncer-sized douches readying to hold me down and rip out my fingernails.

There aren't any, but I'm still watching.

"Aria." I can hear the annoyance more than I can see it on Fin's sighing frame as he leans back in the seat and stares at me like *I'm* the one with thirteen heads.

He rolls his eyes and tugs the keys loose from the ignition, pushing the door open with his shoulder and stepping out.

"Fin, I swear to God—" My words cut off with the slam of his door.

I growl in frustration and slam my body into my own door to release its hold on me.

"You are a dickhole." I slam it shut, stomping my feet as I walk, following Fin's annoying ass up the concrete stairs.

"And you're fucking infuriating." He pushes open the large entrance to the house, disappearing inside, with only the jingle of keys smacking a countertop announcing his presence.

I pad in after him like it's my sole purpose on this earth to irritate the shit out of him.

The house is pitch black inside, pausing me in my tirade to make Fin's life miserable when the heavy wood snicks shut behind me.

Blinding white light surrounds me, and I groan, reaching up to shield my eyes from the onslaught.

"See? No fucking torture chamber."

I blink.

And I fucking blink.

Tall ceilings and exposed red brick encase a living area bigger than the entire building my shop is in, and it's filled with plush leather sofas.

Yes … Sofassss

As in plural couches.

Strategically lining the walls, so as to not cover too much of the surface, are different memorabilia protected by heavy frames and thick cases. The first one to my right is a poster from As Above's first world tour, signed by each member of the band and then a few more names.

Like Leo's.

Then there's a guitar affixed to the wall and surrounded by a glass case that allows you to see almost every angle of the mangled instrument.

"Wow." It's all I can say as I wander about the room, taking in everything about As Above that I can see from this level. The rest of it expands way above the second story, well beyond my sight constraints.

The only break in the brick and collectibles is a bar that opens to the kitchen on the first level, a balcony above that on the second floor.

Fin stands on the kitchen side of the bar, a whiskey tumbler in his hand and a look on his face that I want to slap right off him.

"You done fangirling?"

I flip him off with an eye roll and sidle up to my side of the bar.

"Fuck off," I respond and steal the drink right out of his hand. I shoot the amber and set the glass down with a gesture that suggests another round.

His entire frame lifts with his sigh, the eye roll flying all the way to Mars and back, but he pulls the bottle closer and produces a second glass.

Filling both tumblers with more than two fingers' worth, Fin grasps his glass like I might steal it again, sipping the liquid.

"You really shouldn't do that," he tells me when I tip mine back and swallow the contents in one gulp.

"Why the hell not?" I demand, the bottom of my glass smacking the marble again.

"Whatever floats your boat, kid. I'm not your fucking babysitter." With a shake of his head, Fin leaves me and the bottle alone at the bar.

It doesn't take long to feel the effects of the alcohol warming my blood and for me to ditch the glass, only to replace it with drinking straight from the bottle.

The more I drink, the less shitty I feel and the more comfortable I become. The house may not belong to me, but it doesn't stop me from stretching out on one of the many couches like it is.

It also doesn't stop me from pulling out my phone and opening the text thread to Rex.

Me: I hate that you're famous.

The little dots at the bottom of the screen illuminate almost immediately, and I sip from the bottle.

SexyMane: Right now, so the fuck do I, babe.

SexyMane: Where are you?

I can't believe I never changed that name. It's ridiculous. *Sexy Mane.*

I laugh to myself and slide down into a prone position, only spilling a little of the amber on my hand.

SexyMane: Tell me where you are, and I'll come get you.

Me: S'oky. Fin's here somewhere.

Me: I think.

I swing my head about the room to check for my companion, only to come up empty.

SexyMane: Just tell me where, and I'll be there.

SexyMane: Please, baby.

SexyMane: I love you, Aria. We can figure this out.

Chapter Fifty-Two

Rex

WHEN MY LAST TEXT goes unanswered, I call Fin.

Swear to God, he better not do anything dumb.

I grip the device to my face as it rings and *rings*.

"God*damn it*." I cock my arm back and throw the thing against the wall. It bounces off the plywood, plastic pieces splintering from the device and scattering all over the floor of the treehouse.

"*Hey*." Mac ducks and covers his head as shit rains down on him from his spot on the brand-new beanbag. "What the fuck, duck lips?"

Throwing my hands up with a growl, I run a tight hand through my hair and turn on Ian, who's perched in the corner, making the small space seem broodingly claustrophobic.

"*What?*" he barks at me from behind his crossed arms, the biceps bulging ridiculously beneath his too-tight shirt.

"Find her," I hiss.

"No."

My nostrils flare at his automatic response.

It's the same response he's been giving me for the last hour and a half.

They've been gone all fucking night.

"What if—"

"They're fine, Rex. She's safe. Give her some space." Ian's words only enrage me more, that emotion driving me straight into my bodyguard's face.

"If the paps find her, it's on you." I spit as I gesture to the tablet set up next to his massive frame that runs a special software made specifically to scan the internet for threats based on provided keywords.

Like "Aria."

The screen illuminates, exposing the bullshit we've been dealing with since before Aria ran out.

As Above is trending on all social media platforms.

And not in a good fucking way.

The bodyguard hashtag has blown up with the scandal video that had leaked prior to the videos of me slamming a fucking vagrant with a gun.

The one trend that's beating out all of those, though, is the one that's got me most on edge.

#Rexsnewvines

My tattoo. Of my girl's name.

It's already started a new shift in what people are calling their ink.

All over the internet, people are embracing the term and referencing their own as *vines,* making the discovery of dangerous content for Aria that much harder to wade through.

"No one's figured it out yet, Rex." Ian's tone is softer now, gruffly whispered to me in some sense of reassurance as he scrolls down the list of bullshit people are suggesting my new ink says.

Close-ups litter the web, screenshots from the videos of me taking a graze from a goddamn bullet in a sad attempt to pry into my life and know me better.

I hate all of it.

It puts Aria in danger, the videos and the ink, and that was the last thing I ever wanted for her.

Pushing a hand into my hair, I huff and pace the tiny room.

"I fucking knew better." I mumble the words to myself, more thinking out loud than addressing the room, but that doesn't stop my brother from kicking a foot out and tripping me up enough to send my ass careening to the floor.

"Shut up, rat breath," Mac says over his phone as the floor shakes with my impact. "Here." My twin slaps his phone with Aria's number lit up on the screen into my hand.

I take the thing in disbelief as my brother eases out of the beanbag and ushers Ian out of the treehouse without another word.

I mash the call button as soon as their heads disappear beneath the floor, silently begging for her to answer.

"Mac," my girl calls out excitedly from the other line, sending my heart palpitating with the confusion of when the hell my brother let security in his phone and why she sounds so slurry.

"Where are you, baby girl?" I ask into the mic and pray she responds to my brother.

"Oh, I'm just—Wait." She cuts herself off, and my eyes go to the ceiling in frustration. "Say that again. I've had a few."

I ditch the act and growl my next words into the receiver. "Where are you, baby?"

"I *knew* it," she shouts like she just won Jeopardy. "I fucking knew it."

I grunt a warning into the phone, one that suggests I'm not up for fucking games right now.

"*Babe*," Aria grunts back mockingly. "You sound so badass, Rex." She *giggles* and tests my fucking patience.

I smear my free hand down my face and sigh, her laughter calming my mood, and I ditch my frustration to be dealt with later.

"Let me video with you?" I ask, calmer now that I know she's okay.

I just want to see her face.

The line goes dead, only to come back a moment later, the screen filled with her gorgeously drunk face.

Aria lies on a leather surface I catch in the background through her fanned out waves, her eyes red and puffy, her adorable nose red. She laughs into the screen, tears streaking down her face.

"What's so funny?" I can't help the smile that begs to pull at the corners of my lips, even more so when she grunts back at me.

"*My name's Rex, and I'm a badass,*" she mocks in a deep tone, then bursts into hysterics. The view vibrates with her movements, her camera capabilities clearly hindered.

I can't help the chuckle that escapes me when she rotates, the entire world spinning on its axis along with her.

"Oh, this is a good view," she comments, staring into the camera. At first I think she's talking about me, but then she leans back to push her smashed tits toward the camera and flips her hair over the side of her crown like she does when I finish fucking her.

Fuck me.

"*Aria.*"

The sight alone makes my cock spring to life, the ring through my head catching on my boxers and tugging in just the right kind of way. I adjust the thing in my shorts, my sight not leaving the cleavage on full blast of my screen.

She's been drinking.

The little weasel voice in my head reminds me when she pouts her full lips, but I take a screenshot anyway and log it for safekeeping.

"There's nothing to eat in this house," she comments, her eyes looking over the screen instead of at me. "Nothing but fucking alcohol."

"Is Fin there?" I ask, hopeful that it's not someone else stealing her attention.

"Dunno," she responds and reaches past the phone, pushing her tits right up close and personal.

"Damn, that is a good view." My chuckle is cut off when I hear a clatter from the speaker, my girl coming back to full view with a bottle in her hand.

She takes a full swig, the amber liquid dripping down the side of her mouth, and she swipes it away with the back of her hand. "Oops."

I run a hand through my hair, my pounding heart and pulsating cock turning my brain to absolute mush, as I watch my girl take another pull from the bottle.

I'm so at odds with everything right now that it doesn't feel like there is a right answer that leads us to a happy life together.

It's so much sooner than I anticipated when I started this tour.

Is it too soon?

"Do you think Cedar tatted you because you're famous?" The words tumble out of Aria's mouth in slurred syllables, breaking into my psyche and bringing my attention back to her gorgeous face.

"Uh ..." *How do I say yes without ruining her friendship?* "Does it really matter *why* she did it?"

"Yes. Really does," she slurs, my palm scraping over the scruff lining my chin.

"Aria, I can't say that she didn't, but I think it's more about her making sure I'm in it for you." My chest swells at the thought, the darkness swimming away the longer I see her face lighting up my screen. "I'm glad that you have people in your life who are willing to take shit for you. It doesn't matter if she gets anything out of it in return."

"You're too sweet." Aria flops back onto the couch, her hair fluffing around her face.

"Is that …" I squint at the screen, desperately trying to make out a frame on the wall behind my girl's head. "Is that *my* fucking band's tee?"

Aria doesn't answer, she just snickers as a smile forms on my lips, and I jump up from the beanbag to haul my ass down the ladder in search of Ian.

"I should've fucking known Fin would do that. Damn."

I shake my head, my feet carrying me across the brilliantly green lawn to the lit-up house, my brother's phone still firmly planted in my hand.

"What's that?" Aria brings her face to the screen, blocking out the shit in the background with a grin.

"I'm coming to you," I say as I take the steps up the porch. "We still need to talk about you telling me *no*." Her eyes widen in the screen at my words when I step into the house. "Ian."

"Nope." I hear his grumble from the sitting room, his attempt at finality futile and hilarious.

"Don't I pay you, dickweed?" I brush his feet off the chaise and square my shoulders when his tired eyes meet mine.

"No, you don't."

I roll my eyes and tap his knee with the back of my hand.

"C'mon, Ian. It's with you or without you." I turn my ass around and head back to the front door, tossing my twin's phone at his head on the way. "Sleep in the car."

"Fuck you," he grunts, his heavy footsteps catching up with me faster than I thought he would, mine hitting the sidewalk to the driveway. "Safe house, right?"

I nod, the jingle of his keys breaking the otherwise silence of the nighttime air.

Or morning time. Pretty sure it's late as balls.

"You fucking knew?" I take up the passenger side of Ian's SUV when he automatically goes to the driver's side.

The only answer I get is a throaty grunt as he shuts himself in and turns the key to bring the engine to life.

"Asshole," I mutter, more for my satisfaction than for him to hear.

"Again, fuck you."

Another eye roll leads me to staring out the window at the passing landscape.

Ian drives smoothly but quickly in the direction of the highway, then our hidden property at the back of the industrial park.

The very same one I disappeared to when I left Aria behind in that hotel room all those weeks ago.

It takes some time to get there, my lids getting heavier with each passing mile of concrete and asphalt.

There's no tail this time—*thank fucking God*—but Ian still circles around different blocks, going in opposite directions, then back again.

Once he's done fucking around, we pull up to the place I haven't set foot in since I wrote the ballad album for the same woman who's harbored inside.

The soles of my boots hit the pavement before Ian can put the SUV in park, carrying me to the front of the house and up the few stairs to push open the heavy door and march inside.

"*Aria*," I shout into the house, skidding around the bar and into the room I know she was in at one point tonight.

Cursing when I find it empty, I run to the kitchen and nearly take Fin out in the process.

"Yo, *watch it*," he snaps, cradling the carton of eggs over his shoulder, narrowly removing them from meeting my chest. "Precious is in the fucking back room."

I grab a fistful of his tank and bring his nose to meet mine. "The fuck you call her?"

"*Precious*." Fin shakes his head and spins away from me, muttering shit under his breath.

I don't care.

I take off at a dead sprint to find my girl.

"Babe."

Chapter Fifty-Three

Rex

L IGHT SPILLING IN FROM the hall, I stand in the doorway and watch Aria's full chest rise, then fall in a steady rhythm that sets my heart at ease.

She's beautiful lying there, still in borrowed clothes, with her mouth hanging open and tracks of drool racing from her lips.

I snicker quietly to myself, knowing that the sight would drive her insane, but I love it.

I love every inch of this fierce woman, every trait, every piece of her that she thinks is a flaw.

It's fucking not.

Silently, I slip into the room and close the door. I walk to the bed and step out of my boots, my shirt going next, then the pants.

She groans when I slide in next to her but settles into my warmth when I pull her to me.

I take my time pulling up the discarded blanket to cover her body.

"I love you, babe."

I kiss her hair and let my heart rate settle against her back.

"We're going to figure this out."

The words send a twinge of pain shooting across my chest, but as long as she allows me to have her, to be with her, then I'll deal with whatever comes at us.

"I'll make it all okay. I promise."

Her whispered words break the silence so quietly I almost miss it.

Almost.

"Aria?" My heart kicks back up like I've just stepped on stage and am in charge of entertaining a crowd of tens of thousands for the next several hours. "Baby?"

Aria flops to her back when I sit up, the barricade of my chest no longer holding her up.

Soft snores sound from between her gorgeous pink lips, sinking my heart into my gut.

Dammit.

Blowing out a breath, a hand racking through my hair, I sink back into the mattress beside her.

"I'll marry you whenever you're ready, Aria."

My arm goes across her waist, my chest to her side.

"Just say the word."

Nose to her hair and inhaling her scent, I drag my thigh across hers and settle my calf between her legs.

Her heat radiates through her pants, a small groan escaping her parted lips when my thigh bumps into her groin.

Her hand finds my thigh, and despite my weight on her, she rolls beneath me until her ass is pressing into my crotch and her hair fills my face.

My eyes close, and I groan. I can't help myself.

Arm across her chest, I tuck her soft frame into mine with heavy lids and a hardening cock.

Purplish light begins to spill in through the sides of the drawn curtains, the dark room getting lighter with each passing minute.

Aria's skin glows more with each passing moment, time I don't want to miss despite my exhaustion.

I should've passed out at Ma's, but the adrenaline of living my life has kept me up well past what should be acceptable for any human.

Now, I just want to watch her.

See her.

Feel her.

Be with her.

I glance over her as I tease my thumb across her chin, her bottom lip. Aria's tongue darts out in response, swiping over the pad of my thumb.

My cock hardens.

"Damn, baby," I say, my voice gravelly, and kiss her hair.

She arches back into me, the extra pressure on my cock making me pulse with need. Instinctively, my hips push forward, my bare erection sliding between her covered thighs and creating the perfect amount of pressure to drive me insane.

"Oh, *fuck me.*"

My groan is met with a small whimper and parted lips as I slip my hand beneath the fabric of her tank. My palm finds her breast with peaked nipples and cups it, my fingers itching to pinch and tease her.

Aria groans, her hips rocking back against me like I'm already inside her, and it's a race to see how fast we can make her cum.

Shit.

This woman really does make me squirm.

"Aria," I moan into her ear as the seam of her pants flicks over the head of my cock, her thighs gripping my length, sending shockwaves of pleasure up my spine. "Wake up."

She goes still for a moment, my throbbing dick begging for more action.

Looking over her shoulder at me, she slips me the most devilish grin before sliding down her sweats, causing my erection to bob back up and slap right against her pussy.

"Fuck, yes."

I grab her hips, arch her back into me and sink my cock inside my gorgeous girl from behind.

We moan in unison, that same sense of euphoria coming back and enveloping around us.

Like this is where we're supposed to be.

I curl and uncurl my hips, moving my cock in as far as Aria's ass will allow, then back out.

The feel of her tight heat around me, slick with arousal, makes my balls weep and my cock harden for more.

More of her body.

More of her heart.

I want her to be mine, in every sense of the word.

"Aria," I moan desperately, a sheen of sweat building over my bare skin, my hips moving against her.

She groans a response, pleasure building, hips arching.

I want to ask her again. The need building with each thrust of my hips, heightening at the rate of my orgasm as if it's a race to see which one I can get out first.

"I want you," I moan into her ear without abandon, driving my words into her ear as much as I drive my cock into her slick pussy. "I want you for the rest of my life." My hips speed up, my body clearly chasing the orgasm over the answer, so I grip her shoulder to keep her steady against me. "Only you."

Aria grips the sheets at the intrusion, her mouth stuck open in the perfect little O I'd like to stick my cock in.

She moans, deep and loud, as her hips slam back to meet mine.

It almost feels like a battle. A fight of who will win.

My body pushes forward until she's in the mattress, lying on her stomach with her ass up and her face smooshed into the pillow. Straddling her thighs, my hips slap against her ass, my balls making contact with her clit.

"*Rex*," my girl moans for me, her pussy slicking with even more need, coating my cock and my balls with her arousal.

"Yes, baby." I grip her hair and yank her head back to feast on her neck. "The only name I want you moaning ever again." She breathes heavily beneath me, my weight crushing her into the bed. "Tell me you'll fucking marry me, Aria," I growl into her ear, my hips pounding into her, my emotion getting the better of me. "Tell me you're *mine*."

Her eyes roll, her fists tightening on the pillows above her, as her pussy clamps down on my cock in the most glorious of orgasms. I grip her hip and ride her as the waves of ecstasy intensify between us.

"Yes, Rex. *Yes*." she screams, and I blow.

Deep inside her slick pussy, I pulse with pure pleasure and release my cum on a primal growl.

"Tell me again," I pant, my cock still jerking and emptying.

"Yes, I'll marry you, Rex," she breathes for me, sure and clear.

"Thank *fuck*." I pump my hips with a swollen chest and an enlarged cock. "And you're not too drunk? Enough to warrant amnesia in the morning?" I brush her hair back from her face, my excitement splitting my face wide.

"Not too drunk." She giggles up at me, then her laughter and her smile fade, seriousness taking hold of her beautiful features. "But I'm going to need some things from you before we even tell anyone. Okay?"

"Anything, baby." I shower the side of her face in kisses, knowing that I'd do damn near anything to keep this woman in my arms for the rest of my life.

Strike that, I would do anything. Period.

"You already said yes. *No take backs.*"

Aria laughs and swats at my thigh so that she can tug her pants up and sit facing me with her back to the headboard.

When she runs a hand through her hair and tosses it over one side of her crown, my cock twitches. I ignore the thing and sit cross-legged in front of her, giving her my undivided attention that does not go without a grin I can't remove from my face.

So much so that my cheeks are aching.

"I want you to wear something for me," she mutters, my brows shooting up at the thought that crosses my dirty mind.

"Is this a kinky something?" I wag my brows at her. "A role-play kind of something?" I lean forward, using my forearm to brush back my own hair from my face.

"No." She shakes her head, her minuscule grin unmistakably reacting to my questions. "You'd be into that?"

I chuckle, a note of seriousness washing over me. "I meant it when I said anything for you. Any-fucking-thing at all." I palm her jaw and press a gentle kiss to her soft lips. "Just say the word, and you got it. It's all yours."

Flush rushes up my girl's chest to her ears as her eyes dart to the mattress beneath us in some sort of shyness I'm not entirely used to seeing on her.

"I want you to wear something I made," she whispers, oh so quietly, to the bed. "Is that wrong?" Her eyes dart to mine, becoming erratic. "That's wrong, I shouldn't ask you that." She goes to move away from me, but I stop her with both hands to her face.

"Baby." I press a kiss to her nose and grin. "I'd love to wear an Aria original." Her eyes search mine for a moment, her thoughts taking her to all the places and reasons why not to do something so extreme. "Dress me like one of your French girls, babe."

A furrowed brow meets my comment, then a burst of laughter as the words settle into my girl's overworking brain.

"Damn you." She giggles with a hand to her forehead as I settle back into my seat. "And why the hell are you naked?"

I shrug. "You didn't seem to mind about ten minutes ago." I wink. "Or when I asked you to marry me. Again." My giddiness plasters to my face as my girl's flush grows deeper and redder.

So I grab her ankles and pull until she's under me again.

"Dear God, what have I done." Her hands run down her face to hide her grin. She's not fooling me at all with that move, but I'll let her think she did.

"No take backsies," I remind her with a fake seriousness to my head-shake. She slaps my bicep with a smile she doesn't hide from me.

Aria's smile fades, her hands finding my skin and planting against my shoulders. "You understand why I'm asking you, right?"

Pursing my lips in thought, I nod.

"Fans are going to find out about you, and you're choosing to show them first. To set the narrative. Direct the attention from this"—I touch the colored vines on my neck—"to who you actually are."

Aria's lungs expel as if my answer lifted weight from her chest, and her eyes mist over. "So, you're okay with that? Wearing an outfit so I can post a pic or two?"

Confused, I dip to meet my girl's—my fiancée's—nervous gaze and shake my head.

"Aria," I start when I see the dread filter into her face, her walls starting to build right back up. "Just a pic or two is not good enough." I press my forehead to hers when she goes to push away. "Design the rest of the tour. Plus the award show at the end, something formal."

I glance at the clock on the nightstand, then back to Aria's fallen face.

"You've got about sixteen hours."

"No way." Shaking her head, her hair sticking with static cling to the pillowcase. "No fucking way."

"Yes, way." I lean back and pull her trembling body into my lap. "Give me what you got now that'll fit me, and I'll help with the rest."

Cradling her to my chest, she blows a hefty breath over my skin.

"Still too damn sweet." Aria wraps a hand around the back of my neck and pulls me in for a long kiss.

Panting, I lean back with a smirk for my girl.

"You got work to do, and I got a ring to buy."

With another wink, I stand her on her own two feet and slap her ass.

"Let's go, *wife.*"

Chapter Fifty-Four

Aria

I watch in shock and awe as my fiancé struts across the stage of my laptop, donning the masterpiece of masterpieces I've been designing in my head since before I knew I wanted to take a stab at the fashion world with shit I found at fucking thrift stores.

He sings of me—as if that isn't enough of an ego boost—on stage to forty-six thousand fans.

That's right … 46,000.

Not counting the number of people streaming the event live like we are.

It's been six weeks since he challenged me to create his entire wardrobe for the next six months, six weeks since I sent Rex to the store with the inspiration to find me the missing pieces, and he came back with the perfect fit.

Acid-washed black jeans that I ironed midnight-blue patches beneath, a destroyed leather jacket with the As Above emblem hand stitched into the back, and an equally destroyed white muscle tee beneath that.

Rainbow studded belt lines his ass like all the alt kids did in the early 2000s, and heavy boots cover his feet.

His right hand, clad in a matching leather glove, lifts the mic to the crowd for them to finish the lyrics. Rex bangs his head, his boot smashing the sole into the stage to the beat of the song, encouraging the crowd to keep it going.

They don't disappoint.

My heart seizes as the voices of thousands of people sing to me words of love and affirmation I never expected to hear from a metal show. The emotion that I thought only soul could bring me hangs in the air around me and my girls, their eyes glued to the screens as much as mine are.

"He's damn beautiful," I murmur into my palm, my words too soft to be heard over the thumping music and chatter surrounding me. Cedar's hand is on my shoulder, her eyes trained on the bigger screen my laptop is slung to for the rest of the room's viewing pleasure.

"Did you see that shit?" someone screams with pure excitement, but I don't see anything except my man leading the way into the next song, his back shimmying against Fin's as he plays air guitar.

They jimmy and jostle together for a few beats, then Rex breaks away to go to his brother, pounding his way around the drum set.

Literally.

Mac's drums are set in the middle of a rotating platform that his ass is strapped into to keep up with the beat while it turns.

Why you ask?

Because he fucking can.

Because why the hell not?

I grin when Rex grins, the camera catching his movements as if I'm right on the side stage with them and lifting my spirit right out of my body.

"This is amazing. I'm so glad Rex did this." Aurora vibrates beside me, her hands gripping my bicep and shaking the shit out of me.

It's amazing how time can ease the jagged edges between all the people who care about me.

"Me, too." I toss the words over my shoulder, too afraid to remove my eyes from the screen.

"Guhhh," Aurora adds when the Rex on the screen she's watching does a backflip in the middle of the stage.

"How the fuck is Mac keeping up?" I catch Jon's comments as we all admire flashes of the tireless drummer.

"He's a fuckin' badass." Jordan's words are soft, subtle, but they cut right through the noise of the room.

I think there's more to Jordan than my future husband thinks.

He levels Mac out perfectly.

Excitement erupts in the room and on the screen when the final song comes on, but Rex addresses the crowd directly.

"Oh, here we go."

"Damn, you guys look good tonight." The crowd roars in response, Rex prowling to center stage.

He pauses there for a moment, his smile so damn wide, and absorbs the love thrown his way.

Mic back to his pierced lips—yeah, I love the snake bites he's rocking—he chuckles when the noise level rises before he can utter a single word.

I so admire his ability to command an entire room. Stage. Stadiums.

The entire internet.

"I want to say thanks to the crew for making sure this shit streams live." Applause drowns out any other words, so Rex pauses.

The band keeps tempo, though, repeating the intro to the song however long they need.

"So, there's an award thing." Another roar sends Rex's grin skyward, but he continues with more gusto into the mic as he gestures on his left to

Fin. "*And this talented motherfucker has been nominated.*" Rex grips Fin and shakes him like my sister just shook me.

Fin nods, sends a wink to the audience, and goes back to playing without missing a single beat.

"*Aw, he's shy.*" Rex chuckles into the mic and addresses the crowd once more. "*Ya like the new threads?*" He tugs on the lapels of the jacket, popping the collar and posing like some kind of misfit runway model.

Hot dayum.

"*Ask Scarlett. She's phenomenal.*"

Rex bounces about, the name drop he's been doing since his first show wearing my designs shot off into the crowd for their own homework.

They fucking delivered.

With nothing more than the name, my sales doubled overnight. Then doubled again by the end of the week.

Shit is so high right now I've already hired a seamstress and am looking at an assistant designer to start *yesterday*.

I've got a shoot I need to be at to dress someone in less than two hours.

And another twenty *threads* shipping out by morning.

God, I miss him.

Back at center stage where someone like him belongs, Rex stands with his arms stretched out, his eyes closed as he absorbs the pulse he helps create.

"He's spectacular," Aurora mumbles beside me, her hands cradling a bowl of walking taco ingredients, earning herself an elbow to the gut.

"Eyes to yourself, sis."

But I can't take mine off him, the alluring and talented Rex Thompson.

More like the ink standing proud at the base of his neck.

"Rude," she mutters but shovels more food into her face.

The beat drops, Rex coming to life as if in sync with the melody, the first verse screaming out past his lips.

The masses before him join in, so much that he's almost drowned out, lyric for fucking lyric.

Goose bumps.

"It's almost as good as being there," someone comments as the room I'm sitting in adds to the vocals, clapping to the beat.

Biting my lip, I rotate the ring on that special finger of my left hand, knowing that he's all mine.

Helps that he has called me wife *since the moment he slipped it on my finger.*

The glint of the sapphire there catches my eye, reminding me that I have a shit ton of planning to do and secrets to keep for a while.

Rex is going to shit a brick, and I'm almost glad that he's on the road right now, so I don't spoil the surprise for him before it's time.

But hey ... It's all about embracing the moment ... right?

"I'm sorry I gave him so much shit." My sister crouches next to me, pulling my attention from Rex and furrowing my brow. "I just ..." She pauses, looking down into the bowl she holds as if it's full of all the answers she seeks. "Didn't want to see you hurting all over again."

"I know," I whisper, wrapping an arm around her shoulder and pulling her tight against my ribs. I peck a kiss to her temple and release her back into the wild.

"Love you."

"Love you back."

Epilogue

Aria—Six months later

Nerves rack my body, sending me into fits of chills combined with the sweats, which I need exactly none of right now.

I've done everything I can to cover it up.

There's just no hiding it anymore.

The floor-to-ceiling mirror now seems like a terrible idea, when it seemed like the greatest thing before it was *me* standing in front of it.

Because right now, it shows the exact thing I don't want Rex to notice until I'm ready to say it out loud.

It's terrifying but also so fucking exciting.

We've come so far, and I can't help but adore the grin I find on my face more often than not these days.

"You're fucking stunning, Aria." Rex's massive arms snake across my shoulders and pull me back into his broad chest.

"Thank you," I whisper, spinning in his embrace to focus on him instead of the visual before me.

He's bulked up a lot since he's been gone, not that Rex was small in any sense of the word.

I'm not complaining.

I guess boredom and a raging sex drive with not enough satisfying ways to relieve it will do that to a guy.

"Are you ready? You still wanna do this?" Hands to my hips that hold me close when I spin to face him.

Rex's starry gaze bores down into mine, a smile tugging up his pierced lips.

"I love you, Rex." I cage his face between my palms and press a gentle kiss to his lips, the rings there chilled to the touch. "I'm nervous, I won't lie about that."

"We don't have to do this if it's too much."

I shake my head with a smirk, my meticulously done curls bouncing around my cheek, the ends tickling the tops of my high cleavage on the one side.

"It's not too much." I step back from his warmth to do another once-over in the mirror.

I take a moment to admire Rex, all his tatted and pierced glory, in a three-piece suit tailored to fit his huge frame.

Wild curls fall around his shoulders in contrast to the classic attire adorning his body, yet somehow coming together to scream *this is me, here I am, Rex Motherfucking Thompson.*

"You look so beautiful, babe." He trails a hand down my arm to grip my wrist and pull me back to him.

"I was admiring you." I snigger and smooth the lapel of his sport coat down.

This is one of those moments where I'd normally have to adjust his tie even though it doesn't need it, but Rex refused to wear one. Instead, the pressed silk shirt beneath has the first several buttons undone, displaying his glorious ink for the world to see.

Except tonight ... the world is going to have a chance to put the face to the name that's been streaming since the night Rex proposed to me.

The night a grubby mugger attacked him.

The night I told him *no*.

And then *yes*.

I snicker now at the thought as I run my hands down the front of his torso.

I desperately ache to reach beneath the fabric, feel the steel rings I know are beneath, but I know that if we stand here any longer, Rex is going to undo all the work I've done to get us ready.

I can see it in his eyes.

"Let's go." After a gentle peck to my lips that leaves a hint of red behind, Rex intertwines our fingers and leads me out into the hall to find our little group waiting for us.

"Pony up, princess." My eyes snap to Fin at the use of the nickname, his attention unexpectedly on Cedar.

She rolls her eyes and slaps away his outstretched hand. "I'm not paying you."

"Then why'd you fucking bet?" he sputters, his eye roll more obnoxious than hers.

"Bet what?" I ask, smashing the call button to the elevator.

"That you were humping and wouldn't be ready in time," Mac answers as he passes me and piles into the lift. The rest of us follow suit, leaving me to face the closing doors.

"That was earlier," I say with a wink to my almost brother, my baby sister hooting somewhere in the elevator behind me.

"It's bad for the baby." Rex's hand jostles mine at his words, his smile unmatched by anyone else in this whole damn building.

"Whatever." Toby scoffs from somewhere in the back. "That's not a real thing."

I shoot a look at Rex, his knowing smirk plastered to his face as his eyes travel subtly down my body to stop on my belly.

No way he knows.

He shoots me a wink when his heated sight levels back on mine, his attention moving back to the opening elevator doors.

He ignores Toby as his palm finds mine to escort me out onto the main floor of the hotel.

Does he know? Can he tell?

Trying my best to be subtle, I attempt to check out my reflection in any and every shiny surface we pass along the wide passage to the ballroom where the awards are taking place.

I see it, but I know it's there.

"C'mon, you look fine." Aurora nudges me with an elbow to the ribs as we enter the large doors to the expansive space set up for the event we're attending.

It's gorgeous.

"Thanks, sis," I mutter as I take in the fancy centerpieces, fresh flowers adorning the tables and walls.

Glints of silvers and golds meld into the decor, accentuating the dark greens and crisp whites against the cathedral-esque architecture.

A great place for a wedding if we hadn't already chosen the beach.

I swipe my damp palms along the skirt of my dress and meet a set of blue-green eyes that see right into my soul.

My mouth waters, and my pulse kicks up.

In fact, I'm able to be here tonight because my studio is so successful that I've been able to hire an entire staff that keeps the place running while I sit back and watch.

Except I can't stop. I love it too much.

So, I gave myself permission to work on my passion projects. The special ones that take more time and meticulousness. The ones that allow me to not be stuck behind the sewing machine for twenty hours straight.

"You're breathtaking, babe." Rex's whispered words tickle my ear as we stop at our assigned table, and he pulls out the seat for me to settle my ass into.

The ass that's grown

Has he noticed?

He's gotta fucking know.

No way he doesn't know after this morning.

"Thank you," I whisper back, a slight flush rising on my skin, as he takes the seat next to me and slides his hand onto my thigh. I grasp at him there, unable to keep from touching him so long as he's with me.

The smile he answers me with has my own grin growing.

"So is he gonna win or what?" Toby's words break into our little bubble and draw my attention.

"Of course he is," Mac answers smoothly, a gentle shrug accompanying his words. "Banger's guy ain't shit."

Cedar's nose crinkles at the mention of the *other* band while Toby pretends to spit on their name, which garners a few odd glances from old biddies seated around us.

Sounds about right.

I glance at the patrons that fill in around us and realize my table is full of the misfits, the oddballs covered in tattoos and extra hardware, aside from one other group seated just to the left of the stage.

The Bangers.

A rival band from the west that made their headway just after As Above rocketed to stardom.

Or so I've been told.

I lock on icy blue eyes from across the room that make me want to cause a scene as they bounce curiously between me and Rex.

I see the accusations there, the snooty attitude that screams of self-righteousness and misplaced pride.

"Oh, shit." Rex clears his throat and grips my hand, failing at dragging my attention from the hourglass figure I wanna fucking maul just because she has eyes.

"The hell is that?" I ask through squinted eyes and ragey fists.

"Don't worry about it." Rex's fingers trap my jaw and force me to look into his steely gaze and away from the bitch who's trying to catch these hands.

He pecks another kiss to my lips, leaving more tint on his without a care, and presses his forehead to mine.

"They call her Doll." Cedar sidles right up to me, so close that her chair bumps my back. "Cuz no one knows her real name." Rex's warmth leaves me to send a pointed look over my shoulder at my best friend.

"No one asked you, Cedar," he growls.

"And judging by your response," Cedar mutters as I look over in time to catch her knowing smile, "the rumors are true."

"Shut up, woman."

I clear my throat, tilting my head in Rex's direction despite him still throwing shade over my shoulder.

"Dammit." Rex rolls his eyes and brings my knuckles up to place a gentle kiss there. "She's been around. We've all had a turn." He coughs, a sad attempt to cover up his next words. "Or two."

"Rex." I slap his bicep, knowing that he had a past before me, but I can't help the anger that rushes me. "Really? All of you?" I fling my wild eyes around the table, catching everyone looking away in guilt except Mac.

Cedar giggles behind me, a little too happy about this, earning herself a death stare just like the rest of them. "Ya nasty, all of you."

"What did I do?" Leo shoots back, his feigned offense making my eyes roll all the way to Pluto.

"Like you weren't in on it," Mac snaps knowingly.

I shake my head and slap another palm on Rex's chest as the lights begin to dim and the presenter takes the stage.

"Ow."

"You'll live," I whisper-hiss to my fiancé as the spotlight finds our host for the evening, grinning with a fake white smile and pleated pants.

Gross.

"Welcome all." He speaks too loudly into the mic, sending shockwaves through my eardrums that rattle around in my brain.

He tells us of the rules for the night—no cameras, no videos, blah, blah, blah—the sound guy getting his shit together and bringing down the volume a thousand notches as our host drones on without noticing.

I tune him out with a gentle rub to my temples and do a scan of the darkened ballroom to find *Doll* still glancing in the direction of our table.

Her sleek black hair falls stick straight down her bare back, her sparkling dress completely void of covering her spine.

Even in the dark, her eyes catch mine and shoot daggers my way.

Our way.

My hand instinctively goes to my stomach and gives a little massage of reassurance.

"Should I be worried?" I lean into Rex, tucking his curls behind his ear to place a kiss against his cheek.

"Never, babe." He glances at me with a smirk, his fingers tightening around mine, his sight darting down to my stomach. "I was yours the moment you pulled off the blindfold."

Heat rushes me, boiling beneath my skin for this man.

I have to tell him.

"Now, if you'll join me in acknowledging the nominees ..."

Applause drowns out my thoughts, begging for our attention or risk being the assholes that don't clap.

Rex taps his palm to his thigh as he pulls my chair against his and tucks an arm protectively around me. It makes my stomach flip, and the news burns holes in my thoughts.

I'm going nuts.

Whistles and hoots begin as the nominees stand in thanks, Fin's grin wider than I've ever seen.

I can't hold it in anymore.

"Rex." I lean into my fiancé and whisper the words.

"Please welcome to the stage, this year's winnnnnerrrrr …" The host brags, dragging out his words along with opening the envelope with the winner's name on the inside.

"What is it?" Rex asks, his full attention on me and not on the stage.

At least my attention is on Fin as he stands from his seat on the stage.

I should wait.

Rex grips my jaw, worry furrowing his brow.

"Finland 'Fin' Montgomery of As Above," the host shouts.

Our table erupts. The room busts into deafening applause.

Cedar jumps up beside me, knocking my forehead into Rex's and bringing his shocked expression up close and personal.

"Babe?" He absently rubs the spot on my skin where we collided, but his eyes refuse to leave mine.

Steeling myself with a deep breath, I force my attention back to Fin and applaud for him.

Rex follows suit, but it doesn't stop him from keeping his gaze locked on me.

"Well, shit. Thank you," Fin mutters into the microphone, eliciting a few chuckles from the crowd, and when he rotates to speak to the band, I push Rex to focus on the stage.

Rex tips his chin to Fin in acknowledgment, then refocuses on me.

Wild applause drowns out the rest of Fin's short speech, but none of it draws Rex's steady gaze from me.

I turn and grab my fiancé's hands in mine.

Then I bring them to my stomach, Rex's palms flattening around the swell I can no longer hide.

Everything around me stops.

"I'm pregnant," I whisper.

His eyes flare wide in question, the warmth of his hold steadying my nerves. "Say it again."

"Yes." I nod, tears forming behind eyes with way too much makeup to ruin, but I don't care.

The pure admiration that meets me, the tight arms thrown around my ribs, make it worth ruining hundreds of dollars worth of time and cosmetics.

Rex wraps me up, taking me with him, and we spin.

"Did I just hear what I fucking think I did?" Cedar growls in my ear the moment my feet hit the floor.

"I was going to wait, but it's been eating at me." I swipe at my face unapologetically, unladylike, and I do it with a smile.

Rex's hands go to my stomach, his misting eyes holding me hostage.

"Yeah." I nod again to confirm the questions I see sparking in his eyes, and to answer my sister. "You did."

"Holy shit," Cedar breathes somewhere behind me.

"What she said." Rex's chuckle is watery, and he pulls me in tight, his lips smashing into mine, smearing the red stain all over both of us.

"I'm gonna be an uncle?" Mac's voice echoes along my brainstem as Rex pulls back from me, breathless and a little in love.

"Yeah," he answers his twin without taking his eyes off me and my watery mess.

"I fuckin' told you, potato spud."

"Yeah," Rex smirks. "You did."

Rex's eyes leave mine for just a moment to meet his twin's proud gaze. Something passes between them, some kind of twin love I'll never truly understand, and when Rex comes back to me along with Mac's gaze …

And Cedar's.

And Aurora's.

Then Toby, Leo.

A giddy Fin strides back to us, award in hand, an extra pep in his step.

"What?" Fin pauses with a grin and takes in each of them with their eyes on me, his brow winging. "What'd I miss?"

Epilogue Two

Rex—sometime later

THE PAST FEW MONTHS have been a whirlwind of shit, and that's coming from the lead vocalist of a fucking rock band.

From craziness to great news, to even better days and some fucked-up ones in between, I've never been so damn content to sit at the front of the reception hall with my hand on my *wife's* leg while she beams at me from her seat at my side.

And even better when photographs of Aria and I flash across the projector off to the side of our filled table.

The photographs.

The ones that brought us together, all thanks to Aurora, who sits at the other end of the table and tries her best not to mean mug or make googly eyes at a particular security guard who roams around the room.

"I'm right here, y'know," my *bride* whispers, her hot breath cresting over the shell of my ear when the projector flashes another sexy-ass image of my girl wrapped around my body in a classy yet provocative way.

Aria in that dress?

Delicious.

Her legs wrapped around my waist?

Even fucking better.

Genevie is a goddamn genius.

"Mm-hmm," I drawl, inching my way up her thigh to knead at the muscles close to her groin, smirking when her breath catches and my cock fills.

"Rex," she breathes against me, her hand coming down to cover mine. "We have to get through the rehearsal first."

Groaning when her grip tightens, I flash a smile out to the other patrons of our rehearsal dinner the night before our wedding and curse the fact that they're all here.

I want nothing more than to bend my *wife* over this very table and sink into her as I watch the look on her pretty face from the night we met.

The *awe* reflecting in her face from then to now.

To see the flush I put on her cheeks that day before I even touched her, then to see that same flush accompanied by the love she has sparkling in her eyes when she looks at me now.

"What is there to rehearse, babe?" I grumble back to her when flashes blind me. "You're mine, I'm yours. Now let's go."

"Nuh-uh." She tugs me when I go to stand and flattens my hand back against her covered knee, far from where I want to be. "Once you leave, you're with the boys for the night. You're not getting away from me yet."

Damn traditions.

With an impatient huff, I settle back into the chair and wonder what the hell else there is to do to get ready.

All I give a fuck about is her saying "*I do*" and Genevie or Aurora catching the moment for me to frame to add to the collection of photos that help me remember why the fuck I get up every morning that Aria's not in my arms.

Like the album I have stashed in my bag of all the *other,* more provocative, pics Genevie was able to get from that day.

Ones with her in my lap, her hands on my chest, and others with me hovering over her grinning frame.

The day that changed my life and led me to Aria now tucking herself under my arm and grinning up at me like I hung the moon despite the hellions I helped create.

"Stop looking at me like that." My girl shakes her head at me and turns her gaze out to the people who are here for us.

"Like what?" I ask as I plant a kiss on her warm cheek and inhale a lungful of her tropical scent I'd much rather be licking right now.

"Like you wanna love me for the rest of my life."

I can't help the grin that she pulls from me or the groan that travels over her ear and leaves goose bumps behind.

"Why would I wanna stop doing *that*?" I smirk and cup her face in my palm, my thumb tracing over her bottom lip that I lean down to kiss. "Now …" I lean in close and whisper to her as my eyes flick to the screen filled with Aria standing at the bottom of the wrought iron staircase, me kneeling at her feet to remove her heel. "You gonna let me recreate that"—I nod to the screen—"except with my face up your skirt?"

Bonus Chapter

Aria

"**G**OOD MORNING, WIFE."

The sound of my husband's sleep-deep rumble has my lips turning up at the corners and my hips inching back against the hardness I know I'll find.

Of course, he does not disappoint.

"Good morning, *husband*."

Rex's hand travels its way up my soft belly to settle between my breasts and effectively cocoon me in all things *him*. "I will never get tired of hearing that from you."

My cheeks ache with the smile that has yet to leave me since Rex and I swore *I do* less than twelve hours ago. In fact, I think my smile hasn't left me since I wound up in his tour bus all that time ago and took the leap of faith that my heart kept begging for.

It led me right here, with Rex's commitment to me inked into his skin, his Ma babysitting, while my husband and I finally get the island honeymoon he's promised me.

We're even in a bungalow, set out into the crystal blue ocean, only accessible by the long dock or a boat.

Which means I get to be as loud as I want.

I wriggle my ass back into the curve of his hips. "Then don't."

Rex lets out a low growl when his erection slips between my thighs, his hips working in shallow thrusts against my ass. "You don't have to worry about that, Mrs. Thompson."

Goosebumps break out over my flushed skin.

"Mrs. *Scarlett*," I correct on a half groan and a full grin when Rex's weight pushes me onto my stomach, pinning me to the mattress.

"Oh we'll fix that, wife." One of his hands clamps onto my hip and tugs until my ass is in the air, his other pulling my wrists up above my head.

God, I love him.

Rex straddles my thighs and anticipation flutters in my belly.

When he reaches between us, using his dick to tease along my pussy with that devilish ring, anticipation blossoms into full-blown *need*.

It doesn't matter that he woke me up with his head between my legs less than three hours ago. It doesn't matter that Rex hasn't kept his hands to himself, even at our wedding, only a few hours before that. It *really* doesn't matter that I get the chance to do this for the rest of my life.

I need it now.

They say that having kids changes you.

But in my case …

It's made me feral for my husband.

"Please," I beg on a breathless whisper when my husband decides to tease me. Running his dick just along my seam, he coats himself in the wetness that slicks his plush head.

"Please what, babe?"

I mewl and push back against him, searching for the friction we both crave. "Please fuck me, Rex."

He leans over me, his hair falling all around us, dimming some of the sunlight shining through the sheer curtains as his weight bears down on me. It's impossible to move, to press back into him, to beg him with my body.

"Please fuck me, *who?*"

I let out a frustrated grunt when all he does is keep his dick just out of reach. Just far enough away to not give me what I know we *both* want.

"Rex," I mutter in an attempted warning, but it comes out more like a breathless plea.

Even after all this time, this is what he does to me.

"Yes, *wife?*" Rex asks with an emphasis on the title as he arches his hips, the ring through the tip of his dick ghosting over my clit and making me hiss.

"Oh God."

Rex's throaty chuckle only serves to make me wetter, to tease me more.

"Yes, *wife?*" he repeats, his hips jutting forward and slipping his dick between my thighs, pulling a growl from his own chest.

I know what he wants.

I'm just too stubborn to give into him this time.

"Fuck me, Rex," I mutter, my face digging deeper into the pillow beneath, all while Rex moves his pelvis against my ass.

It's really not fair, considering he's giving himself a taste of friction, a morsel of what he wants, but at least I know that eventually he'll cave.

As if he's in my head, Rex's dick slips further up, the head of him passing just out of reach from my clit once again.

"Oops."

I mewl at the sound of his deep voice in my ear, goosebumps raising all across my skin.

Okay, maybe I won't outlast him …

His tempo increases just enough to leave me breathless, half-frustrated, and a whole lot aroused.

"Please, Rex," I beg into the pillow, my fists flexing.

He leans close, his lips coasting over the nape of my neck, his soft groans vibrating across my skin.

"Hm … maybe since you're begging …" His words trail off as his hips arch and his erection finally slips between, reaching my clit.

"*Oh God*," I moan into the bedding, my body lighting up. "Yes, baby, please."

Rex's sultry chuckle travels down my spine as his head slicks through my folds, still not quite where I need him.

I'm gonna lose this battle.

I'm on the verge of begging desperately, pleading his name into the open space of our honeymoon suite, when the head of his dick *finally* hedges against my entrance.

He thrusts forward, sinking to the hilt, and I gasp.

"Oh shit, babe." He lets loose a sexy, throaty chuckle in my ear. "I slipped."

He's full of shit and he knows it, but I don't get a chance to call it out with any coherent words before he's slipping free from my body, only to slam back home again.

Over and over.

"Oh *God*, Rex," I choke out, my hips working against the weight of him and arching back to meet his thrusts.

The precipice builds higher and higher, dragging me along for the ride of my life as warmth blossoms low in my belly. It slowly spreads, taking over my body until I feel the heat of Rex down to my toes.

I'm close. So damn close.

But then Rex leans back, taking the heat and the orgasm along with him.

I pop up on all fours when his grip leaves me and push back against his hips, desperate to finish what he started.

"Spread your legs," he demands, leaning to one side and then the other when I push my thighs apart so he can settle between them.

Rex's hand finds my ass, smoothing over my skin and pulling a frustrated keening from deep in my throat.

"*Rex*, I need you."

I glance over my shoulder when I feel his gaze heat up my back and nearly cum at the sight of him knelt behind me. His cock is thick in his tight grip, his blue-green eyes scorching a path up my body, his chest heaving.

When his gaze finally snaps to mine, it's like the heat of the room expands, taking my breath with it.

"I'm gonna watch you fuck yourself on my cock, *wife*."

My eyes roll back when Rex lines back up to my entrance and slips the head of him just inside me.

"*Yes, God. Fuck.*"

His hands slide up my back, tracing his fingers along my arching spine, and thread into the hair at the base of my head.

"I'm all fucking yours, wife," he growls, his grip tightening in my hair and pulling a moan from between my lips.

It's exactly what I needed to push back, taking all of him inside me, and riding him until we're both gasping for air.

"Fuck, you're so sexy with my cock buried inside you. Wrapped around me. *Fuck.*" Rex's fist pulls on my hair, my neck arching back with a gasp that fills the room.

The sting in my scalp adds to the pleasure consuming my insides until I'm falling apart around my husband with a scream.

"*God, yes, husband!*"

"*Oh fuck*," Rex grits out, his hips grinding against my ass. "Say it again, *wife.*"

"*Husband*," I moan, and push back against him, my pussy fluttering around him. "Rex, my husband."

"*Fuuuuck.*"

Hips pitching forward, Rex's thrusts shorten until he's barely leaving my body, his growl of pleasure filling my soul while his cock fills my body.

It's everything.

"Rex," I mutter, and push up on shaking limbs.

"Shh, babe," he mumbles in return as he pushes back on his haunches. "Stay still for me."

I listen—of course, I listen—and let my head fall back down to the pillow just underneath me while my ass hangs out in the air.

He leans back, still lodged inside me, and mutters "You're fucking beautiful, my wife."

My eyes flutter closed when I feel him move, his cum following his path as he slowly withdraws from my body.

I'm so content, halfway to falling asleep, when Rex's growl slices through the room.

And that's when I feel it. The drip of his release leaking from my body and sliding down the length of my pussy to tease along my clit.

Shivers rake down my spine, my lips popping open with a soft gasp.

"*Fuck*, baby. You're even more perfect with my cum dripping out of you."

My lips tug up into a smile and I wriggle my hips.

"Maybe you should do something about that, husband."

He growls and grips my hips, stilling my movements.

There's a long enough pause that I'm about to lift my head from the pillow when I'm struck with the brilliant idea to sneak a hand between my legs instead.

"Since you wanna watch," I mumble, and spread my legs further apart.

Using my husband's cum, I circle my fingers around my clit with a gasp.

Then I push them inside my pussy and nearly cry out.

"*Fuck*, baby." Rex's grip flexes on my hips. "I'm still fucking hard."

I go to pull the digits from my body when his grip tightens.

"Nuh-uh," he breathes out. "Scissor your fingers, Aria. Stretch that pussy open." My chest heaves with my breath as I listen, slowly widening my fingers with each stroke. "That's it, baby."

I feel Rex move closer, the heat of him warming my ass, his groans getting deeper with each pass of my fingers inside me.

"Okay, okay," he practically pants. "Go down to one."

"*Nooo*," I drag out. "So close."

"I know, baby. But gimme one."

Hearing him breathless and demanding like this … it's got me so close to the edge that I want to fling off.

Instead, I pull one digit from my pussy and leave the other to work in slow strokes that sends my pulse skittering.

It feels so good to just have him watch me, having him near while I play with myself, but it's even better knowing that it's *his* cum that's coating my fingers.

My hand …

Bliss threatens to take over, pulling me into that beautiful space between orgasmic euphoria and happiness, only to pause its tug on me when my husband's dick grazes over my knuckles.

"What're you—"

"Since you wanted to tease me," Rex rumbles out, his plush head hedging my entrance. "Then I'm going to fuck you with that finger in there."

Shivers rake over my skin and that familiar heat blossoms low when he advances, the crown of him stretching me further open.

It's slow and deliberate, teasing and filling all at once, as my husband begins to sink his cock inside my pussy along with my finger.

"*Fuuuck,* babe. So goddamned *tight.*"

I'm panting by the time he finally seats fully inside me. Ready to burst. Moaning incoherent shit when he rocks out and then back in.

"So … *full.*"

"Uh-huh," Rex huffs out, his thrusts building. "So gonna fucking cum."

I nod against the pillow, desperate to fly off the edge I've come to once again. "Cum with me, husband."

He grunts. "I'm right there, baby. Curl your finger."

I do and nearly scream.

Hello G-spot.

The orgasm slams me in waves, and I can feel my body clenching around where Rex and I are joined. It's so close and intimate to feel what he feels when he's inside me as my body flexes and my mouth hangs open in a yell against the pillow.

"Fuck, that's it, baby." Rex's erection hardens along my finger, the rest of him stiffening behind me as his movements tighten and his dick explodes inside me. "*That's it, Aria.*"

I feel him coating me from the inside out and moan.

With my husband's pleasure-filled roars etched into my memory, and his warm grip holding me together, I smile.

I've never been so happy to embrace the fucking moment.

"Babe," Rex gasps out, his open mouth pressing into the nape of my neck. "I swear I have more than sex planned."

I snort and nod. "*Sure,* you do."

Rex chuckles and forces a deep breath before leaning back and smacking my ass.

He withdraws slowly, carefully, then steps off of the bed, leaving me ass up on the mattress.

I'm ready to pass back out. A hard sleep attempting to claim me all over again that I don't hear what my husband is doing until the bed dips beside me and a towel swipes away the mess.

And then the familiar sound of a shutter flicking has my eyes popping open.

"You *didn't*."

I flop down on the bed, turning slowly to find Rex's grinning face mostly covered by a professional grade camera.

Click, click.

"I need new spank bank material," he mumbles through a grin from behind the lens. "G said he'd show us how to develop these when we get back."

Leaning up on my elbows, I blink at him. "You asked your friend to use his camera to take spicy photos of me?" I cock a brow.

Click.

"No," Rex drags out. "I asked him to borrow it. For honeymoon pics. That's it."

I roll my eyes at the smirk he flings my way.

Click, click.

"You're beyond ridiculous, husband." Sitting up, I steal the camera from his grip and turn the lens in his direction. "He's never getting this back."

The End!

Acknowledgements

H OLY SHIT.

If you've made it this far, then you just read the first book I ever finished writing. The first book I ever published, and then *re*published just over a year later. The first story to come to life in my head and never leave me.

Coming back to this book after two years away was like coming home. There were frustrations. There were tears.

But it was so fucking *sweet*.

So good.

So … *nostalgic*.

If you read the original version of this book, and came back for a second round, *thank you*. I hope I delivered this story with more passion, more experience. All the *umf* that Rex and Aria's book deserves.

Thank you.

If this is your first round reading this book, then I want to show my appreciation for you as well. There are millions of books out there, and you chose this one. That means *everything* to me. This is seriously a dream come true and I wouldn't be able to justify doing this if it weren't for each of you.

Thank you.

I hope Rex made you fall in love, and Aria helped you see your potential. I hope that Mac reminded you to laugh, and Ian gave you the fuzzy, but sexy, poppa bear vibes.

Like they did me.

I could name a million things that these guys managed to make me feel while writing this, but that would probably be an entirely other book. With all the love and angst and humor, it's just … *chef's kiss*

I miss them already.

But not to fret, they're all coming back for more in Fin and Cedar's story—The Rush. Which is available now on Kindle and Amazon!

If you enjoyed this book, please consider leaving a review.

No author ever does this deal alone. There is always an amazing support system, a team, a family, behind each and every one of us that make this shit possible.

For me, that first person has turned out to be my greatest cheerleader, my biggest fan pushing me to get the words to paper, and slapping high fives with each word count accomplishment. He has been my rock when I felt like crumbling, and my Devil Dog when I couldn't fight anymore. My lover when I needed soft and my friend when I needed the ear. His undying support made this shit possible and I am forever grateful for this love of mine.

I fucking love you, Danny.

Then there was Brook. My ride or die author bestie. My editing menace. I appreciate your late night revisions and last minute assistance more than you will ever know.

Next is the besties—Bev and Jorge. The greatest fucking inspiration on a forever kind of love. Your encouragement from the moment you found out about my book, my writing, has been phenomenal. I love you bitches.

To my momma ... See, I told you it wasn't a phase! But seriously, thank you for all of the music. All of the lessons. All of the freedom to figure out who the fuck I was. Who I am. You did what you did, what you had to do because it's all you knew. I know that now. I love you.

To my sisters ... I may not be the oldest. But if there's anything I could ever ask for in this world it would be to be an inspiration to you. I hope I encourage you. I hope I help you. I hope that you grow and learn and see my mistakes and make shit better because you knew me. To the fucking moon and back!

And to the readers. To the women and men out there that ever felt like you couldn't. To anyone who ever felt like they weren't good enough. That you wouldn't make it.

You can. You are. And you fucking will.

I believe in you.

And, lastly, to the younger version of me. The version that didn't know better. That didn't think I could. The scared one on the bathroom floor, riddled with panic attacks, terrified of what comes next. The toxic version that kept to herself and didn't speak up because it never felt like the words mattered.

It matters so damn much that there's a whole ass book full of 'em now.

I'm so damn proud of myself for how far I've come.

Content Warnings

Content Warnings include on page references to the death of a spouse, anxious tendencies (namely overthinking and negativity bias), grief, drug and alcohol use, car chase and car wreck, gun violence.

References made for **off page** content include sickness of a loved one, mentions of hospital stays, mentions of past manipulation.

Not everyone deals with trauma or grief in the same ways. This book is character driven and while the issues shown on page are mostly mild, this is just a representation of how my characters have dealt with their situations / mental health. This is in no way any sort of reference for real life use.

The Moment is meant for audiences of 18 years or older.

<u>Also by Rae Stone:</u>

As Above series
The Moment
The Rush

Turn the page for a peek of The Rush, As Above book two.

Sneak Peek

If you prefer to go into books blind, then skip these next pages. If not then I hope you enjoy this little teaser for what's to come. The band, the banter, the *tension …*

This is your final warning :)

"What the—" Freezing in place, my face falls when I find Peach leaning over Cedar's curled-up body. She's in the chair, her face hidden from me, her feet kicking in little pedaling motions that make the heat rise up my chest and my words growl out past my lips. "You have three goddamn seconds to step the fuck back."

"Not so hard!" Cedar throws her head back, her mouth wide, her blue eyes scrunched up and hidden from me.

My hands are already clearing to wrap around my bodyguard's neck when the sound that ratchets its way past Cedar's red-stained lips registers in my foggy brain.

"If I lighten up at all, you do this shit."

"Because it tickles—"

Cackling.

She's fucking laughing?

"Who the fuck thinks a tattoo tickles?"

My lungs heave. My fists clench. And my boots stop right behind the man with orange hair and a death wish.

"I do. Because it does!"

Breathe. Don't kill him.

Don't. Kill. Him.

The hum of the tattoo gun leaks into my ears as the show outside of the tent comes down. But that doesn't do much to bring me down from the adrenaline spike set to murder.

Because that means he's inking my—

About the Author

Rae Stone is native to the Midwest, from a town called Springfield, OH. While she no longer resides in the City of Roses, Rae is definitely a misfit of Suburbia that would rather paint her nails black and annoy the neighbors with her loud rock music.

When she's not elbows deep in writing, Rae can be found attending concerts with Mr. Stone, consuming romance novels like water, and letting her fur kids run wild.

Wanna connect? Find Rae on socials below!

Facebook | Instagram | Tiktok | GoodReads | Amazon | BookBub | Newsletter | Website

Need a place to discuss all things As Above?

Check out Rae's reader group here → Rae's Misfits of Romance